Pr

"Ann Bancroft writes with brave honesty about some of the more difficult human experiences. In her excellent novel *Almost Family*, she takes on the complicated struggles of a woman fighting cancer, along with the consequences of some of her recent life choices. Bancroft takes us into Liz's world and holds us close as Liz finds comfort and healing from some unlikely sources. It's a beautifully crafted story, well told."

—RUSSELL ROWLAND, author of *Cold Country*
and *Fifty-Six Counties: A Montana Journey*

"Ann Bancroft gives voice to thoughts most of us don't dare say out loud, writing as only someone who has 'been there done that' could. There are so many poignant truths in this book. I would highly recommend it for anyone who is facing a metastatic cancer diagnosis, or anyone close to somebody with cancer. *Almost Family* is rich with humor and wisdom, with deep themes of fractured relationships and how to go about healing them. It was very hard for me to put it down."

—CASS BROWN CAPEL, PhD, cofounder of
Save Ourselves Breast Cancer Organization

"Gritty and absorbing, Ann Bancroft's *Almost Family* introduces us to three Bay Area residents struggling with terminal cancer. The author portrays her characters' hopes and dreams, as well as their frustrations and fears, in spare but fast-moving prose. This remarkable debut novel will enrich your life!"

—LEE E. DIRKS, former newspaper executive
and author of *Religion in Action*

Almost Family

Rhea—
Thanks!

Ann Bennett

Almost Family

A Novel

·

Ann Bancroft

SHE WRITES PRESS

Published 2024

Printed in the United States of America

Print ISBN: 978-1-64742-666-8
E-ISBN: 978-1-64742-667-5
Library of Congress Control Number: 2023920691

For information, address:
She Writes Press
1569 Solano Ave #546
Berkeley, CA 94707

Interior design and typeset by Katherine Lloyd, The DESK

She Writes Press is a division of SparkPoint Studio, LLC.

For Tom Spanbauer

Prologue

*A*ll my life, if you'd said, "Join a support group," I'd have said, "I can't think of anything worse." Two hours in a circle of folding chairs, trapped with all that angst. The on and on and on of it all. Bad parents. Drunken husbands. Jobs not only shitty but so low paid you can't even afford your own shrink, so there you all are in a group session, talking about your shitty jobs. God, no. It's bad enough just getting through these things. You want to waste more time whining about them? Staring at them in other people's faces? Yet here I am, going to a support group, after having just trashed the whole concept out of hand.

In my defense, this group I'm in is about *the* thing, the thing you can't get over or move on from or leave behind. It's the thing that makes you leave everything else behind, not just school or city or friends. No next new stage, no trying any different way to be. Just this one last adventure. So I figure none of the usual admonitions apply. Yes, we're a group, and we do sit around. But you really can't tell us, "Get a life," like I used to say, or think, anyway, about any other kind of support group. Say it about ours and you'd be even more of an asshole than I was.

Strange thing is, that's exactly what we're trying to do here. Get a little life, even if we are dying. And who's to say we're dying anyway, so long as we're still walking around?

*T*he first time everything fell apart was late on a Friday
afternoon in August 2008. I'd skipped out of work at four
thirty, a first, and was still unpacking boxes in my supposedly
temporary postdivorce apartment. Just a week earlier, I'd left
the beautiful Oakland Hills home I'd shared with my husband,
Bradley, for twenty-three years and had moved into the bottom
floor of a borderline-shabby Tudor-style fourplex on a leafy street
near Lake Merritt.

I unwrapped my half of the silverware, the mugs, and put
them in a cupboard sticky with too many layers of semigloss
paint. Aretha was on the cheap CD player I'd brought in from
my office, and I raised a fist to "Respect," shouting the letters to
no one but me. It hadn't really hit me yet, the finality of my decision, or the things I might mourn. I hadn't even figured out why
I'd stayed married to an alcoholic for so many years even after our
daughter, Marisa, was out of school. But I did know what finally
gave me the courage to leave.

Lyle.

The first man I ever really opened up to, the first man who
knocked my socks so far off he made me want to sing out loud.
I was giddy with possibility, even if my grown daughter wasn't
speaking to me as a result. Even if Lyle wouldn't be leaving his
wife for at least another year.

I was on my way to the kind of life I'd thought was reserved
for others. People who knew love because they knew how to feel

at home in places, people who didn't have to try so hard to be perfect, to fit in, to do the best job, be the best parent, clean up after everyone else's mess.

When the phone rang, I thought it was Lyle calling to confirm he'd be in that week from New York. We'd have sex for the first time in my own place instead of at the Excelsior, that dumpy hotel with saggy drapes. He'd stay all night long. Maybe I'd even get the kitchen together in time to cook him dinner.

It wasn't Lyle on the phone, though. It was my doctor, his usual lighthearted voice slowed down to the point where I knew something was off.

"Liz, I need you to come in . . ."

It was breast cancer. Stage One, but aggressive. I'd need surgery right away.

I did what I always do when a crisis hits, whether it's a PR client caught in a felony and I have to come up with a positive spin or a tree blown down on our house or my parents getting their own cancer diagnoses. I went into full-on Army brat mode, froze my emotions, and did what I had to do. I made plans for someone to take over my workload when necessary, assured my boss it would hardly *be* necessary. I'd be working through this thing.

I went on a binge shop at Macy's, ordering a shaker coffee table, a cheap sling-back chair, and a green leather sofa that was too big for the living room. I took from my house, temporarily my ex-husband Bradley's house, Grandma Millanova's overstuffed chair, the one we never got around to refinishing after our puppy Boris chewed on it, not even after Boris got old and died.

I didn't cry until I called Lyle to tell him the news. I cried just as much because he wouldn't be spending the night that weekend, and who knew when I'd see him next.

"Oh no!" he said. "Darlin'—" But then his wife must've come home because he started in on a fake business conversation: "Yes, that sounds like a good rollout plan. I'll go over the schedule with Ron."

After that first diagnosis, I stood up tall in my kitchen, a glass of wine on the counter, and called my daughter, Marisa. She was in her third year at Georgetown Law, slammed with studies and law review.

"No, really, I'm fine, honey," I said. "Prognosis is great. This'll just be a blip, nothing to worry about."

Instead of saying, "Honey, would you consider flying out so we could have a weekend together, just us?" I said, "Don't worry, I'll be working right through treatment. Don't even think of coming out here. Patsy at work has already put in an advance order of a whole week of take-out meals, and Kate will be over all the time." Not exactly true—Patsy, my assistant, didn't know about the surgery yet, but I was sure my best friend, Kate, would be around.

There was a pause on the line. I had the fleeting hope that Marisa would insist on getting on a plane, but she didn't press. Marisa was mad at me about the divorce, mad at me anyway, I suppose, for being too interested in her life, for years of imperfectly trying to keep everything in our out-of-control household in perfect control.

"Glad you have such a good attitude, Mom," she said. "That'll help, for sure." Then, "Sorry, I'm late for study group, but we'll talk soon."

I could have told her I was scared. I could've told her, again, that I was sorry about the divorce. I wanted to give her as much time as she needed, but also, I didn't know what I could say to make things better between us. How do you start talking, really talking, after brushing things under the rug for so many years? How do you mention a new man—especially a married man—in the same breath as divorce and expect your daughter won't judge you harshly for that?

"How's my sweetheart?" he asked. That South Carolina drawl never failed to calm me down.

He came out from New York to see me again after my first chemo, when I still had hair and felt good enough to have sex, desperately fantastic sex, despite my still-healing scar, the punch-holes under my arm where the lymph nodes were taken. I told him we should savor that weekend but that I wouldn't see him again until after chemo was done. I didn't want to be a drag.

My face turned gray and I had no eyebrows and only wisps of hair, like a baby bird. Kate and my new neighbors, Linda and Stu, were plenty attentive—Kate, another military brat, knowing me enough to pretend she was the one who needed to share laughs over a meal on the concrete patio. Treatment went by in a blur. Surgery, back to work, chemo, back to work. Wearing a wig made getting ready for work easy. Just put on your hair and slap on a smile.

In the in-between moments, dragging myself from one meeting to the next, or in that sliver of preconsciousness after sleep, I had Lyle to think about. Finally, he could call me at home. Finally, I could email him at midnight, and I did email, morning and night, revealing my every up and down, always concluding on a positive note. Lyle fantasies stretched through my days, lightening my spirit when my body was wrecked. I lay in bed exhausted but reviewing down to the finest detail our first working lunch that turned out to not be about work. The pale stripe in his shirt, the way his eyes, always intense, suddenly became intent upon me. What we ate and how quickly we went up to bed when I saw him in New York, at the Roosevelt and that one time at the Algonquin. That day we sat with sandwiches on a bench at Lake Merritt and talked about how we'd quit the firm and move up to Oregon someday, after his son graduated and he and his wife could have the kind of talk I'd had with my husband. Bradley and I didn't fight. The tension and secrets between us had crowded our marriage for so long that they had become like a third person to be finally rid of, so that we could get along. I even remained in the house while we had it on the market, sleeping

6

in our bed while he slept in Marisa's room or cheerfully headed "out" somewhere else.

With Lyle, I imagined a different life, coloring in the specifics of it until it became more vivid than the one inhabited by my body. When we moved to Oregon, I'd find a job at something nonprofity, and he'd build fine furniture in the refinished garage of our Craftsman house. My daughter might even come up to visit a week at a time, and we'd grow close, taking a watercolor class together or hiking along the Columbia River. Lyle and I would make friends. Have people over. Discuss books and politics and maybe get to know a few people really well. My cancer? A bummer, sure. A waste of a year, but lucky to get through it while he was still with his wife.

I've gone over and over it in my mind and figured out that this was the time that must've done it: Before starting radiation, as soon as I could travel after chemo, I put aside my initial reservations and went to see Lyle. We planned to meet in Kansas City, where neither of us had ever been. I was still bald, but my color was back, and I couldn't wait. We'd giggled over messy room service ribs, and after sex I went to the shower in our hotel room, taking off my crooked wig. For the first time ever, he did not want to come in with me. That look on his face just before he turned away to shave, when he dropped his smile and pulled in a deep breath. I saw fear in his eyes and then, when they narrowed, disgust. How could I have gotten so used to my cancer self I didn't prepare for what a turnoff it would be to him? How could I have let myself become so gaga over anyone that way, believing that giving my whole self would make him happy?

Three weeks later, with twenty-three of thirty-three radiation treatments to go, Lyle dumped me. By email. That is, the romantic email he sent was addressed to someone named Ellen. And when, heart racing, I asked who Ellen was, he wrote a pathetic, defensive apology, explaining in too much detail how he and his old girlfriend had reconnected and, you know, rekindled. It felt as if, just as we'd been singing along with the radio on a road trip, he'd pulled over on a freeway in empty, unfamiliar territory and told me to get out.

Call it the last straw, after divorce, then cancer, then treatment. When he dumped me, Lyle's lies and the truth of cancer punched so hard I could barely get out of bed. I called in sick every day after each of my twenty-three remaining radiation treatments, and another whole week after the last one, something I'd rarely done through the months of chemo, when I actually was sick and not just heartbroken and fatigued. All that time off after the breakup, I stayed home and obsessed. Almost fifty, obsessing like a high school kid. I'd google Lyle and his college girlfriend, stalk them both on Facebook, and then I'd google Medline and breastcancer.org, cutting and pasting all the worst-case statistics into my very own document of doom. I convinced myself I had two years left, max. Two years, and I was spending them humiliating myself.

Kate was the one who forced me back to work.

"For God's sake! You're cancer-free! Forget about the bastard," she said. We were having Greek takeout on the rickety patio table, celebrating the end of my treatment. She blew her cigarette smoke away from me into the juniper hedge.

The next morning, I brushed my teeth, imagining it was Lyle I spat on.

I slapped on my fringy Halle Berry wig and squeezed into stilettos, the black pencil skirt Lyle thought was so sexy, the drapey sage-colored top that looked great with the reddish tint in my synthetic hair. Lyle was in town for our monthly all-hands meeting on the SoClo account. Our goal: produce and market credible studies showing the health benefits of salt, using doctors who'd say low-salt diets had been dangerously hyped, athletes who swore by salt supplements, that sort of thing.

If I'd stayed home, claiming radiation fatigue, I wouldn't have to face Lyle. But then he would run the meeting, instead of me, and that thought propelled me with rage. *Remember, he dumped you in the middle of cancer treatment. By email! Fucker could've waited another six weeks.* Three minutes till ten, I exited the elevator on the twenty-first floor, into the bright cubicle-filled headquarters of Star Solutions. Head down, I ignored the normal morning greetings, brushing off Patsy when she inquired, "I thought you were still off? You feeling okay?"

"Had a checkup, but I'm here," I fibbed, heart beating too fast. "I can take the meeting."

"You look great," she said, soft round eyes lifting behind wireless glasses as she smiled. It's what people say to cancer patients no matter how awful they look, but Patsy knew me and my bullshit detector well enough not to kiss up. I was so grateful for the compliment I felt tears coming on.

I closed my office door behind me long enough to take a breath and look out the window. That view—Bay Bridge, across to San Francisco. Whenever I felt like a fraud, I looked out the window to remind myself I got there by being good at my job. Kate's words replayed as a pep talk. Lyle was merely a coworker now. I headed to the conference room and hesitated two breaths before entering. *Howcouldyou howcouldyou howcouldyou you bastard.*

I opened the door. Eight people sat at the walnut table that could hold twenty: four colleagues from my office, two thick-bodied white men representing SoClo, and a beautiful young woman I didn't recognize who must've been the new hire from the Manhattan office, the new hire who now sat next to Lyle. My cheeks burned, stomach roiling with jealousy, and this wasn't even the old girlfriend he'd dumped me for. Smooth Lyle. Beautiful gray Italian suit, as usual more formal than his West Coast counterparts but impeccably so. I could hear him inhale sharply as I settled into my chair, but then he immediately lifted his shoulders and flashed me a brilliant smile. "Why, Liz, so good to see you," he said. "You doing okay?" The note of concern made me want to puke. "You'll take the meeting? Or shall I . . . ?"

I looked him hard in the eyes before returning the fake smile and then offering it to the room. Lyle fiddled with his pen.

"I'll lead," I said. "I've prepared."

I was certain that day, the first day I had to face Lyle again at work, was the low point.

Fifteen months later, my hair had grown back thick and curly, better than before I'd gone bald. Lyle was mostly back at the New York office, but thoughts and images of him still ping-ponged around my brain, no matter what mantras or breathing tricks I tried to make them disappear. The thoughts would stop my breath, freezing time to let shock, humiliation, and grief have their turn. Still, I got my work done. If I had to talk to him, I made myself sound so breezy I almost believed he didn't matter at all.

"You're looking good," Lyle said one day while he was heading toward me in the hallway. *Insincere son of a bitch.* But then, before we passed each other, he looked at me in the old way, heat in his eyes, and I startled with a sharp inhale. *No response required*, I told myself, though something like a smirk involuntarily appeared. I walked on, using a file folder for a quick wave.

The SoClo rollout went so well that we picked up Agricorp as a client. I'd just had a stultifying lunch in Jack London Square with two of the company honchos who'd flown out from Des Moines to see how we'd go about rebranding high-fructose corn syrup.

I took a hard look at Buzz Nyland, who'd called me "young lady" twice since we'd met, and then at Pete Crawley, so cowed by his boss he seemed to shrink during lunch. It was all I could do to resist getting up from the table, going to the restroom, and leaving for good. But then, these new clients came with a big bonus and salary bump. I'd been looking to buy a condo on Lake Merritt, with a grown-up kitchen, office nook, and bathroom big enough to fit a tub. I'd have a guest room, too, so maybe I could convince Marisa to stay with me some weekend. We could talk, really talk, like we hadn't done since, well, honestly, ever.

How to explain my relationship with Marisa? I was just figuring it out myself, but so much of what we'd become had to do with Bradley, and his drinking, and both of us covering for him and denying to each other and ourselves that there was a problem—you do that long enough and what's true and what's a lie becomes hard to discern. Of course, my lying about Lyle and leaving Bradley for a fantasy didn't help any. But she played her part too. Marisa was tough.

This is what I was thinking as Buzz droned on, displaying a mouthful of crab cake. I reached unconsciously up to my collarbone, where a dull pain had emerged the day before. It grew sharper when I touched it there at the lunch table, and my breath stopped.

It wouldn't be the first time I'd come up with symptoms mimicking a cancer recurrence. I'd had the coughs (spread to my lung?), the headaches (to my brain?), even the suspect yellowish cast to my skin in a department store mirror (liver?). We all do it. Anyone who's had cancer has had a symptom that comes with the gut-stabbing terror that this is it, the metastasis that will kill. I'd been prodded, x-rayed, MRI'd.

I pressed my collarbone and heard my dead father's voice say, "It's nothing." My dead mother chimed in, "Don't be a hypochondriac, for gosh sakes!"

I have no idea what Buzz said during the rest of the meal. "Sure thing," I told him, as their limo pulled up afterward. "I'll be back to you with a proposal." Patsy was going to have to get on the line with his assistant, "just to confirm" what was discussed.

I went home instead of back to the office, dialed Dr. Wong's number, and made the first available appointment for a CT scan of my bones. For once, I was taking my stoic parents' advice with grains of salt. Healthy, healthy salt.

The day of the appointment, I drove all the way to the Hayward suburbs, where, in a faux Tuscan mall, a diagnostic center was stuck between a camera store and a Michaels hobby shop.

I passed through the tiny lobby with Florida rattan chairs and plastic philodendrons and into a prep room where a man named Tarik stuck an IV in the usual spot on my hand. Dye pumped into my bloodstream but needed time to circulate. "Come back in three hours," he said. "There's a Starbucks."

I sat there in the Starbucks, staring out the window, coffee growing bitter and cold. Across the parking lot sat a group of middle-aged women, gathered around an outdoor table in front of the Applebee's. Their lunches heaped on trays before them, they clasped hands and bowed their heads. Instead of thinking, *Maybe now's a good time for me to start praying*, or at least facing up to my life and the possibility of it coming sooner rather than later to an end, I started in on obsessing about Lyle. Was it the obsession itself that'd led me to where I was? Or was the obsession a way of escaping the fear of this day coming?

I needed to think of something else, so I fiddled with my pad and pen and wound up writing a prayer of my own:

> *Lord, why hast thou forsaken me*
> *in the shadow of Rubio's fish tacos?*
> *I thank you, oh Lord, for the sustenance*
> *of Texas West BBQ pulled pork*
> *And ask your forgiveness for stuffing the temple of my soul*
> *till these shorts are an abomination on my thighs.*
> *I pray for the resurrection of Scrapbook World*
> *and for the financial health of Ritz Camera too.*
> *Yet, surely, I shall not wander till the end of my days*
> *in the wilderness of Tuscany Roads.*

Its porticos are dark, Lord, and also fake.
Lead me to the path of something better to do, Lord.
Give me time, Lord, and I'll do things differently, some-
where else. Somewhere more pleasing in your sight.

And then, stupidest thing ever, I emailed the prayer to Lyle. I hadn't contacted him in months—by then we were working on different accounts—but there, in the worst possible moment, my most vulnerable moment, I emailed him.

I wrote him a little note saying I was waiting for the results of a bone scan "because of some complications," and that in my boredom I wrote this fake prayer I thought he might enjoy. I pressed "send," still hoping he'd be there and be real, that I could touch him, somehow, and everything would be back to the way it used to be. What an idiot. What a liar, telling myself I was so over him. That things had been perfect in the first place. What a lie everything about Lyle was. I didn't even want to think about all the lies in my life.

Seconds later, my email buzzed:

Liz, you are hilarious! Thanks for sending this. And do let me
know the results of your scan. I'm sure you'll be just fine!
    Take care,
    Lyle

I dug in my purse for a rubber band. It had been nearly a year since I threw away the thick red one I'd put around my wrist to ward off my obsession. The band would snap, and I'd think, *Forget him and the sting of him; make my wrist sting instead.* So that day in the parking lot of Tuscany Roads, I dug through my purse, the wadded-up pink-ribbon tissues, the Tylenol and codeine pills, shoulder-sized Salonpas, too many lipsticks, and the purplish-brown polish I kept thinking I was going to take to that new Vietnamese nail place on Twelfth. No rubber bands.

The man simply couldn't handle anything uncomfortable, any hint of real pain or fear. I couldn't believe I used to think all that denial was just optimism, that he was just a positive guy, not a chickenshit passive-aggressive two-faced southern asshole. This was the very thing that had attracted me most when we'd first met at work—his always-upbeat South Carolina southern-gentleman charm. Never a fucking discouraging word, never facing up to anything real, his "manners" keeping tough conversations at bay. He'd made it so easy, and sure, I'd been complicit, but still. Fucking Lyle. To think that he'd been my big goal in life. If I had any life ahead of me, any time left with my health, I needed a better goal.

*D*r. Wong confirmed what I knew the scan would show: metastases—"mets"—in my collarbone. As I stood in the paper robe, mouth stuck on open, she handed me a piece of paper with the information about Mercy's Thriving Survivors. A support group. For me. I'd never in a million years.

Out of habit, I suppose, I called Bradley first.

"Everything okay with our little girl?" he asked before I even said hello. Our little girl had just turned twenty-six and had started work as a lawyer in a big-time firm in LA.

"It's been a while since we've talked, but I assume so," I said.

"Well, I talked to her last Thursday; she sounded great."

I felt the corkscrew twist in my stomach. She always called him, never me. Twiddling the cord on the old-fashioned wall phone, I looked out through the tiny living room and into my bedroom. Sycamore leaves banged against the bay window above the bed where I'd lain like a block of cement after chemo, sweating a chemical smell, drifting in and out, in and out.

"Actually, this is about me. I wanted you to know first, so after I tell Marisa and she calls, maybe you can buck her up and help her through this?"

"Through what?"

"My cancer's back. Metastasized. In the bone." Not "my bones" but "the bone"—the way doctors describe it. Part of a nameless body. Already closer to cadaver.

"What?" Bradley acted as if he hadn't heard me, but I knew

he was just buying time. He hadn't the slightest idea of how to respond when serious issues came up.

"I'm Stage Four, Bradley. It is not good. I'll be okay for a while, maybe a few years, but most likely this is going to kill me, barring a Mack truck or heart attack, you know . . ."

"Jesus. Liz. My God, really?" A pause. I imagined him reaching for a flask. "Hold on. Don't be such a pessimist. Practically every day I hear of new treatments. If anyone can beat this, you can! I wouldn't want to take you on. I bet cancer thinks twice too."

"Ha ha," I said. Always the sales pitch with Bradley. The optimism that really means "please don't make me uncomfortable."

"You're right," I said. "I've got a whole shitload of pills to take. I'll probably outlast you. Anyway, just wanted you to know. Let me be the one to tell Marisa. I don't want her getting upset. And it may take a while, because she's so slammed at work. I want it to be the right time. Not that there's precisely a right time, but she's so busy, you know? I'd hate to set her back . . ." I was babbling. Even though we were divorced, and even though Bradley was more often than not too high to really listen, there I was, expecting him to be my sounding board. The one thing I knew he'd understand was my worry about Marisa.

"Okay, I won't tell her till you tell me it's okay."

"Thanks, Bradley."

"You give 'em hell, kiddo." I heard the catch in his voice.

"You take care of yourself," I said.

Right then I realized that I wanted him to comfort me. And right then I realized what I hadn't realized in our years of marriage: he couldn't.

I needed a walk. I locked the kitchen door behind me, stepped down the three concrete stairs, and walked down the driveway to Park Boulevard, flicking and shaking my hands at my sides. As if I could make the cancer fly out through my fingertips and, with it, all the failed relationships of my life.

What a mess I'd made. Mistaking Lyle, of all inappropriate people, for the one who could rescue me, mistaking great sex, the excitement of secret meetings, for that elusive thing other people seemed to have in their lives without any effort at all.

Perhaps as a way of putting it off, I told myself the news would be better delivered to Marisa in person. Whether I was protecting her, or me, I honestly don't know. I'd set it up so she could grow up to be even more tightly wrapped than me. I'd always thought of those as good qualities—don't let your emotions get the best of you, because the men in your life sure won't; tough stuff passes, so don't dwell on it; whining is not to be tolerated; keep your complaints to yourself. Now that I needed to talk to her about a Big Thing, a thing I really couldn't brush aside, a thing that wouldn't pass until I did, how would I start?

The next day, I asked Patsy to hold my calls, closed the door to my office, and paced. I tidied the files on my desk, noticed two dying roses and a shriveled lily in a vase on the bookshelf, put those in the trash, and rearranged the remaining semi-fresh blooms. I played out the conversation my daughter and I would have, how I'd be straightforward, but not needy, when I asked her to come up to Oakland for a visit.

I moved a file from the stack to my briefcase, pretending I'd have better luck focusing at home. I breathed in purposefully, then picked up the phone. It was Marisa's direct number, but after three rings, her assistant picked up.

"May I tell her what this is about?"

Seriously. I'm her mother. "Please just ask her to return my call when she has time," I said.

At home, I sat numbly on the couch, no TV, no food, just staring, waiting for the phone to ring. By 8:00 p.m., stomach clenched and mind ricocheting from one fear to the next, I put the flip phone in the pocket of my fleece and walked again down noisy Park Boulevard toward the lake, hunched in a stiff

March breeze. Streetlights and traffic lit the way on the route I'd taken many nights after work. People were out, darting into the 7-Eleven, jogging in sweatpants and hoodies, dragging themselves home after work, but suddenly I did not feel safe. I hurried the two blocks back, double-locked my door, and closed the kitchen blinds before making a cup of tea. At nine thirty, Marisa called. I could hear the exhaustion, the exasperation, too, in her voice.

"What is it, Mom?" She thought I was being needy already. Wait until I told her the truth.

"Oh, nothing, really. Been a while and I'm just thinking of you . . . Listen, think we might plan a weekend together, or even a day? Could you come up here? Or I could fly down there? Just to play tourist, go out to dinner?"

"Oooo-kay? What's this about?"

"I have to have a reason?"

"No, I guess . . ." I heard a shuffling sound, a loud exhale. "I could come up in two weeks, Saturday the twenty-eighth," she said. "Just for the day, though. I have something that night."

I stifled my disappointment. An afternoon would be a good start.

"Well, great, then," I said, overly chirpy. "I'll find someplace nice for lunch, and we can—"

She interrupted me. "Yeah, we'll figure it out. Can't talk more now though. Just got home and still have piles to do."

"Okay, honey. You'll get through it. Sleep well." But she'd already hung up.

"You'll get through it"; I'd said this so many times to my daughter. In elementary school, when she was determined to be the lead in the school play and the goalie on her soccer team at the same time. In middle school, when she kept a straight-A average and ran for student council and also on the track team. Overbooked in high school, stressed with SAT prep, applying to colleges, applying for jobs. Why did I always say, "you'll get through it"? Shouldn't I have said, at least once, "give yourself a break"? No, I encouraged her frantic schedule to keep her from feeling the tension at home. If she came home late and tired from practice, Bradley's absence wouldn't be as felt.

Too late to change any of that. At least we'd have an afternoon. The thought made me giddy and at the same time scared. Afraid of my own daughter, of blowing it somehow. I always seemed to blow it. But now, ashamed as I was at the thought, I had the cancer card. What daughter wouldn't drop everything, once she knew her mother was Stage Four? What a twisted silver lining. I was determined not to use it.

I sat at my kitchen counter, picking at the remains of a Whole Foods salad, noticing the cracks in the tile and remembering the smooth expanse of granite, the Wolf range in our old house where, on good nights, I'd cooked for Bradley and Marisa. I touched my collarbone and felt it throb. There were pain pills in my medicine cabinet, but I did not want to go there yet. So I climbed down from my stool and went to the refrigerator for the bottle of chardonnay. I knew it wasn't good for me, but really? Did I give a shit at that moment? I did not.

I didn't want to call Kate, or my sister Louise, who'd just be waking up in Amsterdam. Chitchat with the neighbors was out of the question. I had big things on my mind, like what was looming ahead, and I didn't know my neighbors Stu and Linda well enough for that kind of conversation. I thought for the briefest second of calling Lyle, not even caring about his wife. Doesn't a Stage Four diagnosis trump everything? But a hot rush of humiliation and shame rose to my cheeks. All that lying. All that pain, and only myself to blame.

I drank half a glass of wine and considered for the first time in my life that I was approaching the end of it and did not have the tools to proceed. Usually, without even thinking, I knew how to fit into a situation, how to be the way people needed me to be. But this? It was mine alone. Even as the wine warmed my belly, the fear of somehow blowing my own life lay hard in my chest. I opened the refrigerator as if the answer might be inside, and I stared at the empty shelves. Finally, I dug in the pocket of my fleece jacket for the piece of paper Dr. Wong had given me, the one with the support group information on it. I'd suck it up and go.

Chapter 3

*M*ercy's Thriving Survivors gathered Wednesday nights in the Nordstrom Employee Training Room, because someone must've thought a hospital conference room would be too depressing. To get there, I walked through the Designer Studio, past all those beautiful expensive things, all those ways of being in the world that I'm not and never will be. A silk blouse on a mannequin caught my eye—simple and sensuous, the color of dark cherries. *It would work under a blazer too*, I thought. I fingered the beautiful fabric, noticed the fine stitching at the collar, the way the first button would rest just barely above the décolletage. *Eat your heart out, Lyle.*

I reached around the mannequin for the price tag pinned discreetly to the back of the blouse. A hundred and seventy-five dollars! I'd never spent nearly that much on a blouse. But wasn't that the sort of devil-may-care thing someone in my position was supposed to do? I turned to a rack, lifted from it the identical blouse, and held it in front of me before a mirror. My sallow cheeks seemed to brighten on the spot.

The young salesclerk, made up and dressed to the nines herself, asked, "Will this be on your Nordstrom Card?" I detected a dismissive air, perhaps because of my sweatpants or the fact that I didn't have a Nordstrom Card. Then, as she folded the blouse just so and wrapped it in white tissue, it hit me: a $175 silk blouse. Some legacy! A struggling family could buy groceries for a month with that amount. I'd planned to get around to altruism at some point in life, but when had I done anything like pay for a family's groceries, even though I could've afforded it? A cloud of shame and regret hovered between me and the clerk as she handed me a thick-handled shopping bag.

"You'll love this," she said. I carried the bag past dressing rooms, past elegant knits and $1,000 handbags, then down a hallway, where a door opened into a square beige space with nothing in it but two long plastic tables, one in the room's center, surrounded by folding chairs, the other against a wall by the entrance to the room.

I noticed the four people in chairs and thought, *This is it, the moment I can turn around and leave.* I'm still not sure why I didn't. Ahead of me at the wall table, a woman in a flouncy, flowery long skirt, a thick sweater camouflaging her too-thin frame, bent to fill out a name tag, her long, streaky blonde hair giving her the look of a teenager. When she rose and turned in my direction, though, I stifled a gasp. Then I smiled too big, hoping to cover my shock at the horror-show moment. Of course, the long blonde hair was a wig. It took me a minute, standing there smiling too wide, to realize her scarred, dented face had been pretty, before.

Her name tag said Rhonda, an old-fashioned name that befit her, somehow. I stuck my hand out and said, "Hi, I'm Liz," but with an odd, crooked smile she lifted a skinny elbow toward me and said, "Rhonda. I'm sorry, but, cancer-shake?" I lifted my elbow to hers, apologizing in turn. "Of course."

Settling in with Rhonda's face, I saw shiny french blue eyes. Beautiful eyes, above still-high cheekbones and mostly creamy, cared-for skin. She was just older than I expected her to be when I saw that long blonde wig from the back. The right side of her face was pink and indented at the cheekbone, and a half-inch tunnel threaded with a scar stretched from chin to ear.

I followed Rhonda to the table where others were taking their seats and pulled out a chair between a pallid young man in an Army-surplus jacket and a large woman with gray, post-chemo fuzz peeking from under a paisley turban. I stuck the bag under the table by my feet, a flush heating my cheeks.

Everyone in the place was wearing sweats or the equivalent; my own baggy cardigan and T-shirt fit in just fine. What had I been thinking, buying that blouse?

Rhonda, who'd taken the chair across from me, was the only one who'd made an effort, wearing a scarf in a bright swirl print over a pale-pink cable-knit sweater. She pulled from her big yellow hobo bag a plastic spray bottle, the size they allow you to carry on airplanes, then lowered her head and spritzed her mouth, setting the bottle on the table in front of her. I thought she might be a little OCD about bad breath, but then she quietly explained.

"No salivary glands," she said. "Radiation. It's the only way I can keep my mouth moist. I'm so sorry it's intrusive." So sorry to bother us with the sound of her spray. Didn't want to inconvenience anyone, didn't want to offend our sensibilities with her spray. I felt a strange warmth toward this woman. If she could sit in this awful room with her mouth spray, surely I could suck it up and stay.

In walked Christine, the facilitator, grinning as if we were all about to have the very best time talking about our cancer and how we're getting ready to die. I knew she was the facilitator because hers was the only plastic name tag pinned instead of pasted on, and because of that too-eager smile. She sat at the head of the table and arranged a binder and pencil in front of her.

Crap, were we going to have to do worksheets? Circle our pain levels from one to ten? Put an "X" on the frowny face or the smiley face? Or was she taking notes on our attitudes, passing them along to our oncologists if anyone sounded ready to jump off a bridge?

The man pulling out the chair next to Rhonda was huge, thickly built and maybe six foot four. I figured he'd chosen the seat next to the delicate Rhonda so he'd have more room to manspread; a man that big couldn't help it.

He nodded at the facilitator, who gave the big smile back, and I suddenly wanted out of there again, never mind sweet Rhonda, but it was too late. Leaving would cause me to make a scene, and one thing I never, ever do is make a scene. So I lowered my head and took a deep breath. *I have nothing in common with these people*, I thought, and then I remembered, *Oh shit*. The thing we did have in common was the biggest and worst possible thing. So why were any of us even there? Why didn't we all just run the hell out of that room, past the designer blouses and out the door to our cars and our own houses, where we could try to forget?

We did the round-the-table introduction thing, which I always hate. Thank God Christine didn't make us do one of those "one true thing and one lie" icebreakers, or pass out ridiculous little toilet paper squares on which to write something about ourselves nobody would guess.

"Just your name, and please tell us what brought you here," she said. Was she kidding?

The big guy, Dave, boomed out an answer so loud it shocked me out of my nervous thoughts. "Kidney cancer!" he announced, loud as a ranting radio talk show host, as if kidney cancer were the call-in topic and the audience was queued up to weigh in. He added, "I'm an ex-Marine, a Vietnam vet, and also? I'm gay. Getting that out on the table, case it comes up." He gave a sardonic little salute. Quiet chuckles moved around the table.

Rhonda answered easily after that. "Squamous cell of the jaw," she said. "Three surgeries, chemo, radiation, now some maintenance therapy. I'm thinking positive, though. I am!" Her high, sweet voice; she should read children's stories with that voice.

Rhonda lifted the bottle up to her mouth with one hand, covered it with the other hand, and sprayed two to three times behind it, as if that way no one would notice.

The young man in the oversize Army jacket, Raul, sat hunched over the table, his post-chemo hair frizzy like a grandma's perm.

He oozed sadness; I could barely stand looking at him and at the same time wanted to rock him in my arms.

Christine got the ball rolling with a question that made me wish for the icebreakers after all.

"Let's talk about how you felt when you were told your cancer had metastasized," she said. "What was going on with you at the time?"

You know when, on the TV news, the hot young blonde sticks a mic into the face of a mother whose child was just lost in a fire? The mother has purple bags under her swollen eyes and her hair is flying everywhere and she's still in a dirty pajama top from two days before. The twenty-four-year-old reporter scrunches her face just enough to look concerned but not enough to give herself a scowl line on camera. "How are you feeling right now?" she asks the mom. Lips glossed, pouty with concern.

That's how it came out when Christine asked us the question.

All cancer patients remember in slow-motion detail what it was like when our doctors called and we heard the word "metastases," not as question but as fact. I don't like to dwell. Maybe the shrinks who trained Christine knew something, though, because all of us wound up talking on and on. I was glad she called on Dave first, so I'd have time to think about what I'd say.

Dave stood up when he was called, and I remember thinking how impossible it seemed for such a big man to have to fight for his life against little tiny cells, even an army of cells—a big man like that should have been able to take them down with one swat. He stood up, six foot four in his burnt-orange canvas shirt with the plaid flannel lining, hair shaved off just the one side of his head. Somewhere unseen, those tiny cells were taking this enormous man down. I thought, *Crap, now we all have to stand.*

Dave said he'd been pumping on the elliptical at 24 Hour Fitness, with his flip phone on the plastic book holder where no cell phones were allowed. He was bargaining with the phone: if he did five miles or 350 calories, the doctor wouldn't call because everything would have looked fine on his MRI. He'd be showered and relaxed enough to make the call himself, and then the receptionist would say, "Oh, I'm not supposed to tell you, but the tests came back fine."

For good measure, Dave did 5.2 miles, but still no vibrating phone. He blamed the cell reception in the gym and panicked that he'd missed the call. Without showering or even grabbing his jacket, he went outside to make the call himself.

"I'm standing there shivering in my sweaty wet gym clothes, on musical hold. Some goddamn '50s nostalgia station was playing 'Runaway.'" He began to sing in shrieking soprano like a taunt, then stopped right in the middle of the song and stood there like he forgot the rest but didn't care.

His voice was so loud, and he was so big, that even across the table from me Dave felt too close. Maybe what he was saying made it feel that way, made me want to cover my ears and look away. I looked down at the Formica table, reflecting in a long line the fluorescent lights set into dingy acoustic ceiling tiles.

"I was on musical hold through the whole stupid song," Dave continued, "and then the doctor's assistant answered and acted like I was her best friend, so happy I called, so I figure it's good news. I hear her tap-tapping on a computer. Tapping forever."

Dave told his story like he'd told it a thousand times.

"Then she comes back on and sounds like a receptionist, all officious and cold, not like my best friend at all. She says, 'Let me see if I can get Dr. Artoonian right now.'"

We all knew where it was going from there. He could've sat right down, but Dave took a deep, defiant breath and pulled his shoulders back, and he wasn't stooping anymore. He wasn't finished.

"I wait through another song, and that one I don't remember because in the middle of it Dr. Artoonian comes on and says, 'I'm sorry to tell you . . .'"

Dave lifted his big palms up in the air. He must've gotten

cold telling us this, cold on that bald side of his head, or else he didn't want us to see him about to cry, because he looked down to his jacket pocket and pulled out a black knit cap, raised his head up, and pulled the cap down almost to his eyebrows. It broke my heart, the way it puffed out on the side where he still had hair, and how, just at that moment, Dave looked lopsided and small. Then he sat down. His chair squeaked hard on the linoleum, and he splayed his elbows on the table.

Fucking cancer. Dave's was kidney, and after his surgery he'd lived with it fine, considering, for more than three years. He'd beaten the odds! Now it was back, just like Rhonda's. Just like mine, and Raul's, and just like it was for Margi in the turban and Todd and the woman who I couldn't see on my side of the table, plus the guy with the bandanna whose name was a scrawl I couldn't read.

The room began to feel stuffy. I was relieved Rhonda stood up next. What if I just didn't stand when it was my turn?

Rhonda's long curly wig fell over half of the indented part of her face. She spritzed her mouth two times and put the bottle down. I wondered if it was hard for her to eat. Could she eat at all? It looked like her teeth were normal, just super white. I wondered if she had to put up with a thousand appointments having dentures made on top of all those radiation treatments, and if she thought it was worth it for the crooked brand-new-dentures smile. Rhonda's optimism made me a tad suspicious because it seemed so genuine.

Rhonda had the kind of radiation where they make a head mask out of mesh just an inch bigger than your skull. They actually bolt the thing down to the table, with your head stuck inside, and you have to stay there under the mesh head cage while you get zapped. They zap you for a long time, too, stuck in that mask. Zap you day after day, till your skin's a purplish red. I thought, *Jesus, I would be so claustrophobic with that kind of radiation.* Breast radiation was a picnic compared to that kind. On my back, arm above my head, cushioned and held still in a custom mold. Then a single buzz, like halftime at a basketball game, and you're done for the day. Just thirty-three days of that, breast and underarm burned to a crisp by the end, but still, no mesh helmet bolted to a table.

The way Rhonda's cheekbone caved slightly in made her smile look lopsided, and her radiated skin showed pink even under makeup.

I wondered if it hurt her to smile at all, but Rhonda smiled a lot, that best new-dentures smile. I swear she glowed serenity, Rhonda did, standing there telling us how she found out her cancer had spread.

"My doctor made me come in to see him so he wouldn't have to deliver the news over the phone," Rhonda said.

He gave her some vague bullshit about anomalies of concern, as if she wouldn't know what that meant.

I had barely looked at Dave when he spoke—it had been too much, too loud, too close, right there across the table for the first time. With Rhonda, though, I couldn't turn away. I figured most people do turn away, whether they want to or not, and wouldn't it feel horrible to have everyone turn away? It would be awful to not fit in because of the way your face was. I always knew how and when to smile, be quiet, laugh, disappear, but how would I act if people turned away? So I made a point of looking right at her, right into her eyes and at all the rest of her face. Rhonda faced Christine when she talked, and Christine fiddled with the bottom of her sweater.

"He thought that was the kind way to deliver the news," Rhonda said. "I felt sorry for him for having to tell me. He said it was the worst part of his job. Poor guy, he's got to be only thirty-five, forty years old."

"And how did you feel, Rhonda?" Christine held her chin for a second. She seemed intent on chewing her hair, pulling it across her cheek with her thumb and index finger. I thought, *For*

God's sake, sit still and quit fidgeting. You're supposed to be the fucking facilitator.

Rhonda said, "Well, of course, I was shocked." She turned her head to the right, good side toward the table. "Even though, you know, I kind of expected it for a couple years. I had a *good* couple of years. I'm really grateful for that." Grateful. That's how she felt. I swear she was trying to make Christine and the rest of us feel better too.

All I could think was that I'd wasted the time between my first diagnosis and my mets. I didn't get any smarter and spent all that time working and obsessing about Lyle, never really focusing on my relationship with my daughter or anyone else.

The only person besides me in there with breast cancer mets was named Happy Calloway, and she was a shining example of why parents should never set a kid up with a name like that. Her voice was a lament—the sound of it, everything she said with it, the echo of her nasal whine lingering in the room after she spoke. If there was one word to sum up everything Happy had to say, it would be "alas." One gesture? It would be the back of her hand, held to her forehead. *Alas. Sigh, alas.* Of course, she was the one who couldn't stop talking. Not only about her breast cancer but her whole miserable life story. Her face drooped, heavy lids, heavy cheeks, hair the color and weight of steel pushing her shoulders down. Alas.

You can go ahead and think what a bitch I am to criticize a so-called sister survivor for being a downer in a support group for dying people, because, sure, if anyplace should welcome downers, shouldn't this be it? Understand, though, that by way of introduction, Happy started in on complaining. Not about dying, not about feeling pain or sickness or all the things she'd be sorry to leave behind. For that whole first ten minutes, Happy complained about her life. Not even her current life, but the life she resented having in the past. How, before she quit working, her coworkers didn't appreciate her. All the times she'd come in early and stayed late to tidy up. All the times she'd straightened shirts on shelves and cataloged the boxes no one else was bothering to catalog. I could barely stand it. How on earth could a person let a simple introduction turn into a lifetime of complaints? I could've bored everyone to tears with how I'd wasted years on the SoClo account, but nobody wanted to hear that. It was hard enough to stay focused on things that were important at that moment.

Christine affirmed Happy's lament, her head moving slowly up, then down, mustering the merest hint of a smile. Happy went on and on, and I wished to God that Christine would think, *Screw the facilitator's manual*, and interrupt.

When Christine finally stepped in and cut Happy off, leaving me the last to go, I was determined to be upbeat. When I said "breast cancer, second time, bone mets," I heard my voice come out squeaky high, as if I were about to giggle, for God's sake. And, looking pointedly at Happy, that's all I said.

I stood, nervous, wishing I'd worn something other than sweats and a T-shirt, and wishing I could wear a bra, but it wasn't worth the nerve pain I got under my left breast and all the way around half my back, ever since they'd taken my lymph nodes and must've hit a nerve.

I wasn't nervous to share the part about Tarik, the Metastasis Hunter, or the part about imagining the worst. I was nervous to share that, while Rhonda felt sorry for the doctor who told her about her mets, I felt guilty. And there was no way I was going into all that, not in front of all these strangers, even if all of them had troubles as bad or worse than mine. If I didn't want to, I wouldn't even have to see them again. Still, I wasn't ready for a tell-all. But Christine pressed.

"And what happened that day?"

"When my doctor called, she told me straight out," I said. "She said, 'in the bone,' and right away I thought, *This is my fault. I did this to myself.*"

That was too much information, but it was too late. I stared at the clock while I thought about the rest of the story, the part I couldn't say.

I fiddled with a tissue in my right hand, looking down at the table instead of at Christine or Rhonda or Dave across from me, thinking of a lie I could say instead of telling them I'd put off radiation treatments for a whole month just so I could spend a weekend with Lyle, having sex in a New York hotel room, fantasizing about a future over room service filets.

"I mean, after my first diagnosis, I went around like cancer was nothing," I said. "I got so caught up in work, like nothing was different, because I didn't want things to be different. I was so busy working that I actually put off radiation treatments as if it wouldn't matter, and . . ." I babbled on without pause, staring at the clock, above and behind everyone in the group.

"Things just weren't going well . . ." I omitted the details, how I'd left my husband after falling for a married guy, how my daughter barely spoke to me as a result.

"But I did wind up going to radiation, and a year after that, well, here I am anyway."

I made the mistake, then, of looking at Rhonda, who covered her mouth and shook her head. Then at Dave, eyebrows raised, hands clasped before him. And then, damn it, so much for getting off with the minimum, I felt tears coming on. Shit. I so didn't want to cry. Particularly not in front of all those people with worse stories of their own, not senseless melodramas like mine with Lyle. With what I'd told them, it didn't even make sense to cry. How would they know what was bringing forth the tears? I'd come across as hysterical. So I sucked in a breath and made myself stop before a tear actually ran down my face. I took a swig of water from my plastic cup.

"Anyway," I said. "Dr. Wong told me, 'Let's get you in tomorrow, okay?' She said it gently, and that worried me because the last time I'd seen her she was a little pissed off. About the radiation delay, I mean. This time her voice wasn't too gentle, but it wasn't cold either. It was like someone who cared, like she wanted me to know there was a next step, even though she couldn't tell me about it over the phone.

"At least that's what I remember. I drive myself crazy trying to replay that phone call over and over and over in my mind. I don't remember the exact words—and what difference does it make? I replay it anyway, making myself nuts."

Christine looked me straight in the eye but then took her glasses off and wiped them clean on that long black skirt, the kind of skirt a Greek widow would wear. When things got tense in that room, Christine wiped her glasses every five seconds on her skirt. Of all of us sitting around that table, she was the one who looked the most uncomfortable. Because she was the only one who could go home after the meeting and not have to think about dying.

I felt a ball of panic in my belly, as if everyone could read in my mind the whole story about Lyle, and Marisa, as if they were examining in horror the woman who'd traded a month of treatment for a weekend of sex. I felt naked. Exposed. So I kept my sight on the wall clock instead of looking anyone in the eyes. It was 7:40 p.m.; we had fifty minutes to go.

"When I went to my doctor's office the next day, I was sitting on that white tissue paper on the examining table, freezing in the green paper robe," I said. Someone laughed at that, so I looked down from the clock and at the group for a second. I still couldn't look anyone in the eye.

"I said, 'I'm sorry, Dr. Wong. I should have listened about the radiation.' She told me not to think about it. She said, 'In all likelihood, it made no difference.'"

I'd been so grateful when she said that, whether or not my own stupidity really was to blame. I was doomed anyway, by something way bigger than Lyle. My father's skeletal, final-days face appeared in my mind, as did my mother's tumor, pushing through her neck. I knew what doomed looked like. It was in my genes.

I didn't want Christine to probe me about my feelings, so I headed her off. "So I felt relieved in a way. 'In the bone' scared the crap out of me at first, but it really doesn't even hurt yet, unless I press on my collarbone here." I touched the place where the scan had lit up, just to the right of the hollow in my throat. I touched it hard enough to make it hurt.

"I feel lucky about that," I said. Those words—"scared," "lucky"—were safe to say in front of this group, even if the rest weren't.

I didn't say the part about being doomed out loud because I wasn't sure if everyone at the table felt that way. Some people go all the way to the end without believing they're doomed. They say, "I'm going to be the one that beats this!" Not me. I'd seen enough cancer to know the drill. I just wanted to be brave enough to make it through. I sat down.

After talking about how we felt when we heard the worst news of our entire lives, as if that weren't bad enough, Christine wanted to know about our support systems at home. The way she said that, "support systems," made me think of the guy you call in Bangladesh when your hard drive craps out. And I mean, why were we in there in the first place if our support systems were so great? You could tell none of us were exactly going home to *Modern Family* by the way we kind of shorthanded our answers.

"Friends, good friends," said Dave. "Family's not in the picture." That's all he had to say. Nothing more about what picture his family *was* in, or why. After that, Dave just snapped his head away from Christine and looked straight at Raul, next to him, making it clear it was Raul's turn.

Raul told us he had his mom, and she had "health issues," too, but they were getting on fine. Then Raul did what Dave had done and stared at Rhonda so she'd have to go next.

"Oh, I have a partner," Rhonda said. "He's wonderful." She lit up with a lopsided grin. Then her face got serious. She took a deep, resigned breath. "And a daughter," she said. Then back with the smile. "Oh, and lots of support from my church."

That figures, I thought. Church. It explained the trying-so-hard-to-be-sweet thing. So maybe Rhonda did have oodles of support and just needed someplace to go where her face wouldn't shock everyone. Where people wouldn't give her that look.

I expected Christine to take charge at that point and either probe Rhonda some more or tell me it was my turn, but before she could say a thing it was Rhonda who took charge.

"And how about you, Liz?" Rhonda put on her extra-super-sweet voice and smiled across the table at me like I was three years old. Christine pushed her hair away from her mouth and looked at me too.

So I went. I didn't exactly lie, but it wasn't exactly the truth either. I said I had my daughter and some friends. Blank, bland looks on faces at the table.

"Well, one good friend, but I do know a bunch of people. I'm still working, and that takes up most of my time." I didn't say that I hadn't let on about my cancer at work, or that I had to see Lyle there, or that my daughter was the ache in my heart, the one big thing I hadn't figured out how to get right. Or that, two years into all this cancer shit, the people who were really more acquaintances, lunchtime friends, drinks-after-work friends, had mostly stopped asking how I was doing. My sister called from Amsterdam every few weeks, between trips with her oil-exec-utive husband all over Europe and God knows where. Did that qualify as a support system?

There was Kate, and that was about it. And I loved Kate, but even she didn't get what I was going through with cancer. I didn't think anyone could, unless they'd been there themselves.

I didn't want to discuss my support systems. I didn't know the others well enough yet to get into tangled family messes. But Christine wasn't giving up. She was determined to run this group, even if she didn't really know how.

I went home that night unsettled, slightly depressed, slightly ashamed. Those nice, open people—sweet Rhonda, sad Raul, and big, loud Dave—what had I to offer them? Showing up at that one meeting felt like a commitment, but the thought of going back made me queasy. I was used to running meetings, not going to them and being put on the spot.

Then, just as I was unbolting the door into my apartment, I heard the phone, and I bounded across the kitchen to answer it before even closing the door.

"Oh, great," I said, after Marisa's opening word. "I was going to call you to get your flight information." I wasn't, actually, but I liked the sound of her arrival being real, as if weekend flights to see her mom were part of a normal routine.

"I hope it's the nine thirty Southwest," I said. I'd checked the schedules, fantasizing how it would be to meet her, how we'd get through the initial awkward conversation and wind up having a marvelous time, how I'd treat her to a great lunch in North Beach, then a little shopping at Union Square. The image lifted my spirits, and I found myself smiling at the phone.

"Actually," she said, "I can't come after all. I'm sure you understand. I have a brief due Monday morning. In fact, we're all working through Sunday, so it's just not gonna happen."

Her voice was brusque, unapologetic, as if having to call me to cancel was itself an imposition. I noticed, too, that she didn't say "Mom."

"I'm sorry, Marisa," I said. Sorry to have bothered her with the idea. Sorry to have gotten my hopes up. The lump of disappointment dropped from my heart to my belly, and then anger took its place. "You tell me, then, when you feel like coming up. I won't interfere with your schedule." It came across as harsh, not understanding, and at that moment I didn't care. I was the one who needed understanding, damn it. I pictured myself taking my last breath, in a hospital bed, Marisa still in LA, hunkered over a legal file.

"Okay. Will do," she said. "Bye now."

I clutched the phone, mad at her, mad at myself for the melodramatic thoughts, contemplating calling her back, screaming the truth. But that's not how I wanted to tell her.

A wave of fatigue hit me then, as hard as any since chemo. Before cancer, I never understood the difference between "tired" and "fatigued." It's this: "Tired" suggests that when you wrap up what you've been doing, or when you get home, or when the workday is done, you should put your feet up and rest. Fatigue demands it. Not when you're done, but right now, drop everything, lie down where you are, even if where you are is not yet home, not yet done, not anywhere comfortable at all. Fatigue is in charge. After that phone call, my body barely made it to the bed, but my mind wouldn't rest. I couldn't stop thinking about Marisa's distance, my same old job, the sharp pains in my collarbone and in my heart over all the things I hadn't gotten right.

Chapter 4

The few times I've returned somewhere I've lived after years have passed and major life changes have taken hold, I've been struck by how disappointingly different the place looks and feels. How little our once-huge house on base in San Antonio. How shabby the housing at Fort Ord, where as kids we'd had such fun. How dull my once-hilarious friend from middle school had become.

After my diagnosis, work was becoming unbearable. All day, it seemed, officious men made needless comments just to get in the last word, to be clever. Wasting my time. Precious hours devoted to hawking and hype for companies making unnecessary things. And on top of it, I had to deal with Lyle.

"How're you feeling?" He leaned on the doorway to my office, pale-blue dress shirt and a green tie that I'd given him, god damn it. Forehead creased as if worried on my behalf. No more "darlin'," just syrupy extra-southern insincere solicitude.

I glanced up at him for just a second, then returned to reading something on my desk, exhaling at the interruption. I'd stopped myself a dozen times from calling or emailing him—no, I'd want to see his face—or pulling him aside when he was in Oakland for meetings. Like right then. There was my opportunity, right in the doorway, to say it. I could look at him, straight, hard, cool, and say, "Oh, that bone scan? Not good. Metastases. Stage Four." Take that and spin it, Lyle.

But then what? More drama, more insincere remarks. And he'd be the one getting the word out at my job that I was sick.

Lobbying to replace me so he could move out West. I looked up again from the file.

"Let's just stipulate from here on out that the answer is 'Fine,'" I snapped. "But thanks for asking."

His chest rose with a sharp inhale, but then, naturally, he smiled. "Good. Glad to hear it, Liz."

It was only 4:00 p.m., but after Lyle rounded the corner down the hall I decided, *Screw it. I'm done dealing with this for now.*

"Heading out early, today, Patsy," I said. Her face registered equal parts surprise and concern. I was always the last to leave, even on Fridays.

"Know what? Why don't you pack it in too," I said. Her jaw hung open, but she must not have wanted to jinx the moment by questioning me.

"Have a great weekend," I said, over my shoulder, because I was already on my way.

I'd just changed into sweats, splashed water on my face, and determined to shove the aggravating workweek from my mind when Kate arrived in a cloud of her expensive, old-fashioned Van Cleef & Arpels scent. She'd brought over a pizza, and the moment I opened the door for her, the perfume-over-cigarette smell made me a little queasy.

"Why don't we eat outside?" I suggested.

We brought out paper plates on the rickety wrought iron table, along with a bottle of Chianti for Kate and water for me. I felt shitty enough in the mornings without risking a headache.

"You always look so clean and pressed, even on Friday after work," I said. Kate in her jeans and a crisp white blouse. "Did you go home and iron that?" Ironing was a habit neither one of us had been able to break since childhood. I swear she'd ironed the jeans too.

"Growing up, I ironed my dad's uniform shirts for ten cents apiece, and pillowcases, even the tops of sheets," I said. This was the opener for one of our shticks, the one about growing up as military brats. How what we grew up thinking was normal, wasn't.

"Didn't everybody?" Kate asked with her big-toothed grin.

"Didn't everybody shop only at the PX?" I asked.

"Didn't everybody play in the bivouac just beyond the sign that said, DANGER, AMMUNITION, because some of the spent shells might still be live?"

I raised my water glass to her at that one. My turn.

"Didn't everybody stand and say the Pledge of Allegiance before the movie started?"

She raised her Chianti glass to me.

"Didn't everybody ride their bikes in the spray behind the DDT trucks on base?" She lowered her chin and raised her brows.

"Got me," I said. "Jesus. See you in the chemo lounge one of these days. Must've been an Air Force thing."

"MacDill, in Tampa," she said, then took another sip of wine, a big one this time, and dug into the pizza box for a second slice. She'd ordered The Works, and we'd forgotten about the pineapple. Yellow chunks of it piled into a corner of the box. She'd lost too much weight since the most recent of her messy breakups, this one particularly searing as they'd lived together nearly a year. I was glad to see her plowing into the cheesy, greasy slice. Sitting there with my best friend, the impatience of the day began to slip away.

When Kate and I met, in 1977 at San Francisco State, it was that tribal connection that made us instant friends. After class in college, Kate asked me if I wanted to have lunch with her, maybe because she'd noticed I was the only other one in the room who wasn't nodding earnestly at the professor as he decried American atrocities in the Vietnam War. Walking to the cafeteria, we talked about everything—school, the TV show *Mork & Mindy*, the new tourist trap Pier 39, the movie *Annie Hall*—before getting to the one question both of us were afraid to ask and have to answer.

I went ahead and asked it first. "Where'd you grow up?"

That day, Kate's lips pressed together in a tight line and she took in a deep breath. "I grew up in the Air Force," she said. "All over the place." She stared at me hard, as if daring me to criticize, but instead I actually shrieked in relief.

"Me too!" I said. "I mean, the Army. But all over the place!"

All the things we knew about each other, before they were even said.

It was always like that with us—she understood things about me I didn't have to actually own up to—probably one reason I loved her. But when it came to cancer, the biggest thing in my life now, we had no common frame of reference. If I wanted her to know about how cancer felt, I'd have to tell her, and that felt like a new weight between us. So I made the mistake of telling her about Marisa instead.

"She can't come up after all," I said. "Work."

"You're kidding me." Kate took another bite of pizza and scowled.

"Well, you know, she's got to prove herself in this job, and that's the price you pay at a big firm like that," I said, covering for my daughter like I'd always covered for Bradley and his drinking.

She took a long sip of Chianti.

"For God's sake, Liz. Isn't this the second or third time she's blown you off? And you still haven't told her about your diagnosis?"

"I thought it'd be better in person. You know, she's got all these resentments from the divorce. From everything, it seems, growing up . . ."

Kate slashed at her mouth with a napkin. "Well, that's just a crock," she said. "She's got nothing whatsoever to complain about. You should just quit tiptoeing around her bullshit. I mean, how dare she, even if she doesn't know what you're going through!"

I pulled a shawl tight around my T-shirt, suddenly feeling a chill.

"It's perfectly normal," I said. "Her age, her job. And she doesn't know. That's on me. When she's able to come up, I'll tell her."

"Hope you live that long," Kate blurted, then gasped. "What a horrible thing to say. I mean, I am just so pissed at her, and pissed at you for letting her get away with it, again. You've let her treat you like that for years."

It wasn't her faux pas that made me angry. My relationship with Marisa was a button I could not tolerate her pushing. We'd had the argument before, only not as directly, when the stakes weren't as high, the hurt not so close to the surface.

"You have no idea what you're talking about!" My voice rose. "You have absolutely no idea what it was like keeping it together in that house, or what it's like now. I don't need your judgment about my most painful thing at the very worst fucking time!" I saw the light in the neighbor's kitchen turn on.

Kate's face dropped; her shoulders too. I knew we'd both said the kinds of things that can ruin a friendship, but at that moment my fury held sway.

"I'm going in," I said. "Thanks for the pizza."

Chapter 5

*K*ate apologized over the phone that Sunday, and I apologized in turn, but I knew there'd be coolness between us for a while. Not because we'd hang on to resentment but because emotional flare-ups like that were so rare, for both of us. We hadn't had one in years, and, come to think of it, that argument was about Marisa, too, and my constant worrying about her even after she'd entered high school. Kate didn't have children, so that was another thing she didn't get.

I hadn't made up my mind about whether to go back to the Thriving Survivors, but I did want to be around people who got it. People who wouldn't judge my story—well, at that point, they couldn't, because they didn't know it. Maybe I could make a clean slate with these people, just as I'd done at every new school. They'd know a different version of my story, just as I entered its most consequential chapter. Or maybe I'd go back and just keep my mouth shut, more like Raul. Nobody could make me say anything.

I arrived early, like I always do, and saw Dave and Rhonda at the table alongside the wall, the table with the green tea and flax bars on it. The flax bars tasted like particleboard, but we ate them anyway—me for something to do with my hands, others because flax is supposedly good for you, or so they remarked.

Dave kicked off the conversation with the cancer icebreaker "Who's your oncologist?" And Rhonda said hers—she called him

Peter, not "Dr." anything—had become "not only a doctor but a dear, dear friend." Envy sliced through me as I tried to imagine Dr. Wong and I having the kind of conversation such friends must have.

"I swear I can't focus on a single thing these days, can you?" Rhonda asked me directly.

"Focus?" I flushed at the thought of the botched presentation, the lunch meeting with Agricorp, where I'd spaced out everything from the moment I felt my collarbone throb. And then the last big meeting I'd chaired after that, where I'd lost my train of thought right in the middle of a sentence. It was awful, thumbing through a binder as if the thing I meant to say needed data that was in there somewhere, to back it up. "Let's just move on to the next item," I'd said. But everybody knew. We hadn't concluded the last item. Worst of all, Lyle was there with his goddamned worried brow. At meetings, I'd always been the one who insisted upon recapping each item, getting everyone to agree about next steps. I felt their eyes on me, concerned, and was that a smirk from Jeannine, that snotty, ambitious new associate?

I blinked at Rhonda. "Focus? Oh, God, yes!" What a relief to not be the only one.

"I swear I haven't been able to finish reading a book for an entire year," she said. She wore another long, full skirt and heavy sweater, this one embroidered with a line of daisies. I'd upped my game with clean jeans and a white blouse, à la Kate.

"You wouldn't believe the stack of books by my bed," I said. "People thought I'd have all the reading time in the world during treatment. I could barely get through a newspaper article!" It was the first time I'd admitted that to anyone.

Rhonda's bright eyes softened as she nodded. "Well, maybe we're saving our focus for the important things," she said.

"Thanks," I said. "That's what I'm going to tell myself from now on."

Dave broke in, practically bellowing, "Do you gals meditate?" Another surprise from this giant macho-looking man. Maybe that's what intrigued me about Dave. We'd both spent years hiding ourselves. Me as an Army brat, him pretending not to be gay in the Marines.

Rhonda said she prayed every day and, yes, meditated too.

"Most I do is go for walks," I said. "I find it hard to sit still. If I wait till night and just sit there and breathe, before I know it my head's on the pillow and I'm asleep."

"I haven't been able to sleep in years." It was Happy, joining in. "So much to worry about. And then my husband snores." Her sigh was so deep I thought for a second it was a parody, a joke, but her look was contemplative. "Forty-three years of marriage. It's just not what I expected."

Forty-three years, stuck on what you expected when you were sixteen. It was the saddest thing I'd ever heard, and it also struck me as funny in a way it wasn't supposed to. Looking at the others, I could see Dave and Rhonda thought that too. Dave's lips pressed tight together in the way they do when you're trying not to smile. Rhonda put a fist to her mouth. I swear she wanted to laugh too. I pretended a cough to cover my chuckle, and my chest warmed with the odd connection.

At ten after six, Christine gathered her no-wrinkle, ankle-length black skirt over thick black ankle boots and settled her plump behind into one of the folding chairs. That was the signal that we should sit down too. I brought a flax bar to the table, crinkled the wrapper open, and set it on a little napkin in front of me for something to look at in case things got tense.

Christine smiled too big and slapped on that compassionate face, leaning her neck toward us, brown hair with the too-blonde highlights puffed out on top, tapering in points below her chin, long enough to fiddle with but not to chew. She had already pulled out of us how we felt about our side effects, about work lives interrupted or ended for good, about getting our affairs taken care of. The way she put that—"getting your affairs in order"—made me think of my affair with Lyle, about my divorce, my daughter, and how none of it would ever be in order at all.

After we were all settled into our chairs, Christine looked down at her four-by-six-inch spiral notebook and then back up at us, one by one around the table.

"Today I'd like us to talk about something many of you may have on your minds. Something that can heal our spirits and bring peace—forgiveness." Christine asked if we wanted to talk about things we'd thought about forgiving "in the recent past." Why didn't she just say "since you found out you're terminal," or even "as you contemplate what lies ahead," if she wanted to be euphemistic about it?

Damn. I could forgive Lyle for hurting me when I was most vulnerable, for the chickenshit way he left. Bradley, for hiding behind the bottle all those years. But then I'd have to forgive myself for cheating with Lyle in the first place. For hiding my own self from Bradley and staying with him way too long. And for Marisa, spoiling her rotten and then expecting her to be considerate. Buying her too much stuff, programming her every hour when she was growing up. Letting her get away with being so distant. Being so distant myself.

The room was silent for a long moment, and I stared into space, having those thoughts. Rhonda's head was down and I could tell she was fiddling with her cardigan under the table, but when she looked up she turned to Christine and started right in.

"I know Jesus wants me to let go of some things, and there are some things I just can't," she said. She said it so softly I'm sure most people at the table couldn't hear her. She didn't elaborate but kept looking at her lap as if holding a rosary under the table, saying a prayer for penance. The Jesus stuff usually made me squirm and want to run for cover. I'd been asked too many times—out of the blue by a friend's mom while baking cookies at her house, by the chaplain's daughter, by my own mother's Oklahoma cousin—"Have you accepted Christ as your personal savior?" The question made me freeze. If you say no, you know the person asking has consigned you to hell in their mind. If you say yes but you know for a fact that you made that declaration as a kid and that nothing resembling God has been in your life for decades, you're the kind of hypocrite you hate. I finally figured out a response: "Oh, my faith is so personal," I say. Read into that what you want.

I didn't have the guts of my big sister, Louise, who is much more direct and doesn't seem to worry much about what people think. I heard a distant cousin corner her with the Jesus question, about the time Louise was studying to become a nurse. "Let me ask you a personal question too," she responded. "When was your last Pap smear?"

Our own little family went to a Presbyterian church for two years in Monterey, when I was seven, and I loved Sunday school. But just as we were about to move, the minister took his own life. My parents whispered about the horrible thing that had happened that first Sunday we didn't go to church, and by the next week our mother said it out loud.

"Well, if that doesn't make a person lose faith, I don't know what could," she said. I don't think she liked church in the first place, but after that we never went as a family again.

So usually when people bring up anything smacking of religion, I think, *Oh no, here we go*, but with Rhonda, for some reason, I didn't. Maybe because she admitted to not being so perfect. And so far, anyway, she hadn't tried to shove Jesus down anyone's throat.

Nobody said anything for the longest time, so finally I did.

"Forgiveness is hard."

I said it in a kiss-ass way, trying to redeem myself to Rhonda but also because it was true.

I was still replaying the Lyle breakup, and every time I thought of my years with Bradley, another incident popped into my mind that made me think, *How did I put up with it for so long?*

Marisa asleep on a school night, eighth grade. Bradley "heading out for a bit" at 10:00 p.m., fresh clothes, checking himself in the mirror before giving me a peck on my cheek. His real estate deals at the bar. Me wanting to believe they were real estate deals. Next morning, waking up to find a stranger passed out on our living room couch. Bradley half-dressed and snoring like a leaf blower in our bed, his breath—beer and scotch and meat. Me punching him in the shoulder and saying, "Get that man out of here before Marisa wakes up!"

Should I tell the Thriving Survivors about all that? Or tell them the story Marisa and I used to tell instead? That one begins with me coming home from work the next day. Ann Taylor suit, Louis Jourdan pumps. Mom in execu-drag. How I saw the hotel-sized floral bouquet on the dining room table, twigs curling above lilies like petrified smoke. Bradley in the kitchen, apron on, calling out, *"Voilà, mesdames!"* Shaking the pan of filets mignons, the sizzle and flames from the brandy in the pan. Then, at the table, Bradley's toast: "To the most beautiful women in the world!" Bradley lifting a wedding-crystal glass.

Marisa's adoring look at Bradley. "Daaad!"

She gets up from the table to give him a big hug, daddy's little girl. I push the steak around my plate, silent, fuming, while they talk about Marisa's friends, kids I knew nothing about. Bradley knew, though, about their crushes and cliques, who was whose best friend that week.

Before I left Bradley, I'd tell people the story of the flaming filets mignons like I was actually part of the festive surprise. Thrilled by it. I never did tell the part about the stranger with the greasy hair passed out on our living room couch. I didn't want to face the shame of it myself, let alone admit it to anyone else. And somehow, despite all those nights, despite all my attempts to control the story for Marisa, it was me she wound up resenting, not her dad.

But we were talking about forgiveness. I didn't tell the group I wanted to forgive for Jesus, and I hope Rhonda didn't think that. The truth was I wanted to forgive just to bring peace to my own selfish self. To be free of those memories, make some new ones while I still could.

The guy in the bandana said he wanted to forgive his father but couldn't to his face because he's dead, and I don't know why, but I tuned out there, all through the bandana guy talking, and then Margi and Raul. It was feeling pointless, really. Or maybe it was just getting too damned sad.

The group was still talking, but I felt suddenly desperate, like I should leave the room and call Marisa that very moment. No, no. I knew how that would go. Not well.

I still hadn't gotten up the courage to tell her about my cancer being in the bone. She'd already bailed on coming up just for the day, so how would I ask her to come stay with me longer than a weekend? If she thought I was asking her to take care of me, she'd probably come, but I'd hate that. It would be out of obligation.

Maybe she just didn't want to deal with me at all. Truth was, Marisa was more like me than I cared to admit. Ever since she'd been little, Marisa had worked so hard, had been so focused on being the best at everything. How typical of an alcoholic's kid! She'd grown up to be one of those people you admire and hate at the same time.

I looked across the table at Dave. He looked tuned out too. When it got to be his turn, he said, "Forgiveness." Bellowed it like it was the title of a speech he was about to deliver in an arena. He took the deepest, longest breath.

"I hate to say it, but that sounds arrogant to me," he said. "Like something you'd dispense, forgiveness. Like you're God. I'd rather just stick with acceptance. That's my goal. Accepting all the little things and the big ones too." He'd lowered the decibels now to DJ with a mic. His words seemed to echo.

Christine looked up at the wall clock and took off her glasses to clean on her skirt again. Did she not hear him? Did she not get it? She showed no acknowledgment of how awesome it was, what Dave had just said.

No. She called down the table to Raul and asked what his thoughts were on the subject of forgiveness. Her pursed lips, eyes boring in. She might as well have asked for his thoughts on the subject of mitosis.

He was the youngest in the room, maybe forty, with that curly chemo hair and a chin that sloped toward his neck even when he didn't have his head down. His pallor looked like late nights at drunken poetry slams, but apparently it was an effect of non-Hodgkin's lymphoma. When Christine called on him, he pulled on the collar of his faded retro Army-surplus jacket and dropped his chin even lower. He licked his lips and then looked around at us all as if begging for the answer. I thought, *For Christ's sake, Christine, give him a pass.*

"I don't know," he whispered. "I guess." Rhonda dug in her purse like she'd just remembered something. Christine kept staring at Raul, and his head dropped even lower.

"I don't know," he said again. I thought he might cry. He sounded so sad, as if not knowing the right answer would keep him from heaven for sure.

Margi and the bandana guy were having their own whispered conversation at the end of the table. I could hear, ". . . port put in Wednesday" and "Really? They took mine out."

I fiddled with my cup, Rhonda fiddled with her purse, and Dave looked up at the ceiling, then at Christine.

"It's okay, Raul," Dave finally said. "None of us know."

I knew Christine was doing what she'd been trained to do, everything by the book. Look your patient in the eye. It is important to affirm what the patient is expressing. Validate the patient's feelings with a nod but do not interrupt. Smile only to express warmth and connection with your patient, being careful not to appear dismissive of emotions. Your patient may be experiencing sadness, anger, or fear.

Christine was so busy validating and nodding and not interrupting, so busy trying to empathize, not sympathize, I could barely stand it. Someone tells the truth, goes deep down about how they're feeling, and all she does is bore her eyes into them and, lips squeezed into a line, move her head with excruciating slowness. Down, then up, then down. Then she remembers she's supposed to smile and she does, just ever so slightly, without teeth.

I thought about leaving at the break but then considered how hard it would be to come back if I did. As dreadful as it was, at least it was something different to do. Oddly enough, being there with a bunch of people with cancer took my mind off my own troubles somehow. Compared to them, I didn't have it so bad, right? I felt mostly okay, most days. My prognosis was better than most. Also, Dave fascinated me, and Rhonda too. That big, proud man, that sweet, fragile woman, and both of them brave enough to show themselves to strangers.

Raul hunched into himself on one end, Todd and Margi yakked about insurance, the bandana guy sat in the middle and made tiny accordion folds in a straw. For the final half hour, Christine closed her spiral notebook and, thank God, let us talk about whatever we wanted. No more interrogations. I could sit and observe. The group got to talking about chemo, and Rhonda told us how a nurse almost put someone else's bag in her IV.

Everyone reacted, of course, mouths open and "Oh my God" and "Oh! Rhonda!" All around the table. Dave, though, went ballistic. He pounded a knobby fist into the palm of his other hand, so hard it freaked me out. His faced purpled, and out from his bottom teeth came a deep growl, I swear. I stiffened, wondering if he was going into some kind of fit, if he had some mental condition he couldn't control. Rhonda's blue eyes opened so wide, and she leaned back, as if she thought Dave's anger was directed at her. Happy gasped, and Raul actually looked up, scanning the table to see Dave and everyone's reactions to him. Dave leaned forward in his chair, elbows tight to his ribs. He worked his jaw around, gray eyes getting smaller and the lines between them running up his tall forehead in deep, angry grooves.

Then he looked around at the rest of us: Raul, head raised, eyes big with fright; me, stock-still; Rhonda, leaning back. Dave closed his eyes and breathed in deep and slow. He relaxed his jaw and opened his eyes, and those forehead grooves softened to thin traces. We watched him transform right in front of us, from exploding Dave to big mellow wise Dave, and the whole room went silent for a long minute. In the silence, a barely discernible hum and click of the electric clock. People looked down at the beige laminate tabletop or across the room at a single poster, Scotch taped to the wall. It said, "Our Customers Come First!"

I couldn't take my eyes off of Dave. What passion, what discipline! Here was a man who could go deep and not drown. He didn't care if people started looking at the poster and drinking from plastic cups and rustling into handbags and pockets for paper or Kleenex or a business card suddenly missed.

Christine tugged at the right side of her dull brown hair so her scalp showed where it was parted, like someone with too-tight braids. I waited to see if her hair had grown long enough to finally put in her mouth, but it hadn't. She just tugged it tight across her cheek. Right at the moment when I was thinking she looked like a little girl in over her head, she must've figured out I was thinking that. She flicked the hair away from her face and pulled her chair in closer to the table, straightening her back. Professional. "Dave, that seems to have made you angry," she said. *Brilliant, Christine.* "What is it that makes you so angry about the incident between Rhonda and her doctor over meds?"

That was the moment I'd had it with Christine. If Dave wanted to tell us, he would, without her interrogating. I raised my eyebrows and examined the acoustic tile. Dave grinned, just for a second, just at me. He was the one who should have been leading this group. He'd have us all telling it like it was in no time.

"Yes, Christine," he said. "I will explain." His hands flat on the table, I could see the age spots and a scar all the way down one thumb from his wrist. His fingers started to curl under as he spoke.

"It's like I've got only so much time to get it right in the world, and, damn it, I just can't tolerate people getting the important things wrong. Being so incompetent they could put the life of my friend at risk." He took another of his Zen breaths. His hands relaxed, his brow lines thinned, gray eyes grew steady and soft in a spacey mid-distance look. I loved how he called Rhonda his friend. How he'd rush in to save her from that incompetent nurse.

"I get so impatient, but I've got to be tolerant—of every-thing," he said. "And there's only so much time for that too."

He was dead right: we didn't have time for bullshit. Why didn't Christine realize that?

"Tell me. Do you all have the same conflict?" he asked.

Dave had a way of making it okay to say what you were really thinking, a lot more than Christine. So, before I knew it, I was speaking right up.

"I'm not sure I'd call it a conflict," I said. "For me, it's about patience. I am incredibly patient now about stuff that used to make me crazy, but on the other hand, some things I never even bothered to think about make me want to scream. I can wait forever in a grocery store line behind an old lady, digging in her purse for a checkbook, pulling it out after her bill has been rung up, sloooowly writing the check. That used to drive me nuts. I'd be crabby after work, standing in line behind her, rolling my eyes at the checker.

"You'd think, wouldn't you, that I'd want to grab that time, not be forced to spend it in a checkout line? But I get that it doesn't matter. It feels good that it doesn't matter." It felt good, too, sitting there and telling the truth out loud. I turned to Dave, saw him nodding at me, and I lifted my shoulders back.

"The thing is," I said, "something like that will make me believe this disease has made me so wise and aware, you know? Someone who takes it easy, who feels compassion for every being. But no. Yesterday I went completely off on my best friend, just for being impatient with *me*, and really, she was trying to protect me." I suddenly felt a hot wave of shame, blabbering all that personal business to these strangers, even admitting I'd argued with Kate. What if someone pressed me to say even more? But then Happy saved me.

"Nobody has patience with me," she said. "My mom always had more patience with my sister. My husband gets impatient with me but not our son. No matter how hard I work, no matter what I do, nobody wants to give me credit." Her head, slumped, wagged slowly back and forth.

Rhonda reached an arm around Happy's shoulder and gave it a squeeze, then moved back, either for fear of germs or because she didn't want to go overboard sympathizing with Happy's lament.

"Seriously, Happy? You're still thinking 'Mom liked my sister best'?" I felt a hormonal surge of anger, the kind that, since chemo, had shown up unbidden, uncontrollable, and usually at the worst possible times. "In middle age, in Stage Four? Can't you give it a rest? Move on?" My cheeks got hot and I puffed out a breath.

Christine opened her mouth, then closed it. Perhaps she was going to chastise me for lashing out. Can they kick you out of a support group?

Dave gave me a look of such calm acceptance, as if to say, *It's okay. But you can cool down now.*

My body was just beginning to cool and mortification set in. "I'm sorry about that, Happy. Really inappropriate of me.

Patience is not my strong suit lately. Sometimes I get myself so agitated, I can feel my face burning up," I said.

Good God. I'd said it without thinking, with poor Rhonda right there in front of me, half her face burned up, radiation, surgery, God knows what else.

"Amen," said Dave, rescuing me. "I mean about your friend."

Rhonda's sweet, children's-story voice fell over our rising anger like a blanket: "I'm sure your friend will forgive you," she said to me, then turned to face Happy.

Like a four-year-old caught in a lie, Happy, her head still drooping, whispered, "I forgive you."

"I think we have to forgive ourselves sometimes too," Rhonda said. "I've done things to be ashamed of since this all happened. I get impatient. Just last week, getting coffee in my neighborhood. I wasn't even in a hurry. Everyone was on the way to work, but I wasn't, so I should have let others go first. I should have been patient like you were, Liz, at the grocery. But a businessman cut in line in front of me, and I just couldn't let it go. I poked that man right in the back. Hard!"

Rhonda jabbed a skinny finger in the air. I hoped she couldn't hear me gasp. *This* is what I'd hoped was under all that sweetness. Rhonda went on. "Out loud so everyone could hear, I said, 'I guess you must be very important to think you can cut in line like that.' As soon as I said it, I was so embarrassed." I loved the image of Rhonda telling that guy off.

"I was about to apologize to the man when he turned around," she said. "In one second I could see him go from angry to flat-out terrified when he saw my face. Like, 'Oh, Lord, she isn't just crazy, she's got some kind of contagious face cancer!' The man practically jumped backward and bumped the woman ahead of him in line. The way he looked at me made me not want to apologize for the outburst after all. So I didn't.

"I've never done anything like that before," she said. "It was mean, but I forgive myself." Two sprays into her mouth, the bottle behind her hand.

I made a point of looking her right in the eyes, not looking away, and I smiled.

Christine glanced at the clock. Five minutes to nine, time to wrap it up. Before she finished telling us all to have a good week, Christine announced that our next meeting would be "something special." She went on, "Mercy has acquired a block of tickets to an A's game, Saturday. Enough for all of us to go! Sign up at the table, please. We'll meet at the valet parking at ten, and a bus will take us to the game."

I pushed my chair back from the table, then felt a poke at my shoulder and turned to see Rhonda.

"You'll go? I hope you'll go. It'll be fun!"

"Um, I'll check," I said, leaving myself an out.

As soon as I turned from my chair, there was Happy Calloway, slack-faced and glum, releasing a deep sigh just for me. I figured she'd be mad at me, but before I could apologize again, she said, "I'm so glad someone else here understands." That's the thing about people like Happy. You can insult them to their face and they don't get it. "I mean breast cancer," she said. "I keep thinking, *Why me?* But seeing you here, knowing I'm not the only one . . ." Her voice trailed off.

I thought, *Just you, me, and forty thousand dead a year,* but I said, "Yes! I mean, in this group you see people having an even tougher time than we are, you know?" I said it like we'd won the lottery. "It gets me to thinking how lucky I am, all things considered."

Happy's forehead creased. I gave her a conventioneer's clap on the shoulder.

"Seems like you're doing well too!" I said. Then I gave her the upbeat brush-off, the worst kind because it leaves a person with nothing to say but thanks, when you've done nothing for them to thank you for at all. The worst thing you can do to someone depressed about cancer is force her to smile. "Keep taking care of yourself!" I said.

Happy smiled. "See you next week," she said.

Would I? Watching her thick gray hair heading toward the exit, black bag clutched tightly to her hip, I was ashamed of myself and relieved to have her gone. The idea of another round-table with Happy, with Christine, sad Raul . . . nope.

Chapter 6

*B*ut scoring those tickets and suggesting we go out must've been the best idea Christine ever had.

The minibus picked us up outside Mercy Cancer Center, under the covered driveway where the valet parking guys take your car for free when you have to go in for radiation. Free valet parking, and they don't even accept tips. It's one of the perks. Probably has something to do with liability, too, not wanting people with chemo brain wandering around the parking lot, rear-ending some doctor's Mercedes on the way to the pay gate.

But that warm September Saturday of the field trip, everyone was wide-awake, raring to go, even me, although I could give a crap about baseball. I didn't want to let Rhonda down. We were outdoors on a sunny afternoon, connected, on the same team. Nothing to do with cancer, just a day at the ballpark.

Raul was there, and I hardly recognized him standing up straight with a smile on his face and his hair washed and combed. He wore an old Oakland Athletics shirt and even brought a catcher's mitt in case of foul balls. Christine was in jeans instead of the Greek-widow skirt she'd worn at the meeting, and an extra-long A's sweatshirt to cover her butt. I felt like the skunk at the garden party, wearing a red sun-protective shirt over jeans, not even thinking about red being the color of the opposing team, the Boston Red Sox. Duh. And there was Rhonda, decked out in an extra-large vintage Reggie Jackson jersey, gold with green lettering and a white number 9. She wore skinny jeans and an A's cap over her wig. Rhonda punched Raul on the arm and said, "Go, Oakland!" Raul fist-bumped her back. "Go A's."

Then Dave got out of his forest-green Subaru in the parking lot and headed toward us wearing a San Francisco Giants cap. I asked him if he wanted to get killed.

"It's the A's, not the Raiders," he said, palms out and eyebrows up like what else didn't I get about sports.

When everyone got there—Raul, Happy, Margi, Paul, and the bandana guy plus me and Dave and Rhonda—Christine opened the minibus door and waved us in. Rhonda got in the van first so she'd be the one sitting in the way back. Dave got in next so he could sit by her, and then I got in to sit next to Dave.

Everyone else loaded up, and as soon as the bus pulled out of the cancer-center parking lot, Dave said, "Are we all in for junk food?" He looked at me with a wicked smile.

I could already taste it. "Keeeel-basa," I said. "And a beer."

"Garlic fries! Oh, man!" Dave yelled. He was hunched over, knees up practically to his chin and elbows pressed into his sides. I shouldn't have let him take the middle seat, but Dave had a way of making you forget how tall he was. He had that bad posture that big men get when they're kind and are used to leaning down instead of forcing people to look up at them. "What about you, Rhonda? You in?"

I could see her forehead puckering. *Oh no, here we go,* I thought. *She probably has a thermos of kombucha in that black drawstring bag. And kale chips.*

But Rhonda turned to us with the biggest grin. "Churros!"

I laughed out loud. Deep-fried dough crusted in cinnamon sugar. So bad.

I expected Christine to turn back and *tsk* at us, but I don't think she heard because Happy was talking in the seat right behind her, boring everyone shitless.

Dave tapped my knee with his right hand and Rhonda's with his left. "I've got gratitude items to report, ladies!" That was bald-faced mockery of the gratitude drill Christine put us through after the forgiveness bit at Nordstrom. I don't think Christine heard, though.

"Number one," Dave said. "Yesterday's CT scan. Stable mets! This new Sutent stuff they're giving me is doing the job! Nothing growing in the past three weeks. One of 'em is even a little bit smaller."

Overall, Dave looked pretty healthy. He took off his baseball cap and ruffled his half head of hair with both hands, touching the ceiling of the bus. His hair was growing out a nice silvery gray on the one side, thick stubble covering the side with the scar and radiation tattoos. With the cap on, there was nothing out of the ordinary at all. His coloring was still a little off, olive faded not quite right, but his face looked soft and younger outside that dismal meeting room. He had no whiskers yet, but wispy steel brows, and the whites of his eyes were clear. Not bad, not dying, just a big man with his gal pals, heading to an A's game on a Saturday afternoon.

Rhonda smelled faintly of lavender soap. She turned to high-five Dave. Blue eyes sparkling, biggest, crookedest smile.

"Only numbers!" She said it with a little squeal. "Those statistics you read. The odds. That's all they are, you know. Only numbers."

"Only numbers!" Dave and I yelled. And from the seats in front of us, everyone yelled back. Even Happy yelled it. "Only numbers!"

After the big high fives, after the smiles that stayed on our faces too long, Dave's cheeks sagged a bit. Maybe it was just my imagination, just my cynical don't-get-your-hopes-up self, but in the silence after the numbers cheer I heard it sink in. Our good news, when you got down to it, was bad news with a happy spin. Dave sat up taller and pressed his hands down on his thighs. "Second item," he said. "Lewis!" He smiled then and took five years off his face just like that.

"Lewis. My neighbor who got mad at me for blasting Guns N' Roses?" I vaguely remembered him complaining about his neighbor at one point by the flax-bar table. "He asked me over for dinner. Tomorrow night."

I smiled blandly. "Nice," I said.

But that apparently wasn't the response Dave was looking for. He stuck his chin out and pretended to look through the window in front of us, examining the freeway traffic. "Not sure you could call it a date," he said. His voice was quieter than usual. "Not that I want a date."

Ah. A date! It never occurred to me any of us would be thinking about dates.

I leaned forward and looked over at Rhonda. Her lips parted for a full, long breath; then she squeezed them tight together. I thought for a terrible second that she might be one of those churchy right-wing homophobes. She lifted her wig and pushed it back, showing bald for just a second, then pulled it too far forward like she always did. She reached into the drawstring bag for her spray. When you don't know what to say, find something to do.

"I mean, that's great, Dave," I said. I smiled at him, wider than necessary. And big tough Dave looked so relieved, his smile wiped the lines right off his face.

But I was wrong about Rhonda, because once she finished with her spray, she turned to slap Dave on the arm, and then she actually winked at him. He reached his arm around her and gave her skinny shoulder a quick squeeze.

It shocked me, Dave's excitement over a date. Made me feel awkward and apart because I couldn't imagine it, at this point. Not that I wouldn't be all over Lyle if we hadn't broken up. But someone new, now. That shock of new attraction. Trying to look your best for him, wondering whether your best would be enough for him to be attracted back. I wondered if Dave really felt those things or if it was something he just wanted to feel one more time. Maybe he just needed to prove he still had it in him. Was it important that we all go through the motions, at least as long as we could?

Then I thought about Rhonda and if she was even going through the motions with her boyfriend. "Partner," she'd said. The way she'd looked practically gaga that day when she'd told us her partner was her support system, I bet she was still having sex. The way she suddenly seemed excited for Dave, not confused, like I was.

That's when it hit me for the first time. You'd think something so big would've hit me before, but it hadn't. I guess I was so busy working, going to doctor's appointments, getting over Lyle, worrying about Marisa, making sure my shit was together so down the road she wouldn't have to deal with it all. What hit me was, what if I'd had sex for the very last time?

I didn't notice Dave or Rhonda or the people up front or where we were on I-880 South. What was the consequence of no more sex? I wondered if it was more consequential or less because I knew my time was limited. Had I had enough sex for a lifetime? What a ridiculous question. There is never enough and there is always enough. Sex and life, both.

The minibus pulled into the parking lot of the gigantic concrete oval they called "O.co Coliseum," which was a dumb name but better than some of the corporate names it could have been called. People had been tailgating in the lot, and the smell of barbecue lingered. Fans packed their picnic gear into cars, dumped charcoal in trash cans, and headed toward the entrance. It took us no time to get in line behind about a hundred people, nearly every one of them wearing some Oakland Athletics team gear—an A's cap and a rock-band T-shirt, construction-company cap and an A's shirt, Harley jacket with an A's shirt underneath. Old hippies and teenaged hip-hoppers, every age and every race, old-school tattoos like semper fi and crosses and snakes, and brand-new six-color tattoo sleeves. Babies with earrings and moms with nose rings, grandmas in green sweatpants with white stripes down the side. That's what I love about Oakland. How diverse it is, how unpretentious. I suppose it's like the Army. You can root for it, feel a part of the team. You can know half the world looks down on it and not care.

Dave and Rhonda and I stayed together in the line. Even though we didn't know each other well, we started talking to one another like we'd already gotten close, like we knew somehow that we shared something more intimate even than we shared with the rest of the group.

A scruffy gray-bearded guy in an A's propeller cap and green cape walked by, playing a banjo for the fans in line.

"Woo-hoo! Banjo man!" It was the last thing I expected to come out of Rhonda's mouth, loud and out of the blue, but there she was, practically jumping up and down.

"Who knew you were such an A's fan, Rhonda?"

"Growing up in San Leandro? Of course," she said. "I gave this jersey to my dad for his fiftieth. Best times ever with my dad were right here at the A's games. My mom didn't approve, but I think it was the only time my dad ever had any fun."

I tried to think of having fun with my dad. There was that one time we all went camping, in Big Sur. Whooping with excitement under the stars, and then embarrassment after being shushed. I'd disturbed all the others snuggled in their tents. We never went to any games.

"I was never that into baseball," I admitted.

Rhonda looked up at the Coliseum, around at the crowd, back at us, a smile on her uneven face I couldn't quite describe, like wonder and satisfaction at the same time. We moved ahead in line, fans yakking all around us, unzipping their backpacks for security.

"I pitched Little League," Dave said, "but my dad didn't come to a single one of my games. And that was a good thing, given the kind of scene he'd 'a made if he had shown up." The

Giants cap shaded Dave's eyes, but I could tell he wasn't looking at Rhonda—he wasn't looking at anything but the memory in his head.

"My brother, Brent, played in junior high," Dave said. "For those three whole years, Dad was on the wagon. Every game Brent played, I was there and Dad was there. No scenes. Good times. Brent was the best hitter on the team."

Dave made an "O" with his lips and pulled in a deep breath. "Anyhoo. By the time Brent was a sophomore, Dad was back in the bag! Worse than before." Dave pulled that out of himself and let it sit there in the air a minute. Put a fist to his face, arm across his waist. Then he loosened his arms and pulled his shoulders back a bit.

I knew that feeling. How hard it is to look back and admit how it was. Like when I could no longer deny that Bradley's drinking was out of hand when I found the greasy stranger passed out on our living room couch. Right then I felt I knew Dave in the way growing up in the Army let me know Kate. There are things you just understand.

The line behind us grew to another couple hundred. I saw A's gear from every decade, the names of players even I remembered. Rhonda wasn't alone. There were Rickey Henderson and Mark McGwire jerseys from the eighties, old A's T-shirts celebrating playoff wins, and several people wearing Coco Crisp shirts, a couple of them in giant Afro wigs. I'd been so tuned out of sports for so long. I thought maybe Kellogg's was sponsoring the A's now and those Coco Crisp shirts were advertising a new brand of cereal. Didn't figure out until the second inning that Coco Crisp was actually the name of the center fielder; the fans were crazy for him.

A couple brave souls ahead of us wore Red Sox gear. They were die-hard East Coast transplants flying the flag for Boston, and nobody gave them a hard time. Nobody gave Dave a hard time about his Giants hat, either, because the A's-Giants rivalry doesn't really cut deep. It's hardly a rivalry at all. If you live any-where in Northern California, the teams to hate are in LA.

We followed Christine into the dungeon of the Coliseum. A dark, dank tunnel, sweaty people elbow to elbow, shouts bounc-ing off concrete. It smelled of beer and hot dogs, but the light was so bad and the walkway so crowded you could hardly see the hot dog and souvenir stands. I looked up high and saw stains in the concrete from when the pipes broke in the Loma Prieta quake. That day the A's were playing the Giants in San Francisco. Battle of the Bay World Series, 1989. That terrifying day. Marisa was six, and I'd just picked her up from school. We pulled into the garage, and when I took the two steps up into the kitchen I all at once felt the jolt, saw the kitchen light fixture swaying wildly over the table. I grabbed Marisa and huddled over her, under the doorframe like we'd always been taught.

"Mommeee!" she screamed.

"It's okay, honey. It's just an earthquake. Whew! That was exciting, wasn't it?" Just like my mother, I knew when to pass off fear as adventure. When the shaking stopped, adrenaline set-tling, I lifted Marisa up and carried her to the living room, like a toddler, her pigtailed head hiding in my shoulder. The door to the china cabinet was open, but, oddly, just the cups had fallen onto the carpet below, and it seemed only one was broken.

"Look! How lucky. Most of them didn't even break!" I said.

"Mommy, look! The swing is swinging by itself!"

In the backyard, a ghost swing, squeaking. The phone rang, Bradley calling to check on us and tell us he was okay. Right about then, far out our window, a section of the Bay Bridge col-lapsed. The bar Bradley went to had the news on TV, he told me after closing time. It would've been upsetting for Marisa to watch the footage of the freeway and bridge collapsing, buildings in rubble. I'd finally gotten Marisa to sleep with songs and an extra story. Daddy had extra work because of the earthquake, I told her, but he was fine and would be there in the morning.

Dave pressed in on one side of me, Rhonda on the other. Even in that claustrophobic walkway, there was a comforting sense of being together, us and the crowd, all in the same boat, pushing and being pushed along, healthy, sick, every class and every color on Earth, all for the same team.

"This may be worse than Candlestick," Dave said.

He was talking about the dingy old SF Giants ballpark, deep in the fog belt, where the team played until 2000. Bradley was a fan, so before Marisa was born we'd drive across the bridge with hats, gloves, jackets, and a sleeping bag to put over us in the freezing August fog. The sticky orange plastic seats. Gulls circling above, scouting for fries. My head on Bradley's shoulder, fuzzy orange Giants cap over my ears. Even then I didn't care much about baseball, but there didn't seem to be a better way in the world to watch a baseball game.

It surprised me, that image of Bradley and me. I hardly ever remembered times when we were happy like that.

We emerged from the walkway to section 122 and had to stand a second and blink in the searing sunlight. What a glorious green the baseball field was under that sun! Whoever gave Thriving Survivors the tickets must have had some pull because the seats were great, just a few rows behind the A's dugout on the first level behind third base. It was just before the 1:00 p.m. start of the game, no shade in the entire stadium, so thank God we all brought hats and sunscreen. I dug in my backpack and pulled out the dorky big-brimmed SPF hat with the long neck flap in the back. I put it on. Dorky or not, the one thing I couldn't take since radiation was getting blasted by sun. It felt like I was being burned alive.

Rhonda pulled a green cotton scarf from her drawstring bag, put the scarf over her head, and tied it at her chin so almost all her face was covered, like a particularly observant Muslim. Then she put the matching green A's cap on top of the scarf. It was an odd look, sure, but it had team spirit going for it. Dave didn't bother with anything but the Giants hat. He wore a Grateful

Dead T-shirt, the gray one with STEAL YOUR FACE! written under the skull.

We stood up for "The Star-Spangled Banner." Hand over my heart, automatic, and tears sprang to my eyes. I couldn't help it, standing up there with everybody in the whole stadium singing. It just meant so many things. Growing up in the Army, standing up at the movie theater when the flag waved in black and white across the screen. Every game at every school, a dozen different schools, standing up in assemblies during the anthem, feeling I belonged. Fathers and brothers off to Vietnam, bombs bursting in air. Standing up with Bradley at Candlestick before the Giants games, happy. Standing up with Rhonda and Dave and Raul and Happy and Margi and Todd, and right then I remembered—the guy in the bandana was named Craig. Standing and surviving, all of us, oh beautiful for spacious skies.

We sat, and half the people in the stands shouted, "Mar-co! Scu—taro!" as Marco Scutaro came to the plate for the Sox. Dave leaned toward me and talked behind his hand. "Used to play for the A's," he said. "They still love the guy."

Two balls, two strikes, and then he grounded out. I remember it was Marco Scutaro because the name rhymed so nicely and I was determined to pay attention to the game. But by the time the second batter was on strike two, ball two, Dave opened his mouth to say something about the game, and I saw that his tongue was coated white.

"Is your stomach okay, Dave?" I figured the white coating was Maalox.

"Side effect," he said. "White tongue. Blisters. Scaly feet." He raised his palms, then looked down at his feet as if the rough skin would show through his tennis shoes. I don't know why, but the way he listed his side effects seemed like a challenge, and I went with it.

"White tongue?" I said. "Blisters? You call those side effects? You should see me in the morning. Like the Tin Man getting out of bed, my joints are so sore." I gave him a big smile. *Top that.* Dave picked right up on it.

"You don't even want to know how many times I pee at night!" Dave roared it loud enough for everyone to hear. Someone had just singled, and I jumped up and cheered even though I hadn't seen the hit. The third batter was up, and it was my turn to one-up Dave.

"You think pee is bad? You don't want to know what goes on in my bathroom!" Dave and I laughed so hard I almost had to pee right there. It was the first time I'd told anyone about my side effects. How creaky they made me feel, and how queasy, the hour after taking my meds.

Dave turned to Rhonda to pull her into the game, our game.

"Liz thinks she's got side effects! Tell her about your side effects, Rhonda!" He slapped her on the back and stuck his tongue out. "Look at this tongue!"

In that second it hit me that maybe we shouldn't be joking about side effects with Rhonda, but in the very next second the guys behind us shut the whole thing down.

"You guys oughta pay attention! Cripes sake, you're missing the game!"

I turned and saw a white guy with a thick black beard glowering at me under dark bushy brows. A hot dog crumb stuck like dandruff in his beard. The smell of garlic from his fries hit me in the face as soon as I turned around. Before I could get an apology in or even let him see me looking contrite, he was standing up and yelling, "C'mon, Anderson!"

I turned back to face the game, and apparently there'd been a single for the Sox because everyone in the stands was yelling "Awwwww!" so loud it didn't matter whether we were into the game or not. Bases loaded. Guys behind us clanging on a cowbell, trying to get the batter rattled.

The drummers in the right-field bleachers pounded so loud we could hear them across the Coliseum, and a whole section of fans in the left-field seats waved big green flags in unison, up, down, and to the side. Even with all that going on, and bases loaded right in front of my eyes, my mind kept going back to the thought I'd had in the minibus about sex. Wondering what it would mean if sex was over. For good. There was the awkward sex in college, the uninspired sex with Bradley, the voracious sex with Lyle, the longing it left. And that was it? Nobody else to get excited with, nobody to help me put Lyle in the past?

"Aaaand out!"

When the inning was over and the fans settled down some, I tapped Dave on the shoulder and reached across him to Rhonda and tapped her on the knee. I hunched down, my head at the level of the drink holder in front of me, and motioned for them to hunch down with me. We inhaled the smell of stale popcorn, spilled beer dried into the concrete.

"Can I ask you a personal question?"

The minute I said it, I regretted saying it. There were some things you just didn't need to say. We were at a baseball game, for God's sake. Still, I expected them to get quiet and pay attention after my question. Instead, Dave yelled "Ha!" so loud I jerked back into my green plastic seat. Rhonda's smile started slow, but then she started laughing too. For a second I felt hurt, them laughing at me that way after I'd gotten them to hunch down to hear my confidence. I thought we were supposed to support one another.

"God, no, Liz!" Dave said. "Personal? You want to say something personal? *Ha!*" He stared into me, gray eyes sparkling and open wide.

It sank in. How much more personal could we get? What's more personal than knowing you're on the way out and getting together once a week just because of that? Of course I could tell them about anything, and they could tell me, and we would tell everything important we could tell, wouldn't we?

None of us were paying any attention to the game. Rhonda shrieked, "Personal!" and kept on laughing at the thing no one would get but us. Rhonda laughing that way made me start laughing too. Dave put his arm around my shoulder, and we all sat there laughing with our bodies shaking and our heads down. I gulped a breath. The guys behind us yelled, "Way to go, Ellis!" and the crowd clapped at another strikeout.

I took a deep breath and leaned across Dave's chest so Rhonda could hear. "It's about sex," I said.

A gray-haired woman in front of me turned around and stared. I stared back at her—a "mind your own business" stare—and she turned back around. Then someone on the A's must have made a base hit because everyone around us jumped up and screamed. This time Rhonda and Dave stayed in their seats and leaned in toward me. Sex trumps baseball.

"Sex? Oh nooooo!" Dave said, in a whisper so loud he might as well have been talking full volume. That set Rhonda off.

"Nooooo!" Rhonda said in a loud whisper. We'd all been skewered, sliced, poisoned, and burned in cancer treatment. We'd been disfigured, wasted, given terrible odds. And I was too timid to talk about sex?

"Okay, okay," I said. "Lean down. It's just this." I calmed myself, took a breath, and didn't feel nervous anymore.

"Two years ago, after I got through chemo, I hated cancer so much for ripping me off of my sex life. Everyone's so worried about you staying alive, you know? Nobody mentions that breast cancer rips you off that way. The meds just suck you dry. I mean. Here's personal." I looked up at the back of the older woman's head and then over to the guy in the electrical workers union hat, and glanced behind at the diehards in green. Bottom of the second, and one of our guys struck out. Everybody was intent on the game but us.

"There is now no part on my body that's any more sensitive than my knee," I whispered.

I'd cried that time, reaching down and trying to get stimulated, trying to excite myself, specifically without thinking of Lyle. Feeling nothing.

Rhonda had her palms together and her lips down on her fingertips, like all she could think to do was pray. Dave clasped his hands tight at his waist. I guessed I had managed to make him uncomfortable after all.

"Although," I said, "I don't have a Lewis next door to give that premise a valid test." I poked my elbow into his arm. God, I guess I was nervous after all, or else why did talking about sex turn me into a locker-room jock? Dave elbowed me back, though, jock to jock, and that was a relief.

I didn't expect them to say anything, and they didn't, not right away. We just let the baseball sounds take up the space. Shouts of "Cott-on candy!" and the announcer and the organ chords pounded some tension into the game.

Sex. I thought back to the time when Lyle and I first met for a work lunch and looked at each other knowing it wasn't about work. He'd come in from the New York office and we were supposed to be strategizing on the SoClo account. I bounced off of his ideas and he bounced off of mine and somewhere in there I noticed how tall his forehead was over those icy eyes and thought, *Sexy in an Ed Harris way*, and I couldn't think of another idea about SoClo at all. Next day it was his plan for us to have lunch at the Marriott, instead. Where he was staying.

Around that time, way before I got sick, Bradley was out at the bar and Marisa was off at law school and I was in my bedroom taking a good, honest look at myself naked. It had been years since it had mattered.

I looked at myself sideways and from behind in the full-length trifold closet mirror. I squeezed my boobs together to see them make cleavage and then I let them drop to see how much they'd begun to sag. I took a good look at the pouch under my belly button I never could get rid of even at twenty and had given up entirely trying to get rid of around the time I turned forty. I turned around and discovered the dimples in my butt. I hated those dimples in my butt. No number of glute squeezes would get rid of those, not that I did glute squeezes in the first place. As I pulled some clothes on, I gave myself the pep talk. Not too bad, for forty-nine. Small enough to escape the big droop of middle age and fit enough to stand looking at my behind at all. Still a size eight, sometimes six, and a fringy new haircut everyone raved about at work. Not bad. But not sexy, either. It had been so long since I'd felt sexy. I didn't know why I'd bothered with the mirror at all.

Some nights out of habit Bradley and I would wind up sleeping entwined, me in my old sleep shirt and panties, him in his jockeys and T-shirt smelling like beer and smoke. Not that our sex life had ever been the swing-from-chandeliers kind of so-hot-he-devours-you-on-the-kitchen-floor. We were never like that. I was so young when I started going with Bradley. I'd had that kind of sex once in college but somehow thought it was okay not to have it that way with him, since he was ten years older and so sophisticated compared to me. Bradley didn't have to ravage me in bed to have me want him. He didn't really have to do anything but a sales job, and Bradley was the best salesman in the world. By the time I was inspecting my butt dimples, though, we'd been married twenty-three years. His drinking had gotten worse and worse. We'd gone three years without any sex at all, and the last time was awful, so frustrating and sad. I went through the motions, trying to get him aroused, but really I was more pissed off than aroused, trying to prove a point, I guess. The point being that all that drinking wrecks your sex life. When he apologized I did the worst thing a woman can do, which is get all huffy and turn away. I punched the pillow and went to sleep. We never talked about it. We just never tried again.

But that day when I was in front of the mirror inspecting myself, a spiky, growly mass of anger grew in my gut. Goddamn Bradley. He was ruining my life. But also, god damn it, I was so deep-down angry, how could he ever want me? I was just figuring out how angry I was.

Within weeks of that body-evaluation day I was in a hotel room with Lyle, making up for all that lost time, devouring, being devoured, and the main thing is I was believing what my body said was true. That if the sex was so spectacular, it had to mean more, infinitely more—souls merged forevermore. That's how dumb I was. Three months later I turned fifty and filed for divorce without a single tear.

I came out of my Lyle reverie when everyone around me screamed, "Yes!" Though I didn't know what for until I saw an A's jersey with "Hermida" on it running for second base. Rhonda was out of her chair with a fist straight up in the air, then Dave was up, clapping his hands above his head and yelling, "Ho!" I jumped up and started clapping too. Funny how excited you could get about a run even if you weren't really watching the game. Once we sat down, though, the next batter ended the inning and it was still 0–0.

Between innings, the IBEW union guy and the woman next to him left their seats, and the bearded man behind me left for a minute too. A hip-hop song blasted over the speakers, and people waved their A's cards in the air, hoping to get picked for a prize. If we huddled close enough, Dave and Rhonda and I could have an intimate conversation amid the chaos. I leaned across Dave and motioned to Rhonda to lean in again. Dave turned his baseball cap backward, Rhonda pulled her scarf down to uncover her mouth, and both of them hunched over with me by the drink holders.

"I faked it the last time I had sex," I said. Dave gave a slight shake of his head. I hadn't told them the half of it—my divorce, Lyle.

"After chemo, you know? When you're still so incredibly wiped out, still bald?" Rhonda's head went up and down, her lips scrunched to the side.

"It's almost impossible to even fake it," I said. "But I wanted so much to think we could go back to the way we were before cancer. You know. Wanting each other all the time, feeling sexy all the time." I looked around to make sure nobody other than Dave and Rhonda was hearing this.

"You know how, when your body's working right, you can't help it? Random lustful thoughts, constantly? That craving all through your body even when you least expect it?" At least that's how it'd been those two years with Lyle. Those two years when lust was heightened by waiting weeks or more between rendezvous.

I kind of hoped Dave and Rhonda would pooh-pooh the random lustful thoughts, that they'd say something like, "Oh, that was just when we were young." But they didn't. Rhonda smiled; Dave smiled, in that far-off way. Meds and mouth sprays and dentures and neuropathy and all, I could tell their minds were still connected to their parts. We waved off the guy selling popcorn.

"I'm glad I'm not lusting that way anymore, I guess. It has hardly occurred to me I'm not lusting. Not that there's anyone in my life to lust after." I looked over and saw that the IBEW guy was back. He was talking to a frizzy-haired woman next to him.

"You're not supposed to feel this sexless until you're really, really old, and *then* you die," I whispered loud to Dave and Rhonda. "If you die young, shouldn't you get a pass on feeling so old?"

I was immediately ashamed, not for telling them but for feeling sorry for myself. My God, it's not like they didn't have their own troubles, worse than mine.

Dave leaned even closer to me, and Rhonda moved closer to him. He spoke in almost a whisper, first time I'd ever heard him be that quiet.

"My suggestion?" he said. "Go down to Velvet Sensations over on Ninth and Judah. I know Lisa, who owns the place. They're very sensitive, you know. First woman-only sex-toy store in the city. Maybe you just need to work a little on getting your mojo back."

Rhonda blushed on the sliver of good cheek I could see past her scarf. But she stepped up, woman to woman. "He's right, Liz," she said. "You don't need to put up with a sexless life. It's not over yet. Try everything, you know? As long as you're feeling well enough otherwise."

My face heated up too. "Thank you," I said. "You guys are so . . ." I didn't know how to put it. "Such a relief." A sexless life. How I'd wasted all those years, and now? I couldn't imagine taking Dave up on his suggestion, but I was overcome by his compassion, and suddenly sad.

I knew for sure then that Rhonda was still having sex with her boyfriend. Of course it must've been different, how the head and neck cancer would make you feel. Not so crazy on your hormones. Nothing at all to do with hormones, far as I knew. Still, Jesus, I counted my blessings.

I couldn't remember ever being so personal. Even Kate and I had never talked about vibrators. When you're with people who've been through one medical indignity after the next, I guess nothing physical is too personal to discuss.

It was bottom of the third, and I got the stink eye from the lady in front of me again, so I asked Rhonda and Dave if I could get them something to eat. Least I could do after they'd wasted the whole inning listening to me.

Boston scored in the third and was ahead 1–0 for what seemed like forever. By the time I got back to our seats balancing the cardboard box with two beers, a lemonade, a kielbasa for me, garlic fries and a hot link sandwich for Dave, and Rhonda's churro, it was already the fourth inning and Boston had scored again. Rhonda was off in some heavenly place, taking one slow bite of churro at a time, not even noticing me squeezing into my seat with the rest of the junk food until I settled in and Dave handed her the lemonade. I should have offered something to Raul, but there's only so much you can carry. He looked happy enough sucking a blue Slurpee through a straw.

Dave gulped his Sierra Nevada and yelled, "God! This is so good. First beer in more than a year!" It was worth the $7.50. I took a sip of mine and let the cold, sweet, and bitter taste rest in my mouth before swallowing. First for me, too, in I couldn't remember how long. But the real magnificence, the juicy, perfectly spiced, crunchy crumbly, fatty mustardy soft-bunned bite of nirvana, was that first taste of kielbasa from the Saag's sausage stand. I closed my eyes and let a piece of grilled onion dangle from my mouth. I was so happy I thought I was dreaming the announcer's voice when he said, "A big A's welcome to the Thriving Survivors from Mercy Cancer Center!"

I turned toward Dave and Rhonda and saw next to Raul a woman with a badge on her A's shirt, standing in the aisle with a mic in her hand. Next to her, in an elephant costume, the A's mascot, Stomper. And next to both of them, a guy carrying a big TV camera, pointed straight at us. Then I heard Dave's voice, yelling, "Look at us!" He pointed across the Coliseum, up at the Jumbotron. There we were, on the screen, me stuffing the sausage in my face, Dave pointing at the camera, Rhonda blissed-out with her churro and blinking, confused, under her scarf and hat. I chewed fast as I could and covered my mouth with a brown paper napkin. Then I lifted my hand, stupidly, at the woman with the mic. It was mortifying.

In the row ahead of us and a couple seats to the side, Happy was giving a little half wave, fingers pressed together like the Queen of England, mouth drawn down to look sufficiently tragic. Raul looked like he always did, at first, a little bewildered and sad, but then he noticed himself on the screen and sat up a little straighter and smiled. Christine swept her hand in our direction, making it clear the announcer was talking about us, not her.

The stadium got quieter than it had been the whole game.

I felt a hand on my shoulder and saw on the screen that it was the crabby bearded guy behind me, so I turned around to give him a little grin. I should have expected it, but it caught me by surprise when I saw his thick brows coming together under the A's cap, his dark eyes all soft like he might even cry.

"Hey, sorry, man," he said. "Really sorry. Can I get you guys some beers?"

The Look. The one where they expect you to keel right over in front of them and die. We'd been outed, and suddenly the whole row of cowbell-ringing, green-flag-waving A's diehards were giving us the Look.

"Or Coke, maybe?" the bearded guy said. "Whatever you guys want. I mean, I'm going anyway. Really."

I stood up and turned to face him, to show I could stand just fine, for God's sake. Nobody was hauling me off to the hospice just yet. I glanced over at Dave, and he stood up and faced the guy too. I'd rather face the bearded guy than have to look at us on the big screen, and I was glad Dave stood with me. Rhonda had her head bent down practically to her lap, and Raul, having had his reflexive wave-to-the-camera moment, put both of his hands over his face.

I don't know what made me decide to do it, but the moment was so embarrassing and the screen was screaming "cancer!" anyway. There was no way around it, so I went ahead and played the cancer card.

"Sure," I said to the bearded guy. I turned to Dave. "Beer?" and he nodded, no smile, his eyes growing hard. I didn't even bother asking the others what they wanted.

"Two beers and two lemonades," I said. "Thanks a bunch. Really sweet of you." He squeezed his bulk in front of the row of knees, and Dave and I both sat down.

The first beer had already settled in with a warm, fizzy haze. I never drank beer even when I did drink, so the second one, from the bearded guy, sat in the cupholder getting warm. A nice seventy degrees outside and a slight breeze, taste of kielbasa still delicious in my mouth, the fans shouting and announcer calling out names, and I didn't know what inning it was and didn't much care.

The A's turned it around in the seventh, though. The blaring music and announcer's shouts rang in my ears, and Dave hugged Rhonda and they both jumped up and down. Final score was 4–3, and even if I didn't follow the whole thing between yakking and getting buzzed on all that beer, even with the Jumbotron moment, that game with the two of them was the most fun I'd had in I can't remember when.

Chapter 7

*W*e piled into the minibus, same order as before, so exhausted and squished together I accidentally dozed on Dave's shoulder half the way back. The driver let us out at that same concrete bench by the valet drop-off, and everyone said their goodbyes and see-you-next-weeks. Dave and Rhonda were still talking by the bench when I went back into the minibus to get my hairbrush, which had dropped out of my purse. I always forget to zip my purse.

I wanted to be part of whatever they were talking about, to hang on to that connection we'd made in the bleachers, but I stayed back a few feet the way you do when you hope someone will ask you to join in.

Dave picked up on it right away.

"You okay to drive, Liz?" he asked, and motioned me over.

"Sure," I said, and I moved in next to Rhonda.

Then Dave said what I'd been thinking. He said it out loud, and I mean loud, but the volume didn't matter because we were the only ones under the overhang by the concrete bench. The sharp lines running across and down his forehead looked as if they were drawn with charcoal, drawn dark to make him look fierce, not just sixty-three.

"See? That's the kind of day we need to have," he said. "Sunshine, some fun, some real communication in between." He waved an arm at the cancer center. "We've gotten too used to these guys telling us, 'Go here for blood draw, lie here for the

78

scan, put this on, take that off, give me your arm, give me your butt, hold still, breathe, don't breathe,'" he said. He stuck his arms out like Jesus, imploring, and then he pulled them back in, fists to his waist. "We're like fucking cattle. I don't know about you, but I'm not going back to that meeting room, ever again."

"Amen," I said. Oh, the relief in Dave's words. "I don't need someone telling me how to talk about how I feel. I know perfectly well how I feel, and Christine doesn't have a clue."

I looked at Dave, at Rhonda, and realized that even though we'd all been in the group more than a month, we still didn't even know each other's last names. Of all the Thriving Survivors Stage Fours, I liked Dave and Rhonda the most, liked them in almost a desperate way, at that moment in the cancer-center valet lot. That way when you meet someone for the first time and want to know everything about them and tell them everything about yourself even if you wind up talking till three in the morning, days in a row. Rhonda, Dave, and I were all so different, but somehow we just fit.

So, even though I'm never one to make the first move about anything, never one to take charge of a social situation and expect others to go along, it felt perfectly natural then and there to speak up to Rhonda and Dave. The idea thrilled me, but I said it almost in a whisper, and the two of them leaned in toward me like we were still at the game.

"We don't have to meet in the employee training room at Nordstrom," I said. "And we don't have to meet with Christine. Let's just meet on our own. Just us three."

"We can be our own support group," Rhonda said.

It wasn't only about Christine; it was the whole scene back at Nordstrom that had bummed me out, one precious minute after the next. I knew that meeting with just the three of us, it would be different. Friends, supporting one another. Choosing this, together.

Rhonda turned to look behind and around her as if Christine

might suddenly be there. When Rhonda's head turned, her long, stiff curls stayed in place.

"Christine really is so sweet," Rhonda said. "I hate to hurt her feelings." Then, so low we could hardly hear, "And what about Raul?"

By then I was used to the way Rhonda's mouth looked when she talked. Her teeth were perfectly straight and Hollywood white, and her lips were full and pretty, red lipstick always fresh, but everything looked a touch crooked because of that cheek.

"We could ask Raul," I said. But I knew what he would say. Poor Raul was so hunched into himself, so stunned by what had befallen him, I couldn't imagine him coming along. Perhaps I was afraid he would and then bring us all down. Selfish of me, I know. Rhonda was just flat-out nicer. Sure enough, Rhonda was nice to me, and she didn't press the point.

About every time Rhonda talked, her sweetness irked me at first, and then what she said started worming its way in, like a new arrangement of a song that's annoying because it's not being played the familiar way, until you let yourself really listen and it starts sounding just right. Just two meetings into knowing Rhonda, it was okay by me if she wanted to be all pious, when usually pious people made me want to turn and run.

Who was I to say that Jesus plus affirmations plus kombucha plus organic cauliflower mash wouldn't buy her another year? Rhonda had been through so much cancer hell she could believe Santa would save her, and you wouldn't hear me trying to talk her out of it. I wished I could believe me some of that.

Dave's eyes opened wide under sparse brows—wisps of steel growing in several directions at once.

"Right on!" he yelled. "We could meet wherever and whenever we want. We could meet outdoors! We could take more field trips and go hear some jazz or something. Get out of that fucking room. Sorry, Rhonda."

Rhonda got a strange look on her already-strange face. All

soft-eyed, like she was seeing inside and outside at the same time. It almost scared me. She flattened her baggy jersey over her thin belly and pulled her shoulders back like she was about to recite a poem in front of class. I'd noticed that usually when she talked, she turned her face to the left, hiding the side with the scar, but at that moment she looked straight at me and then straight at Dave, big, deep-set blue eyes opened wide.

"I've grown to love you all so much in such a short time," she said. "I want us to be there for one another." She looked shy and proud at the same time, eyes sparkling, seeing right into me, then into Dave, and her face was just the way it was, not scary or ugly or wrong.

I didn't know what to say. I felt warm and open but scared at the same time. No one had ever said they loved me right off the bat like that, just so plain and simple and sincere. I wanted to say, *You, too, Rhonda*. I don't know why that would have been so hard, but it would have sounded fake coming from me, so early on. Instead I reached over and put my right hand on her pointy shoulder. I said, "Thank you, Rhonda," and I wished I had just left it at the shoulder squeeze. Saying "thank you" after someone says "I love you" sounds so one-sided and dismissive, like, *you* can love, but don't expect me to go there with you. So I squeezed her shoulder another second and felt her streaked blonde synthetic curls, stiff as a Barbie doll's, grazing my fingers. Dave moved toward us then and I stepped back to give him room. He wrapped both arms around Rhonda without hesitation.

It was a big man's hug, a generous, authentic, not-a-Marine hug. "I love you, too, Rhonda," he said. Even that was a bellow, so loud I was surprised Rhonda didn't cover her ears. I looked around the parking lot to see if anyone was watching.

Dave leaned the shaved side of his head down on Rhonda's good cheek. He stayed there a good long minute, not self-conscious, not anything but just pure sweet Dave and Rhonda holding each other because they wanted to. When it came to Dave, Rhonda had forgone the germ-free elbow-shakes. No one could've resisted a hug like that from Dave. Besides, I was getting the feeling those two would be safe in their bubble for the long haul.

Dave was a good foot taller than Rhonda, and they looked like a couple at a junior high school dance, awkward guy catching up to his growth spurt, picking the daintiest girl in class. He rocked her gently side to side, next to the concrete bench.

"Lovely, lovely Rhonda," he said. A tear rolled down from his eye to the shaved side of his temple, then onto Rhonda's wig. A tear from this big, loud guy.

"Right," I said. I'd meant it to sound gentler than that. Not so damned curt. It seemed like I should join in, but I couldn't bring myself to make it a group hug, to say, "I love you guys too." Even though the craziest thing was that I did love them already in a way I'd never loved before. It felt weightless, easy, matter-of-fact. Not the look-over-your-shoulder, careful-what-you-say-and-how-you-say-it kind I had with Bradley. Not the keep-it-to-yourself kind I had growing up. In our tight, nomadic family, nobody ever said, "I love you." Ever. It was the thing that just went unsaid. Perhaps because there's loss where love is, and life in the Army already comes with so much loss. Perhaps because there just wasn't room for emotion in people raised to carry on through depression and war without examining or expressing how they felt. Love was read between the lines.

Bradley was extravagant in his gestures, overspending, showing off with dramatic surprises, but neither of us were easy with quiet, intimate moments of affection. After we'd been married a short time, without much thought or mention, we stopped sharing simple, daily affirmations of love. No "darling" or "smoochkins" in our marriage, no stolen kisses in the hallway. I was better with Marisa, but too often I expressed love by spoiling her or expecting her to be perfect because I believed she was. Now that we were so distant, I was just beginning to figure that out.

With Dave and Rhonda, it was easy to feel love, if not yet to tell them about it. Just being with them made it a little safer. We were all really in this, like it or not, getting ready for the light or whatever it was on the other side.

The three of us decided the first meeting on our own should be outdoors, and I suggested Lake Temescal, a woodsy oasis above the city I hadn't visited since Marisa was still at home. We'd all been so enthusiastic about the idea, I even told them I'd take the day off, so we could go on a Friday and miss the weekend crowds. I immediately felt guilty about that, and sure enough my boss called a staff meeting for Friday morning. Did a support group count as a medical absence? It would have to. It shocked me how liberated I felt telling Patsy I'd be out. Still, I worked some at home on Sunday, and in the days leading up to our meeting I started having second thoughts. What if, away from the ballpark, the beer, the enforced confessional of Christine's group, we discovered our differences, interesting as they seemed, were just too great to bridge? What if it turned out to be too much effort, too awkward to keep revealing ourselves the way we had begun to? Or we found out things about one another we didn't like? What if they didn't like me?

But I'd made the commitment, so I stuck to it just like you stick with commitments in the Army, just like I stuck with Bradley some twenty years too long. I got to the lake early to find the perfect table. There were some nice ones up high, with a good view, but I wasn't sure Rhonda could climb the steep gravelly hill to reach them. I walked all around the lake, through redwoods, oak, pyracantha, and birch trees. Past empty little fishing piers, and past the swimming beach, closed since Labor Day, the life-guard station covered with a tarp.

It was a typical Bay Area morning, a little damp chill in the air but a patchy, hopeful sky. The geese were wound up for some reason, sounding like a traffic jam; then they all stopped at once and I could hear the gentler trills of other birds. I wished I'd gotten around to knowing the names and sounds of more birds.

I walked to the far end of the lake, where a chain-link fence separated the path from a golf course. Most of the way around the lake, if you looked up you could see big houses checkerboarding the hill, woods cleared around them for fire protection. I didn't remember those houses being there the last time I was. But that had been years earlier, a family picnic for Marisa's senior class at Head-Royce School. It was the last time we'd had fun as a family, and maybe that's why I'd picked the place that day. At the picnic, Bradley was gregarious as usual with the other parents, but not drunk, Marisa not ignoring us, not embarrassed by our presence but seeming to enjoy the rare occasion of our talking with the parents of her friends. It was a day when we could all believe everything was fine. That night when Marisa went out, Bradley did too. She obeyed the midnight curfew; I don't know when Bradley got home. But I remembered the day, and the place, fondly. How it felt like we were far out of the city, in a special, natural place, easygoing as I hoped to be with Rhonda and Dave.

But Lake Temescal wasn't as I'd remembered. Here I'd suggested we meet someplace in nature, and I'd chosen a place with houses looking down on it, a golf course next to it, and a freeway nearby. Dave and Rhonda might think, *Sheesh, can't we do better than this?* Anxious, I walked the whole mile around the lake, almost to where I'd started, and wound up back at the first picnic table I'd seen.

Tall grasses fringed the lake, and the water was a deep murky blue under the clouds. The table was right at the water next to a big rough boulder, a good ten feet above the water's edge. Granite, I was pretty sure. A sign by the worn redwood table said, THE BIG ROCK, as if it weren't obvious. In just that spot, though, not a single house, road, or building was in sight. Enormous cedars and oaks circled a spacious lawn behind that table. Trees blocked the freeway; I tried to imagine the *whoosh* of traffic as ocean waves. It would do. And there was Rhonda, on the first little fishing pier. I smiled at the sight of her feeding ducks out of a plastic bread bag, her streaky curls over a brown puffy jacket, with a long knit skirt and flat-heeled brown suede boots. I took a seat at the picnic table and watched her a minute. I could hear Rhonda's laugh, clear and deep from her lungs.

Rhonda smooched and quacked to the mallards, flinging pieces of Oroweat into the water and laughing as the ducks quacked back, butting one another for advantage. You're not supposed to feed the ducks; bread really isn't good for them. Surely if Rhonda knew, she wouldn't do it. I turned to make sure no one else was around to see her.

Dave's baritone startled me from behind.

"Lovely Rhonda," he said. She looked so much lovelier outdoors. Light shining off the lake, her face bright, standing tall and confident in her long floral skirt.

"Dave!" I said, excited as if we'd been friends for ages, reunited. Dave wore his black knit cap and a royal-blue fleece jacket with a black down vest over that. He looked healthy too. All of us had layered up—me in my silk long johns under sweats, gloves in the pocket of my REI vest, light rain jacket over that, and Rhonda puffed up in her down—we'd all be fine despite the cold. It was nearly sixty degrees, but layers are a habit with people like us. Chemo puts your metabolism out of whack.

Rhonda waved to us, said goodbye to the ducks, and tossed them what was left in her bag.

"Perfect place!" she called out. Her best smile, crooked on the right. She carried a paisley cloth zipper bag that looked overstuffed, and she put it down on the table.

"Sandwiches," she said. Leave it to Rhonda. I hadn't brought a thing.

"And a surprise."

Dave pulled his cap off and raked his hair back. It was growing out on the one side, and he'd cut it closer on the other so it was almost even.

"My God, Rhonda," Dave said. "You didn't need to bring us anything. I was thinking we could go out, maybe. Find some flax bars. Ha!"

It was a thrill to be hanging out in a park on a weekday, playing hooky with these new friends. Not a soul at the lake yet except us. My anxiety lifted and I felt giddy with possibility.

Dave looked different, but it wasn't just his hair. We all seemed somehow different, out of that awful room once again. More alive, and more exposed. I was the only one whose scars didn't show, but all three of us were lopsided, each in our own way. Dave with his hair, Rhonda with her face, me with my boobs.

Ever since radiation two years before, it hurt me to wear a bra. I'm not even sure why, since the burn was long gone. Maybe it was a chemo thing. Nerve damage, whatever—and what was the difference, anyway? Most days I just wore a thin undershirt instead of a bra. The effect was that, on the left, I looked like my grandma, small tit hanging like a change purse halfway down to my belly. On the right I looked sixteen because that breast was pulled up when they took the tumor out and had to sew the skin back together. So it was perky but indented where the scar was. Rhonda looked so pretty on the left side of her face, but when she turned to show the right, well, I've already described that side of her face. Dave would look normal once the hair grew back, unless it didn't grow back all the way over those pencil-dot radiation tattoos and the smudgy red scar running from his right temple to his scalp.

Rhonda pulled from her bag three extra-large T-shirts in Day-Glo green. Extra-large would be perfect for extra-loud Dave.

"I had them made," she said, holding them up with a proud, shy smile, like a child showing off an art project.

THE METS was written across the front in orange and blue script, OAKLAND above it in gold.

"We're the only ones who'll get it," Rhonda said. She winked at Dave.

I got it right away, the joke in the shirts, and it made me think there was more to Rhonda than I'd given her credit for. "Mets" was for metastases. Bone mets. Brain mets. Liver mets. Whatever other mets might come along. Oakland was where we lived, except for Dave. I hadn't figured out yet why Dave drove across the bridge from San Francisco just to attend our group.

"That is so cool!" I said. Our special, slightly snarky inside joke. I loved it.

She lifted her elbow and leaned across the picnic table. Dave did the same, and their elbows tapped. Back to remembering immune systems. "T-shirts and a secret handshake," Dave said. "Bonded for life, ladies."

That remark took the breath out of me. Much as I was tickled by the shirts, the bonding part felt like a suffocating reminder of why I'd never joined clubs. Because if you joined, you were expected to stay, and what if you made the commitment and it turned out badly?

Dave lifted one steel-toed boot over the bench, then the other, and settled himself down at the table. He stretched the T-shirt out in front of him on the redwood planks worn gray, and he smiled wide as he looked at the name. You could see the years of coffee and cigarettes on Dave's teeth when he smiled, but when his eyes crinkled up and the crags down his cheeks disappeared, he looked ten years younger just like that.

"The Oakland Mets. Ha! Sounds like the Chinese knockoff

factory screwed up on the teams. Ah, Rhonda. This is too much. The hell with elbows."

He stretched across the table to give Rhonda a cancer hug. Hugging is okay if you can turn your face away from the other person's face, and that's what Dave did. He reached around Rhonda's shoulders and clasped his forearms across her back, and he turned to me with a smile. They made an arc over the table, Rhonda's face looking sideways at the lake, Dave's face looking sideways at me.

I felt I should hug Rhonda too. At least a cancer hug, not the bullshit one-shoulder hug, that WASPy kind I usually do, half in, half out. The kind Marisa still did with me. I couldn't blame her. Nobody ever hugged in my family, so it never came naturally to me. I guess military families in those days weren't big on hugging; it didn't go with the underlying ethos: suck it up and always be prepared to leave or be left. It wasn't until I was in high school, my dad finally out of the Army, that my parents hugged their lifelong best friends, Ed and Arlene.

"People are hugging now," Ed said as they prepared to leave one night after a bridge game and too much booze. "Even men are hugging. Have you noticed? I think we should hug." And the two couples awkwardly embraced. I looked on, astonished, from the top of the staircase, where I waved goodbye. I wished they'd had that conversation when I was little. Wished that hugging came naturally to me from birth.

I was tempted to scooch off the edge of the bench and go over to Rhonda and Dave. But something held me back; all I did was smile.

"You are so good, Rhonda," I said. I took off my rain jacket and pulled the shirt over my head, and Dave and Rhonda did the same. Extra-large went practically to Rhonda's knees and hit me mid-thigh but barely went past Dave's waist. I immediately felt self-conscious in the matching shirts. No T-shirt looked good on me, least of all an ill-fitting one in unflattering, screaming green. Would we have to wear them all day? Every time we met?

All of us giggled then, and Dave's giggle turned into a "*Ha!*" and a loud smack on his knee. In that moment I wanted never to take the shirt off again.

Rhonda had made a couple extra shirts because they were five for the price of three, she said. That way, if anyone decided to join us, they wouldn't feel left out. We probably wouldn't wear those shirts more than a couple times, for fun, but having extras seemed generous and welcoming, just like Rhonda. I wondered how I'd feel if someone else did join us, though. It felt right with just three. But my prognosis was better than theirs—a year or more, maybe several more, with all the new meds for breast cancer coming along.

I imagined myself in a year, alone at that table in the shirt, and felt a wave of sadness followed by guilt at imagining them gone. Dave and Rhonda were doing well on their meds. Rhonda was so hopeful; why shouldn't I be, on her behalf? None of us could be sure how long we'd have. The important thing was that we all felt pretty good at that moment.

Before I realized what I was doing, I jumped into running the meeting, out of habit.

"So, do you think we should have a format? I mean, Mercy's Thriving Survivors Stage Four had some structure, and structure isn't bad, so you don't run the risk of babbling on and on about meds and headaches and joint pain . . ." I noticed Dave rolling his eyes—whether at the idea of structure or babbling, I wasn't sure, but all of a sudden I saw what I was doing and regretted my suggestion.

"Maybe we should just start with some things we're grateful for," said Rhonda, rescuing me.

Rhonda and Dave sat on one side of the table, facing the lake, and I sat on the other, facing the oak tree and the lawn. Rhonda with her spray bottle in front of her. Kleenex box on the table, just in case. Dave started us off. He pulled his shoulders up and back, so even sitting down he looked six feet tall. He sucked in his breath, long on the exhale. Meditation breath.

"First thing," he said. "I'm grateful for Lynette." He paused, as if contemplating that, honoring its truth.

"She's my ex, but she's stuck by me longer and better than most wives stick by the husbands they don't divorce. She stuck with me trying to be so macho I went off to Vietnam, and when I came back crazy pissed off. She stuck with me through vet school. Then she even stuck with me six years after that, when I came out."

Rhonda looked up at Dave with something like amazement. What people can get through. The things love can survive. She would be just like Lynette, I bet.

Dave told us he and Lynette had one of those seamless breakups that went from married best friends to unmarried best friends, and the way Rhonda looked up at him, eyes open wide, as if that was just the greatest thing she'd ever heard, made me feel sad for Bradley and me. I made a little sound with my throat and then, I swear to God, raised my hand like we were in school. I just didn't want to jump in, is all, when Dave was talking. They both laughed, but they weren't laughing at me.

Dave made his voice high and stern at the same time. "Liz? You had a point?"

Something about Rhonda being so sweet and generous, something about Dave being so open and unashamed, something about our silly shirts and sitting there under the trees by the Big Rock and the lake, all of us Stage Four, nothing left to prove, made me want to face the truth in my life. Made me want to say things out loud that I hadn't even said quietly, to myself. It hadn't occurred to me until just that moment that maybe that's how you get to the bottom of things.

"My husband and I never were, and sure aren't now, the way you and Lynette are, Dave. I mean, we're friendly. We get along fine. But there's the booze, and then with cancer? You can imagine how well a man who needs to get high to deal with the slightest emotion deals with cancer.

"'You'll beat this thing! Call if you need anything!' But I won't hear from him, guaranteed."

"Oh, hon," Dave said. "I wish it were different. Want me to talk to the guy?"

He looked right at me then like a bouncer just waiting for a word from the boss. *He has to be joking.* I thought of how protective he'd been of Rhonda, back at the Nordstrom employee training room, when she told us how she was almost given the wrong chemo.

"It's okay," I said. Dave's exhale, out with a big puff of air, made him sound relieved.

He stretched his arms out on the table and slumped down on his elbows.

"Oh, God, I was in and out of love a million times in just six years, and Lynette was the one solid surface in my life," he said. He sighed. "But then, in 1984, Robert came into the Family Pet Hospital. He came in needing me to put his cat down. That's always so horrible. It's more horrible putting animals down than it is for us. They can't choose like we can. They don't have to live with the uncertainty like we do. And when they're ready to go, there's no regret over what they could've done, no blaming themselves for smoking or sex or eating too many steaks.

"Hell," he said. "I smoked from the time I was sixteen till I was nearly fifty years old." He looked over his shoulder at the lake, then back at us. Rhonda put a hand on his shoulder, her body rocking slightly, slowly, a physical manifestation of "it's okay." I thought the sadness in Dave's eyes was about the smoking and about Robert's cat so long ago. He sucked in air again and let the breath out in a big, slow, angry puff.

I tried to remember the last time I sat and talked about my love life. Ever? Lyle was a secret, to everyone but Kate, and I talked with her about the secretiveness of our affair. But not deeply about him, about us, or love, exactly.

Dave's eyes lit up as he stared into mid-space. "Robert lived right around the corner in the Sunset, on Irving, and I'd never even seen him all those years. I don't know how that could've happened. He's such a gorgeous man. That day, after we euthanized Ernest, I closed up early and made Robert a cup of tea. He wanted to sit awhile, with the body still there. We drank another whole pot of tea, and then I went upstairs to get us a bottle of wine. This was all so not the way I dealt with my clients, but Robert was just different. I couldn't just let him go. We sat and drank and talked about everything, till it was after nine and restaurants were about to close. I put Ernest back in the clinic freezer, waiting for cremation in the morning, and Robert and I went out for Thai. That night we went back to my apartment above the clinic. Buried Ernest in the backyard the next day." Rhonda's blue eyes welled as Dave locked his hands together and held them to his chest. "We lived upstairs in that shambles of a building for the next twelve years, listening to the streetcars rumble by."

It was the sweetest love story I'd ever heard.

He put his head down so I couldn't see his expression, and he left it down so long I thought maybe he was crying. I shot Rhonda a nervous look, then turned to gaze at the lake, give him some privacy. But Dave raised his head with a loud sigh, not tears, seeming far away somewhere in thought. How lucky he was to feel so deeply about someone, for so long.

"Couldn't live without Robert," he said. I wondered what Robert thought about Lewis next door, and how excited Dave was about being asked on a date, but you never know what arrangements people may have. Two men; maybe it was different.

Dave reached across the table for Rhonda's sack of sandwiches. "Mind?" he asked, but he was already spreading out the choices.

"Please," Rhonda said. "There's PB and J, and tuna, and cheese—all cut in half so we can share, but I didn't know who could eat what."

"Thanks, hon. I can't eat cheese," Dave said. Even though we'd all gone off the wagon at the A's game, sugar was probably off-limits for both of them. It should have been for me, too, I suppose. Good nutrition can keep your energy up, and a lot of cancer patients swear that sugar feeds cancer cells. It's one of the myths that makes you feel there's something about cancer you can control. I ate pretty healthfully but ignored much of the cancer-diet advice, which changed every time I turned on the news.

"Ever notice," I said, "that the people telling you 'carpe diem' and 'go ahead with the bucket list' are the same people telling you to avoid butter, sugar, wheat, rice, wine, meat, dairy, and anything from a box or can? We're supposed to have beans and kale for breakfast, lunch, and dinner but then go off and have a ball zip-lining in Kauai. I'd rather just have a glass of wine or a burger once in a while and forget about jumping out of a plane."

"Or something in between," Dave said. "F'rinstance, I've lived in San Francisco nearly fifty years, and I've never been to Alcatraz. Because, you know, I could go anytime. So I guess now's the time." He had already started in on the tuna.

"We could do that!" I said. Suddenly the possibilities seemed vast.

I reached for the PB and J and watched Rhonda. Sure enough, she looked relieved at my sandwich choice. That left her with the cheese, easy to eat between spritzes, and no cancer-loving sucrose there. I took a soft, sweet bite. Peanuts and strawberries and spongy whole wheat. Exquisite.

You live long enough, and get to a point where you're thinking how much life is left, and little things like the taste of peanut butter can put you in another world.

"This tastes like picnics with my sister when we were kids," I said. "Sitting in a tree."

How does it happen that you can be so close as kids and then barely speak years later, not because of any blowup or rift but simply neglect? It would've taken just a little effort.

"I'm grateful we're out here too," Dave said, out of nowhere. "Today. Just us. In this place." I felt myself flush, unexpectedly, as if discovering a middle school crush.

"Me too!" Rhonda said, no embarrassment at all, just frank, shared gratitude.

I nodded, pointing to my mouth full of peanut butter. The things I was grateful for seemed so small. A cup of tea. A moment of peace. Damn. I wasn't prepared with a speech about gratitude, and wasn't this supposed to be different from sitting around back at Nordstrom?

"Are you guys up for a walk?" I asked.

I don't know why, but it's so much easier for me to talk when I'm in motion. It's as if moving my feet helps me form words faster and get them out of my mouth. Walking, you don't have to stare right at a person's face when you're talking and get all tongue-tied trying to respond to the way they're responding to you. You can just let it rip. Anything you say is left behind you by the time you've said it. In the air, back on the path, not just sitting there like a stone on the table between you.

Rhonda immediately started gathering our trash, folding her uneaten crusts into the Saran Wrap and stuffing it all back into her zippered cloth bag.

If any of us worried about making it the mile around Lake Temescal, we didn't say anything about it. If we got tired, we could just turn back. I'd already scoped out the bathroom situation; there was only the one at the entrance to the lake, but Dave and Rhonda didn't seem to have bathroom issues, so far.

We headed through the tunnel of trees, under the houses perched high, up the grade where they put a handrail along the gravel path just in case.

"I've been thinking how grateful I am for the most basic

things," I said. "Food, shelter, insurance, enough money to get by, maybe leave a little for Marisa if I don't blow through my entire 401(k)." The last ten years of our marriage, Bradley and I kept separate accounts. We'd had years of arguments over his overdrafts, his reckless spending while drunk or in apology for having been drunk. Thank God I earned enough to make the mortgage payments. Bradley's pending sale of the house would be a windfall for me.

"Talk about silver linings," Dave said. "No worries about how you're gonna stretch your money out till you're ninety-five, like Lynette and half my friends are doing. They're like, 'Shit, I forgot to save!'"

"True," I said, not just to agree with Dave but because I meant it. Every once in a while since all this happened, I felt like I'd walked into a warm, soothing sauna, relief steaming through the walls. I breathed it in deep and felt a hidden tightness release in every organ, every vessel, every vein. I'd think, *Money doesn't matter anymore. Making enough, saving enough. Losing, spending, giving it away. Doesn't matter!* This must have been how monks got to feel, letting all that go.

We all stopped on the path for a minute, taking a break. Rhonda grasped the handrail with both hands and bent over it, watching a duck's butt disappear into the water below. Dave rested one of his hands on the small of Rhonda's back. Birdsong, leaves fluttering, a tiny patch of blue behind wispy clouds, the soft lapping of the lake.

I pulled my T-shirt down flat over my lopsided tits and bunched it up at my hips. Something to hold on to. Then I turned to start us off walking again. Rhonda walked with her arms crossed under her own full, even breasts. Dave had a hand on his hip, like it was hurting, like he was hoping the pressure of that hand might stop the hitch in his step. We'd come halfway around the lake. Better to keep on going than to turn back.

"You okay?" I asked Dave, and I could tell that irritated him.

He pulled his hand away from his hip and lifted a palm like he had no idea what I was talking about. "Of course," he said. Rhonda glanced up at the trees and pretended not to notice that exchange.

I imagined walking round and round the lake a dozen times, telling them everything, from the minute I married Bradley to the minute I called Marisa on her twenty-sixth birthday and she was too busy to talk.

If only we could slow down real time as well as our memories speed it up. The highlight reel played in my mind again as it had, over and over, the same scenes, a million times. Marisa and the time she caught me kissing the neighbor, how she never let me braid her hair again after that night. The time I sat her down to talk about alcoholism and how she reacted: "It's your fault, Mom. He wouldn't drink if you were nicer to him." How I bought into that.

Bradley, bringing drunken "clients" home after closing time. Me, scrambling so Marisa wouldn't see. That fantasy I couldn't shake for a whole year when she was twelve, about a man I'd met only twice. The budget-blowing vacations we took as a family—skiing in Tahoe, condo in Hawaii—to convince ourselves all was fine. Keeping a lid on it. The nights after Marisa left, when Bradley didn't even bother coming home. How I worried he was dead, and the times I wished he were. Lyle.

My shoes scraped at the gravel path, slow, easy steps. I smelled redwoods and algae, wild fennel and pine. Dave walking with his hitch, Rhonda silent, tiny feet under billowing skirt. I thought about both Bradley stories and decided I didn't want to tell them. Bradley was past, done. It all seemed too tiresome to go through with Rhonda and Dave. A waste of precious time.

Instead, I tried to sum up that part of my life for them, the whole married part, in a way I hadn't been able to sum it up for myself. None of us had said anything for about a hundred yards, so I guess when I spoke it seemed out of the blue.

"Everybody's craziness always seems so special to them," I said, "but when you get down to it, ours was a run-of-the-mill, garden-variety alcoholic family." It surprised me when I said that. The truth of it. The simplicity, after all that chaos and confusion in my mind. On the highlight reel, there with Dave and Rhonda by my side, it was clear as day. Bradley covering up, me hiding his drunken episodes from Marisa, excusing them to myself. Trying so hard to please Marisa, Marisa working so hard to please her dad. A daughter so perfect at everything, both of us trying to keep things ordered and controlled. Both of us codependent like mad. Right out of all the cheesy codependent books that show how one way is to be a doormat, another way, a control freak. I managed to be both. Putting up with Bradley's disappearances, scrubbing the counters like mad before bed. Spoiling Marisa with gifts she didn't want or need, demanding she show me her homework. Glowering and leaving the room when Bradley interrupted Marisa's work with playful banter. Telling her she should shoot for the stars and then deciding which stars she should shoot for. ("Student-council president would be more rewarding than head cheerleader, sweetheart." "Sure, UC Santa Cruz would be fun, and close, but Georgetown . . .") Garden-variety alcoholic family. What a relief to say it out loud.

"Keeping things together to look normal," I said, "you get into so much denial and spin, pretty soon you believe your own lies. The biggest one is that none of you are crazy and no one is a liar at all."

When it came out of my mouth that way, I thought it was kind of funny, or at least not whiny in the way I so didn't want to be. It felt like a weight beginning to lift, but when I looked over at Rhonda, she'd stopped. Her chin down on her chest, a hand pressing against her fake bangs, covering her forehead. I guess we all needed a rest.

"I'm so sorry, Liz," Rhonda said. And she looked sorry too. Sorrier even than I felt. Such sadness in those eyes. I felt bad that she seemed to take it all to heart, but I guessed that was just Rhonda, taking everything to heart.

Dave, though, just sighed deeply. His cheeks sagged again as he looked at me, shaking his head back and forth slowly.

"You got it in a nutshell, babe," he said. Of course. He'd been through his own alcoholic crap.

"Anyway," I said. I didn't want to leave off with my whole married life sounding so bitter and bleak. We'd had our times. "There wasn't violence or anything. Mostly we got along. And my marriage was great training for PR!" I said it almost as loud as Dave might. "My last client, the salt guys? Spin and denial galore."

I made my voice go deep like a radio-ad man. "The mineral most treasured through the ages: salt! Makes junk food wholesome and nutritious!"

Rhonda's laugh was a high "Hmmmm!" She was playing along with me, trying to lift the mood, showing she didn't judge my meaningless career. Dave, not so much. He pressed two fingers against his lips to show he wasn't going to say what he thought. The thought of Dave judging me put me into kind of a panic. I felt rejected and naked all of a sudden. There I was, having done nothing for the greater good, not even able to make an impact on the little family I had.

I started walking, wishing I hadn't told them so much. Keeping silent is a way of holding on to your own version of reality, and generally that's what I preferred. Anyone I told about Lyle would've had a boatload of criticisms to offer. And anyone I told about Marisa's estrangement might judge me a terrible mother.

We made it back to our table, and settled onto the bench seats. The wind made dark-green ruffles in the lake. We pulled our jackets over our shoulders. Rhonda fluffed back her long curls. She stuck her index fingers inside her wig on each side of her forehead. "Straight?" she asked.

I gave her wig a tug on the left, straightening the part.

"Perfect," I said. Without a mirror you can never tell if your wig is on right. Sometimes it puffs out at the sides or rides up too high above your forehead. When it's crooked, you look like a tipsy matron in a British sitcom. It's embarrassing to ask someone who doesn't get wigs, someone who's pretending you're not wearing one. Patsy and other people at work would always say, "Looks great! Can't believe it's not your real hair!" Then I'd go into the bathroom and see it sticking out on one side, notice how the reddish, fringy bob didn't really go with my olive skin. Going red seemed fun when I bought the wig, but my eyebrows, before I started brushing them on, were closer to black. I was glad my wig days were behind me and was happy to help Rhonda with hers.

Rhonda patted her wig around the sides of her face until I made the "okay" sign with my fingers. She flattened her shirt over her skirt at waist and hips and then pulled her shoulders back.

"All those years of court reporting," she said. I hoped she didn't think we were mocking her. "If you don't watch your posture, sitting all day at that machine will put your back out by the time you're forty. I saw it all the time. Carpal tunnel this, tendinitis that. Frozen-neck syndrome and whatnot.

"I was real careful with the back and shoulders, sitting all day like that. Twenty-five years in the Alameda County Courthouse. Homicides. DUIs," she said. "Drugs." Her shoulders dropped a bit, and she was quiet a moment. "Anyway, I watched my posture, and I'm grateful for it!"

Rhonda gave us her big best new-dentures smile again. I thought, *Really? Is that what she's going to say she's grateful for?* But I don't think she even realized she'd used the word "grateful." It was the kind of word Rhonda used in casual conversation. You didn't need a group to get Rhonda talking like that. Blessed, grateful, the whole bit.

"You must've heard about some hairy stuff," I said. "This county in the 1990s."

"Yes," she said. "Terrible stuff." Rhonda put her elbow on the table and covered the bad side of her face with one palm, pink nails over pink skin, circle of tiny square diamonds on her ring finger. She looked up at the cedar branch hanging above the table and uncovered her face so she could reach for it, then twisted off a piece of cedar the size of her palm. She rubbed it between perfectly manicured fingers, held it to her nose, and breathed in. I imagined Rhonda's nails were cut short and unpolished when she showed up at nine sharp in courtroom number six. Could see her pulling her shoulders back, spine straight, chin up, face normal, creamy skin, even on both sides. Never looking down at her machine but cocking her head just slightly at the judge. Looking straight at the witness to catch every word. Those slender fingers, tapping away. Tapping, tapping, defendant to death by injection. Tapping the autopsy result, the angle of the body of victim number two. Tapping the number of kilograms, powder identified as cocaine. Tapping the sobs of a witness. Tapping the drunk driver's lies.

I felt it then, the welling of love for Rhonda I had wanted to feel back at the meeting room at Nordstrom, when we had just barely met and I thought her dignity had grown from illness. I thought it was just something she wore, like optimism and her best, crooked, brand-new-dentures smile. Extraordinary. My heart expanded, just like that.

Rhonda breathed in the cedar smell and passed it across the table to me. Such a sharp, clean fragrance that I imagined if the essence of all life could be distilled into a single scent, that would be it. And that nothing bad could happen if we could only keep on smelling that smell. I rubbed a bright, nubby leaf between my fingers so the smell would linger on my skin; then I passed the branch across the table to Dave. He breathed it in, too, his face growing rounder, softer.

"So, what about your family, Rhonda?" I asked, because it seemed a reasonable thing to ask, but apparently it wasn't. Rhonda slumped for a second, crumpled into herself, diamond-ring hand over the bad side of her face. Then her head turned down and her hands went under the table. She lifted from the bench to her lap a bright yellow leather hobo bag with a heart-shaped metal closure and unnecessary buckles on both sides.

She dug in the yellow bag and pulled out a wallet, in matching yellow, thick with credit cards and photographs in plastic holders. Rhonda flipped through the plastic dividers and pulled out two worn photographs, both of a small tan shaggy dog. It tugged at me. Six years since our cocker, Boris, died.

"My puppy dog, Cremora," Rhonda said, holding one photo in each hand and displaying them, first to me, then to Dave. I wondered what other photos were stuffed into that wallet.

"Cremora knows just when I'm down," Rhonda said. "No matter where she is in the house, if I'm feeling a little down, she comes over to snuggle up. She somehow knows where my sore spots are, and she only snuggles on the other side. We get on the recliner together, or she hops right up on the bed. Sometimes Cremora knows even before I do when I'm tired like that. I love that darned dog. Never a problem, like kids. Ha!"

I tried not to show how that stung. It was one thing to tell them about my divorced husband. Another to admit that I barely spoke to my daughter.

Cremora had a tiny-toothed underbite and big filmy eyes. It turned out Rhonda's puppy was eleven years old.

"Sweet!" I said. I could imagine the dog snug in the curve of Rhonda's belly at night, Rhonda in a fuzzy sleep cap, long curly wig on a stand next to her bed. Pill bottles and dog toys, a row of photos in frames.

"Looks like a wheaten with some English bull," Dave said. He held the picture of Cremora up close to his face with both hands. "Goooood girl," he said.

"You must be a wonderful vet, Dave," Rhonda said. "Cremora's probably wagging her tail and wanting to jump in your lap right now, from miles away. If I ever need a new vet, now I know where to go."

"Not unless you want to hang with the homeless guys at the Tenderloin Free Veterinary Clinic," Dave said. He raised the steel threads of his eyebrows like he was daring her, and then he smiled all the way across his face. Tobacco teeth.

"I quit my practice after treatment the first time," Dave said, "but Tuesdays and Thursdays I put in a couple hours there. Homeless guys love their dogs. They'll buy dog food before food for themselves. The addicts, only thing they do take care of are their dogs."

Rhonda's brand-new-dentures smile disappeared, and her forehead creased. Homeless. One of those things you just can't do enough about.

I thought, *So Dave works with homeless pets, and I wouldn't be surprised if Rhonda washes the feet of their masters.* My job? Vice president of a corporate-whore PR firm. *Is God laughing his ass off,* I wondered, *putting me with sweet Rhonda and kind, protective Dave?*

Not that I was sure I even believed in God.

I thought Rhonda was still troubling herself about the homeless people, the way her eyes looked somewhere far off, her shoulders slumped like she'd given in, not like Rhonda at all. She came up with another thing to be grateful for, though, starting off robotically, still looking at nothing in front of her. She said she was grateful for people in her church, who kept bringing food to her house even though she was done being wiped out from radiation weeks before.

"I wish they'd save themselves," she said. "I mean, in case it gets worse someday."

Always "in case." She fluffed up those streaky blonde curls, like a belle reveling in the attention of one suitor after the next.

"I don't know if I even remember how to cook," she said. She was back to herself again. That bright white smile and good side of her face to the world. Still making the effort. No wonder she had casseroles lining up at her door.

"A lot of the attention has to do with Eldon," she said. "Good and bad." She lifted her brushed-on brown eyebrows at that, as if we were supposed to know what she meant. Who was Eldon?

"Oh, Lord, chemo brain," Rhonda said. "I thought I told you all about Eldon, but I didn't, did I? My boyfriend," she said. The left side of her face turned pink. It almost matched the right side, red and covered with foundation, powder on top of that. "He's the sweetest, kindest man. Only problem is—you wouldn't think it'd be a problem, but it is, sometimes—he's the pastor's brother. And the pastor is Everett Lester. You know Everett Lester? Alive! Ministry of the Word? In the church, we just call it 'Alive!'"

If you lived in Oakland, which I did, or San Francisco, which Dave did, or even if you lived in New York but you knew anything about gospel music at all, you'd heard of Everett Lester. His choir had won two Grammy Awards, for heaven's sake. As turned off as I was by the idea of going to church, a gospel choir was another thing altogether. If I could justify going to church just because I liked the music, even I would go.

"It's the best thing in my life," Rhonda said. "Singing in that choir."

"Holy crap! Rhonda!" I said. "You're *in* that choir?"

"A star in our midst," Dave said. He slapped the table hard and flashed Rhonda a fanboy smile.

I said, "Are you the only white person in the choir?"

Maybe I was right about groups; you're bound to say stupid stuff and risk becoming the one person everyone wants to be rid of.

"Almost," Rhonda said, like it wasn't a stupid thing at all. "I was only the third white person, and it was because of Eldon."

She went court reporter on us again and lifted her chin, so for a second I thought she was going to belt out a hymn. But then she kind of collapsed into herself. She lost a couple of inches right there at the table, like she'd given up on the good posture, the choir robe, the gratitude, all at once.

"We were going to get married. He wanted to get married, still does. But of course with this . . . no way I'd put him through that. That's not fair."

I wanted to say, *Of course you should get married!* and *Oh, it'll be wonderful!* but I couldn't. It wouldn't be wonderful for me, anyway. It would feel, I don't know, cheesy and melodramatic. The tear rolling down the groom's face, the bride, what, dragging along an IV pole? You just couldn't know. It wouldn't be fair. But oh how I wished I had a partner in my life. Too late. Too late for a close family. Too late for a legacy of good works. Too late for a love like Dave and Rhonda had in their lives.

I looked at Dave and bet he was thinking about marriage at the end of life too. His big hand covering his mouth, elbow on the table, holding the weight of his head.

"I'm sorry, Rhonda," I said.

Maybe the first time I said something right.

The dampness in the air chilled me, and I hadn't brought my warmest jacket. What an idiot. Twenty-five years in the Bay Area, and I still expected the sun to come out by eleven o'clock. This was one of those drippy-all-day days. Cedar tree still wet, lawn still wet, everything wet not from rain but from the heavy gray sky. I crossed my arms under my breasts, pushed the saggy one up level to the perky one. Squeezed around my ribs to get warm.

I was glad none of us filled in the silence. No "Getting a little chilly!" No "So much for the sunny East Bay!" How can you go from talking so personally to the kind of meaningless chitchat I'd always fallen back on? Out of habit, I opened my mouth to say something inane, but I realized I was done for good with that kind of nervous talk. I guess they were too.

All of a sudden Rhonda's super-whites showed all the way across her face. Her eyes got as big as Christmas.

"Listen," she said. "I'd love for you to come one Sunday to hear us at Alive! I promise not to proselytize, honest. Dave, you can bring Robert," she said. "I'd love you to."

What was she thinking? A gay white couple in a Black Christian church where even being a white woman is dicey if you're dating the pastor's brother? Sweet Rhonda. I wished I could think the best of people the way she did.

But something about what she said was even worse than I thought, because of the way Dave looked when she said it. Wounded, like I'd never seen him. He put his fist to his mouth and squeezed his eyes shut. Was it the mention of marriage? Talk about unfair. Two people together for that many years when they weren't even able to make the choice. It occurred to me I didn't even ask if Robert was Dave's husband. Didn't even think to call him that. I looked down at the table and fiddled with the cedar branch.

"I mean, it'll be okay if you both come," Rhonda said. Even she was getting nervous at how Dave looked. It got so quiet that the traffic behind the trees sounded like it was getting closer, louder. Rhonda spritzed once, twice.

When Dave finally looked up at me, then over to Rhonda, his face was all crumpled up the way a face gets just before tears, his mouth in a hard, tight frown.

Rhonda reached over to him and put her skinny arm around his thick back.

"Dave. Oh. I'm so sorry, Dave. I didn't mean anything hurtful. Really," she said.

Of course we didn't get it. We couldn't possibly get it.

"I should've told you," Dave said. It was the second quiet thing Dave had ever said. His face wasn't twisted up anymore, but tears dropped down the crags in his cheeks and to his chin. "I guess I wanted someone on this earth to know me, and hear me talk about Robert, and think of him being there when I got home," he said. "I wanted him alive in your minds, but he's not alive. Robert died of AIDS in 1998."

Dave said the last part into his big right hand. He heaved in deep. "I guess I wanted to pretend he was still around here, still with me, just this little bit."

It was the saddest thing I'd ever heard. Holding back something so big, pretending the love you'd had was still alive. I'd pretended a lot when I was married, but I'd never had a love like Dave did with Robert. Dave wiped his face with his sleeve, smudged the wet under his eyes with two fingers. We sat there, still for a moment, Rhonda's arm around Dave, Rhonda looking like she herself had just lost the person she loved most in the world.

"That many years ago and I still think of him every day," Dave said. Everything about him looked old, emptied out. His head dropped back down almost to the table, and the hump of his back in the Day-Glo T-shirt shook. Shook the bench, shook the table, shook Rhonda, shook me.

I looked at Rhonda, hoping she could get us back on track, say something that would make Dave feel better and stop his tears.

Rhonda said nothing though. She leaned into him and put her head on Dave's shoulder, her yellow T-shirt on his matching one, and then she, too, started to cry. Quiet tears, rolling down the good cheek onto Dave, making his shirt wet.

I couldn't just sit there, watching the two of them leaning in, their soft sobs. Without thinking, I rose up, reached across the table, and put a hand on Dave's other shoulder. I felt its warmth, felt it rise and lower with his sobs. And then my other hand moved on its own, up and onto Rhonda's thin shoulder, a position so awkward and so right at the same time, so astonishing, the three of us there holding on, that tears welled up in my own eyes and, before I knew it, dripped onto the table. I didn't even try to stop them. Dave put his arm around Rhonda's shoulder, and his whole body started to shake with it. My heart opened, somehow, as his shoulder lifted and lowered my hand up and down with his tears. None of us pulled away.

Cheeks, chins, tabletop, three little puddles, drip, drip, drip. Nothing was there to stop us, so we just cried softly together for the longest time. Cried in a way I'd never cried before, warm, comforting tears for Robert and Dave and Rhonda and me, right there on the bench by the Big Rock at Lake Temescal.

Chapter 9

*A*fter all that crying, the plan to meet Dave in San Francisco for our Alcatraz trip felt momentous, almost like planning to meet a potential lover after a first promising date. We'd fallen apart together, known one another in a way I wasn't used to being known. I'd never even cried with Lyle, or Kate. And never, ever in front of Marisa. I'd cried in anger and frustration at Bradley, on predawn mornings when he'd just arrived home from a bar, smelling of scotch and someone else's cigarettes. When my parents died, I cried quietly, in my room. But crying together with Dave and Rhonda was different. It cracked my heart open.

I tried reaching Marisa twice on the phone that weekend, feeling ready to really talk, but each time I got her voicemail, my resolve weakened. I played out the conversation in my head, imagining telling her my news outright, no sugarcoating, no whining. Imagining how she'd feel—shocked and perhaps resentful at the same time. If I felt that way about my own cancer diagnoses, surely she would feel that way about it—this big thing, not in her plans. She never called back.

After Lake Temescal, walking into my office Monday morning felt like entering a stale and dusty stage set. What was I even doing there?

Patsy, my assistant, hunched over her desk, tapping away. Men in ties talked too loudly in the coffee room, and the door to the boss's oversized corner suite was closed portentously, a silent announcement that a Big Private Meeting was underway.

109

Even my own office looked different. The mauve-colored walls, a dated pretension to hip. The gray leather sofa, rarely occupied but now a sickening reminder of stolen naps after chemo treatments. How could I have let those files pile up so high? Obviously I'd been letting things slide despite spending too many hours of too many days in that room. Hours. Days. For what? I thought of the conversation with Rhonda and Dave, about not having to worry about money anymore.

Perhaps it was the sight of the couch, the expansive view that seemed to mock me and my years of burrowing behind a desk while all that beckoned outside. All at once, an uncontrollable physical sensation came on—that familiar, post-chemo hormonal surge, rising from my belly to my face, flooding my body with unfocused anger.

It was the same sensation that occurred when I went off on Happy that night at Nordstrom. In the past I'd treated the rare episodes at the office as challenges to be overcome with deep breaths and isolation, on that couch, or hidden in a bathroom stall. That morning, though, pretending calm, hiding behind those piles at my desk, was out of the question. I turned back out of my office and stalked toward Roger's closed door, agitated, but with no clear idea of what I'd say.

Erna, his assistant, lifted her chin to greet me, but before I snapped my demand to see Roger, his door opened. He was ushering someone out, a man whose back was to me as I focused on Roger's florid, self-satisfied face, clapping the shoulder of his visitor. It was Lyle.

My breath stopped and the heat rose, flaming in my chest and onto my face. Lyle wasn't even supposed to be in town. What was he doing in there with Roger? Bringing in a big new client? Something nobody told me about? Seeing his body and the easy way it moved, his impeccable suit, the silver threading through that thick dark hair, a pang of heartbreak and humiliation slammed me still.

In that moment, all the pushed-down rage, all the effort of slapping on a smile, of impressing Lyle, pretending I cared about nothing but doing a great job for SoClo and Roger and all the others I'd allowed to waste my precious time—all of it rose up, demanding to be heard.

I took two long, solid steps toward Lyle, who spotted me mid-turn, his steel-colored eyes startled wide. Roger, too, noticed me, with a raised brow and curious half-smile on his face.

"Good timing," I said, facing Lyle. "You're here. Might as well hear this along with Roger. It might affect you, too." He flushed and his body tensed—did he think I'd say something incriminating, for God's sake?

I paused a beat and took a breath. Roger's curious look turned to one of impatience, and suddenly, astonishingly, what I'd gone in there to say became as clear as if I'd practiced it weeks in advance.

"Roger," I said, steel replacing the heat in my belly, "I'm sorry for the short notice, but today has to be my last day. Health, personal reasons I can't go into, but I'll be talking with HR today."

Once it came out of my mouth, all the remaining heat dissipated, like steam releasing from my scalp. I inhaled deeply, as the consequence of what I'd said began its descent.

"You what?" Roger said. It was the first time I'd seen him flummoxed. The words "health" and "personal" must've stopped him. I saw him back up, his body erect, and could read the thoughts on his face: *Better not go into it, privacy laws and all, but fuck.*

He squinted in concern.

"Well, this is a shock, but, I hope you're all right, Liz."

"Yes," Lyle chimed in. I made my face blank but thought, *You will never know.*

"Anyway," I said, chirpy as if I'd just been dispatched for sandwiches. "Sorry again for the short notice. And thanks for everything. It's been . . . quite a ride." I just couldn't keep myself from kissing up till the end. But then I turned and walked back toward my office to clean out my desk.

"Why? Why so soon? Who'll replace you?" Between questions, Patsy's mouth was agape. I'd given her the same notice as Roger, and I felt bad about it.

"Come on into my office," I said. When she closed the door behind her, I lowered my voice and told her the truth.

"Cancer's back, Patsy."

In her look, sad but not shocked, I saw the truth of my own situation.

"I'm so sorry, Liz," she said. "If . . ."

"I'm okay. I'll be fine," I said. "It's just . . . there's a lot I want to do, and while I'm still feeling good I can't see myself here. Can you please keep this between us?" Patsy's lips squeezed together as if to hold back tears. "Listen, I'm planning that trip to Alaska!"

It wasn't entirely true, but ever since the day I sat waiting for the scan that would reveal metastases, the fantasy I returned to was Alaska. Impossibly vast, remote Alaska. Dying people don't plan rugged wilderness trips months in advance, right? Maybe planning it would prove I wouldn't be sick and dying for at least a couple years. Magical thinking, like buying the $175 blouse at Nordstrom.

I wanted Patsy to imagine me hiking in a gorgeous rainforest, not hooked up to an IV. I would have to think of a gift to send her, acknowledging her support over the past decade, but at that moment I simply said, "Thank you. For everything, Patsy. I sure hope Roger comes through with that raise. I did push him on it last week. And if you ever need a recommendation . . ."

Then, seeing her eyes well up, I put my left hand on her shoulder, letting it rest there a long second before saying, "Let's just go over a few loose ends, okay? And then I'll start packing my things."

At home, there was a message from Marisa, left on a morning when she knew I'd be at work. "Sorry I've been so busy, Mom. We'll talk soon," she said. Now I had two big things to tell her, but obviously she was putting me off. I brushed away irritation and then sadness, picking up the phone instead to invite Kate to celebrate with our usual pizza on the patio. My stomach fluttered, adrenaline churned; I'd done this big thing, diving over a cliff. I couldn't deal with Marisa until it fully sank in. I had to call Dave.

"I was thinking," I said. "We don't have to do Alcatraz on Saturday. It'll be crazy crowded on the weekend. Can you make it Thursday instead? Because, y'know why?" I waited a beat before erupting like an excited ten-year-old. "I *quit*! My job!"

Dave's bellow nearly shattered my eardrum.

"*Ha! Yahoo!* Liz! You're free! About time! I mean, didn't want to lean on you or anything, but that job was eating you up! Who needs it, right? Your time is yours, babe. I swear you'll have more of it ahead of you, now that you've quit."

I could only giggle in response.

"Would you tell Rhonda?"

"Soon as I hang up I will."

"So hang up then! And one of you call me back with what Rhonda's got planned."

Plans. We were friends making easygoing plans, and at that moment it felt as if we had all the time in the world to make, change, and fulfill them. My whole body felt expanded and light with possibility.

Rhonda was just as supportive as Dave, but, being Rhonda, she was also concerned. At first, she asked gently if I'd been experiencing new symptoms, or too much fatigue at the end of the workday.

"No, nothing physical, Rhonda, it was just . . . the job itself. I told myself that it was good money, a good title, challenging, nice coworkers, but suddenly I just couldn't bear spending more precious time in that job. And I'm lucky enough that I don't have to. It seemed, I dunno, a sin somehow to stay there if I didn't have to." Even if I didn't believe in the concept of sin the way Rhonda probably did, it felt like the right word.

"Well, that's what I'd call a healthy decision, then," Rhonda affirmed. "And I'm betting you'll be blessed with a longer life because of it." They both, then, believed that quitting would buy me time. I wasn't sure I believed it, but I wanted to. Maybe after spending more time with the Mets, I would.

Rhonda counseled that being free from work might feel a little weird at first. "It did for me," she said. "All those years when you feel like what you do is who you are? It took me a good year to get used to retirement, but of course I was preoccupied with all the surgery and whatnot."

Her words sank in slowly, and I began to worry. Did freeing myself from work mean I was heading down the chute toward dying? Should I rush out and try to start a new career, just to fend off what lay ahead? I missed some of what Rhonda said next.

". . . but then I got used to this new life. I mean, you might just have to be uncomfortable sometimes without the structure of work, because you've always had it, right? And sometimes not having structure gets you to thinking too much, but if that happens, you just call me, okay?"

Thinking too much about the future, she meant. She'd already put the thought in my mind about getting sicker and about not, in fact, having all the time in the world. Rhonda's offer was genuine and meant to be a comfort, but after I hung up I looked around my supposedly temporary apartment and wondered if I'd been too rash.

Chapter 10

*J*ust two days after quitting, a deep panic overtook me, the kind where it seems if you don't put one foot in front of the other, you might just stay frozen in place till the day you die. I'd gone in for a bisphosphonate injection to keep down the calcium levels in my blood and to keep more bone mets at bay. My apartment felt foreign with the late-morning sun streaming into the kitchen window, the sound of the neighborhood elementary school's recess bell piercing through the whoosh of weekday traffic. I wondered, was this how I was going to spend the rest of my time? Puttering around at home, feeling like crap between one doctor's appointment and the next?

I had to contact Marisa but kept putting it off, as if there were only one call to be had and that call had to be perfect because it would change everything between us. It would cement the reality of my diagnosis in a way I wanted to avoid, at a time when I was already losing my footing. Telling her could wind up creating a new kind of distance, I feared—that distance cancer places between people—when already we'd grown so far apart. I was at loose ends for the first time in my life, completely out of control, and I needed some kind of equilibrium before I called.

Time to straighten up. I ripped the sheets off my bed and put them in a pillowcase to wash. Mopped the kitchen floor, vacuumed. Dusted the Japanese woodblock print and the framed photos I'd taken on our honeymoon in Morocco. *I should've known then*, I told myself. Even then—on our honeymoon!—Bradley had invited a group of vacationing Spaniards to join us after dinner in the café by our hotel one night. I enjoyed the group, even though I didn't speak Spanish and Bradley did. It was a high-spirited time, wine bottles emptied as we laughed and conversed in two languages badly.

"Mind if I stay down here?" Bradley asked when, after midnight, I told him I needed to get some sleep. I didn't mind. But he stayed in the bar nearly all night and slept half of the next day, the last of our trip.

How could I not have known? Alcoholism is obvious if you know what to look for, but if you don't want to see it, and most people do not, it slides into your life and stretches your boundaries until the unacceptable becomes the norm and the norm becomes something you hide.

The one time I tried to sit Marisa down and talk about her dad's drinking problem, she let me have it. She was fourteen and already distancing herself from me, a typical sullen teenager, holed up in her room most of the time. The night before, Bradley had invited a couple guys over for dinner without even asking me—a first. It was a Saturday, and they'd all come from an afternoon at a sports bar.

"I knew there'd be plenty of food," Bradley said, planting a sloppy kiss on my cheek, a showy embrace, wrapping his arms around me while looking at his new friends, both construction workers in stained T-shirts and jeans, men in their late twenties hanging with Bradley, then forty-five.

"And here's my beautiful daughter, Marisa," Bradley said as she emerged from her room. "Come meet Reg and Michael," he said. She flicked her long bangs aside and stuck out a hand to shake theirs. Cute guys, old enough to be forbidden, safe enough to flirt with in front of her parents.

I was in that horrible, familiar place. I had to be sociable, welcoming, *mi casa es su* fucking *casa* to Bradley's whole disheveled world, or be the party pooper, the shrewish wife who'd just made a gigantic lasagna with enough salad to feed the room but would rather freeze or toss half of it than share with a couple of sweet, tipsy, hungry guys.

I put the lasagna on the table and gritted my teeth through dinner around the kitchen table, one of the dining room chairs shoved in. Marisa giggled at the guys and eyed me, Bradley droned on about the crappy economy and the Heaven's Gate suicide cult, and the guys talked about Nintendo games. I got angrier and angrier, the smile frozen on my face. After ten, when they'd finally gone, Bradley and I fought. I threatened to leave. He called me an uptight bitch, a word he almost never used. Bradley rarely got angry, only pompous, pedantic, and sloppy, and then he'd pass out, drunk. I went to sleep in the guest room, tiptoeing so Marisa wouldn't hear. When he awoke at eleven, he cheerfully offered to take Marisa and me out to brunch.

I'd tried many times to get Bradley to stop drinking. Usually, we'd have a blowup like that, and then he'd be contrite and moderate for a while, proving he could control himself and making me question my own sanity for wanting to leave this perfectly nice husband. I had a stable home, for the first time in my life. It wasn't really that bad, was it? After all, he never beat me. He never cheated with other women; I was almost certain. Everybody had issues. Half the world got by fine with arranged marriages, for cripes' sake.

So that morning, rather than confront Bradley, I went in to talk to Marisa.

"I'm sorry if you heard us fighting last night, honey. You know, your dad has a bit of a problem with alcohol. We don't talk about it, but I guess we should."

"He has a problem with you, Mom," she said, looking up at me through bangs she'd refused to cut. "If you'd be nicer to him, he wouldn't drink so much."

I was outnumbered. I tried to tell her alcoholism is a sneaky disease, that nobody chooses to have a drinking problem but they can have one and not even know, and then things like that night happen and everybody suffers.

"Just quit blaming him, Mom. If you don't love him, you shouldn't have gotten married in the first place."

"Of course I love your father, Marisa," I said, wondering as I said it if it was a lie. After that, I decided she just wasn't ready to hear about it. My job would be to protect her as best I could, making sure she wasn't exposed to that kind of fighting, making sure she was busy, and making sure I kept a happy, healthy face on, no matter what.

After I did leave Bradley, and then got my first diagnosis, Marisa came out from Georgetown for Thanksgiving. Since I'd just gone through chemo, the two of us went out for a fancy San Francisco dinner at the Fairmont Hotel, me in my fringy frosted wig and Marisa looking thin and edgy in East Coast black with high-heeled boots. I thought going out would make it easier for her than eating in my small apartment, where we'd have to improvise with a coffee table and a beanbag chair. Aside from the unsuitable table, it'd be her first Thanksgiving dinner without her dad. There'd be no strays from Bradley's work, or his mother, whose attitude generally morphed from snippy and put-upon to sloppy and maudlin after two glasses of wine. At those Thanksgivings, Bradley held court and raised sentimental toasts. Marisa, instead of getting annoyed, looked adoringly on while I'd get more and more uptight. In my defense, I'd done all the shopping, cooking, cleaning, decorating, and setting the table while Bradley charmed, carved the turkey, and made the toasts.

On her trip out from Georgetown that year, Marisa stayed with Bradley in his smaller, funkier house in Montclair, a densely wooded area of the Oakland Hills. She had high school friends to visit and studying to do, so Thanksgiving afternoon was the only time I saw her.

At the Fairmont, just the two of us, Marisa started out stiff, silent as the waiter poured her wine and my sparkling water and brought the rolls.

"I know this is a weird Thanksgiving, honey. But I have to say it's nice not to work so hard on the meal."

She twisted her mouth, turned to the side as if anything in the restaurant would be more interesting than me.

"So what's *he* doing?" she asked, turning back and staring hard. "Your boyfriend."

Blood rushed to my face. I hadn't told her, but Bradley obviously had, damn him, driving a wedge . . . I was about to stammer excuses. Apologies. But the hard look in her eye told me this was a pivotal moment and that I should not be ashamed.

"I'm not sure what your father has told you, but I am seeing someone, Marisa. I wish it could have come out at a better time, a better way, but I guess there isn't one, is there? I'm sorry if it hurts you."

"That obviously wasn't part of the calculation when you took up with him. Hurting me or Dad," she said.

"Listen, Marisa. Your dad and I had issues having nothing to do with Lyle . . ."

"Oh. Lyle? What is he, some buff guy you met at a bar?"

Ooh, I wanted to say something nasty about Bradley, but thank God I took a breath and refrained. "Stop it, Marisa. I don't need permission to live my life the way I choose."

"How many boyfriends have you had, anyway? I only know about two, but it figures there'd be more."

My stomach lurched. "What are you talking about? That one kiss, that one time?" But she'd pushed my button and I burned with guilt. A slut for a mother. Poor Marisa!

"I'm sorry," she said, squeezing her forehead. "Jeez. You have cancer. And I'm pissed about your boyfriend. It's just . . . a lot."

The waiter brought plates heaped with turkey, stuffing, the works. Marisa picked at hers, and we ate mostly in silence, my attempts to change the subject landing flat.

"Well, you certainly won't get overstuffed like I always do," I said, digging into mashed potatoes as she picked at her creamed spinach. Marisa was so thin I worried she might have an eating disorder, but mentioning anything to do with food or weight always set her off.

"Would you quit it with what I'm eating?"

"I'm sorry, Marisa. I really am. Just enjoy what you want. It's Thanksgiving."

I raised a cut-crystal glass, she raised hers, and we each took a sip.

But I'd blown it. The rest of the meal, she barely touched her food. I tried to draw her out about school, and she said, "It's hard. It's good. I'm going to have a lot of reading on the plane." I'd set her back. I should've told her not to come.

After our early dinner, she asked me to drop her off at her dad's, where he'd ordered a turkey and all the fixings delivered in. I was sure the party was just getting underway.

"Take care of yourself, Mom," she said, leaning into the car window. The sky glowed pink through eucalyptus and pine. I could smell the woodsmoke from Bradley's chimney. His Craftsman house, woodsy and compact, looked warm and inviting, and I had to force myself to smile.

"Have a good time, Marisa. Safe flight, and please call me when you get in."

I went home to my apartment, feeling shabby and alone. Kate was with her extended family in Burlingame. It was before dawn in the Netherlands, no time to call my sister, Louise. So I turned my thoughts to Lyle, to the wide-open smile he'd have on when I saw him next. To the feel of his biceps, the way my head nestled so perfectly into the crook of his arm, my leg wrapped over his after we made love. That day was six weeks after chemo, and I'd been feeling pretty well, working full-time but collapsing into bed by 7:00 p.m. Radiation was supposed to start the next week, but I'd put it off two weeks longer, hoping I'd grow a bit more hair. Because before that last phase of treatment started, I was going to reward myself with a trip to New York. A trip to see Lyle.

All of that was Before. Before he dumped me, before metastases and the Oakland Mets, before quitting, before who knew what was to come.

I stretched toward the ceiling and touched the floor. I needed to quit it with the Lyle reverie and get outside. Something Rhonda had said back at Nordstrom came to me: it was the mundane tasks—washing dishes, paying bills—that gave her comfort, made her feel grounded and useful in life. It was beginning to dawn on me how that might be true, how organizing a closet might be as satisfying as anything in my self-important working days. I could make a Zen experience out of washing my clothes.

Truth is, I'd always liked going to Sudz Eze on East Eighteenth. It had become my Saturday-morning routine, dropping off the week's load with chatty, kind Gabriela, staying a bit for a muffin or soup at the Sudz Eze Café. Mostly Gabriela would "fluff and fold" my clothes and have them ready by 4:00 p.m., while I raced around on errands and did work brought home for the weekend. The one time Gabriela was out, I sputtered in irritation at the idea of being forced to sit and read or twiddle my thumbs. But once I gave in to the situation, settling in to read a book or simply look around, it seemed a gift.

Quitting my job meant I could stick around and do my own laundry any day of the week. Like Rhonda said, it might be comforting, sitting quietly with strangers as the laundry went round and round.

It was two in the afternoon on a Wednesday, and just one other person was in there, a sharp-faced young woman with tattoo sleeves coming out of her black T-shirt, sitting on the wooden bench reading a paperback.

I put six quarters in for a box of Tide, dumped my clothes into a top-loader, and sprinkled in the detergent. Shoved more quarters into the washer, heard them clink down, and pulled the quarter-loader out, empty. Everything predictable, the clicking and humming of the machines, clothes getting clean. Being out in the world and tuning it out at the same time.

I waited to hear the satisfying spray of water in the machine, and then I walked through the peach-colored alcove by the library shelf and into the Sudz Eze Café. Two people were there at tables working on laptops, one by the window and one at the back by the counter where Gabriela stood, just in case anyone wanted to order coffee or a stale cookie, or the soup of the day, homemade in a tiny kitchen in back.

Gabriela could be forty or fifty-five; you couldn't tell with that beautiful bronze skin and how carefully she put herself together. She gave me a big smile and a little wave, bright-colored stones on her bracelet matching the necklace over her sweater in peacock blue. She didn't ask what I was doing there in the middle of the week, or why I was stuffing my laundry into a machine instead of handing it to her. As usual, though, she asked how my daughter, the lawyer in LA, was, and was she seeing anyone yet? Gabriela's dark eyes opened wide. One of the reasons I liked Gabriela so much was that when she asked you a question, it was not just to be polite. She really wanted to know. She'd even pried me open about Marisa, and it surprised me how much I'd told her.

That day I deflected the boyfriend question because I didn't want to tell Gabriela that I didn't know. Instead I told her about Marisa finishing the Los Angeles Marathon and working too hard as usual; I said it with the mixture of pride and bafflement I always felt about Marisa.

Gabriela said, "Oh! No!" which is her way of saying, "Wow!" and is what she says in response to news both good and bad. The way she exclaimed about Marisa, whom she'd never met, you'd think Gabriela had known us all her life.

Gabriela had no idea about my cancer, though, and that was another reason I liked seeing her. At the Sudz Eze, all that mattered was that we whiled away the minutes between customers, and meantime my clothes were getting clean. What a relief, being around someone who cares but isn't worried about your health. Someone who wouldn't give you that Look. Hanging out with Gabriela, I pretended I never had cancer at all.

"New grandbaby pictures?" I asked. She pointed to the one that had been stuck on the wall by the cash register for at least six months. A curly-haired toddler, arm in arm with her big sister, pigtails in red ribbons and a missing front tooth.

"Any word on if they'll be able to come visit this year?" I asked, and then I was sorry because of the way Gabriela's face shut down. I knew it was the same old story and that the answer was no, she couldn't go to Bolivia if she wanted to come back to the United States, and they couldn't come to see her here.

I said I was sorry and asked if she wanted me to write a letter, but she said she didn't know who I'd write it to; did I know? I didn't, actually. I'd ask Marisa, I said. As if I talked to Marisa every day. But now I had a reason to call again. Maybe asking help for Gabriela would make Marisa think better of me, and maybe then she'd agree to spend some time, and then I could tell her, but not before we reconnected about something other than cancer.

Then Gabriela asked about my plans for going to Alaska next year.

"You getting excited?" she asked.

I'd told Gabriela about my fantasy trip, as if it were really in my plans.

"Oh! No!" she had said when I'd first told her. She'd gotten so excited along with me that even on my recent visits to the café, I kept on pretending the trip was on. We had talked about how big Alaska was and how it really wasn't covered mostly with snow, just in the winter, and how supposedly you could just look out your window and see moose and bears.

But that day, I just couldn't keep up the lie. I couldn't keep on talking about going to Alaska when Gabriela couldn't even go home to see her own child.

"Oh," I said. "I'm not going after all. It's a long story, but maybe someday . . ."

She looked so genuinely disappointed, as if it were her own fantasy dashed, I couldn't bear to add cancer, Stage Four cancer, to the news.

"It's okay," I said.

I told her I needed to put my clothes in the dryer and take a walk around Lake Merritt for some exercise.

On the walk, I practiced what I'd say to Marisa. First I'd tell her how I had this friend, Gabriela, and she'd be surprised that I'd made a friend at the Laundromat and impressed by my desire to help her see her family. "Speaking of visits to family," I'd say. "Maybe we could plan that weekend, if you don't have too many cases, or if by some miracle you get ahead in your work . . ."

No, too guilt-trippy and sarcastic. I'd just ask her straight out if she'd come, say straight out that I wanted to see her.

But of course I was sent to her voicemail. Stupidly, I left a long message asking advice about how Gabriela, my friend at Sudz Eze, might find an immigration attorney who could help her visit family in Bolivia without getting deported. Marisa wouldn't even know what the hell I was talking about, I realized after hanging up. She'd just have to call me back.

But no. About two hours later, instead of a call from Marisa, I got an email. It contained a whole long memo of names and numbers to call. Reputable lawyers who might handle the case pro bono. Appeals officers at the INS. Legal code numbers that would apply in this instance or that instance.

"I hope this is helpful, Mrs. Millanova," the memo ended. "Please feel free to give me a call should you need anything else." It was signed Lucinda Greaves, paralegal. Marisa had pawned me off on her assistant.

*R*ight under the email from Lucinda Greaves was a notice
from Facebook saying Rhonda Fleese wanted to be my
friend. I clicked the link and saw that Rhonda used a profile
photo of Cremora instead of one of herself. It was the same
cloudy-eyed, ears-cocked, shaggy-faced photo she carried around
in her yellow wallet, the one she showed us that day at Lake
Temescal. When the photo came in the email with Rhonda's
Facebook-friend request, not long after we'd sobbed together at
the picnic table, I sat looking at it for the longest time.

I hesitated before pressing "accept." Almost shut the laptop
down so I wouldn't have to make the decision right then. It just
felt like too much, rejection from my own daughter at the same
time Rhonda, who I was getting to know in such a personal way,
wanted to connect with me in this public but impersonal way.

It shouldn't have been a big deal. I hardly went on Facebook,
after a big obsessive flurry a couple years back, when I'd friended
everyone I'd ever met and then friended all their friends too. Days
when I was just coming out of chemo fog, it made me feel connected without having to really focus or expend much energy. I'd
post something funny or link to an article—any article—to show
how together I was, when really I was lying there all afternoon
like a block of cement, sweating chemicals and fantasizing about
Lyle. At least, until I had to unfriend Lyle to keep myself from
going batshit crazy over all his flirty comments to his old girlfriend and all of her flirty comments back to him. I wondered,

Doesn't he even care what his wife sees? I wasted hours and hours on that crap and had to back off Facebook altogether to stay sane.

But I couldn't say no to Rhonda, even if I wasn't sure how I felt about getting to "know" her friends and family so late in the game, and letting them know me in such a casual, unreal way. It felt so odd, almost like a backing away from how close we'd been since we met at the table back at Nordstrom with the flax bars and green tea.

When I pressed "yes," the first thing I saw on Rhonda Jean Fleese's Facebook page was that Dave Bondereaux was also her new friend. I clicked on Dave and invited him to connect with me so we'd all be in it together on Facebook too. Our smiling faces there, connected. Friends with two mutual friends apiece. Oh, it was good to see. What a lift! Why didn't I think of inviting them on my page in the first place? *Of course we should be connected, outside our Mets bubble, too, if only on the screen.* Maybe I'd reconnect with other people online too. People from when I was married, people from when I was growing up. Suddenly it seemed like a good idea. Leave it to Rhonda. I smiled.

Dave's Facebook hair was more brown than gray and there was more of it, his face fuller, sometime before the crags down his cheeks had carved in deep. Dave in his canvas shirt with the plaid flannel cuffs, sitting on a boulder by a creek somewhere in a redwood forest.

My profile photo showed thick, curly, after-chemo hair dyed auburn that had grown brassy in the sun. I was bundled up at Baker Beach, and my best friend, Kate, had just said, "Three!" as the waves crashed big behind me. Me smiling. "Yes! See?" thinking I looked pretty great with my hair and color back—*Take that, Lyle.* When really it was only given the circumstances that I looked almost okay. I kept that photo up there, though, because it was better than I looked now. Same face, nose too wide and chin too big, dark eyes that compensated some, and a smile so enormous that maybe you gave the rest a pass. But I'd put on a good twenty pounds since that picture, with the hormone treatments and all, or maybe it was the antidepressants, or maybe for the first time in my life I was just eating too damned much and didn't care.

And then there was the picture of Cremora, not Rhonda. I clicked on Rhonda's profile photos to see the ones she'd put up there before. One was taken at a fancy event. An ostentatious chandelier over a buffet table with hors d'oeuvres on tiered silver trays. There was Rhonda, her entire gorgeous ivory-skinned face lit up, her smile looking so different with her real teeth still in. Hers was no "say cheese" smile, you could tell. I stared at her beautiful face, the small, slightly upturned nose, chin pointed but not severe, blue-gray eyes spaced wide and looking so enormous set above both high cheekbones that way. It was an entirely different face, but it was Rhonda's, still.

She was thin but not skinny then, in a black cocktail dress cut low, pearls knotted in the curve of her breasts, wavy blonde hair just above her shoulders. Her tiny hand around the elbow of a beautiful Black man with a thin mustache, receding hairline that made him look distinguished, dazzling teeth. That had to be Eldon in the impeccable suit, beaming with Rhonda at somebody's wedding like he was thinking of his own.

I stared at the next picture, Rhonda in her green choir robe, Eldon in his, set apart by a half dozen others in their choir robes, most everyone's face but Rhonda's Black or brown, everyone, including Rhonda, belting it out for Jesus. In the foreground, a piano player caught by the camera as he lifted his elbows high above the keys.

The third photo showed Rhonda and Cremora at Lake Merritt, sitting on a beach towel on the grass. A toddler next to her, chubby with blonde curls, reaching into the air for something only she could see. Of course you didn't post on Facebook the pictures where you looked sad, but Rhonda looked just so supremely happy in all of hers. I wondered if it was just the comparison that made it seem that way. The comparison with the way things were when I met her, after surgery and the mets weighed her down, and left her with the forced new-dentures smile.

Finally, there was a picture of a teenager doing a cartwheel on a lawn, long ashy-blond hair covering her face, gangly legs in shorts arcing above her. I assumed it was Rhonda's daughter, and that Sally must have been her name, because that was the caption, just "Sally." In the next photo, Sally after the cartwheel, wearing a cheerleader outfit, little white pleated skirt and a big "R" on the front of her sweater, holding turquoise pom-poms high in the air. Rhonda had never mentioned anything about a daughter or high school.

On Dave's page, I looked for a picture of Lynette, his ex-wife, and found her with long silver hair wisped in humid curls around her face, a face that had been around, seen many things, laughed at most of them. You could see it in her eyes and mouth, the way the lines were set by laughter. You had to do a lot of smiling to get good lines like that.

There was Dave in green scrubs next to a sandwich board: "Tenderloin Free Veterinary Clinic."

Dave posted a quote of some kind each day: "'All that is hurrying soon will be over with. Only what lasts can bring us to the truth.' —Rainer Maria Rilke."

Every few days, though, Dave would go on a rant. After the real estate crash in 2008: "They didn't see this coming? With all that development from here on out to Fresno?" "Sons of bitches at Countrywide, AIG, they're off counting their money while working families are kicked to the curb!!"

Rhonda had 93 Facebook friends, I had 272, and Dave had 469. I guessed that most of Rhonda's Facebook friends were actual friends or close acquaintances, and maybe one or two— Eldon and a girlfriend—knew her well enough to talk intimately about cancer and everything else. Dave knew a million people, and being so open, I imagined he let people in and cared enough about them to be let into their lives. In any case, the Facebook numbers meant nothing. When it got right down to it, there were fewer than half a dozen people on my page I could count on as real friends. With Dave and Rhonda, I was starting to figure out why that was. I'd never made an effort, really, to stick with people I didn't know well long enough to truly become friends. I hadn't given it much thought, but growing up, we moved so often that close friendships weren't worth the risk. Keeping intimacy at bay is part of the package when you're married to an alcoholic too. And then Lyle. The way that ended seemed to prove me right.

Dave and Rhonda were becoming a different kind of close, and our time together felt like a different kind of risk. The very premise of our commitment was that it would lead us to loss, but we didn't have to deal with that, just yet.

Chapter 12

*R*honda was right about adjusting to freedom from work. Other than the laundry, I couldn't even tell you what I'd done the past few days. A little reading until I lost focus, which was about five pages into anything. Organizing my closet and the kitchen shelves. A trip to the grocery, a walk around the lake, a nap.

Even though I didn't really miss my work colleagues, it was strange not having anyone to talk to during the day but Gabriela or the checker at Safeway. It was starting to feel depressing, as if I didn't know what to do with my hands or what steps to take next. I procrastinated on calling Marisa because I wanted to feel confident, satisfied, when we talked and not have her grill me about my decision. For a fleeting second, I even wondered if I should've asked Roger about something part-time, but no, that's not what I wanted. It's just that I wasn't sure how to proceed.

But on the first Thursday after quitting, I woke to the alarm at six, just like on a workday; jumped out bed and into the shower; then dressed in jeans, Mets shirt, and a fleece jacket. Workdays, I never thought to listen to music, but that morning, coffee still sputtering in the pot, I put on a P!nk CD and rocked out to "So What." Na-na-na-na! A strange mix of giddy, guilty pleasure and cliff-hanging anxiety came over me. It would be my first real outing since I quit, and also the first time I'd spend with Rhonda, one-on-one. The two of us would take BART over to San Francisco and meet Dave near Fisherman's Wharf, at the pier where boats ferry tourists to Alcatraz. The kind of thing old friends do, the kind of thing you get to do on vacation, unlike the tense vacations I'd had with Bradley—him spending half the day sleeping off the night before, me on my own or with Marisa, touring some museum, looking at my watch, anger rising.

I scrambled my one egg right in the pan, buttered a piece of toast, and then, screw it, pulled from the refrigerator the slab of strawberry-rhubarb pie Kate and I had left the night before.

She had brought champagne with a meal of chicken marsala and roast veggies, plus the whole pie, my favorite. In her grand entrance, extending bottle and bags with a loud "Whoop!" she'd put on a good show at celebrating. Over dinner in the living room, though, she peppered me with questions that made my stomach knot.

"I don't know, Kate," I finally said. "I have no idea, to tell you the truth. Maybe I'll volunteer somewhere. Maybe I'll find a book club. It's only been a couple days, so cut me some slack, okay? It's just . . . weird."

Before you knew it, I was the one consoling her, for feeling bad about making me feel bad. We got tipsy on the champagne and wound up laughing about how predictable we were, even when life wasn't.

That next morning, I let the sweet-tart-crumbly combination roll around slowly in my mouth and actually moaned out loud. Then a bite of the egg, for protein, then another big forkful of pie. When had I ever allowed myself such decadence?

At the MacArthur BART Station, I spotted Rhonda right away, slanted morning sunlight bouncing off the synthetic fibers of her wig. She raised her hand in my direction, and as I approached and saw her arms extended, I decided, yes, we should hug. I lifted my arms slightly and nearly pulled back but then felt her easy embrace, stiff curls brushing my cheek, her shoulders bony even under the puffy down of her jacket. I gave her two quick pats on the back before pulling away, but still, it felt right, hugging Rhonda. Natural, like I was the kind of person who went up to other people and hugged them all the time. As if I'd grown up hugging and hugged my own daughter whenever I felt like it.

When we separated, Rhonda beamed at me. "Happy retirement!" she said. "Now we can really get into some trouble!"

She'd dressed warmly for the trip, in one of her long flouncy skirts, brown paisley with brown tights under it, socks rolled up over the tights and thick-soled, purple-striped Asics shoes. Her Mets shirt stuck out under the same puffy jacket she'd worn at Lake Temescal.

Rhonda wore red lipstick that morning, and she pulled it off just fine with those blonde curls, her face flushed from the cool morning breeze. I'd even call her pretty right then.

The train screeched toward the platform, and we squeezed onboard together. I charged ahead to the one available bench, saving her the window seat. She scootched in beside me and patted the black drawstring bag on her lap.

"I printed out the self-guided tour," she said. I could see the pages rolled and sticking out of her bag. It was Dave's idea for us to be tourists in his hometown, but leave it to Rhonda to come prepared. I'd always been too busy to even think of a trip to Alcatraz and never had tourists visiting from out of town. But why not? Wasn't this a chance to explore a bit while we could? I was always the one holding things together in my life, and to tell you the truth, the idea of just having fun made me nervous. When I was married, all our casual friends—and all our friends were casual—thought Bradley was a blast. Alcoholics have all the fun in the world! I was the one who stayed home with Marisa, or stayed at work, or stopped by for just one glass of wine. No fun at all, but then, belting out slurred show tunes at 2:00 a.m. gets old after your twenties. The fun I had with Lyle was mostly in bed, or fantasizing a life we didn't have.

Now I had the time, the companions, and a sense of urgency.

I was determined to lighten up. It's what Bradley had begged of me, but in his case, that meant quit worrying about his extravagant spending, his not showing up on special occasions, his closing the bars on work nights, his bringing home greasy-haired strangers who smelled of cigarettes. *What will it be like to lighten up on my own terms?* I wondered.

Rhonda smelled of lemon and peppermint. I was on her bad side, and I noticed a smudge in the makeup she'd put on her scar.

"I brought PowerBars," I said. I didn't tell her I'd brought nine for the three of us. I always got carried away, but what if everyone liked the same kind and you only brought one of that kind? It was good to have options.

Then Rhonda asked, "Whatcha been up to?" and I don't know what made me do it; I could've just answered with an innocuous list of chores done, my dinner with Kate, pigging out on pie. Instead, deep in the tunnel halfway across the Bay, I told her.

"Mostly," I blurted, "I've been avoiding talking to my daughter." It was only as I said it that I realized it was the truth. Right there on the crowded train, I said it out loud.

The thing is, Rhonda didn't probe, didn't look surprised. In her deep breath and slow nod, I read understanding, but how could she understand?

"I mean, I haven't even told her about my mets yet," I babbled on, in case she hadn't figured out that part, and I expected her to jolt in alarm. "I kind of want her to want to see me first and to have things, I don't know, on a better footing. Not that it's horrible, but it's just that, since the divorce, you know, we've kind of grown apart. And she's just incredibly busy at the law firm. I hate to interfere with her work when she's doing so well, plus she must be under such intense pressure there; it's one of the top firms in LA . . ."

"Hmm, well, you may *want* things on a better footing," she said, her voice low, "but sometimes you don't get to choose. Sometimes reality just doesn't follow our plans." Well, sure, we didn't plan for cancer, but I was talking about Marisa. I expected upbeat Rhonda to say something encouraging, but it was as if she'd determined things would not go well, and that gave me a little chill.

"Call her," she said, blinking and then looking directly at me. "Go visit, or insist she come up here. Don't let it wait."

She made it sound so dire. I assumed she was talking about the possibility that I'd get sick and run out of time, and that scared me. What was I waiting for? I was blowing it, big-time, holding out and expecting Marisa to be available. I needed to push more, and fast. My gut clutched with the panic of being out of time, of not being able to fix things. Rhonda seemed nonplussed, though, spritzing her mouth, gazing at the black tunnel through the window as if there were a view.

"You're right," I said to the back of her head. "I'll try her again tonight."

Then, as if coming back onstage as a new character altogether, Rhonda smiled and started talking about her dog, who'd eaten an entire stick of butter off her counter that morning.

"Naughty girl! Good thing she has an iron stomach. One time it was an entire pan of brownies, and you know they say chocolate can be deadly for dogs, but no, Cremora was just fine except in the poop department!" I missed having a dog. Was it also too late to get a dog?

Outside the station, we passed a line of panhandlers, their cardboard signs advertising hunger, that they wanted work, that they were veterans. A woman of about fifty, in greasy cargo pants and a Guatemala missionary-trip T-shirt, held a simple message in thick purple marker: HELP ME.

I passed with my head down, thinking, *This is a problem I cannot even begin to solve*, wishing I'd done more in my life for the needy but rationalizing, too, that giving cash could be a mistake, could keep them on the streets when they should be getting real help. The crossing light at the Embarcadero turned green, but

Rhonda was no longer beside me. She'd stopped and was saying something to the woman while handing her a $5 bill. I felt ashamed. When was I thinking would be a good time to start being generous?

We spotted Dave's giant shoulders stretching across the back of his Mets shirt at the front of a line bunching behind the Alcatraz ticket booth. Rhonda and I picked up our pace, practically running toward him, calling his name. Rhonda hugged him, so then I did, too, a second righteous hug in one day, making me feel unfamiliar but not in a bad way. I breathed in Dave's smell of leather and sandalwood, let his chin rest a second on the top of my head. Hugs right out in the open, waiting in line, like Dave was my brother and we hugged all the time.

"Freedom, eh?" he shouted. Then he turned to the couple behind him in line because, in greeting Dave, we'd cut in front of them.

"You don't mind they're with me?" His brows raised innocently, but I saw the woman twist her mouth in a sour expression. "Our cancer group," Dave added. "Field trip."

I heard Rhonda's quick inhale a second after my own. We both smiled lamely at the couple, who pulled back and extended their arms to let us in, words stumbling out of their mouths: "Sure, of course, oh my, absolutely, great!"

Tickets in hand, we posed before a green screen as a woman in nautical stripes and a captain's hat waved her hand, called, "Cheese!" and took our photo. A sea lion barked close by, and I breathed in the oily, briny smell of the pier. On the gangplank, I elbowed Dave and gave him a ration for his cancer remark. "Poor couple didn't know what to say!"

Dave grinned. "Public outreach," he said. "People need to get comfortable with it."

We made our way to the stern, and once the boat pulled away from the pier, a powerful churn of foam behind us, cold breeze slapping our faces, Dave laughed out loud.

"Best trip to prison, ever!"

The wind chill picked up with the speed of the boat. Rhonda pressed in close to Dave, and I stood next to her, the three of us leaning against the railing and taking in the city as it grew distant behind us, the Golden Gate half-shrouded in fog to the west, shadows of puffy clouds over indigo water whipped with white. I had a sudden longing for Marisa to be there; maybe we could make this trip when she came to visit, and maybe it would be easy, like this moment, huddled in the breeze, watching the city recede.

Rhonda shivered and pressed one hand on her wig. I hunched in and pulled my fleece hood tight to my ears, but Dave, jacket flapping open in the wind, hair blowing in wild spikes, seemed to lift and expand, mesmerized by the powerful, sudsy wake. I'd never seen him so happy. It was freezing, but neither Rhonda nor I made a move until Dave turned and noticed us, said, "Jesus, let's get you inside!" and led the way to a table and two benches belowdecks.

The smell of burnt coffee and engine oil took over from the briny sea air. I excused myself to find the head and on the way saw, in the narrow corridor across from the women's room, a couple stealing a passionate kiss. She was pressed against the wall and he against her, the two of them kissing desperately, as if just reunited, soon to be parted again.

I ducked into the bathroom, my stomach churning and cheeks flaming with the sudden memory of Lyle. That led to a spike of anger, and then, unbidden, another memory I'd tried for years to keep at bay. That kiss in my kitchen, when Marisa was nine. Washing my hands, I shoved it away, racing back to Rhonda and Dave, determined to have a good time.

Waves slapped against the side of the boat and splashed the window as the big rock came into view and a muffled loudspeaker directed passengers to the exits. The three of us merged into the crowd—families, a Chinese tour group, kids in matching T-shirts from a private middle school. Rhonda put her arm through Dave's as we walked up the stairs. I watched them from behind, her head leaning to tap his shoulder, his head tapping back, mimicking the two children in front of them, horsing around.

"Welcome to the most infamous island in the world," a baritone recording intoned. "Walk in the footsteps of the world's most dangerous criminals and the men who guarded them."

I noticed a hitch in Dave's walk, that bad hip bothering him again, and saw Rhonda's too-thin wrist as she held fast to the gangplank railing. On land, Rhonda hooked an elbow into Dave's, so I did the same on the other side.

"Three musketeers, in for life!" Dave shouted, clearly pleased with his double entendre. The moldy concrete of the prison loomed high above us, and we entered its lower level, down a corridor named Broadway.

We crowded around the cells, reading quotations from famous inmates, staring into hardened faces in black-and-white photographs. We learned the inmates played checkers, took open showers in a vast and cold cement room, worked in the laundry, pitched softballs on a field in their few precious hours outdoors. Mostly, they bided what must've felt like endless time in small cages with scratched metal bars and open toilets.

Dave read from the printout Rhonda had brought. "'We are all our own jailers and prisoners of our traits.' No shit." Dave shook his head and I wondered what trait confined him. Or me. What was I afraid of, now that I didn't have work to worry about? Being alone? I looked up at Dave, still musing, and over to Rhonda, who seemed to be taking in every word of the exhibit, a look of sadness in her eyes I read to be her innate kindness, a concern for lost souls.

Leon "Whitey" Thompson, inmate number 1465, coped the way I imagined I would.

"I was a man who was dead inside," he said on a prison audio. "You couldn't hurt me no more, see?"

On New Year's Eve, some inmates could see, through a slit of barred window, lights flickering across the water in San Francisco. They could hear the faint strains of dance music played by an orchestra at St. Francis Yacht Club.

"If that isn't the saddest thing I've ever heard," Rhonda said, shaking her head. Then she added, almost under her breath, "I wonder how many of these men were mentally ill."

"You'd have to be," Dave said.

"And if they were mentally ill, would this be better, in a way, than just being on the streets? At least they'd be safe here. At least they'd be fed."

"God, Rhonda, how could this be better than anything?" I said, but Rhonda seemed lost in her thoughts and didn't respond.

We left the crowded main prison to find the sky cleared of fog and clouds, and we blinked against the bright late-morning sun. Down some stairs and several yards from the main prison complex, the amorous couple I'd seen on the boat nuzzled against a boxy green building, once the prison morgue.

"Love abides," Rhonda whispered.

"Lust finds a way," Dave said.

"God, I can't take it," I said. "Let's find a place to eat our snacks and look at the view. Someplace not the morgue."

We headed down a path to a garden that had been maintained by inmates and restored by a nature conservancy. Sharp-scented orange lantana mixed with sage and native grasses, fragrant pink lilies growing wild. We found a crumbling wall wide enough to sit on, away from the crowds but with a spectacular view across the Bay to the western part of San Francisco and the Golden Gate. Gulls shrieked and circled overhead, ready to dive for unattended snacks.

"So was it the morgue or the lovers that got to you?" Dave asked.

I wasn't used to people figuring out my emotions, pressing me on how I felt.

"It was the couple," I said. "It's almost like I'm being forced to deal with a certain moment I'd rather forget." I shouldn't have said that last part, and I knew it as soon as I did.

"Oh, we've all had regrettable romances, haven't we?" Rhonda said. It hadn't occurred to me that Rhonda had her own rich history of love and heartbreak.

"Sounds like this one stuck around," Dave said. Always compassionate, Dave. But they'd both gotten it wrong.

"No, no. Not a romance," I said. "Just a mistake. A gigantic mistake that broke my relationship with my daughter."

I told them the story about that Fourth of July when Marisa was nine. Bradley had invited his usual bunch of Coldwell Banker buddies and their families to a barbeque at our house in the Oakland Hills.

As the company looked across the yard at fireworks lighting up the East Bay, I switched Bradley's two-shot margarita for one with just a hint of tequila. He'd already downed four. Bradley was the kind of hollow-legged drinker who could outdo anyone at a party, but there'd come a point when he'd get too loud, too hilarious, and then stumble upstairs to bed no matter who was still at the house. I couldn't let it happen with this work crowd, so I was monitoring his drinks and he caught me. Took a sip of the drink I'd made; glared at me, his jaw tight and mean; dumped the drink on the lawn; said, "Oops"; and went back to the drinks table to pour himself a stiff one.

Bradley passed me with his drink, whispered, "Cunt," and then smooth as could be joined a cluster of men, starting in on a story. He could tell stories better than anyone, but I'd heard all his stories and was shaking, furious. He'd never used that word. I considered packing a bag and driving to a motel for the night. But there was Marisa, standing on the lawn apart from all the little kids, yelling up at the Zuckerman twins to quit pushing on the play structure. She was tall for her age, a bit nerdy then, bookish and awkward, and precocious in the way of an only child.

She wore a navy-blue fleece hoodie with a big glittery star on the back. From the back she'd look like a teenager if it weren't for the braids and red corduroy shorts. She'd insisted on the red, white, and blue and begged me to wear those colors, too, because she cared about being patriotic at that age and also she wanted us to dress alike when company came. Bradley obliged her with a ridiculous flag-striped shirt, and I went along with a navy T-shirt and white jeans. Marisa found a red bow from the wrapping-paper box and pinned it on my shoulder to complete the ensemble.

Marisa in her red, white, and blue had her hands on her hips, and she looked around to see if I was in earshot after she yelled at the other kids. At the last party we'd had a talk about her being bossy.

I couldn't leave Marisa. So I snuck back into the kitchen just to get away from everyone for a second. What made me turn around was hearing the screen door shut behind me, the deliberate click of the latch.

I turned and saw Norman, the man from two doors down, standing right there in our fancy new-granite-countertop kitchen, with his hand behind him on the door. Norman was a computer guy who worked from home, and I kept running into him walking the dog or at the Montclair Market. He and I were friendly in a neighbor-you-run-into way, and, yes, he was attractive if you like that teasing, tousle-haired Peter Pan sort of guy. The guy who knows he's attractive with a face that's still boyish at fifty, the guy who charms until someone else winds up paying the tab.

That night at the party, when I saw it was Norman coming into the kitchen behind me, I freaked. My body jerked back and adrenaline shot to my toes, not just because he'd flirted with me at the store but also because he hadn't even been invited to our party. I didn't know why, but seeing him there made me feel guilty, not angry or afraid. I looked out the window at Marisa, hands on her hips.

"Crashed your party," Norman whispered. That Peter Pan grin. I looked down, looked out the window.

He looked straight at me, one of those sexy laser stares. He said, "May I see that for a moment?" He was pointing to my wineglass, and before I could say anything, he took it from my hand and put it on the counter. There he was, standing too close to me again, right in my own kitchen. I could have said something, but I didn't. I was waiting for him to ask for a drink or something, but instead he pressed me against my own refrigerator and kissed me hard.

Sitting there with Dave and Rhonda, I stopped the story, realizing I'd said too much, heat flushing my cheeks. Dave gave me that conspiratorial look you give when someone's been naughty but in a harmless way, chin down, eyes up. Rhonda shook her head like the adult in the room, wanting no part of this foolishness.

"The thing is," I said, "I didn't push him away. I could have said something, but I didn't. The truth is, I was thrilled." I couldn't believe I'd confessed this to them. It was embarrassing, and at the same time it felt like such a load lifted. I'd only ever told Kate, and she didn't seem to get what a big deal it turned out to be.

I remembered that the refrigerator magnets felt like hard gumdrops moving across my back. Marisa's artwork and her fourth-grade class picture fell to the floor. He squeezed my butt and tongue-kissed me hard. I was woozy with his sandalwood-soap smell, his taste so different, that specific taste of a man never tasted before. The taste of lust in his breath.

Outside, loud pops and red streamers in the sky. That's what I was feeling, too, along with the whoosh in my ears and a dizzy, crazy rush of desire. I hadn't felt that sexy since before Marisa was born. I never did feel that sexy again until Lyle. I opened my mouth wide and let Norman's tongue in and put my tongue on his.

"We kissed, hard, and for the longest time. Then I stopped to take a breath and looked around Norman's shoulder and down to the floor. That's when I saw them; I'll never forget."

I paused a second there, wishing I hadn't gotten to the point of having to tell the whole thing. I couldn't look at them when I did.

"Marisa's red Keds, just two feet away from us. Her skinny long legs in those red corduroy shorts. She was looking right at us."

Just as it did that day, my heart stopped pounding and everything went very still. When I finally looked up, Dave didn't look like he was about to wink at me anymore. Rhonda let out such a big puff of air it was as if she'd been holding it in the whole time I was telling the story. When she turned to look at me, it was the same as with Dave. That blank you put on your face when you don't want a person to know what you think because it is not anything kind.

I was sure they both thought I was the worst mother ever.

"The thing I remember most is her braids," I said. It seemed important to tell them about Marisa's braids, how I'd made them for her that morning and how in the kitchen that night they were half undone, sprouting little auburn spikes.

"Her face went so pale under those freckles she had." Marisa's enormous brown eyes fixed on something that wasn't me and wasn't Norman but something shocking she could not fully absorb.

Dave and Rhonda looked like they were picturing Marisa, too, wanting to go to my little girl, make it all right.

"What happened to Norman?" Dave asked. He said the name like it was sour in his mouth.

"I don't know," I said. "The front door slammed, and he was gone. I avoided him in the neighborhood and never talked to him after that."

I remember standing there for the longest time with that empty space between Marisa and me, and then I took a step toward her. Sitting on that hard prison wall with Rhonda and Dave, I put my hands out in front of me as if I could grab Marisa right there. "When Marisa wouldn't let me hug her, I knew I was screwed," I said. "What do you say when your daughter's seen you kissing a strange man? A million explanations went through my mind, but what I wound up saying was the stupidest thing of all.

"I said, 'Honey. Marisa. We were just playing around.'" I put my head in my hands, and blood rushed to my face as the whole episode replayed. I couldn't look at Rhonda and Dave.

"I thought she would cry and I'd comfort her, but it was much worse," I said. "She crossed her arms in front of her and then shoved me away.

"Oh, God. That look in her eyes. That nasty Joker smile. I'd never seen her look that way. Those teeth still too big for her face, not cute, just mean. I saw right that second how hurt turns to hate.

"She said, 'You weren't playing.'

"The door slammed behind her and I stood there a moment, staring through the screen. Marisa ran to the play structure and climbed up the ladder. Little Matty Bodle was up there, waiting his turn for the slide. She shrieked at him, 'Get off of here! It's mine!' He turned around to look at Marisa, and she pushed him away from the slide. 'I said get off!'"

My daughter trying to run the world, all by herself. Me just standing there, not being able to go to her, to lift her load. Maybe it seemed a simple thing. An incident. One of a thousand little traumas of growing up. I wondered if that's how Dave and Rhonda saw it, and suddenly I couldn't bear that possibility. I felt the tears coming, like they always came when I thought of Marisa being lonely and messed up, that night and still. I tightened my whole body to hold them back.

"I should have gone out there in the yard and told her not to behave like that," I said. "But for the first time ever, I didn't have a leg to stand on, you know?"

Rhonda closed her eyes and did that praying thing with her hands. Like I was so hopeless that was all she could think to do. Dave wagged his head. "Damn, Liz," he said.

"Damn," Rhonda said, so low I could barely hear. First time I'd heard her curse. I had no idea what was behind that curse.

I was afraid they'd judge me, of course, like Marisa did. Mostly I was afraid of what Rhonda would think. Being so Christian, I just didn't see how Rhonda could relate to my fucked-up life. She was the type that didn't say anything at all if she couldn't find anything nice to say, and she wasn't saying a thing. She didn't even look at me. Just picked at the cuticle of her thumb. Then I felt Dave's arm around me, his hand giving my shoulder a squeeze. I looked over at Rhonda again and thought maybe she did understand. Her curls stayed stiff as her face made slow, tiny nods.

We'd already experienced the way sympathy can make you want to cry. I guessed it was a self-pity thing, letting yourself feel bad when others feel bad for you. But when it came to Marisa, that I would not do. No, when it came to Marisa, I was responsible. I wouldn't let myself fall apart because of the ways I'd failed.

Rhonda finally spoke up, and it sounded like she was accusing me, impatient with me. "Did you ever try to talk to her?"

"Yeah. Of course," I said. "I tried a bunch of times, right after the party and a while afterward. But that girl was steel. She looked up at me like she was already practicing to be a lawyer." Those serious eyes, that jaw of hers, strong like Bradley's, the way it jutted forward.

"She interrogated me. Over and over. 'Do you love him?' she'd ask me. I said, 'Oh, God, no! Marisa. No, I do not love him. I hardly know him.'"

I told Marisa the truth, even though she was only nine. I said, "I don't know him, hardly at all, and I don't want to. I was just standing there at the refrigerator and he came up and kissed me. I didn't know what to do. I just made a mistake and let him do that. You never, ever want to let a man fool around like that with you, do you hear? You need to think about these things, and I should have thought about them, but it just came up so fast and I was so surprised it was happening and I'm so very sorry, Marisa. I'm sorry I upset you."

I thought I'd had it all planned out, what to say and how to say it, but instead I just wound up babbling at her.

I told Dave and Rhonda how one night, a few weeks after the kiss, I stepped over to Marisa's bed and leaned down to hug her, and how she held her body stiff and straight. How I held on to those skinny shoulders, pressed my cheek against hers for just a second. I wanted to smell her baby smell, but it seemed that in just a few weeks Marisa had lost that smell. Her pudgy little nose was already starting to get oily, and I smelled on her for the first time that sour-sweat puberty scent.

I said, "I love you, Marisa. I hope we can get past this, okay?" I squeezed her shoulders once more, then pulled back. She wasn't having any of it. Wouldn't loosen up in the slightest.

"She was wearing a new red barrette that day; either someone gave it to her or she used her allowance to buy it. Her hair was parted in the middle, pulled to the side with the barrette, and it hung down straight and lank over her shoulders. She never let me braid it again."

Dave's hand rested on my shoulder again, just for a bit, just long enough. "Oh, hon," he said. I thought Dave's touching me might get me tearing up again, and I expected Rhonda to weigh in with her sympathy too. I tightened up against that, squeezed my eyes shut. But Rhonda caught me by surprise.

"You know, Liz, you've got to quit beating yourself up over things that happened in the past like that," she said. No sympathy at all. "Yeah, it was a mistake. You're not perfect; surprise! And it happened so long ago! She's probably over it, and you should be too."

Rhonda was wound up like I'd never seen her. Every bit of sweetness out the window. Side-chopping with her palms at "over it." I half expected her to lean across Dave and slap me right there on the wall at Alcatraz. She dug in her jacket pocket for the spray bottle and spritzed three times into her open mouth, not bothering this time to hide behind her hand.

"My gosh," Rhonda said. She put the bottle back in her pocket and pulled her shoulders back. "Sure, you feel bad about the kiss, Liz, but you can't allow Marisa to keep manipulating you over it."

I had no idea how to respond, but what she said seared. Manipulated by Marisa. I'd never thought of it that way.

Rhonda kept staring at me like I'd better have a good answer. I turned to Dave, hoping he'd rescue me, but he was nodding at Rhonda as if he agreed.

"Marisa is a grown woman," Rhonda said, her voice lower. "If she carries resentment from something like that? Well, it's up to her to let go of it. She thinks her life is tough? Poor baby, only a lawyer in a hot-shit firm."

Rhonda said "shit." And she said it with a sharpness that I'd never heard from her. Then, making it worse, Dave said, "She's right, Liz."

The breeze kicked up, and I shivered, my stomach tight. They were trying to comfort me, but my gut reaction was to defend Marisa, to pretend that her behavior was fine, that everything was fine, really, except for that thing I did when she was little and how now she was so busy we'd grown apart. But, sitting there between Rhonda and Dave, it hit me. Protecting Marisa was what had led us to that place. It's what I'd always done. Pretending it was fine that her dad showed up at the ski cabin two days late, fine all the nights we wrapped his dinner in foil and ate on our own. I enlisted her in shoving Bradley's alcoholism under the rug, keeping her extra busy and keeping an extra-watchful eye, and she'd turned into a not-too-likable version of me: a control freak, never letting on how she really feels.

And there we were, the three of us Mets, in a situation none of us could control. A big tear plopped down onto my lap.

"Thank you," I said.

"If you must, you can tell Marisa you're still sorry about what happened," Dave said. He had no idea what a huge shift was going on inside me. "Ask her to let it go, so you can too. You can say it's eaten you up all these years. Ask her to forgive you, now that she's grown."

"You need to stop letting it eat you up," Rhonda said, reaching over to touch my arm. "You gave Marisa all you could. Now it's time for her to give to you. But she won't do that if you won't reach out to her. Please do." Her bony fingers squeezed my arm as she said "please," as if Rhonda would be the one to suffer from Marisa's estrangement.

"I'll do it," I said. "I promise."

The thing that had weighed me down for years, that stupid fucking kiss, was nothing I needed to carry at all. My impulse to defend, or walk away, lifted, and I just sat in a strange, neutral place of not wanting to hide, run, or fight. We were all on the same island, going back on the same boat.

It took four days for me to reach Marisa. She was in meetings, or wasn't home, or was just running out the door and said she'd call back. When she didn't, and the next day her assistant put me through, a guilty-sounding sweetness came through in her voice.

"I know, I'm sorry I've been hard to reach, it's just . . ."

"Don't worry, honey. I know you're busy," I papered over my anxiety and annoyance, then immediately regretted it. It was time for me to stop covering for her when she was inconsiderate. And sure enough, as if she'd just remembered she was supposed to be mad at me, her voice rose, exasperated.

"You're right, I am busy, crazy busy, Mom, so I really only have a second," she said. I could hear fingers on a keyboard even as she said that. Multitasking, returning emails, no doubt, while on the phone with me.

"Well, I wouldn't intrude if it weren't important," I said. "And it *is* important, Marisa. I need to talk to you, and I'd like it to be in person." The keystrokes stopped.

"Oh, good God, are you getting married?"

"Ha! Oh, Marisa!" I nearly doubled over and had to catch my breath. "No. Not even close!" I needed to sound less loaded, less ominous. Didn't want her to worry or be upset.

"Just, listen, we haven't really talked or caught up in such a long time, and our one weekend didn't work out," I said. Oh, God, that sounded whiny. I tried to recoup. "Look, I'd like to carve out just a day, no big deal. I could come there if you don't want to come up here."

I knew she wouldn't want me to go to her turf. She'd be stuck with me there. I didn't know LA or anyone but Marisa who lived there. In Oakland, she had friends, her dad, multiple possible escape routes.

"I'm sorry, Mom," she said, and she really did sound sorry. It floored me. Silence between us for a moment. This time, instead of jumping in with reassurances, I let the silence be. And then, after more keyboard clicks, she offered me a date, a Saturday twelve days away.

"I'll come up," she said. "I'll stay with Dad since he has more room, but you and I will have the day, okay?"

"Wonderful," I said.

"I'll send the flight info soon, okay? Gotta go now, though. Bye, Mom."

"Bye, Marisa. I love—"

She had already hung up.

Chapter 13

*W*e had a plan, Marisa and I, and even though the details hadn't been filled in, even though I was apprehensive, my heart was bursting. First thing I did was dial Rhonda, even though we never talked on the phone. I just wanted her to know. But Rhonda wasn't home, and I didn't leave a message. I'd try again after my walk.

I put on my hoodie and headed down Park Boulevard and onto my usual path, to blow off steam. One of the things I loved about Oakland was that Lake Merritt was smack in the middle of it. Around the lake was the courthouse, the museum, the Oakland Auditorium, and that show-offy modern glass cathedral. The walk around the whole lake was 3.4 miles, and before I got sick that was how I'd shake off my workday, especially in summertime, when it was still light enough to feel safe walking till 9:00 p.m.

It was sunny and warm that afternoon, with just the right breeze. I figured if I couldn't make it the whole way around, I'd rest a bit at the cathedral, and then maybe get on a bus or, worst case, call a cab.

So I walked the quarter mile to Lakeshore and got on the path that circled the lake. I passed a young man in track pants and sleeveless shirt, gold chain, lost in his headphone music, shouting random lyrics in the air. A couple of women power walking, punching their arms forward with their strides, and dishing. I wished Kate were retired, so we could walk and dish.

A gangly guy with Rasta hair sat by the Grecian pillars on the lake's north side, leaning against his backpack on the grass. Same guy, always in that same spot, pretending not to be selling the handbags and jewelry he had carefully arranged on a blanket, several yards from where he sat.

I made my way through a noisy line of kids on a field trip to the Rotary Science Center, and I stopped at the restroom there because you never knew. A mom in the next stall spoke to her whining toddler in Spanish, telling him over and over again to pull up his *pantalones*. I thought of Marisa, and how strangely time moves, one day helping her go potty, the next begging her to leave her law firm just for a day.

The restroom door slammed behind me, and I was once again out in the sun. I looked to my right and could see the playground through a wire fence that surrounded a small vegetable garden. Through that fence, over thick leaves of chard, I saw a little girl of about four, chubby legs in pink-striped tights under denim shorts, purple shoes with sparkly butterflies on the toes. Her blonde hair flying as she did a somersault on a patch of grass.

The girl shouted in a high, breathless voice, "Look, Mama!" She hunched her body down onto the lawn, somersaulting with legs in the air.

"Look! Mama! Eldon! Look!" she yelled. Her sideways somersault and screams for attention reminded me, too, of Marisa at that age. Yelling for my attention as I was in a fog, worried about Bradley.

I peered past the girl toward the swing set and saw a handsome middle-aged man approaching. His hair was close-cut gray, receding over a smooth, dark-brown forehead. He dressed preppy in creased khakis and a tucked-in polo shirt. The man smiled a big, indulgent smile, head bent down low as he approached the girl.

"Yes, yes, we see," he said.

Eldon. It was Eldon. And only then did I put together that the woman sitting on the bench behind him, the woman the girl

150

called "Mama," was Rhonda. Rhonda in the flouncy skirt, thin white hoodie, fresh red lipstick, looking in my direction but not seeing me because of the fence, the garden, and the girl wanting her attention right then. Rhonda in her stiff blonde curls, Rhonda's melodic voice calling back to the girl.

"Wonderful, sweetheart! But now we have to go home."

I don't know why I didn't call out to Rhonda at that moment. Why I didn't race back around the Rotary building and over to the playground so I could say hi and meet Eldon and the little girl. I was transfixed by the sweet scene, but watching them in it, I felt somehow like I'd intruded, just by happening by. Because why hadn't Rhonda told us about the little girl? The girl did another somersault, then another. Rhonda stood up and walked toward her.

Eldon's back was to me, but I heard him say, "Cassie! C'mon now, when Mama says let's go home, we need to go home." By then Rhonda had reached the little girl. She leaned over, picked the girl up, and raised her high in the air.

Eldon yelled. "Rhonda! Don't be lifting her up like that!" Panic in his voice. Rhonda could hurt herself. He lunged to take the child from Rhonda's arms and lowered her back down on the lawn.

"Nooo!" Cassie shrieked.

Eldon clasped one of the little girl's hands and Rhonda held the other. They took two steps, shouting, "One, two," and on "three," they swung Cassie in the air. A child's instant forgiveness; she giggled and shouted, "Again!" I'd told Rhonda everything about Marisa; why hadn't she mentioned this big thing? I felt a weight in my stomach; I'd thought we were getting close.

I stood there at the fence as they walked away and out of my sight. Thinking that if Rhonda had wanted me and Dave to know about the little girl, surely she would've told us by then? The girl called her "Mama," but she couldn't have been Rhonda's child. Rhonda was fifty-five. The girl was towheaded blonde, fair-skinned like our friend. And something about the way Rhonda had said "home" made me think she wasn't dropping her off.

Then it hit me, and I couldn't believe it took that long. Cassie was Rhonda's granddaughter. Rhonda had never mentioned her, and she'd quickly changed the subject after telling us back at Nordstrom she had a daughter. That one time I'd seen her face turn hard, when she'd changed the subject and dug into her purse. I felt thick and queasy with the thought that Rhonda's daughter might be dead and that she had kept this from Dave and me.

I supposed that sometimes, to keep it together, you just had to hold some things in. Sometimes there just wasn't enough time to explain when the thing that needed explaining was so big it would crowd everything else out. The way cancer did when people didn't know. The way I was afraid it would do with Marisa—that we'd go from no relationship to one centered on cancer. But maybe after our day together, maybe after she knew, cancer would help us cut through the everything else.

I stood there looking through the fence for the longest time. A wave of tired hit me then, as it did sometimes. There was no way I would make it around the entire lake.

I stopped to rest on an empty bench that was usually occupied by a homeless woman with her cart. She was a woman I always took to be about seventy years old, the way her lips wrinkled over missing teeth on both sides, her skin like clawed rawhide. Just a few days before, though, I'd stopped to give her a dollar, remembering what Rhonda did that day we went to Alcatraz. When I gave the woman the dollar, for the first time I looked in her eyes. I looked at her face and realized that she was probably my age—maybe even younger.

The rest of the way back home, I wondered where she might be. Under the freeway at Harrison Street, maybe. The ER. I thought, *There but for the grace.* I thought about Rhonda's daughter, and Cassie, and how we just couldn't know.

Chapter 14

I didn't try calling Rhonda again to tell her about Marisa, and I certainly wasn't admitting anything about spying on her through a fence. She'd kept things to herself for a reason, and she probably didn't care about my calling Marisa, anyway. What had I been thinking? We were a so-called support group, getting together for some fun, coincidentally having cancer, but that didn't mean we had to get into each other's family business. My face burned with the thought that I'd told them that whole long story about the kiss. For God's sake! If I didn't stop yakking, I wouldn't be surprised if they both found excuses to stop meeting altogether.

That Saturday, a few days after I'd seen Rhonda playing with Cassie, I got to the Merritt Bakery early and waited for her in one of the booths separated by pink trellises. Dave was to pick us up for an outing on our turf, the Oakland Embarcadero. It was another place we'd all thought of visiting sometime but never had.

I was already on my second cup of coffee, planning in my mind the visit with Marisa, when Rhonda showed up. Nine o'clock, right on time, in her red lipstick and puffy coat. I waved, and she flashed her bright-white crooked smile and scootched into the seat across from me in the booth.

"So how are you, Rhonda?" The thing I knew weighed on me, and my greeting was overly chirpy.

"Great! Oh, Liz, you look wonderful today!"

I did not, objectively, look wonderful. I'd dragged myself out of bed, leaving no time to wash my stringy hair. My joints ached from one med and my brain was fuzzy from another.

A white-uniformed server named SueEllen showed up with our to-go cups, mine filled with hot coffee and Rhonda's with a Lipton string hanging through the lid.

A big whoosh of cold air blew all the way over to our booth when Dave came through the door. Now we were three, ready for our adventure.

But something about Dave seemed off to me. He was bundled up, in his black stocking cap and some kind of tracksuit jacket, also black, over the canvas shirt with his Mets shirt showing at his neck. His face looked small and angry under the cap, or maybe it was just the black he wore or the way his eyebrows were growing out crazy and wiry all over the place.

"Hey! Dave!" I waved at him with one hand while the other was pressing down to help get my butt out of the booth.

Rhonda called out to Dave like she was in the sixth grade. "Dave! Davey! We all made it! Yippee!"

His mouth gave a sour little twist for a second, and then he pulled in a deep breath like it was an effort to say anything at all. "Hey," he said. "Ready?"

He stood at the door, waiting for us. Didn't come over for a hug or to sit down. What the hell had gotten into him? I had the horrible feeling that perhaps I'd misread all of us.

He led us out the door, into the cold wind and to a Subaru wagon in the bakery parking lot. He went straight to the driver's-side door, didn't open the passenger side, and didn't even mention anything about the fact that the entire back seat of the wagon was laid flat. *For what?* I wondered. *A Costco run?* Dave didn't even offer to fix the back into a regular seat. The back of his car looked like it'd been a truck bed, essentially, forever. There was a metal fence between it and the front seat, and a carpet lay across the space, covered with dog hair. It was as if

154

Dave were on his own planet, and the atmosphere there was even nastier than the one we actually inhabited.

I told myself to quit thinking the worst. With cancer, moods can change on a dime, and nothing's worse than pressure to keep your chin up, keep smiling, make everyone else in the room feel better no matter how you feel. I knew this but hated it nonetheless. It frightened me, the thought that one day we could be close, and then he'd show up and be so distant. *Like everything*, I thought, sinking into gloom. *Closeness doesn't last.*

Rhonda and I squeezed into the front passenger seat, one seat belt squashing the two of us together, my hip in the door handle and her thigh on the gearshift.

Dave finally turned to us when we were all squished together in the front. "You're both skinny enough, and it's a short way, right?" So much for chivalry.

Rhonda shot me a look. Just the teensiest eyebrow raise, but she didn't say anything either. Part of supporting one another should be to let each other be. You didn't have to feel close to be supportive, right? You just had to stick around, whether or not circumstances were ideal. Nobody ever said we had to be best friends. But my heart had dropped to my lap.

It was cold in the car, even squeezed next to Rhonda in her puffy jacket, and I wished I'd worn something warmer than the Mets shirt under the fleece. What was the point, even, of wearing the Mets shirt when it had to be covered up? Suddenly I felt stupid in that shirt. Rhonda's secretiveness, and now the way Dave was acting, reminded me we didn't know each other all that well. Smushed together in that car, I felt lonelier than I had even before we met.

I held the paper to-go cup on my knee and Rhonda did the same with her tea. Dave backed out of the parking space and then jammed on the brake for another car. Scalding coffee sloshed onto my thigh and seeped through my jeans but I sucked it up, didn't swear or say a thing about it. It had been a stupid idea to bring the hot drinks anyway. Rhonda managed to hold on to hers without spilling it all over the place.

Dave drove down Lakeshore and over to Oak Street, then got on I-880 South, and finally Rhonda asked, "Everything okay, Dave?"

"Sure thing," he said. I don't know how many exits we passed after that without anybody saying anything. Nobody says anything when everybody's thinking, *This is not such a great idea because it's freezing outside and maybe we should go on another day.* The second, and I mean the very second I was thinking that, the car started to bump and lurch, and more coffee spilled all over my thigh.

"What the fuck, Dave?" This time I was angry. I was angry at my burning thigh, angry it was so cold outside, and angry I was squeezed into the car way beyond my boundary for personal space. Also, I'd just realized I'd left my phone on the kitchen counter, and I started worrying about forgetting stuff. Were there mets in my brain? Or had I forgotten it on purpose, so I wouldn't be waiting all day for Marisa to call? If she could send me to her voicemail, she could damn well leave a message on mine.

"Oh my goodness!" Rhonda said, which was nearly as irritating as the now-cold liquid on my leg. I'd just said "fuck," so her "goodness" felt like a rebuke.

"Damn it!" Dave shouted. "Flat tire! Hang on!"

Dave moved the car slowly toward an exit, and we bumped and thunked with each rotation of the wheels. I stretched my arm out to the dashboard and rested the coffee on it so it would spill there instead of on my knee. I realized right then that I really, really needed to pee after all that coffee and that we were about to be stuck in a godforsaken industrial wasteland with a flat.

Dave had both hands over the steering wheel, bump-bump-bump at twenty miles an hour, and cars behind us honked, screeched on their brakes, and squealed over into the next lane. Every bump made it worse, I had to pee so bad.

"We can call AAA," Rhonda said. "They usually come very quickly, and then we'll be right on our way."

Both of Dave's hands gripped the steering wheel so hard his knuckles looked like they could pop out of his skin. "I just got new tires!" he yelled.

"It'll be okay, Dave," Rhonda said, making me feel even worse because I hadn't offered a single bit of consolation. We finally reached an off-ramp and bumped slowly down the grade to a frontage road. Dave drove across the gravelly potholed road and parked at the curb. We got out, and he scowled at the left rear tire. It was completely flat. Smashed down under the weight of the car that way, it reminded me of a mammogram, but of course that's not what you say.

"Shit," is what Dave said.

He pulled his cap off as if somehow that would help the situation. His hair sprang out unevenly and in all directions. He opened the back hatch of the Subaru, grumbling something I couldn't understand but the drift was the same: "Shit."

"It's okay, Dave. It'll all be okay," Rhonda said.

I almost snapped, "What makes you think that?" Because suddenly, with this one mishap, this one bad mood, it seemed as if nothing would ever be okay.

There were no people in sight, just the long, flat metal containers of a self-storage place, surrounded by a chain-link fence. A Doberman paced inside the fence. Across the street from the storage place, on the side where we were parked, a two-story building had FOR LEASE signs plastered on it every few yards. A weedy lot next to the building. This, I thought, was my life. A weedy lot, empty, the people I cared about out of reach.

"I'll just be a minute," I said, and I dashed through the weeds, over broken glass, and behind the building, where I hoped nobody could see me squatting to pee.

I made it back to the group, and Dave cursed as he pulled the spare tire from under the dog-haired back of the car, and he cursed some more because he couldn't get the jack out of the trunk well. It was bolted down somehow, and Dave was going at it with some kind of wrench, twisting and banging. "Why don't we just call AAA?" I said, "we" meaning Dave. I figured once we got the tire taken care of, we'd call it a day.

Rhonda stood a couple feet behind Dave, hand clutching her chin. "Dave doesn't have AAA," she said, looking to me with a little apologetic smile. "And he left his phone at home. But I'm sure we'll get it fixed in a second." I remembered, then, that Dave was a stickler about phones, a bit of a Luddite. Didn't want to miss being in the moment, didn't want an outing with friends to be interrupted, for electronic noise to intrude.

Rhonda sipped at her cup of cold tea and looked up at the freeway as if we'd just stopped a minute to take in the view. A pickup truck passed us on the frontage road, its driver looking straight ahead, pretending not to notice we were broken down. Asshole. I considered, for a second, hitchhiking home. I wasn't doing Dave or Rhonda any good, and I felt so depressed over the way the day was unfolding I figured it might be better to remove myself altogether. Of course hitchhiking was dangerous and we weren't in a great neighborhood, but what, really, did I have to lose?

"Ha!" Dave had the jack free. But he banged his head pulling it from the car.

He dropped it onto the asphalt, a heavy metallic *thunk*, then sat down cross-legged, his big shoulders hunched over, and centered the jack under the car. He put the lever into the jack and pushed down hard. With the lever in his right hand, his left hand over that, he pushed down again and again, grunting with each jerky lift of the car. The Doberman kept barking his head off.

"Haven't done this in almost forty years!" Dave shouted. His lips made a tight flat line across his face. "Our dad was a mechanic," he said, "but I was the one who showed my brother how to do this." He breathed in deep, back hunched over the jack, and then grunted with one more push of the lever down, up, down.

The cold air stung my thighs through wet jeans. October was supposed to be the best month in the Bay Area, but out there on the frontage road, it was damp, dark, and windy all at the same time. The only thing I wanted to do was go back home and get into bed. Everything had gone wrong. I felt a headache coming on and was sure it was caused by the same mets that were making me forget things.

Dave got the car jacked up all the way and then started to loosen the lug nuts on the flabby tire, and the wheel started to spin. "Ahhh! Damn it! I can't believe it!" Dave grabbed the lever from the asphalt and started lowering the car again.

Rhonda whispered into my ear, "I think you're supposed to loosen the bolts before you lift the car. But I wasn't sure." I felt a wave of relief that Rhonda hadn't shut me out, and I gave her a half smile. I think we both felt helpless.

Dave got the nuts loose on the flabby tire and jacked the car up again, faster this time, seeming to put all his strength into each shove of the lever. When the car was high enough, he pulled the tire off.

I wanted to be helpful, show Rhonda I could be kind, too, so even though Dave's mood scared me, I picked up the spare and handed it to him. It was one of those "chicken leg" spares, smaller and lighter than I had expected. Dave put it on the wheel, tightened the lug nuts, then lowered the car with the jack.

We all saw it at once. Dave yelled, "Fuck!" and Rhonda yelled, "Oh, no!" and I yelled, "Oh my God, can you believe it?" The spare was flat too.

"I didn't check the air!" Dave yelled. He sat down on the asphalt and shook his fists, his long legs splayed out beside the car. His shoulders slumped forward, and he put a hand over his brow. He pulled his cap off and scratched at his hair.

"I am so sorry, gals," he said. "I guess we need a tow truck."

Dave looked more anguished over the flat tire than I'd ever seen him look, and that was saying something after everything we'd talked about. I couldn't believe he'd get so upset over a flat. *It's impossible to know people*, I thought. Just when you think you did, things like this happened, and the distance between you showed itself to be unbreachable.

"It's okay, Dave," Rhonda said. Always the optimist.

But, bad as I felt at the moment, I did feel sorry for Dave. "I wouldn't even remember to carry a spare," I offered.

I thought of moving closer to him, but Dave stood and took two long steps away from the car. Out of his mouth came a ferocious shout, nearly drowned out by the sound of semis on the freeway, speeding by.

"Fucking Brent!"

I looked at Rhonda and she looked at me. It seemed neither one of us had a clue what was up with him or how we should respond.

"What is it, Dave?" I was glad it was Rhonda who spoke first. Rhonda's sweet children's-story voice.

Dave exhaled with a low growl. He pulled his shoulders back up and turned to us, his hair spiking all over the place, hands stretched out, forehead lines deep.

"Brent?" I asked.

"My brother," Dave said. He'd calmed down some but had that same sourness in his face. He shouted over the freeway noise. "My so-called brother!" His mouth went into that thin hard line again. "Heard from him this morning and I've been pissed ever since." He took another deep breath and blinked a few times.

Oh, family pain. I felt empathy wash over me.

"Sorry," he said. "Go ahead and call a tow truck, Rhonda."

Rhonda, the only one who did bring a phone, had an old Motorola flip phone, so we couldn't even look up where the nearest tow place was. Everyone was so freaked about the tire going flat we didn't pay attention to what exit we'd taken. So

Rhonda called Eldon and explained. She told us he couldn't come pick us up, but the two of them figured out where we were and who to call.

Turned out we were two exits beyond where we should've been to get to the Embarcadero walk in the first place. When Dave found that out, he got pissed at me. "I'm the driver; I thought you were supposed to be navigating," he said.

I stiffened. "You could've told me," I said. "How was I supposed to know if you didn't tell me?" My impulse to shut down, close off, and walk away briefly kicked in, my arms reflexively crossing my belly. Then I remembered we were supposed to be supporting one another.

None of us had paid any attention to where we were going. I'd been thinking about Marisa, Dave had been stewing about his brother, and Rhonda had been quiet too. If we hadn't had the flat, we would've wound up at the Oakland Airport or back in Rhonda's hometown of San Leandro or God knows where.

The estuary was close by, so sea smells mixed with diesel smells in the breeze. I took in a deep breath, and we leaned against the car, facing the elevated freeway, waiting.

It would be at least a half hour till Asa's Tire & Tow arrived, Rhonda said. I resisted the urge to fill in the quiet with small talk. What was bothering Dave had to be big. He paced, thumbs in pockets, to the curb and back.

"When did you last see him, Dave?" I asked.

He stopped, midway to the car. "Oh, Christ. It's been twenty-three years."

Big, loud, self-possessed Dave shrank into himself for a minute, like it was too much effort even to keep his chin out. His neck disappeared and his shoulders squeezed forward. I ached, seeing him that way.

"Now that my time's about up, Brent wants me to go out like we had the perfect family all along." Dave did air quotes around "perfect family." "His kids are grown, so, hey, they're safe from being recruited by the queer. That's what his wife would think. Either Brent thought it, too, all those years or he didn't stand up to it. Just as bad."

"Ah, jeez, Dave," I said, and I could feel my own insides crumpling with his pain. How I'd misread everything! Dave had lived with that pain his whole grown life. From his own brother. No wonder he was upset. Not that I was super close to my sister, but at least we weren't estranged.

Rhonda moved closer to him, rested her hand on his arm, the look on her face as pained as I felt.

"When Robert died, Brent sent a card," Dave said. He dropped his head, took a breath. "She signed it too."

He said the "she" like we all knew Brent's wife and agreed she was a horror. But in that moment it was as if Dave wasn't even talking to us. His eyes were in a different place, and he told us the story in a way that made me think he'd told it in his mind a thousand times.

"It was a Christian sympathy card." Each word its own bitter sentence. Years of pain and anger digging the grooves into Dave's face.

How many times had I sent inadequate sympathy cards, spending no real thought or care on a note?

"That card. It was like, wasn't Robert lucky to be going home to Jesus. Like wasn't it wonderful that their prayers saved him from eternal hell and damnation. Then a signature: 'Brent and Loreen.' That's all. All they wrote, all they did. It was unbeliev-able . . . Sorry, Rhonda," he said.

Her jaw went rigid like I'd never seen. Her voice went down a notch. "Oh, you don't have to be sorry to me," she said. She moved away from us, toward the front of the car, her wig hair blowing stiffly in the wind. For a second I thought she was going to walk off in a huff, burned by Dave's derision of Christian belief, and I couldn't bear that thought. Couldn't we all just hang in here together? But then Rhonda turned and looked at us both.

"I cannot abide that kind of Christian," she said. "Neither can Eldon or any of my friends from church. Most of my friends from church," she said. "All of my real friends, I guess I'd have to say." She braced her hands behind her against the hood.

I could see Rhonda at a loving church, a place like I'd experienced so long ago. Did such a thing still exist? Where you wouldn't feel strangled by expectation, made queasy by pious hypocrites?

"Funny," Dave said, "it didn't bother me so much that they weren't around when Robert was sick. They hadn't been around before he was sick, so why should they be there when he was?" He practically spat the next sentence. "Once I came out and divorced Lynette, that's when the rift began." Rifts. My own with Marisa felt uniquely painful, but of course it wasn't.

I forgot how cold it was, forgot the wind and the noise and the ugly landscape. I was so wrapped up in Dave's pain. Look at how he'd suffered, for having the guts to be fully who he was. But then, look at the love he'd had with Robert. Genuine, risky love. Neither Bradley nor I had ever had the guts for that kind of love.

Dave faced us but stepped away from the car. "They just didn't get it. They didn't fucking get it! They didn't even *try* to get it. Their kids were little then, and even though I lived out here, I wanted to be in their lives. Now they're grown and I hardly know them." Those things you can't get back. Years, relationships.

Dave glared at me, then at Rhonda, a look that said, *Please understand—but fuck you if you don't*. Rhonda moved a step closer to him, but I was frozen in place, wrung out by the emotions I felt, and could only whisper, "You were so strong."

The breath Dave inhaled then was so deep his whole body lifted with it.

"Back there. La Porte, Indiana. I mean, everybody in everybody's business. Not like I relished going back, but still. What are you supposed to do over the holidays? Every Thanksgiving my brother would make excuses, like they were going to the in-laws' and, read between the lines, surely I didn't expect to be invited along! What did they think, that I'd come in drag? Lynette would've even come with, if they were so worried about it."

I'd never seen Dave so upset. Beside himself. Dave's behavior made me understand, for the first time, what that expression meant. This hot ball of anger and sadness just swooped in and took over his body and left the rest of Dave empty beside it. All my life, this kind of upset was my cue to bail. I'd find a reason to leave the room or simply shut down. I shivered to think of the times Marisa was beside herself and I put her down for overreacting or simply ignored her, physically absenting myself until she calmed down. It never occurred that I could simply accept it, ask about her feelings or simply stay by her side.

So Dave snarled, and I sat.

"Will it feel good in some part of yourself to go back to the love you felt as boys?" I asked after a moment. "Assuming you did love your brother when you were a boy?"

"When we were boys," he said. "It was complicated then too." He slumped over again, looking just plain wrung out.

I tried to imagine a hometown. A place where what you did mattered enough for people to talk about, and that being a bad thing. I'd always fantasized about fitting in someplace small and close. What it would be like to feel good about a church picnic, say, every single week. Truth was, I didn't think I could stand it. Not the way I was, antsy and rootless, the way my life just happened to make me. You moved, you fit in, always had one foot out the door, never got attached.

It must've been so much worse for Dave, growing up with everything tight-knit, knowing the place in his bones but still not fitting in. Or maybe it never was that close. Maybe when you grow up with the same people, close together all the time, you've got to keep your distance somehow. People find ways. That's how our family kept it together, nomads on the move, but each in our own world.

Rhonda, as usual, had something sweet to say. "I think you should follow your heart, Dave." Only she could say that without making me cringe.

Dave turned to her. "That's what I'm thinking," he said. "Go with my heart. Purely selfish calculation. If it feels better to have Brent come than it'll feel to keep him away, I'll tell him it's okay. Not that he asked. He just informed me. Sent me an email, told me he's split from Loreen. Well, that's about frikking time. He says, 'I know we've got a lot of catching up to do.' No shit! Including things he is not going to want to hear.

"I'm just wondering, is it worth it? Do I need this drama at this point?"

I wanted to say, *Maybe some things are just best left as is. Maybe you don't get to wrap your life all up in a bow, and maybe that's okay.*

"You could just take it one dinner at a time," I said. "Coffee, even. And really, you don't need to be responsible for him finding a place."

Turned out Dave already told Brent he could sleep on his couch.

"But just for a couple of days. What can I say? It was just reflexive. He's my brother."

I thought about Marisa, and my sister—*Should I ask her to come?*—and things getting wrapped up at the end of life. It would take another lifetime to wrap everything up. You don't get to press REWIND; you can only do what you can in the remaining time. The thought panicked me. Was there enough time to make things better? Why had I been putting it off and letting Marisa call the shots?

Dave yelled, "Finally!" when we heard the sound of wheels scrunching over the pothole right behind us.

The tow-truck driver, a big man who was muscled enough to lift the car without a jack, began installing a new tire, and over the zipper-rip sound of his tools, I asked Dave, "Is Brent still evangelizing? I mean, Christian except for the 'love your brother'

part? It's just—again, no offense, Rhonda—but I'd hate to have
him lay that on you now. Try to save your soul or something. You
really don't need that. Not in your own house, especially."

Rhonda looked full-on pissed off when I said that. She set
her jaw hard that same way and yanked on her wig. It made her
forehead too high; her whole face dared us to look at it that way.
God, I'd offended her. I felt the blood rush to my face. She stared
hard at both of us.

"I'm sorry," I said. Sweet Rhonda. Why couldn't I keep my
mouth shut?

She waited for the AAA driver to pull away. "I already told
you," she said. "That's not the kind of Christian I am. You don't
need to keep apologizing, and please, don't compare. I don't
believe in the religion I was raised in—Seventh-day Adventist, so
strict you wouldn't believe. Ran away from it as soon as I could.
But then there was a time when things got so bad I needed to
find faith again, and I did."

When things were at their worst with Bradley, I felt so lost
that the only thing that kept me grounded was work. But I imagined Rhonda in a bad place, praying on her knees. Hers might've
been a better response.

"So, yes, my faith gets me through, all right. Jesus has never
let me down."

It was automatic, the way that sentence made my body stiff.
Why couldn't I believe in anything?

"I'm sorry," I said again, and I meant it with my heart.
"Shouldn't have judged."

"Right," Dave said. "Me too."

We piled back in the car, and Dave headed toward the
on-ramp. Dave never did answer my question about his brother
evangelizing, and I sure didn't want to bring it up again.

This time Dave knew the right exit, there was no hot coffee
to worry about, and my jeans were dry.

The street where we parked was as empty as the ugly frontage road where we'd had the flat, but the landscape at Union Point Park was much more inviting. We looked across a freshly mowed lawn to the ruffled gray water of the estuary and the island of Alameda. Native grasses and young trees lined the asphalt embarcadero path. Sailboats were moored just feet away, their flags flapping in the wind, metal sheets clanging. I breathed in the sea smells and forgot about the rough start to our day.

"There it is," Rhonda said. "Point of interest number one. The *Sigamé / Follow Me* statue."

We crossed the lawn and approached a statue about fifteen feet tall, an amalgam of twenty native Oakland daughters sculpted into one strong multiracial female. She wore a collage of clothing from the time of the native Miwok to the present. Barefoot and tennis-shoed, in business skirt, buckskin, pioneer ruffles, and slacks. With her arms outstretched in bits of a dozen different sleeves, she looked over her shoulder at her beckoning hand that was both pale pink and clay red.

Rhonda circled the statue and we followed her, reading the twenty plaques at her feet. Dr. Marcella Ford, African American education pioneer. Cagute, a Jalquin Bay Miwok and the last Oakland-area woman to join the missions. A poet laureate, secretary of state, dancer, author, activist. I tried to think of one really good thing I'd done, a meaningful thing that went beyond going through the motions in life. There wouldn't be enough time for me to do anything great, even if I were able. A deep sadness welled up, but I stopped it with the mantra I kept hearing but not getting my mind around: All there is, is right now.

Dave put his fist in the air. "That's you two!" he shouted. "Strong women! Daughters of Oakland!"

I raised my fist to the statue, too, and shouted, "Strong women! Strong daughters!" *May Marisa remain strong*, I thought. *But may she learn to be gentle too.*

I expected Rhonda to raise her fist high like Dave's and mine, but I saw her head bent down, her hand covering her face.

"My daughter," she said. "I'm praying for her."

I suddenly felt the disorientation of knowing you're missing something but not certain what it is. I remembered the little girl, but had I forgotten something Rhonda had told us about her daughter. I was starting to forget things right and left. People's names, what they told me about their kids. Dave wore the same puzzled look that must've been on my face. Just then the Facebook picture floated through my brain. *Sally.* Rhonda had never said her name.

"I've forgotten about your daughter, Rhonda," Dave said. "I'm sorry."

Rhonda lowered herself to a metal bench at a table facing the statue. She stared at the boats as the wind picked up and the clanging of their sheets grew insistent. She put both hands on her scalp, as if she could keep her head together by holding them there.

Dave and I sat across the table from her, close enough to keep each other warm. "Sally," she said. "You didn't forget. I didn't tell you because I didn't want the whole room at Nordstrom to know. People judge, and I didn't want to deal with their judgment." She pulled the spray bottle from her drawstring bag but didn't spray this time, just held it in her hand, ready.

"It's bad enough at church, where I've got Eldon to fend off the ones who don't get it. I'm working on it, but sometimes I still feel ashamed when I think they're judging me, judging Sally." Who could possibly judge Rhonda?

"I shouldn't feel ashamed, I know, but sometimes I still do. Anyway, I want you to know. It's a big part of what's going on in my life. Or not going on. I don't know how to put it, exactly."

I slid my hand over Dave's, resting on the bench, and he reached his other hand across his lap, squeezing mine, without taking his eyes off Rhonda. Hearing Rhonda so flustered, having such a hard time telling us whatever it was she needed to say, seemed to frighten us both.

All of a sudden Rhonda was every day of her age and then some, pretty blue eyes shrinking in her cancer face, curls looking ridiculous hanging below her shoulders. She seemed about to cry again, the way her brow closed in on her eyes. And then she turned away.

"My daughter, Sally, is an addict," Rhonda said. She inhaled deeply and closed her eyes. She opened them on the loud exhale and looked straight at us, steel eyes, rock jaw. "She suffers from the disease of addiction."

I was desperate for this not to be true, not for Rhonda. Not with her daughter.

Dave blew out a gust of air. "Ah, Jesus," he said.

"Oxy. Booze. Crack. Crystal meth. Probably heroin, too, by now." She said the words like she was listing the names of state capitals. "She's been through pretty much anything she can get her hands on." Rhonda pulled her shoulders back tighter, red lipstick in a hard, tight line, and her face seemed to say, *I told you the truth and now I dare you to think anything bad about my daughter.* I could see her broken heart when she made her eyes mean that way. Like a sweet dog growling when it's in pain.

"Oh, God, Rhonda! That is the worst thing I can imagine," I whispered. I worried about Marisa being distant. Rhonda must have lived in constant fear that Sally would die.

I wanted to go over and hug her, but everything about her told me to stay away. I'd been in that defensive place, that place where shutting down seemed the only option, where all sympathy could do was erode my strength. Dave must've felt as frozen as I did. He wasn't breathing enough for his shoulders to move.

"She's twenty-eight and has been in and out of rehab five times," Rhonda said. "I spent everything I had and then some, but nothing worked." She said it like the whole thing still stunned her, like she'd been stunned year after year, stunned again each time she had to say it out loud. "I finally had to give up. Let her go. Sally's back on the streets now, killing herself, somewhere. San

Francisco, I think. All I know is that, last month, she was with a guy named Josh. She asked me for money and I said no, and then she said something like, 'Eff you, Mom! Josh will take care of me.'"

God almighty, what do you do with all that pain? I thought. In my mind, unbidden, I saw Bradley vomiting, me shutting the bathroom door: "Hush! Marisa will hear."

"It was, you know, all of a sudden getting in with the wrong crowd and a boy who got her into pot and then pills, and her grades went bad and she quit school her senior year. That's when I sent her to that boot camp place in Arizona and she ran away. I tried it all. Letting her back in, kicking her out. Counselors, detox. Twenty-eight days. Three months. Two days in and then back on the streets. She stole my jewelry. Wrecked my car. I even got to the point of calling the police on my own daughter. I hoped that would shake her up, but it didn't. She went in, she came out, and she used again."

In the last years with Bradley, I'd felt guilty for not pushing him harder to quit, but see? It would've been pointless. My heart sank with the truth of it. Before cancer, it was the biggest thing I couldn't control.

An egret flew by. Rhonda looked up at the sky. She lifted her chin and took another big breath in, like she'd practiced saying all this before.

"Sally was a cheerleader, for gosh sakes. A solid B-plus student. Those are supposed to be the best-adjusted ones. I was strict, but I was loving. I was consistent," she said. "I raced home every night so we could eat dinner together."

God, all the racing around, the planning and protecting, the pushing, the praise, and still you didn't know how they'd turn out, or whether all you did was what made them turn out the way you wished they hadn't.

"I've just handed my baby over to God," Rhonda said. "There's not a thing else I can do." She looked so tired, so skinny and scared.

I'd been so worried about Marisa, healthy and successful Marisa. Distant, ruthless Marisa. But things were not this bad. Surely we could fix what was wrong between us.

"Can't you reach her?" I asked. Another stupid question. I could barely get Marisa to call.

"It's really hard to explain all this," she said. "How you get to the point of telling your own kid she's not welcome in your home. How you can let her go on out to the streets and change your locks and pray that will bring her to the point of wanting to save her own life."

I got up from the table and came around behind Rhonda and draped my arms over her, feeling her warmth through her puffy jacket, and her head leaned back and her curls pressed against my belly. Dave loomed over the both of us, arms nearly all the way around Rhonda and me, too, the three of us pressed together in front of all the daughters who were strong.

"I hate that goddamned disease," Dave said. "Addiction, man. Hate it like cancer."

Exactly. It had invaded my family like cancer, ate at it from the inside, left it to die.

Rhonda's shoulders rocked us both as we leaned into her. Hating cancer, hating addiction. We were a tribe within a tribe.

Chapter 15

*A*ll the things we knew about one another without knowing
the specifics. How to shove our feelings down, how to pretend, how to take charge, keep a lid on. All the things you get
good at when an alcoholic's in the house. All the out-of-control
things you try to control. I got why Dave struggled to tame his
rage sometimes, and I got Rhonda's being so perfect, her sweetness, and the steel underneath.

And, oh, what a relief to know that if I knew these things
about them, they also knew them about me. Rhonda had my
number, and Dave, too, even if I was just figuring it out myself.
After what they'd said about Marisa, when I got home that day I
knew I had to tell her the truth, about my cancer and all the rest
of it. I'd had no practice, though, telling these kinds of truths
face-to-face. I'd spent years papering things over, putting on a
good face to make an abnormal household seem normal, but no
time simply facing facts.

I wanted to think I could turn things around with Marisa
simply by talking to her straight on her visit. Two things worried
me though. If I waited to tell her about my cancer in person, that
news would overtake everything else I wanted to say. And my
instincts to protect Marisa, and her instincts to protect her dad,
could easily draw us into our familiar, distant roles.

So I pulled out the breadboard, put my laptop on it, climbed
onto the kitchen stool, and started writing to her. I'd mail it, an

actual letter, because I didn't want my news on her office email. Lucinda Greaves would not be putting it in any file.

I started off newsy and positive, telling her about Rhonda and Dave, my new friends. I thought I was starting that way so she'd have a sense of my new life. But I wondered if I just wanted to bring them into the room to buck me up.

I want to tell you about some new friends I've made, I wrote.

You'd never believe your mom has been taking leisurely walks, going to ball games, and talking about the most personal things with a Vietnam vet who's also a veterinarian and a gay man and with a sweet Christian woman who sings with Everett Lester's famous gospel choir, "Alive!" We've actually become close in a way I couldn't have imagined, Marisa.

I started this letter telling you about them because I want you to know I'm not alone.

It sank in only as I wrote that it was true. And because it was true, the next part—the words I'd been fearing and avoiding—flowed naturally. I did feel Dave and Rhonda in the room.

The reason I've had all this time to make new friends, and the reason these are the specific friends I've made, is because of the bad news, Marisa. My cancer's come back. It's metastasized to my bones.

I conjured my stoic father, his "this is just the way it is" deathbed shrug. But that's not all I wanted to convey to Marisa.

My prognosis is good, given it's metastatic cancer, but because it's metastatic cancer, it is terminal, maybe in a couple years, maybe more.

I resisted the urge to jump in at that point and say, *But it's fine! I'm doing great!* I imagined her thinking, the way I had when my parents gave me the same news, *She's dying!* The shock of it, the sense of panic. But I kept going.

I actually am doing pretty well, but this is, obviously, not great. It's not a "blip" like I said about cancer the first time. I'll be living with this the rest of my life, however long that will be.

Would she be crying at this point? Finding some way to

dismiss it, searching links to treatments, diets, clinical trials? I'd leave it at that, let it sink in. I hoped she'd be pleasantly surprised to see me, looking healthy, not miserable, not wasting away. I continued writing.

So—big reveal!—I quit my job. It just became clear to me that my job is not where or how I want to spend my limited life. I get to keep my health insurance and have plenty of money saved in my IRA. I feel pretty good and don't need awful chemo or radiation like last time, just pills and injections once in a while. I joined a support group, believe it or not, and that's how I met Dave, the vet, and Rhonda, the singer, who also used to be a court reporter in Alameda County. We all have Stage Four cancers, different kinds.

It felt so good to tell her about them. And it struck me how I'd kept them from her all this time. It was a way of avoiding the inevitable—telling her about my diagnosis and having that overshadow everything from here on out. I wanted to keep them to myself until I got used to the idea of a support group, of new friends. And also until I believed for sure we'd be sticking it out.

I know this is a lot to lay on you. I wanted to tell you in person, but I decided it would be better for you to have time to think about it before seeing me and having to come up with something to say. Still protecting her! *I don't want my cancer to be the entire focus of our visit. For me, more important than telling you about my cancer is telling you I love you and want for us to find a way to be close.*

It was as simple as that. Why had it seemed so hard to say that before?

You know, we never really, openly talked about our family. It's only recently I've been thinking about the mistakes I made raising you and the ways your dad's drinking affected us both. No, I'm not going to trash your dad or blame him either. His need to drink isn't his fault. I think he must have struggled a lot to keep it together at work and at home. But we both remember times when he didn't, and how we never talked about those times (all the dinners wrapped up and put in the fridge while you and I ate alone, the mornings he was supposed to take you to school and I said I made him let me take you instead, so he could sleep in . . .). You and I did a pretty good job of pretending everything was okay. Of keeping a lid on, staying super busy so it wouldn't seem anything was amiss. I'm afraid that trying to keep everything under control all those years turned us both into control freaks!

There, I said it. Both of us.

I did try to talk to you about your dad's drinking a couple times, and, if you remember, you shut me right down. I don't blame you. We had a system, and I was disrupting it. We were behaving like a typical alcoholic family, without ever facing up to the disease. We got through, and I know how much you love your dad, but, honey, it's important that we both recognize that all that shoving of things under the rug has taken a toll. There were so many things we didn't talk about that we wound up barely talking at all. At least that's the way I look at it. I know you resent me for that one foolish kiss years ago and that it was particularly hard to learn I had found someone else before your dad and I divorced. You probably resent a bunch of things I did when you were growing up. I'm trying to forgive myself, for being so focused on work, for not communicating better, for adding to the tension in our household. I hope you'll be able to forgive me too. And I hope we can start talking more and quit running so much.

No way I'd have the guts to say everything I said in that letter face-to-face without a bunch of backtracking, making excuses, changing the subject. I just wasn't in the habit. I'd fall back on minimizing, keeping things light. Besides, if I did have the guts to say out loud what I'd written, I imagine she'd be the one to shut down. Marisa had a way of shutting down her eyes, like she had the power to pull down a window shade right behind her eyeballs so nothing came out, nothing went in. I wanted to give her a little time to think about my letter so she wouldn't do that with me.

What if it was just too late? What if she simply had hardened into the kind of person who couldn't deal with this sort of thing? Most people couldn't. They ran away or fell back on small talk or pretended there was nothing in the world a positive attitude couldn't cure. It was a lot to expect of Marisa, who was as hard-wired with denial as I'd been.

I'd never said or written the words "alcoholic family" and applied them to us. I wrote it just like that, so the idea would jump off the page and make her pay attention, make her think about what it meant. Now anyone who knew a thing about alcoholic families would say, "Say no more!" I didn't have to explain what "alcoholic family" meant to Rhonda, whose own addict daughter would steal her blind, or to Dave, whose dad was a drunk so mean Dave didn't even bother going home when he died. Bradley hadn't gone nearly as far down as they had, but that was another thing alcoholic families said: "Compared to that guy in the gutter, our alcoholic is doing just great."

Tribe within a tribe, Rhonda, Dave, and me. Same family disease. I hadn't wanted to believe my family fit into the category, only that perhaps we'd brushed against some of the traits. After the divorce, after cancer, after Lyle, it started to sink in. Who was I kidding? Still, I figured that once Bradley was out of the picture, "alcoholic family" no longer applied. Not taking into account Marisa and me and the traits we still had.

After all that time denying and covering up for her dad, I didn't know if Marisa would be angry at me for laying it out like that, telling it straight for the first time. Or whether she knew all this perfectly well and just didn't know how to talk about it.

At the end of the letter I told Marisa not to worry about calling or writing right away. Told her we'd talk about it when she came up for the weekend, if she wanted to. I thought I should give her that out. I worried, though, that if she didn't face up to our family craziness, and how she and I dealt with it, she was just not going to be the kind of person you'd want to know. I couldn't believe a mother could even say that, but it was true.

Ever since she was little, Marisa worked so hard and was so focused on being the best at everything. How typical of an alcoholic's kid! She'd grown up to be one of those people you admire and hate at the same time. A person can be distant and cold and manipulative—and at work, they'll give her a promotion for outfoxing the competition. At home, though, those things catch up to you, so I told Marisa that too. I didn't want her making the same mistakes I did.

And then what did I do? Right after I laid out the truth, after apologizing for the lying I'd done, all the trying to make everything perfect, all the controlling I did while she was growing up? I ended the letter with my full-blown fantasy of how our weekend together would be. Planned everything down to the minute, just like I planned every minute of her time growing up, from the time the school bell rang till the time she was asleep in bed. It was only after I sent the letter that I realized what I'd done.

I'd written that, after a walk through the Arboretum in Golden Gate Park, we'd do a little shopping at that boutique she liked on Ninth Avenue. For dinner we'd go to Tomaso's, just like we did after her graduation, and have the ziti with sausage and red peppers, and the eggplant Parmesan. Then the next day, breakfast in the gorgeous Palace tearoom. I'd made reservations. It was a wonder I hadn't told her exactly what to wear. I'd fallen into old habits without even noticing, right after all that preaching about control.

But the letter was my best shot. If I didn't get through to her, if all she could see after this was the cancer, that would be it. Marisa might soften, might someday have her own sorrows that leveled her to a point where she had to reach out. By then, I could be gone.

I'd printed the letter, folded it, put it in an envelope, and walked down the street to the box. It would arrive before she flew up to see me. The sound of the letter dropping, the metallic squeak of the mailbox, had squeezed my stomach and stopped my breath altogether, long enough for me to understand in a way

I couldn't escape how scared I'd been of simply telling the truth to my own daughter.

The thick pink envelope came in the next day's mail, with my registration number on hot-pink cardboard. Marisa had signed us up for the Breast Cancer Walk for the Cure.

Before receiving my letter, she'd made plans for us, without consulting me. Touché! I was touched that she'd made the effort, that she wanted to walk with me for a good cause. But it was, really and truly, the very last thing I wanted to do with Marisa that weekend. It would be crowded and noisy and impossible to really talk. And nothing about a cancer walk sounded fun to me.

Marisa, vintage Marisa, texted me that she'd be jammed with client meetings until she got on the plane to San Francisco.

"CU Sat. @ 7:30," she said. "T-shirt table."

Chapter 16

It was drizzling that afternoon when I pulled my Toyota into the always-crowded lot of the Piedmont Market, still fuming about Marisa's text. I eyed the only empty spot—a tight space that would require two moves, with cars waiting behind me. *Relax*, I told myself, but I'd angled too far on the second move and would have to pull out a third time. Pathetic. I waved my arms apologetically at the Mercedes behind me and looked around to see if there were onlookers to the embarrassing spectacle. I saw one man, carrying a grocery bag at the bus stop, his head down, laughing. The bastard. I parked, gave a sheepish grin to the Mercedes driver, a woman too young, anyway, to be driving that expensive car. And then I took another look at the bus stop man. It was Bradley.

"Ha ha," I yelled.

He waved and yelled back, "Have I *ever* said anything about your parking?" Which made me smile, thinking of all the times he'd bit his lip and we'd wound up laughing. One thing about Bradley: he knew not to mansplain during parking maneuvers. He was terrible at parallel parking himself.

"What are you doing here?" I asked, crossing the street toward him.

An old man sat reading on the bench next to him. People walked past with Peet's to-go cups, saying hello to the used bookseller, bringing stacks in from a table on the drizzly street.

"The grocery bag is your clue," Bradley said.

"Duh. I mean, at the bus stop? Parking spaces too tight?"

I watched Bradley's face pale and grow serious, from cocky jokester to teen being delivered home by the cops.

"I'm, uh, giving up the car, I decided," he said. "For a bit. Enjoying public transportation. Doing my part for the environment." His smile was unconvincing. I knew him well enough to know when he was hiding.

He changed the subject. "Listen, how're you feeling? Looking good! Told you cancer was no match for you." He flashed his generous grin.

"Thanks. I'm doing fine," I said. Then I noticed his dishevelment, the dirt on his pant cuffs and a little burn hole on his shirt, from a joint, no doubt. A great well of sadness came over me, and then anger began to bubble up. The feelings were so familiar. I looked at him eyeing me closely, determining whether I'd bought what he'd said. Like the old married couple we'd been, we saw right into each other

"You got a DUI," I stated; I did not ask.

His brows, turning to gray, bunched over the blue-green eyes I'd once found irresistible. "Please don't tell Marisa," he said.

Of course. Don't let Marisa know, don't let her see, don't bring her in on the consequences. Here was my chance to do just that, to wave the DUI like a red flag in front of her, to say, "See? This is just what I was saying. This is who we were both covering for. This is where it leads."

I looked at Bradley's sheepish face, took a deep breath, imagining Dave doing the same to calm himself, and felt my rage dissipate. No, I would not be that person. This time, I would not be keeping Bradley's secret in order to protect Marisa. But I would respect Bradley's wishes because both he and Marisa were adults and his drinking was not mine to manage. Forgiveness. No, like Dave said, acceptance.

"I won't," I said. "It's up to you to tell her if you want." I saw relief in his eyes. "And speaking of not telling our daughter, I'll finally be talking to her about my situation this weekend. We're going on the Walk for the Cure." I rolled my eyes while Bradley gave me a look of pity and admiration, as if I were a saint for doing such a thing.

I couldn't let it stand.

"It was her idea," I said. "Anyway, gotta get my groceries. Hope you don't have to wait long." Piteous as he looked, I would not come to his rescue by offering a ride.

Chapter 17

*R*honda called me the next day to make a plan for us Mets to meet at Caffe Trieste the following week, our first evening get-together since Nordstrom. The place had a cool jazz combo on Tuesday nights, not too late, and it was inexpensive. Rhonda told me she used to love going with a couple of women from her church.

"Nobody's asked me to go for a few months," she said. "I'd ask them, but you know." I bet she was afraid they didn't want to be seen with her. Worried about how people would act when they saw her face. Even when people don't say these things, you know. So that decided it for me, and for Dave too. I called him and he called her and then he called me back, four or five phone calls just for the one date, but that's how it goes when you haven't been out in a while.

"Want me to pick you up? What time do we need to get there for a good seat? Do we eat dinner there or after? Is it one of those dressed-to-kill Oakland places where only the white people look like slobs?" I didn't want to be the one slob.

"You'll see everything," Rhonda said. "You'll be fine. Oh, I'm so excited! I really do miss going out."

"You could maybe wear a different shirt, Dave," I said. "I mean than the canvas one with the plaid cuffs. No offense. I love that shirt! Just maybe not out at night? And even if you don't, we'll still sit with you."

As soon as I said it, I wished I could reel it back.

"For God's sake, Liz. I know how to dress when I have to," Dave said.

Blood rushed to my face. "God, I'm sorry," I said. "No wonder my daughter hates me. That's exactly the kind of thing I used to say to her." I hadn't seen it so clearly till just that moment. Marisa must've felt the way I made Dave feel.

Too much time passed before Dave said, "It's okay. I'll be a good date. And, yeah, let's all dress to kill. It's been ages."

Over the next few days, I built up a whole fantasy about things I'd say to the church ladies and what they'd say back to me. How they'd act with Dave and how he'd act with them. I imagined having to shush Dave and his loud voice when the band started to play. I hated it when people talked over live music, even when the music was supposed to be in the background. You should show some respect. I hoped Dave wouldn't be mad at me for shushing him, especially after the shirt thing, and I imagined squeezing his hand so he'd know I didn't mean anything by my shushing. Rhonda's smile, all rapturous in the room with the crowded tables. The church ladies getting comfortable with Rhonda's face. Rhonda so happy to see them there. A soulful saxophone player, an old hippie on drums, and on the bass I imagined a near-elderly African American man who'd played gigs with the greats.

But that's not how it happened at all. It was Thursday morning, not Tuesday evening, when Dave picked me up in his Subaru wagon with the fenced-in rear seat laid down flat, and neither one of us was dressed to kill. We were headed back to Mercy, the place where Rhonda and I had started down this chute. She'd been admitted in the middle of the night.

I navigated. Down Park Boulevard, up Franklin to Broadway, up Broadway to MacArthur. I could do it in my sleep, and I did it while repeating in my mind, *Not Rhonda. Not yet.*

The stubble on Dave's chin was gray and patchy, but he had a new haircut, close and spiky silver. It made his face look rounder and younger. Dave's voice sounded deeper when it was quiet, public-radio smooth, but he gripped the steering wheel tight with both hands.

"Rhonda said it was just a bloody nose." His body hunched forward like he was pushing the car with his own weight.

"I read that happens sometimes, with head and neck," I said. "They can't get it to stop bleeding without cauterization." I'd googled it an hour earlier. As if knowing the details could make me less terrified.

"I read that too," Dave said.

I turned to look through the wire fence behind our seats, saw the ratty carpet covering the back of the wagon. Dog hair.

"You haul a lot of dogs around?"

I knew I shouldn't have changed the subject. Saying anything more about Rhonda before seeing her, though, felt too scary. I wanted it to be just a nosebleed, and for us to go see her, and for her to get out of the hospital right away and come to Caffe Trieste with us the very next night. It was the first thing I had been afraid to say out loud to Dave. We'd talked about things we were afraid of and mad at and regretted and hoped for and hurt over and loved in all our lives. Talked like I'd never talked with anyone before. And now that it came down to it, now that we were heading to a hospital with Rhonda in it, I felt so scared that I could hardly breathe. I needed to talk about dogs.

"Sometimes," Dave said, "I'll treat a dog and it'll need surgery and then some pain meds or muscle relaxants or some such that I can't trust to give to its owner. The homeless guys who are mentally ill, who are addicts, you can't expect them to give a dog meds every four hours when they abuse or can't keep track of their own."

We'd jumped out of our beds around 6:00 a.m., earlier than usual, after Rhonda called. Dave needed a shave, and I hadn't even showered. I thought clean black stretch pants and a red fleece top were passable, but with the dog hair everywhere, maybe not. I didn't want Rhonda to think we were so freaked out we couldn't pull ourselves together.

Dave looked over at me while he was talking, hand on the wheel, voice rising. I guessed he needed to talk about dogs and not Rhonda too.

"I'll take a dog home for a few days, till it's back on its feet," Dave said. "There's no room in the clinic, and we can't keep meds there overnight or we'd get broken into all the time." Brief glance at the road, then back to me, as if I couldn't hear him otherwise. "These guys understand. They're grateful. They're so happy to get their dogs back healthy, they'd kill for me. One guy actually offered to. I'm not kidding."

Dave was delighted with himself for a minute, a grin clear across his face, smoothing the crags away. I bet he was perfect with the homeless guys and their pets. Big guy himself, biggest heart in the world, wouldn't take shit from anyone, not even the addicts. Oh how grateful I felt for Dave right then. Without Dave, how could I face Rhonda? Rhonda, who seemed bound with both of us in a fierce kind of love.

We were stopped at the longest light two blocks from Mercy, people going to work walking every which way, cars running yellow lights. A pedestrian cut right in front of us, and the guy flipped us off. It was a miracle more people didn't get killed, just going from one place to the next.

The light changed but Dave didn't notice until someone behind us honked. He looked through the windshield, but I could tell he wasn't paying attention. That's when Dave got his big idea. He opened his mouth like he was going to say something but instead slapped my shoulder and turned to look at me, his eyes wide open.

"I know how to find Sally!" he yelled.

"Jeez-us!" I shouted, and Dave braked. We came that close to running someone over. Now I wondered if Dave's mets had spread to his brain. He continued driving, more carefully this time, but kept talking.

"Rhonda's daughter, Liz. I think I can find her!"

Oh, for God's sake, of course. I'd been thinking so much about Rhonda and the little girl that I'd almost forgotten Sally's name.

"The addicts at the free clinic!" Dave yelled. "It's like a small town within the city. Homeless people, addicts in San Francisco, they may keep to themselves, they huddle in their own little groups, but mostly they know who the others are. They keep an eye out. And like I said, a few of these guys owe me. If Sally's around, we can find her."

"But we don't even know what Sally looks like!" I said this to the windshield, so he'd look there too.

"Yeah we do," he said, and he turned back to face the road. "Facebook!" He slapped the steering wheel like a game-show buzzer.

Just as he said it, I remembered the picture. Sally the teenaged cheerleader. Though Sally ravaged by drugs couldn't possibly look like the girl in that picture, it was a start. But if we did find her, then what?

I thought of not making things right with my own daughter, how horrible that would be, to die without having grown close, and I realized that of course we had to do what we could for Rhonda and Sally.

Dave looked over at me. I started to speak, then stopped, and I don't know why I didn't tell Dave about Cassie right then.

"Lynette's been a rehab counselor for years," Dave said. "That's how I know this stuff. I have a pretty good idea of where Sally could get good treatment."

I wondered if Dave and his ex-wife had had a run-in with drugs themselves, or if just Lynette did, but it wasn't the time to ask.

Dave parked the car in a space between two SUVs. I squeezed out, holding the door so it wouldn't grind into the door of the

Chevy Tahoe on my side. I heard the metallic crack of Dave's door as it smacked into the four-wheel-drive behemoth on his side.

I was coming around the back of the Subaru when Dave yelled, "What is it about the word 'compact' that these fuckers don't understand?"

He turned and ran his finger across the tiny scratch he'd made in the Explorer. He touched a finger to his tongue and rubbed at the scratch, then peered over the car roof to scan the parking lot. Nobody there to see.

He took three big steps to the back of the car and grabbed me by both shoulders. He started right in, shouting his plan for finding Sally, as if we didn't have someplace to go that moment. I almost expected him to suggest we skip visiting Rhonda and go find Sally first. Oh, Dave. Taking this big risk for Rhonda, trying to *do* something at the end. I loved him for this, but it scared me so much. The prospect of failing with Sally, my own prospect of failing with Marisa.

"What we'll do," he said, "is both of us talk to Sally. Tell her the situation with her mom, because I bet she doesn't even know. Bet Rhonda hasn't even told her the half of it. Once she knows, maybe she'll agree to go to rehab. Hell, no addict *wants* to go to rehab, but sometimes the guilt gets so bad they'll agree to it."

He was practically spitting this at me. Obviously he needed me to get it so bad. But I got it. I could feel the desperation, too, for something big to go right for our friend.

"One more time could be the time it works for Sally," he said. "It's the one thing we can do for Rhonda. Don't you see? We have to at least try."

I didn't have the heart to discourage him, but I really had my reservations. What if we wound up breaking Rhonda's heart again instead? What if Sally went to rehab but then left after a week? What if she relapsed after a year and it wound up that getting Sally clean wasn't the best thing for Cassie? But of course it would be. How could it not be?

It didn't feel right to say those things out loud, not with Rhonda in the hospital behind us.

Dave turned to face the hospital door, but neither of us took a step in that direction.

His voice lowered. "Even if it doesn't work," he said, "Rhonda will have more peace if Sally's in treatment than if she's on the streets."

"Let's talk about it more after we visit Rhonda, okay?"

Truth is, if we didn't love Rhonda, there was no way either one of us would be setting foot in Mercy. No offense to Mercy, and I mean Dave hadn't even been a patient there. It's just that it was a hospital. I'd spent so much time in and out of there, I knew the blood-draw people by name: Wanda, Eric, and DeShawn. I knew Wanda's dog's name: Scoots. She was a chocolate Lab.

That very first time I went in for a scan, put my clothes in a locker, and couldn't figure out how the locker key worked, Wanda came by and helped me. She thought she was being sweet, I guess, when she said, "Oh, don't worry, you'll get used to all this." And I thought, *Like hell I will, chubby lady in turquoise scrubs with the frizzy hair. Don't think I'm getting used to it, because after this one scan I am so out of here, for good.*

Now I asked her about Scoots.

But going to a hospital and being in one were two vastly different things. It was being in one that scared me, and I'd made up my mind for sure that I wasn't dying in one. What happened, usually, was one emergency after another, in and out of the hospital till you died. So I'd decided that the first time I had an emergency—not like all the little emergencies, like dehydration and weird stabbing pains in unexpected places, but an emergency that made the nurse give you that dire look and the doctor say, "We're admitting you now"—that first for-real time, I was calling in hospice, and hospice could deal with all subsequent emergencies. They came, they gave you pain meds, ran your errands. Hospice was a godsend, mainly because they kept you out of the hospital.

I didn't usually pray, but right then I did for Rhonda: *Please let her go home.*

This was Rhonda's first emergency. Room 412B was in the Miscellaneous Wing. They didn't call it that, but it was the ward for adults who hadn't had surgery or heart attacks, babies or strokes, legs crushed between bicycles and buses.

Walking down the long hall to get there, past the noisy nurses' station, past the carts with food under gray plastic domes, all the beeping fast and slow, the smell of overcooked vegetables and bleach and pee, I felt all my muscles go stiff and then weak. I felt so woozy and nauseous there for a second I was afraid I was going to faint. Dave wasn't puffed up anymore, either; he was slump-shouldered and pale. We both stopped cold when we got to 411, the room before Rhonda's.

I pulled my shoulders back, ran my fingers through my hair at my temples, and fluffed it up in back where my scalp still showed through. I reached down into my shoulder bag, feeling for a lipstick, and I pulled out the first one I found. It was a light brown. I wiped the lipstick across my bottom lip, top lip, and smushed both lips together. Rubbed my little finger from the center of my lips down to the corners.

"Okay?" I looked at Dave, chin high so he could inspect.

"Good enough for the hospital."

Dave pulled at the cuffs of his sweatshirt, put out his chest, and fussed with his hair for what had to be the first time that day, scratching his scalp and picking at the spiky gray to give it a $200-bedhead look instead of what it was, bedhead free of charge. We pointed ourselves forward, one step, two steps. On the third step, one step before the door to 412, we both put on our best smiles.

Rhonda was sitting up in bed. Her shoulders peeked out from the familiar hospital robe, aquamarine with the boring navy-blue diamond pattern.

"Oh my goodness, you guys!"

I tried not to look shocked, seeing her for the first time without her wig. Her head was wrapped in an African-print scarf, bright yellows and greens and reds. It was too loud for Rhonda's pale skin, and it made her look sickly and gray. She must've felt me trying not to look because she put her hand up to the headscarf, pulled it down in the way she usually tugged at her wig.

"I'm so embarrassed to even be in here," she said. "It was only a nosebleed!"

It had to have been one that wouldn't stop bleeding no matter what Rhonda did, bleeding into her sink and onto her floor, through boxes of Kleenex and gauze until finally Rhonda called Eldon and he called 911. Her skin looked chalky and fragile as tissue paper, the right side pale pink. In a white plastic "personal belongings" bag on top of the one table in the room with a drawer, I saw a piece of her blonde curly wig sticking out. Next to it, a florist's vase filled with red roses, a "Get Well" rainbow card clipped on to a clear plastic spike. Rhonda's spray bottle sat next to the flowers.

There were two people, a man and a woman, crowded in that tiny room with the one chair and one stool barely fitting between the bed and the wall. The man was Eldon, the same Eldon who I'd seen in the park. Same killer smile as on Facebook, but his hair was grayer and cut close, receding on a shiny scalp the color of warm oak. He was shorter than I'd expected, close-up. About five nine, a good six inches shorter than Dave, but his body was trim and buff. Creamy brushed-silk shirt, pressed trousers. I thought, *Good for Rhonda!* And then I caught my breath when the sadness hit.

The woman standing at the side of Rhonda's bed had the most beautiful skin ever. It was dark black, flawless like a model's, and she wore screaming magenta lipstick that could look great only on her. Painted-on brows sat over wide-spaced deep-brown eyes that felt like they saw right through me in her first quick glance. Her body pushed the privacy curtain well beyond the space that was 412B.

She wore a dress the color of bay leaves, and on her short matching jacket a big silk sunflower drew the eye away from her size. She exuded confidence in the way she held her body up straight, even with the curtain pressing at her back. Her hands locked at her waist and she worked her thumbs around, tsking at Rhonda like what a fine mess this was. After that one look straight into me, she barely raised her head to acknowledge we'd come in. I tried to brush the dog hair from my thigh without looking down.

"Liz and Dave," Rhonda said, "this is Faye, our friend from church. And this is Eldon."

I put my hand out to Eldon, and he gave it a cool, dry squeeze and then pumped Dave's hand up and down.

"Heard a lot about you both," he said. "All good. My pleasure."

"Likewise," Dave said. Then he went straight over to Rhonda's bed and curved his body over it to squeeze her on the shoulder.

I stepped closer and put my fingertips on the edge of the bed, about a foot from her knee. It felt awkward and too intimate all of a sudden. Rhonda in bed, the strangers in the room, me looking like a slob, machines beeping, curtain pushing into 412A. I couldn't bear the put-on hospital cheer, the sweet sadness and sickroom hospitality of her guy, the feeling of intrusiveness with Rhonda there in bed, a stranger dressed for church pressing against the sheet. Part of me was out the door with a fake hospital grin, and the other stood there looking at Rhonda and feeling helpless, speechless, frightened, ashamed. I was becoming one of the people I hated. Those people who wanted to run. I didn't want to be in that bed, ever, and I didn't want to be glad it wasn't me, and I wanted all three of us back at Lake Temescal, Rhonda feeding her ducks. This was not the field trip we'd imagined, but, of course, it was inevitable. I was the one who'd seen so much death, the one raised to suck it up, and there in the hospital with

Rhonda, I wanted to put my hands over my ears and eyes, and I wanted to run.

"How you doing, sweetheart?" Dave's voice was nearly a whisper.

I had a smile plastered on my face but felt faintly dizzy.

"We're just stopping by for a minute," I said. "Leave you to your company."

I gave a rigid super-smile to Faye. I waited for her magenta lipstick to part in a smile back, but it didn't.

"Well, it's so nice to meet you," Faye said. Like I really didn't belong in that room but she knew her manners. She smoothed her hair, black with silver strands, swooping up and away from her face in waves.

"Excuse me, but have I seen you two at Alive!?" she asked.

Please don't let this be about my personal savior, I thought.

"No, Faye, these are my cancer friends," Rhonda explained.

Before she could offer any more details, Dave yelled, "*Ha!*" loud enough to wake the whole ward. He looked at me with his whole face winking. My mouth was paralyzed into that stupid smile.

"I mean, we're all in the same boat and became friends that way," Rhonda said. Color rushed up her neck and into her face. Faye's penciled eyebrows were stuck in the up position.

"Oh my. Oh my. I'm so sorry," she said. She put a hand to her chest, breathed in deep, and looked at me, looked at Dave. She backed into the curtain so far she must've been practically sitting on the poor patient in 412A.

None of us said anything to Faye, first of all because what do you say? "Oh, it's nothing, we're fine"? Okay, there are other things to say, like, "We're alive and feeling good right now, thanks," or some such, things that aren't lies but aren't rude either. But neither Dave nor I said a thing. I liked that for one minute Faye was more uncomfortable than I was. I swear Rhonda liked it too. Instead of jumping in to say something that would make us all feel better, like she usually did, she lifted her head from the pillows and sat up

Ann Bancroft

in her bed like a queen, hands relaxed over her belly, the pink back
in her cheeks, and the most serene look on her face.

Faye picked up a pamphlet she must've brought for Rhonda
and left on the bed. "Hope in Prayer," or something, two pages,
four-by-eight. She fanned herself with the pamphlet just twice,
then held it to her breast as if that might ward off the pestilence
afflicting so many people in that small space.

Dave was the one who finally broke in.

"We just love getting to know Rhonda," he said. "As I'm sure
you know."

Dave the party host, all of a sudden.

"Rhonda was the one who thought up our name and had
T-shirts made," I said, to show that I loved Rhonda too.

It was all I could think to say, and I said it to Eldon because
I didn't want to say it to Faye. He gave a teeny little nod and a
sort-of smile like you do when you already know something but
don't want to be rude by saying so.

Rhonda had probably told Eldon about those shirts before
she even gave them to us. I hoped he didn't think I was discount-
ing their relationship or anything. As for Faye, I wished I hadn't
told her we had a name at all. It felt like giving something too
personal away.

"The Oakland Mets," Dave said, triumphantly loud. "That's
our name."

Oh well. Let Faye figure it out.

Faye clasped her hands and worked her thumbs again. She
was obviously clueless about the meaning of "mets." "I see. Well,
how nice, Rhonda. Rhonda always does do the nicest things."
The corner of Rhonda's mouth went down, on the good side.

"Yes! She does! Isn't Rhonda something?" Dave returned to
shouting, and Faye pressed herself back even more, the curtain
folding in over her head. Dave knew what he was doing. We both
wanted Rhonda to ourselves.

"Well, I'll let you all enjoy your visit," she said. It had worked.

She moved around to the foot of the bed and the curtain hung straight again. "All y'all are in my prayers," she kept on, backing away, short jacket rising and falling with each breath. "Hope we'll see you again," she said.

"Yes," I said. Stupidest smile ever, still plastered on. "But not here!"

I could tell that scared her to death.

"No, no, not here," she said. "Bye now."

Her body filled the doorway and she backed out of it, patting the yellow flower on her jacket. I let my breath out a little. Dave sat down in the one chair, clasped his hands behind his head, and stretched his elbows out.

It felt okay to move back closer to Rhonda's bed now, even though Eldon was right there, hand on her shoulder, Rhonda smiling up at him in a private little bubble, as if on a picnic blanket at the beach.

"Faye's the one who never called," Eldon said to us after a moment. "Never made a meal all these months. Kept telling me how she's praying for Rhonda, oh yes, but never said a thing to Rhonda herself. Now that Rhonda's in the hospital, she's all up in her face."

"Oh, it's all right, Eldon," Rhonda said. "Faye's been so kind about other things. Important things, you know? Some people know how to deal with any kind of nightmare but cancer. Although it did cross my mind that she might be biding her time, collecting casserole recipes for you when I'm gone."

Rhonda was trying to be funny, but at that moment she was a little girl, pale scared eyes looking up at Eldon for reassurance. The pillow folded around her African-print scarf, making her head look so small.

"Stop that, Rhonda. Please," Eldon said. His smooth brown fingers covered the pale sliver of shoulder where her gown gapped open.

The room got very quiet; I listened to the beeps of a machine wired to Rhonda's body, somewhere under the blankets. Eldon put a hand on Rhonda's good cheek, dark mahogany on pale birch. He picked her hand up off the bed and held it to his face for a soft, slow kiss.

"You know I hate casseroles," he said.

"At any rate, you sure don't need anyone cooking for you, honey. Dave and Liz, I don't think I told you what a fabulous cook Eldon is. I am so spoiled, you wouldn't believe it."

Rhonda was back in charge of the small talk, court reporter sitting up straight, just happened to be in bed for a minute, never you mind.

"Ah, baby," Eldon said. Killer smile. "I'll make extra for your friends, if you like. I always cook for a crowd, even if it's just our little family at home."

Rhonda made Dave and me promise we'd still go to Caffe Trieste without her, because that was what we'd planned.

"I can miss one meeting," she said. "Have some fun!" Exactly like Rhonda would say. Then she said something I didn't expect. "Listen." Her voice lowered. "I don't know when I'll be able to go, or if I'll be able to go." She lifted her head to look straight at us, no lip trembling or chin-up martyr about it, just pale eyes seeing a thing clearly, matter-of-factly.

"If you wait for me," she said, "you'll only make me sad. Second thought, if you two don't go because I'm in this place, it'll make me angry."

Eldon turned from the bed and lowered his head at us to fake whisper. "You don't want to see her mad," he said. Rhonda stared up at him in that way lovers do, shutting the whole room out to look only at Eldon, so much love I had to turn away, respecting the private moment.

"If you see any ladies from my church at the café, you tell them I said hi," Rhonda said.

"Oh, we will," Dave said. He said it in a naughty way, crazy eyebrows raising, cooking something up.

Eldon leaned his head down close to Rhonda's face. "Now, sweets, I've got to go. See you in a couple hours, okay?"

I was glued in place as Eldon pressed his lips to Rhonda's forehead for a long moment. He lifted his head and held her shoulder with his right hand. I couldn't see his face then, but what Rhonda saw in it made her close her eyes tightly. Lyle had made me feel that way, that time in the hospital. Safe and loved.

When Eldon turned to face us, the killer smile was gone. His eyes squeezed shut. He opened them, gave a nod to me, a nod to Dave, and walked out the door.

"He could've stayed," Dave said after Eldon was already gone. I noticed the Indiana came out in Dave's speech when things were tense. "Hope we didn't chase him away."

"We can only stay a minute, too, Rhonda," I said. What a chickenshit. "Just wanted to stop by and say hi." So afraid of that hospital, of seeing myself in it, my impulse to run at that moment overriding my desire to see Rhonda.

Dave narrowed his eyes at me just a bit, like you do when you want to signal one person without the other person seeing.

He got up from his chair and beckoned me to sit in it. I told him I was fine standing. At least standing I could move around. Sitting, I'd be even more restless. But Dave rolled the stool from the other side of the bed and sat on that.

I had no choice but to take the chair, so I sat, ashamed of myself. I tried to yoga breathe, quiet so they wouldn't hear, and tried to remember how you were supposed to do it. I breathed in, pretended the breath was going all the way down to my feet and down through the hospital floor all the way to China. Paused, mixed the breath with the earth's energy, wondered if earth energy was bullshit. Pulled the breath back up through my legs, up my torso, out my skull. Good thing Dave started talking because my exhale was so loud. It worked, though. Kept me in the chair.

"So, on the way over we were talking about bucket lists," Dave said.

What the hell? No, we weren't. I hated the whole idea of bucket lists. It wasn't even fair to talk about bucket lists with Rhonda, was it? I mean, unlike us, she didn't have a remission. She had mets from the get-go. I had eighteen months, Dave two years, till our mets showed up. Plenty of time to jump out of airplanes or go to Machu Picchu or whatever fool thing a person might want to do. Plenty of time to go to Alaska, instead of wasting life in my stupid office, like I had. I wished Dave hadn't brought it up. But he couldn't say we'd been talking about Sally the whole ride over. I guessed Dave was nervous too.

"Yeah," I said. "Like I told Dave, I don't believe in them." I gave him a look like he'd given me, out the side of my eyes.

The way Dave's hands pressed into his knees, his shoulders rising all the way up to his ears, I could tell he was wondering what we'd gotten ourselves into.

"Cripes, we don't need to be talking about this," he said.

"Oh, you guys, of course we can talk about it," Rhonda said. Now she sat up, her legs crossed under the covers, as if we were all settling in at a slumber party. "Of course we think about it. You know, I figure I'm lucky. I've got no bucket list, for myself. I don't need a thing. Right before I got sick, heavenly coincidence, Eldon and I took a beautiful trip up to the Canadian Rockies. That's where he proposed."

She closed her eyes a long few seconds, breathed in deeply like it was alpine air.

"I told him I needed a little time, not because I didn't love him enough but because I wasn't sure how hard it would be for him, with Sally and all." Her voice trailed off, and I thought for sure that was the moment she'd tell us about Cassie, but she didn't.

"I also thought the interracial thing might put him in a tough position, you know? Just, some people. Some places." Long slow shake of her head. "He wasn't happy with that at all. Said how white it was for me to act like I knew how it was to be Black, and why would it be any tougher on him than on me? He's used to it in a way I'll never get."

Rhonda gave a little-girl laugh. We all looked at one another. White people. We had no clue.

"So I said yes, and we had the most beautiful trip." She let her head drop back, closed her eyes. "But then, before you knew it, I got sick."

Quiet in the room again, only the beeps.

"Now I worry about Eldon getting codependent, you know what I mean?" She looked up to see us both affirming we knew what she meant: someone gets so wrapped up in someone else's disease that they harm their own life; they get so devoted to caregiving that their own health declines. When Mom had Stage Four cancer, even though she didn't ask or really need me to, I'd stay over at her house a week at a time, working from there, leaving Marisa with Bradley. Every night, both of us in our flannel nightgowns by 8:00 p.m., watching videos in her big bed, looking out her window over Golden Gate Park. It was a closeness we'd never had before. I'd held on to that fiercely, and then she was gone.

I could imagine Eldon clinging like that to Rhonda, could tell how distressed he was. Maybe it wasn't so bad that Marisa was far away and didn't really get it yet. I was afraid to find out if she'd do the same for me.

"When you think about it, I got the perfect part," Rhonda said. She had her best new-dentures smile on, convincing us, convincing herself. "The spectacular proposal, crystal-clear lake and mountains all around, most beautiful place I've ever seen. But then no worries about a wedding and all that! None of the hard part!"

Dave and I both tried half-assed smiles, and Rhonda gave up on trying to make us feel better. She scooched her body down to lie flat, pulled the pillow down so it reached to her neck, and closed her eyes again.

"Must be something in the IV," she said.

"We should be going," I said.

"Oh, don't go. I'm just resting a bit. How about you, Dave? Do you have a list?"

"Well, I did think about it, and I'm with you, Rhonda," Dave said, God bless him. "Robert and I got to go all over Europe, and we had ourselves a blast. And I went back to Vietnam on my own a few years ago, and I made peace with that."

I didn't want to jump out of my chair anymore. Just sat there with the discomfort, tried to let it pass. I wondered what Dave did to make peace, going back to Vietnam, or if it just came to him, standing there in the jungle as a different man.

"I don't need to go to China," Dave said. "I get the picture." China was one of those places people were supposed to have on their bucket lists, I guessed. *I could live without going too.*

It hit me then, the way so many random end-of-life realizations had. I'd not be having sex, or moving to a new condo, or starting a new career. I supposed I could take a trip, but when and who with? Chances were, none of us were going anywhere.

"One day at a time," I said. Fricking fount of wisdom.

I wanted to get off the bucket-list subject and quit saying banal things, so I asked Dave what became of the neighbor he had the hots for. Ask a gay guy about who he had the hots for and you were bound to get the conversation going someplace fun, wasn't that right?

The way Dave sucked his lips in and squeezed his hands together tight, I knew I shouldn't have brought it up.

"Nah, that's nothing," he said. "We did have the one dinner. He's a sweet man, I could tell that. But what it was . . . it was that he'd heard I had cancer and he just felt sorry for me." Oh, God. Dave's palms in the air, trying to make it a joke.

"Wish he'd just lied. I mean, he didn't come right out and say he felt sorry, but you know that look, that 'I'm so *concerned*' look. You just know." He stopped trying to make it funny. It was just a fact.

"He kept complimenting me, how hot I look for my age, which is bad enough. I mean, someone says that, you feel like you're a hundred years old."

I guess it wasn't as easy as I thought for Dave. I ached for him.

"I mean, I could have taken advantage, played the cancer card, right? But who are we kidding? I don't need the drama. I'm long past jumping into bed with people who are practically strangers. And if that's where it wound up? In bed? You know what that's called, and that's the last thing I want."

I'm guessing Dave didn't want to say "mercy fuck" in front of Rhonda, but we knew, and he knew we knew. Another jab in my gut. That last time with Lyle, was that what it was for him?

I wondered if Dave was at the point where I was, thinking he'd had sex for the last time, or whether it had just been wrong with the neighbor that one time, but then he told us.

"I guess at this point if it's, you know, maybe going to be the capper of your whole life, you want to be pretty sure it'll be a great time," Dave said. "Not so damned loaded. And that's a lot of pressure. I just don't want to deal with it unless it's real."

Ever since our talk at the A's game, that's where I was coming from too.

I don't know how it happens, but if you sit in a chair long enough, and listen hard enough, and care about who you're listening to, you can go from the most uncomfortable place ever to the easiest, loveliest place, all in just a few minutes. That's what happened with us. One minute I was so antsy I wanted to run out that hospital door. Dave was awkward and Rhonda was awkward, and the small talk just made me want to scream. Then somebody said something real, and somebody answered with something real, and just like that we were all back to that place of ease, just being human beings, screwed up and vulnerable every one of us, whether we're sick or well or not paying much attention to how we are.

Rhonda asked when I was going to talk to Marisa and when Dave was going to talk to his brother.

"Wonderful!" she said when I told her Marisa would be coming in two days. She seemed so pleased for me I didn't mention the walk or how our plans for the day had collided. She asked about our meds and how they were working and if we were really feeling okay or just putting it on since she was the one in bed. We said we were feeling okay, except for Dave's blisters and his headaches, my collarbone and joint pain, and those times in the day we just had to take naps no matter what.

Rhonda moved sideways on the bed and put the pillows behind her so she could dangle her feet and prop herself up at the same time. She pulled the blanket over her skinny thighs, covered the blue-diamond-print robe up to her waist. There was a big purple bruise all around the IV tape on her left wrist. When Rhonda moved her body around, the tube pulled on the tape, and I covered my own hand reflexively with the memory of IV pain right there where the needle goes flat into the vein. I chilled at the thought of more IVs, and I blinked back tears for my own diagnosis and theirs. Being in the hospital, there was no escaping it. But there was my friend. It was her turn, and Dave and I would sit, knowing ours would come.

Rhonda's eyes closed for just a second. "I've been thinking," she said. "And I want to ask what you think, about the only thing that matters—when you get right down to it. What I think is," she said, "the whole point of life is love. Caring for one another. I suppose I've always thought this, but now I really do."

Oh, Rhonda. To have lived a life like Rhonda had.

"You act out of love, and you pray to do God's will and to accept what he in his infinite wisdom has chosen for your life," she said. "Because most things you can't control."

I'd made a step with Bradley, but letting go with Marisa was an order of magnitude harder.

"I have a granddaughter," Rhonda said. "Sally's girl. Cassie."

She'd dropped it just like that, matter-of-factly. She'd just been waiting for the right moment; she hadn't been shutting us out.

"Cassie is four," Rhonda said. "She's been with us most her life. Sometimes it kills me, you know, not knowing how she'll grow up." Rhonda closed her eyes. "That's when I lean on my faith, and Eldon, and I just have to know she'll be okay."

I understood why Rhonda hadn't told us earlier. It was just too damned much. And where Dave would usually jump up and go over to Rhonda, where even, at that point, I would, something about the way Rhonda held herself up, so strong or at least wanting to seem so strong, so dignified amid all this indignity, it seemed disrespectful to get out of our chairs. Dave lifted his head and nodded slowly at her, and I did the same.

"I can't control Sally's addiction," she said. "I'd give anything to have her well, to give Cassie her mom back, but all I can do is love that child as best I can. Cassie's the light of our lives!" Just saying it lit up Rhonda's face. "That girl has brought us pleasure during the hardest times." Rhonda held her palms up above her blanket. "I can't control cancer either," she said. "But I can love you two here and now, and I do."

Leave it to Rhonda to sum it all up, to announce with such clarity the hardest thing there was to do, which was to let go. Leave it to her to have the guts to do it right there in front of us, to show she could, and to help us do the same.

This time it just automatically came out of my mouth, and it didn't feel fake or uncomfortable at all.

"I love you, too, Rhonda," I said. Looking at Rhonda up on the bed, her wide blue eyes and uneven face, hearing her children's-story voice talk about love, it was the easiest thing of all to say. My heart opened as if released.

Then Dave said it: "I love you, too, Rhonda."

She smiled at both of us. "I've been wondering what you think it's all about, Dave. The point, I mean. Is it something you think about?"

I was so glad it was Dave she asked first. I needed a minute to think about what it was I really believed.

You'd think a person in my position would be pondering the big questions all the time, would have it all laid out with certainty, the Point of Life. You'd think a person who had mets would be somewhere close to knowing where to come down on the totality of things, and that she'd be ready to hold forth to anyone who'd care to listen. When it occurred to me right there in Rhonda's hospital room that I'd hardly pondered at all, I could feel my face getting hot, as if I'd forgotten to study for the biggest test of all.

"The meaning?" Dave's voice carried out into the hallway. Room 412A was sure getting an earful from us. He cleared his throat. "The point? There is none, in my opinion." He said it matter-of-factly, without a trace of bluster, and I wondered if maybe he was reconsidering.

We knew Dave wasn't religious, but I was disappointed, somehow. I'd have thought he'd have some kind of Eastern philosophy to fall back on. Something that helped him through Vietnam, and Robert's dying, and losing his brother to bigotry. But nothing? No point at all? I let that idea settle in for a minute, looking at Dave, his big, placid face, and it began to make sense. When you'd been through what he'd been through, seemingly none of it part of any grand spiritual plan, pointlessness seemed a logical place to land.

"I'm sorry to disappoint you, Rhonda," Dave said. Silence for a second, and then Dave laughed a quiet laugh. "Diss. A. Point!" he said. "Never thought of it that way. I don't mean to *diss* your *point*, Rhonda."

Rhonda gave a little giggle at that, and I exhaled the breath I didn't know I'd been holding in.

Dave laid a big, gnarled hand on Rhonda's bed. The IV bruise on it matched Rhonda's, under the middle knuckle, purple fading to yellow, spread across the jagged ropes of his veins. His voice was gentle, like the doctor bringing bad news. "I'm a scientist.

Far as I'm concerned, life just is," he said. "No reason or point except self-perpetuation. But that's enough."

There's no arguing with what a person believes. I respected Dave for what he said. He didn't reach for anything transcendent just because it would sound good or make us feel better.

"Yes, there's love, endless, boundless love," Dave went on. "And there's moral, ethical belief. There is a code people seem wired to have, with or without religion, because the code's pretty much the same in all societies, primitive or advanced. We take care of our families. Well, mostly. We love others because it feels good to love others, whether or not there's a God that wants us to. If you do believe in God, that's cool. If it helps you to do the right thing. But I'm more interested in the *reason* it makes us feel better when we care for others and do the right thing. I believe it's evolutionary. The more we help others, the better we all survive, right? Evolution! Simple evolution."

Maybe Dave's notion was grand after all. Maybe it was the grandest thing of all.

Rhonda had God. Dave had science. Ashes to ashes and then on up to heaven or just plain dirt on the ground. It had to be more than that, but I just didn't believe in a heaven and hell, in one God separate from us, looking down. Jesus felt like a long-deceased, beloved member of the family that people told stories about at holidays, not that there was any such character in my family or any holiday stories either. We had the decorations but not the substance, so I always felt a hollow sense at Christmas, a sense that we were all pretending to have something we didn't have.

Rhonda looked so tired. I could tell she wanted to pay attention and was working to not fade out. She pulled the twisted covers up over her waist and leaned back against the three pillows so it looked like she was sitting but she was really lying down.

"What do you think, Liz?"

I almost wanted to go back to the small talk. But, maybe for the first time in my life, it felt safe to think and say what came to mind, even if I wasn't certain about any of it.

"Sometimes I think we make it all up," I said. "What we see, what we experience, our past, this bed. Seeing ourselves as three separate people when we're all part of the same big story. I mean, how do we know? What makes us think that what we experience as reality is really reality?"

"Smoke a lot of dope back in the day, Liz?" Dave gave me that eyes-over-reading-glasses look, but Rhonda didn't act as if it was funny at all. Even the word "dope" made Rhonda pull her arms in, grab her elbows in self-defense.

"No. I didn't, actually," I said. But I knew I'd walked right into that one. I knew these woo-woo ideas about consciousness left me wide open. If anyone pressed me about them, I couldn't come up with a sensible explanation. I had no religion to fall back on, no "Here's what it says according to our folks, so I'm going with that." And when it came to science, I didn't know a thing. Still, since cancer, I'd had some ideas and I wanted to try saying them out loud because I never had, till then.

"Seriously, haven't you heard physicists talk about everything being all the same, and everything that has ever happened and that is going to happen is happening at the same time? How much of life seems so coincidental, like we're onstage or in a dream? Look at the way the three of us met and all we have in common even though we didn't know it at first. Maybe we're all just dreaming ourselves."

Dave nodded, but his lips were squeezed together in that desperate I-must-not-laugh-during-the-funeral look. It should have hurt, I suppose, but instead I felt the comfort of being teased by a big brother. Rhonda, I didn't know. She lay sideways in bed, elbow on the pillow and head in one hand, IV hand over the blanket, tube snaking over the narrow hump of her body and up to the bag on the pole. Her face was open, pale, eyelids half shut. I couldn't tell if she was concentrating on what I said or just trying not to fall asleep.

In the old days I would've let Dave's snickering get to me, to the point that I'd take back everything I'd just said. I used to do that kind of backtracking a lot, pretending I agreed after all, with the person disagreeing with me. I'd play whatever role a situation seemed to demand. This time I wasn't going to do that. Dave could smirk all day.

"Sometimes it helps me to believe this, anyway," I said. "That really, it's all a dream, everything put out there on the stage by our subconscious." I purposefully did not look at either of them for a second because I wanted to come up with the words, and they were stuck somewhere way back in my brain and down low in my gut. "In dreams when I'm asleep, I stumble along and wind up in the strangest, scariest, sometimes most wonderful places. How do we know our dreams aren't just as real as we are in our bodies, but taking place in a nonphysical realm we can't understand? How do we really know we're not all part of the same gigantic web?"

That's what came out of my mouth.

Dave grinned. I knew he'd think it was woo-woo bullshit. I left it at that, let my words seep back down into me somewhere deep. It would all come up again sometime privately, when I least expected it. I hoped I'd be able to talk about it with Marisa someday.

"What I wonder," I said to Rhonda and Dave, "is when it's all over, does it go on, all the endless dreaming? Or will we finally get some rest?"

Rhonda spoke up, loud for the first time.

"Oh, that I am sure of," she said. "We'll all get to rest."

Chapter 18

That Saturday, even though it was seven fucking thirty in the morning and freezing, I unzipped my black hoodie just to show I was wearing a pink T-shirt, too, same as everyone else, with the big pink ribbon on the front and sponsors all over the back like we were at a NASCAR race. The fog glowed rosy gold, amplifying female yells and giggles, shouts of "Over here!" "Barb's Boobie Brigade!" "Kittie's Titties for the Cure!" Everywhere, pink. Pink-ribbon ball caps, pink jackets and shirts, pink jogging pants and running shoes, pink shoelaces.

I imagined Marisa reading my letter and regretting the plan to meet there. We could just skip it and walk down the avenues, find a quiet coffee shop where we could talk. I wouldn't push; I'd let her bring up the letter first. I'd gone over it a million times in my mind and was confident I'd be open and honest with her.

Marisa! The excitement grew in my chest. Maybe she'd be more comfortable going ahead with the walk. I could imagine her not wanting to break down or get into a heavy discussion right away. With all those people, all the pink, it might feel less stark for her, talking about what my diagnosis would mean for us, let alone talking about what else I'd said in the letter. Just as I found it easier to talk to Dave and Rhonda that first time while walking around Lake Temescal. Easier than sitting down across from one another at a table, right off the bat.

The event felt like cheerleading camp. Spread all across the polo field as far as you could see, more pink. Pink balloons above and pink ribbons tacked on every possible surface. Boas and tutus and terriers dyed pink. Tables with pink-paper tablecloths, and on the tables pink stickers and pens and tote bags. Behind the tables, pink-shirted, glitter-manicured teenagers, checking off names.

The crowd was amped. Way too much talking way too loud that early in the morning, but I tried to get with the spirit, I really did, as the line moved forward and women crowded into it, joining their friends, not a care in the world, and where was Marisa?

My walking shoes were worn out; gray, not white; not a dot or racing stripe or shoelace on them pink. I felt that anxious, out-of-place, not-belonging sense I got sometimes when I was in big crowds by myself. Particularly this crowd, with all the pink whoop-de-doo about cancer. Jesus, I didn't know how to feel, but "embraced" was not one of the options. Celebrated, for having cancer. Was that how I was supposed to feel? Of course it wasn't about my cancer, or anyone in particular's cancer. What brought people there in all that pinkness was the notion of doing something, because what else could you do about all those cancers infesting so many breasts? The little in situ cells lurking all over the place, or the aggressive ones like mine, fast out of the gate and on their way through the bloodstream, settling in wherever they choose—liver, brain, bones. The ones that inflame the nipples and bulge out under arms and the ones that connect, somehow, with the ovaries to an extent scary enough that women get rid of it all: cut the breasts off, cut the ovaries out, all of it, get rid of it fast if you can. I guessed all a regular person could do about any of it was raise money. And, this being America, brand it. Put it on a product, use it in an ad, and write it off as a tax deduction.

I wasn't surprised Marisa would go in for this, as hyperorganized and highly sponsored as it was. And she must've believed it to be a way of supporting me. The thought brought a little twinge of maternal sweetness, like when your five-year-old proudly presents you with a lumpy homemade ceramic bowl.

I saw the stage a couple hundred yards away. A woman in pink spandex warmed the crowd up with jumping jacks and such, workout bass blaring through speakers, and, oh, it couldn't be but it was, they were playing "Survivor" by Destiny's Child. And after that, "Stayin' Alive"! Surreal. What were they thinking? And what was wrong with me? Where was my sisterly compassion, my sense of solidarity? Why couldn't I feel supported and supportive and lighten the fuck up? I just couldn't. For one thing, all this focus on breast cancer and only breast cancer felt like a betrayal of Rhonda and Dave.

Between the stage and me were tables set up where they were giving stuff away, and people lined up to get the stuff. Business-card holders with pink ribbons on them, along with the logo of an insurance company. Dog kibble in little pink-ribbon packets. Dog kibble! Yogurt with pink spoons. Scarves that from a distance looked like a pretty print, but when you looked up close the print was a car dealer's logo interspersed with pink ribbons and curlicue script: "Drive to End Breast Cancer!"

I went from table to table, turning back to look for Marisa every minute or so. I got a pink-ribbon shopping bag and put into it the dog kibble for Dave, the business-card holder for Marisa, and the scarf. A pink-ribbon teddy bear key chain from the folks at National City Bank. Why I put that stuff in the bag, I'll never know. Maybe it was my pain meds kicking in. Probably the reason I was so crabby in the first place was the pain, not just in my collarbone anymore but across my ribs on both sides—sharp, shooting, take-your-breath-away pain until the meds kicked in completely, and they were beginning to by the time I got to the goodie bags. After the table with pink plastic water bottles from GoMart, I gave up and got back in the T-shirt line. It was a mile long by then. The woman ahead of me was a real Southern California–blonde type. Personally trained flat belly under augmented boobs, giant super-white teeth and pink-diamond ribbon pinned on her $1,000 jogging suit.

"Isn't this festive?" she said. I swear. I stared at her too long wondering what I was supposed to say to that because I was starting to feel stoned by then, stoned enough to just blurt out what came into my head.

"Maybe not as festive as kidney cancer," I said. "Or colon."

Right then someone tapped my shoulder and I turned around and there was Marisa.

I stood back to look at her, and my heart burst open at the sight of my beautiful girl, so tall and lean and with such *presence*, that strong Bradley jaw and her flawless skin and teeth and thick copper-colored hair showing in bangs under the pink baseball cap, ponytail pulled out the back. Lips full and glossed bright pink. God, she looked more beautiful every year. How did it even happen?

I gave her a full-on hug, not the half hug we were used to, and felt her hair against my cheek. The hug felt natural as could be after writing that letter, after opening up and telling her the truth. I was sure Marisa felt it too. I breathed in a lemony soap smell, a new smell for her, and then I stood back and took in her ensemble, brand-new and all pink from fleece jacket over tank top down to New Balance shoes with pink ribbons embossed on the sides. Marisa always did go all out.

"Mom! What are you doing in this line?" Annoyance in Marisa's voice, and something new in her face. Vertical scowl creases dug into her forehead, and when they did, even the sweet pale dusting of freckles across her nose looked harsh. She pointed with her whole arm toward someplace behind me, and the tendons in her neck and her collarbone stuck out over the scoop neck of her pink top.

"Over there!"

I wondered if there'd been an accident, an explosion I somehow didn't hear, but when I turned to see where she was pointing and saw the huge banner that said SURVIVORS, I understood. Marisa was telling me where to go, and telling me to go there right that second. As if the whole event depended on it. As if every one of those thousands of beribboned women would make it to the finish and leave just the two of us behind, all because I was in the wrong line.

Survivors. I didn't know whether I hadn't noticed the banner before or whether it just hadn't registered that I was supposed to be one of those.

"Get in that line, and you'll get a special hat and a better goodie bag," Marisa said. Her voice went up high. It was a command. Then she flashed me that mean Joker smile, the one she first gave me that Fourth of July when she was nine. Bright-pink lips stretched across overbleached bright teeth. It said, *I've got one on you, Mom.* She relaxed the smile and her freckles became sweet dust across her nose again, but right then I knew nothing had changed at all. I swallowed hard with disappointment.

"You go into to the Survivors tent, and they'll give you breakfast and there's a raffle and more stuff. I know you don't want to win the pink golf bag, but there's a ton of spa baskets and maybe a trip to Disneyland," she said.

I didn't like Disneyland when Marisa was five. And the way she was talking this morning made me feel a hundred years old, like it must feel when your adult child tells you it's time for bingo at the assisted living home. *Oh, yes, dear. I'll go even though I hate bingo and am too addled now to even remember how to play bingo but I'm so happy you're here, I'll do anything you say.*

Was she going to ignore all I'd written? Sweep it under the rug like she was so expert at doing? Like I had been?

"I'll see you in front of the tent after breakfast, okay?" This time it sounded like she was speaking to a child. "Then we'll get started on the walk," she said. No *Are you okay?* No *We'll have a good talk after.*

I started making excuses for Marisa in my mind, like I'd always done. Feeling guilty for how I felt when she smiled at me that way. Marisa had calls to make, texts to send. I told myself she couldn't make any calls on the plane and that she'd lost a couple of work hours because of that. She had a big backlog of work to do even though it was barely past dawn on a Saturday.

She pulled her cell phone from the pocket of her hoodie and inspected it through transitional sunglasses darkened slightly to an amber shade.

"It's 7:52," she said. "So, say, 8:20 in front of the tent, and then there's a survivor-recognition thing at the stage. After that you get to start the race off with all the other survivors, but I can come with you. I checked."

All that bloodless efficiency was making me even more addled, and I couldn't think of what to say. My stomach roiled at what had become of her and, worse, the recognition that she'd learned it from me.

Marisa turned to look at the two women behind her in line. "My mom's a survivor," she said.

I had a place in the T-shirt line, and there were maybe fifty people behind me. No way was Marisa moving to the back of that line. She gave a stretched-out pink smile to the women behind us. "She's going to the tent, but she held my place in line."

All those years of catering to her, of pushing her to excel at school but excusing her attitudes because, after all, there was Bradley's drinking and my own focus on work. From my lower back to my stomach, up through my chest and into my face and out my scalp, came a pulsing ball of heat. It was that hormonal, post-chemo heat again, chemicals taking over, flooding my body full of rage, like I felt the day I quit work. Pointless rage. Huge, unstoppable rage shooting through me. It could be triggered by someone forgetting to use his turn signal, or by hearing about a murdered child, or by someone looking at me wrong at the grocery store, or by nothing at all. Now it was triggered by Marisa, pointing me out as a survivor to keep her place in line.

I saw my daughter ingratiating herself with those strangers. The strangers welcoming her, claiming her as special, pinkwashing over cancer to make it go away. To make *me* go away. The strangers smiling at me with that mix of pity and pride. How they were there to support me, and in supporting me to dismiss me, to rah-rah for pink logos and plastic giveaway shit and then to go home exercised and satisfied, good deed done for the year. In the heat I wanted to slap them, all of them, especially Marisa. She had run to one of the goody-bag tables, as if to escape me. I turned to face the women.

"If you want to call metastatic cancer surviving," I said to the women in line, "go ahead. But some of us have trouble with that word. Some of us who *aren't* going to survive." Each word fueled more heat, up through my cheeks and scalp. "Marisa!" I shrieked her name.

She turned, approached me through the crowd, then took a step away, pulling herself back. Tight pink smile all over her face.

"I'm sorry," she said to the women.

Sorry for the way her mother was behaving. Not going along with the program and all—can you believe it? Mothers.

There was a time when I would've heard that and been so embarrassed I would've apologized myself, for making them uncomfortable like that, for embarrassing Marisa instead of helping her to feel, as usual, invincible, unopposed. Days when I bought all her friends tickets to the latest boy-band concert, dropping them off in front, refraining from listing any rules so Marisa wouldn't have to suffer an uncool mom. Days when I'd marched into principals' offices to demand she be able to take three AP courses when the limit was two. But I was past that time.

"Marisa, I'm not going to any tent," I said, low and hard. Dave would understand. Even Rhonda, I had to believe, wouldn't go into that tent. Where were the tents and balloons and banners for them? Never mind for Sally. In a million years, we wouldn't see a corporate-sponsored run to cure addiction. No banners for heroin recovery, even though that takes work, heartbreaking work, not just sitting in a chemo chair waiting for your hair to fall out.

"It feels like some sort of quarantine, going into a tent," I said. My voice got louder. "Survivor-recognition event? Putting us on display? I just can't do it. I won't, Marisa."

There were those lines in Marisa's forehead again. This time they were pleading with the women for support, but the women were suddenly engaged in the kind of decoy conversation you make to remove yourself from a scene.

I smelled coffee on Marisa's breath when she stuck her face close to mine and whispered, "God, Mom! They're just trying to do something nice. I'll go with you, okay?" She put a hand loosely around my arm and stared into me. Those yellow-brown eyes and Bradley's jaw. Then the put-on smile with the bingo voice. "Let's go in and have breakfast together," she said. "After that, we can do the walk. You need to stay in shape to stay healthy, right?"

Stay healthy?

"Marisa, come over here," I said, pulling her away from the line and the women staring at us. I dragged her to a small clearing in the grass, away from tables, the tents, and the teams forming up for the walk. Her lipstick drew a hard, tight line across her face.

"You read my letter, didn't you?" I said. "And this is your response?"

It was just a flicker, a quick sideways move of her eyes, and I knew. I began to shake with the painful shock of it.

"You didn't even read it," I said.

Her lips parted slightly and pulled in air.

I dropped my hands from her shoulders and held them against the dull ache forming in my stomach. Did she hate me that much? Or did I simply not matter?

Marisa turned away, chin to shoulder for a second, then she looked back at me, straight in the eye, no remorse. "I had a ton of work to read on the plane," she said. "I opened it. I started it. I got through the part about new friends and figured I'd finish it later. We were getting together anyway, right? And here we are. You can just tell me whatever on the walk, after the walk."

I couldn't even look at her. Humiliation, insult, pain so deep I couldn't bear to. I'd poured my heart out, and this was all she could give back.

"C'mon," my daughter said, turning to go. "We should go to breakfast."

The heat again. Heat from every pore, pressure building in my head so that my yelling came out with a hollow sound.

"You stop ordering me around!"

Marisa's whole body jerked back and her mouth opened wide, teeth and gums and bright-pink twisted lips enraged. What came out was a whisper-growl.

"What's *wrong* with you?"

Then I did something I had never done before in my entire life: I raised my hand up and back and swung it forward, but I stopped it just inches from her face before lowering it back down. My breath came hard. I didn't fully get that I'd been ready to slap her until I looked down at my palm, as if it were separate from my body and had moved on its own. I looked up as Marisa's eyes grew huge. Her hand held her cheek as if it had actually been slapped, and she let out a short, high bark.

The heat shot through me one more time, then left me damp, defeated. I'd failed. I'd wanted to communicate with my daughter, and that's what had come out. A raised hand.

I lowered my voice but was angry still. "You didn't have ten minutes to read it? I spent hours on that letter, spilling my guts so you'd understand!"

Marisa hunched into herself, that window shade behind her eyeballs letting nothing out, nothing in.

"No, no," I said to her blank face. "You don't give a shit about understanding, as long as you call the shots." I stared at her expressionless face, feeling her shutting down, because I'd done it so often myself. "I am *done* with that, Marisa! Oh, yes, I've made mistakes. Well, so fucking what!" My voice was cracking, high. "I'll admit to my mistakes. But, Marisa? I'm done with your manipulating. Your controlling. Catering to your thought-less, selfish crap."

Years of hardness in my daughter's face began to break down there, right in front of me. Tears pooled in her eyes, and her tight pink lip line turned down, wrinkling her chin. Mad as I was, her tears tore at me. I moved toward her, my arms out for an apologetic embrace, but she stiffened and pulled herself up and back. I stopped and let her be.

Right there is when I should've told her. I don't even know why I didn't tell her. I knew she'd get back on the plane and read my letter and feel bad about it. And at that moment I wanted her to feel bad.

"I am not going on this stupid fucking walk," I told her. Talked that way to my own daughter. "You can call me after you read that letter. Or not."

Maybe I was the one acting like the spoiled brat, stalking off through the teams of pink, past the survivor table and the goodie-bag table and the wrong registration line. Leaving Marisa standing there, alone in the crowd.

Chapter 19

Still damp and shaky, I stood atop the BART escalator and dialed Kate before going down.

"Are you around today?" I asked. "I need to talk, but I'm just getting on BART in the city. Can we meet somewhere?"

"Good, I need to talk too. How about pedicures? I was going today anyway. Place on Twelfth in forty-five minutes? I'll call them."

One of the things I loved about Kate was how she cut to the chase. No *Why are you in the city this early in the morning?* No *Talk about what?* I'd asked to meet, and we would meet.

It occurred to me Kate might be pissed I hadn't told her about Marisa and the cancer walk, but I hadn't wanted to hear what she'd have to say. I'd imagined her telling me to call Marisa back, cancel the walk, and have the meeting on my terms. Which, in retrospect, would've been a better idea.

I spent the entire BART ride in a stupor—had I really blown the one visit with my daughter by getting mad? How was she supposed to know how upset I'd be? Should I call her immediately or wait until she'd had a chance to read the letter, mull it over?

The door to Paradise Nails opened to chimes and the smell of incense layered ineffectively over acrylic. Jenny, whose real name was Trinh, welcomed me by name and pointed to the empty spa chair next to where Kate sat. Her hands rested in a bowl of cuticle-defying liquid, so she greeted me with a "hey" and a chin-raise. Even with her blonde ponytail pulled through a baseball cap, a Sheriff's Department T-shirt over her sweats, Kate was perfectly made up, lips glossed and eyes lightly shadowed in neutral browns.

"God, this is just what I need," I said, settling into the leather cushion. I lowered my feet into warm, bubbling water and fiddled with the massage remote until the chair back pounded alongside my spine.

"So what were you doing in the city so early in the morning?" I knew she'd ask eventually. "Walk for the Cure. With Marisa," I replied.

"Marisa? She's here? How'd that come about? Where is she? You did the walk already? It's not even ten!" So early we'd gotten two spots at the nail place. The footbaths' burbling muffled our voices, soothed my toes.

I told her about my letter and about Marisa's signing us up for the walk. Trihn and Tina scrubbed our calluses, the chatter between them in Vietnamese sounding like birdsong over the bubbles.

"I didn't want to go, but I didn't want to disappoint her either," I said, looking into her face for judgment or offense that this was the first she'd heard of it. I didn't know why I hadn't told her about the letter; I supposed I'd wanted to keep it between me and Marisa at least until we'd worked things out.

Kate shook her head slowly, and I could tell she wouldn't hold it against me. When I told her how, standing there in the sea of pink, I realized Marisa hadn't read my letter, Kate looked as angry as I had felt. Her jaw hardened and lips twisted round.

"I nearly hit her, Kate. I mean, I actually raised my arm against her and came this close to hitting her."

"Don't blame you," Kate said.

"Yeah, but I let it get out of hand."

Then, instead of assuaging my guilt, Kate said, "Good grief. She's going to feel so bad when she does read that letter."

A Vietnamese TV soap opera competed with the sound of the footbaths, the chatter, the chimes of new customers at the door. The chair kneaded my back, and my heart sank to my belly.

"I should've told her there, right?" I said, too loud. "Should've given her a chance to feel bad on the spot and then worked it through from there? But something made me want her to experience her own consequences."

"I get that."

"Also the walk was so terrible I didn't want to spring my news on her there, right in the middle of all that cancer crap. It'd be like, what, overkill? Drama?"

"You did the right thing. You couldn't have known. Regardless, it's done. Just call her and hash it out. I mean, you do have to do that." Kate knew I could put difficult confrontations off.

I reached a hand over to Kate's arm and gave it a squeeze. How comforting it was to be there with her. How well she knew me, and Marisa. Kate made me feel confident I could work things out.

"Thank you for not judging," I said. "Thank you for rushing over here. You know how much I love you, right?" I'd never said that to her, but it felt liberating to say.

I saw a flush of pink in her cheeks. "Ditto," she said. "Goes without saying."

I'd made her uncomfortable, saying what we'd known without saying. My dear, snarky, shut-down friend. We'd been close because of our shared inability to be close. I wondered if it was too late to change.

I slapped flat-footed into my kitchen in bright-yellow throwaway flip-flops and saw there was a message on my landline from Marisa. I supposed she didn't want to catch me somewhere public given what needed to be said, but when I called her back I could hear flights being announced in the background.

"I read the letter," she said. In the pause I could hear her trying to speak, not finding the words. "I just don't know what to do, Mom," she said. "I'm so sorry."

"You don't need to do anything, Marisa," I said. "There's nothing you have to do."

She asked how I was feeling, then said, "Oh, God, I didn't even ask you that before." Then she apologized again.

I told Marisa I was feeling fine on my pain meds. I told her that at the moment I was busy living, so not to worry so much about if or when I'd die. I had some time, plenty of time. I was protecting her again. Then she started in, trying to fix things.

"Did you research clinical trials?" she asked me. "Are you exercising every day? What about nutrition? You've got to watch your diet and keep in shape," and on and on.

I just said, "Marisa." And I let there be silence between us on the phone until she got it.

"Sorry, Mom."

Sometimes it takes getting sick, deadly sick, to take a good look at yourself, and while you're busy doing that, sometimes others take a good look at themselves too. Even if there's nothing else you leave to the world, maybe that's enough.

I didn't expect Marisa to cancel her flight, and sure enough she said she couldn't but that she felt terrible about it.

"We'll have another weekend soon," I said. "How about if I come down there? My time is free. You don't have to entertain me, but I'd like to take you to dinner. Maybe go to the Getty if you have time."

"I'll make time, Mom."

My heart.

Chapter 20

The following Tuesday, I was buoyant all day, even getting my blood drawn, standing in line at the pharmacy, going through my box of receipts for taxes. When Dave came to pick me up I wasn't ready, because I never was on time, not for social stuff. I was in the middle of a clothes fit, taking off the flowy black pants and putting on the black stretchy capris instead. I'd already gone through three blouses and none of them seemed right. They were too prissy professional, leftover office clothes, or the other extreme—stretched-out, faded, who-gives-a-shit going-to-the-grocery-store clothes. And that $175 Nordstrom blouse? I couldn't bring myself to even put it on. I answered the door wearing the nice slim capris and a black tank top under a red cardigan with ruffles in front, and I could tell even Dave, Dave of the same canvas-and-plaid shirt every day, thought the look was lame. Ruffles!

"I was just changing," I said. "Sorry."

"Hey, no rush! Music doesn't start for an hour," he said.

Dave appeared a different person in tight black jeans and a brushed-silk-and-rayon shirt in gray that I noticed right away matched his eyes. So handsome I was embarrassed for a second, because this was Dave at my door, not a date.

"You look great," I said. "I'm having a clothes fit. I've got nothing. Really. Nothing." I knew how absurd it sounded, but I was so stressed out over what to wear I wanted to cry, and Dave looking so good made it even worse. I thought the first-day-of-school terrors were long behind me, those days of panicking over whether I'd fit in whenever we moved to a new place. But for some reason, maybe because I hadn't been out in the evening in so long, I was right back there, paralyzed.

He put his arms around me, pressed my head to his chest. I smelled the fabric softener on his shirt. And with me still pressed against him like that, Dave breathed in deep and said, "Whatever you wear, it'll be just fine." Guys just don't get clothes fits.

Then, without asking permission, Dave walked right across the living room and opened the door to my bedroom, where practically everything in my closet was strewn across the bed. I'd even had a bra fit, and several of them were tangled on top of the dresser. Every time I thought I should wear a bra, I tried them all on—stretchy sports bras, no-wire lacy bras, front hooks, back hooks, no-hook bras, all bought in sizes too big hoping they wouldn't drive me crazy after fifteen minutes with that post-surgery nerve pain shooting breast to back. And every time I wound up wearing the shabbiest, most stretched-out and yellowed athletic bra because it was the only one that could get me through an evening without looking lopsided or feeling grouchy because of the pain. I knew I'd be putting it on as soon as Dave gave me some space.

Dave went right over and picked up the thing on the top of the pile on the bed. It was a plain white T-shirt, scoop necked, thick cotton, Eileen Fisher on sale.

"What's wrong with this?" he said.

Why on earth I'd be taking fashion advice from Dave, of all people, I couldn't say, but just having him there in the room calmed me down. He was right. Anything would be fine. I opened the closet and showed Dave the two hooks on the side where a dozen scarves hung.

"All good," Dave said.

"Not over this sweater," I said. "You can't wear a scarf over a ruffled sweater, Dave."

I still can't believe I did it, but right then I pulled off the sweater and the tank top I was wearing, and I didn't even have a bra on. I stood right there in front of him, naked to my pudgy waist, my uneven tits, scar and all. I took a deep breath, sucked my stomach in, looked Dave in the eyes. He was holding out the white T-shirt toward me, and I couldn't tell if he was holding it like a shield or like a professional shopper just waiting for me to put it on. His brows rose for just a second, but then Dave's eyes went soft, looking right into mine, calm and assured. He reached over and took the tank top and sweater from me, tossed them on the bed. And then he just waited, holding the white T-shirt out toward me, like nothing was out of the ordinary at all.

I didn't take the shirt from him right away. I stood there, breathing shallowly, half-naked, and pointed up to my scar. "So. There it is," I said.

And the really wonderful thing about Dave that moment was that he wasn't embarrassed, didn't turn away, didn't look sorry for me, shake his head, fake pout, or do any of the things that would have made me feel embarrassed or sorry or ashamed of myself. No, he said just the right thing.

"Hell, Liz," he said. "You don't even need a bra. Why would you even wear a bra? You'll look just fine in this." He handed me the T-shirt.

"Well, I need a scarf to cover nipplage," I said when the shirt was on. "I mean. I am fifty-three."

I smiled big and then laughed, and he laughed, too, and then I stuck my chest right out at him, arms up and out to the side. Saggy breast and scarred, indented, upturned breast pushed out for Dave to see. I felt giddy—it was the first time I'd shown any-one besides Lyle, and we know how that went. He'd been so sweet, southern gentleman swearing I looked beautiful, more beautiful than ever, but then I saw that look of his in the mirror when he didn't know I could see. After that, Dave was the safest person I could think of to show. He got it, right away, that it was a big deal to show him and to not be ashamed. With Dave seeing me like that and getting it and both of us laughing, I hadn't been that happy in a long, long time.

Soon Dave was holding out a scarf, the first one he grabbed off the hook, and it was perfect, a simple cotton rectangle in abstract fall colors: olive, black, burgundy, and gold. I wrapped it around my neck and let the ends dangle over my breasts.

"Beautiful," Dave said. It dawned on me that maybe Dave wearing the same canvas shirt over and over again was a sign of his being depressed, not just Dave being Dave. That night in his gorgeous shirt, helping me through my clothes fit, I saw in his face a smooth contentment.

We drove up and down Piedmont Avenue looking for a parking spot and then found one right across the street from Caffe Trieste, in front of the GNC. The evening was warmer than it should've been in late October, one of those Indian summer evenings, so people were sitting at the four outdoor tables in front, drinking coffee and wine. Typical Oakland mixture of scruffy and work casual, faces white and black and brown, middle-aged and college-aged and two moms with kids, chocolate on the kids' faces, moms yakking over the chatter of the kids.

The second we walked inside, I looked at Dave and he looked at me and I know we were thinking the same thing: What the hell did it matter what we wore?

A mic and set of drums stood on the stage, band instruments in cases were set up against the window, and tables were crowded on either side. Tiny round café tables with fake marble tops trimmed in chrome had been pushed together and lined up in the center of the small room, next to the glass counter with the pastries and cash register where you put your orders in for pizza and wine. More tables sat in a jumble by the wall, under 1950s and '60s photos—San Francisco politicians, poets and rock stars, Italian accordion players, and founder Papa Gianni Giotta and the old North Beach crowd hanging out at the original Caffe. None of it resembled the hyper-rich, techy, hipster-heavy San Francisco of now.

That night with Dave, crowded around those tables and in line to order wine and espressos at the bar, I saw the reason I chose to live in Oakland even before the *New York Times* said it was cool. Oakland was never self-consciously hip, never precious the way San Francisco was or like Portland with all its outdoor gear and bone marrow ice cream and $5 cups of exotic tea. The crowd that night was Oakland all the way. A striking Native American woman, big and androgynous-looking in a Hawaiian shirt and slacks, sat with a couple of Latinas in their thirties, one just off work with her green polo shirt embroidered with the logo of the Parks Department, one dressed in a thick hand-knit sweater over loose red slacks. Some white and Middle Eastern kids from Cal, clean-cut in hoodies and Columbia jackets, surrounded by backpacks and squeezed together on a bench and chairs at a table meant for three. A table of African American women with a girl of about fourteen, one of the women apparently celebrating her birthday in a flowery dress and heels. And seated at a table in a corner by the window, four super-seniors. Old people. Three women and a man in their eighties and nineties, one with a walker folded at the wall, another wearing pale-blue cashmere over her shoulders with a manhattan in a martini glass in front of her, a real drink she must've snuck in from the bar next door.

Dave and I took the last table, by the eighty-something woman with the manhattan, who smiled and waved us to the seats as if she were the hostess of the evening. Next to her, a woman even older, apple-faced, bright eyed, wearing a powder-blue appliquéd sweatshirt, was in rapid conversation, laughing. I looked at Dave, who was also taking in the scene, and wondered if he was thinking the same thing. *Several of the people here are getting near the end of their lives too*, is what I was thinking. *And they're having a good time meanwhile.*

The music began, and everyone in the room came together the way you do when there's music—young, old, strangers, and friends, filling up with the sounds of sweet Appalachian fiddle and "Sittin' on the Dock of the Bay" and "Summertime," belted out by the birthday girl at the table by the wall.

By the second set, we'd gotten to chatting with the woman with the manhattan and the ninety-two-year-old and her middle-aged son. This was their Tuesday ritual, music and wine at Caffe Trieste. The two older guys in the trio, she told us, had been playing around the Bay Area since they started on street corners in the '60s. That night, in addition to the Donald Sutherland look-alike on guitar, there was a slender sixtyish man in a fedora, dress shirt, and belted charcoal slacks, playing like a genius on sax, flute, and drums. With them, the headliner—a young Danish jazz violinist—was model handsome and astonishingly good.

"Won a Grammy," whispered the woman with the manhattan, as proud as if he were her grandson, looking at us to see how impressed we were, then back at the musicians with a little wave. The violinist went on a riff, and Dave looked at me and lifted his palms like there was no telling what you'd find when you least expected it, or who'd be there when you found it. The band played "In the Pines," singing in harmony with a haunting fiddle's melody.

Turned out the older ladies didn't know Rhonda at all. When we asked if they were from Alive!, they looked at us like their hearing aids had gone bad. "Alive!?" I said. "Everett Lester's church out on Fruitvale?"

Eloise, the woman with the manhattan, silver hair piled atop her head in great swirls held together with Japanese combs, looked over her nose at me as if to say, *You can't be serious, dear.*

"We're from the Church of Jazz and Justice," she said. She straightened herself tall in the chair, touched her piled-on curls.

Then the whole scene made sense. I'd never been there, not

being a church person, but I'd always told myself I should go because of the name alone. Plus, the history. When I first heard the name, I thought it was a joke, but Jazz and Justice was one of the oldest churches in Oakland, originally and officially called Plymouth Church of Christ. It was diversity itself and was as much a campaign, I'd heard, as it was a church. For equality, against poverty, railing against every injustice like churches were supposed to do. Inclusive, obviously, and more than that, if these eighty- and ninety-year-olds were out getting high on jazz every Tuesday night. Maybe I could go to church. Suddenly it wasn't hard to imagine Sunday mornings with these women, the music. Maybe that would be a place I'd want to pray.

Another violin solo. The musicians, loving with one another, loving with the crowd, the crowd loving them back. Evening falling. Through the café window, a band of pink sky over the Piedmont Bakery and the GNC. Birthday smiles, aging faces beautiful in their wrinkles, not a care in the world. Dave in his silver shirt, silver eyes beaming, knee touching mine under the tiny table. My autumn scarf, no bra. He put his hand over mine and moved his head back and forth to the music, all the world so perfect in that moment.

One reason the older folks came was that the music was done by nine, and I was fine with that, ready for Dave to take me home though we were still amped, so happy to be out and part of a scene where we felt comfortable and not sick, just like regular people who had regular stuff going on. I was sure the old people had their share of troubles, and seeing them out there at the café made me think Dave and Rhonda and I should be out all the time too. Soon as Rhonda got better.

As Dave and I left the café, I thought about Marisa, and how the thing I cared most about was clearing things up with her. Then I thought about Rhonda and Sally. The difference was that Marisa and I had a chance, a real chance, and I knew for sure she'd have a successful life whether or not I was around. I couldn't even get close to imagining what Rhonda had to think about all the time with her daughter, till she couldn't stand it anymore and gave it up to God.

"Okay, let's do it," I said to Dave. "Let's get Sally."

We'd been jaywalking across to his car, and even though I'd said it right out of the blue, Dave banged once on the roof of the car and without hesitation said, "Yes! I'll talk to Lynette. We'll make a plan."

We rode to my apartment in comfortable silence. Dave walked me to my door, and when I opened it, I didn't want him to leave. I knew probably the one glass of wine I'd had at the café wasn't even a good idea, but I thought, *Really, so what?* and asked Dave if he wanted to come in and share a good bottle I had saved.

"It seems like a special night," I said. "Want to?"

His "sure!" was loud enough to wake the kids across the street, but it made me happy.

As Dave slammed the kitchen door behind him, I was already crouched under the kitchen counter looking for the bottle of 2001 Duckhorn cabernet. That night it felt perfectly right to drink it with Dave. I felt almost triumphant, pulling out two glasses and opening that bottle of wine.

Dave brought the glasses to the coffee table, and I brought a place mat and the bottle. He sat on the gray Macy's sofa, and I brought the red leather cube over from the corner so I could sit across from him. That cube. It seemed so right when I bought it in my post-diagnosis furniture binge. I thought the red would cheer me up. That night it just looked like something from a college dorm, space saving but uncomfortable, more orange than red in the lamplight.

Dave swirled the deep ruby wine in his glass, sniffed it like a pro, and took a sip. "Delicious," he announced. "But even better in ten minutes, after it breathes."

I sipped mine, and it was true, delicious, but all at once opening that bottle felt like a terrible mistake. It went down my throat warm and lovely but in an instant awoke to an awful, familiar jealousy and shame. I wanted to dump the bottle down the sink.

"What's up?" Dave asked. I must've looked as stricken as I felt.

"Lyle gave me this wine," I said. "The guy who dumped me in the middle of my radiation treatments."

"Oh, God, Liz." Dave's eyes rose to the ceiling, neck stretched back, smoothed out, and then he looked back across the table at me. "Well," he said. "We should enjoy it for spite, then, huh? Cheers." He lifted his glass to me, taking a swig instead of a sip this time.

Lyle had given me the bottle so we could have it when I was done with treatment, but of course he was done with me before that. Several times I'd looked at that bottle and tried to throw it out. I'd put it in a gift bag to bring to someone's house but then had switched it for something else. And every time I opened that cabinet, even though I'd hidden it in the back, I knew it was there.

"Know how he dumped me?" I made myself take a swig too. "He sent me an email meant for an old girlfriend of his."

"Christ, Liz."

"Yeah," I said. "And then he tells me, 'You've been so brave. I really have admired you so all this time. You've got such a great attitude, I am just positive you'll beat this!'" I sat up straight on the cube and leaned over the coffee table, in Dave's face. "Don't you hate it when people tell you that?"

The wine made my whole body warm, and I could feel that chemical surge up my torso, heat on my neck, my face.

"How the hell do they know if you'll beat it or won't beat it? What, if you wake up with a smile every day, your cancer cells will just go poof?" I was yelling. "And what the fuck does 'brave' mean? What are you supposed to do, crawl under the bed? Run screaming down the street? Why does everyone say you're brave just because you have cancer?"

I huffed out a loud breath but then immediately felt sorry for what I'd said. The heat subsided and I thought of Rhonda, there in the hospital, and how she probably didn't hate it when people said those things at all. Maybe she said them all the time herself. And all the poor friends and family, people who gave you the Look and didn't know what to say. It wasn't their fault. What were they supposed to say?

But Dave slapped the table hard again and said, "God, yeah. I hate it."

I took a deep, resigned breath. "He wrote, 'Of course I want to remain friends—deeply connected friends! It's always been special knowing you.'"

"'Special,'" Dave said. "Ouch."

"I just could not believe it," I said. "Like you can't believe it when you have cancer. It can't be true. You must have missed something. It'll be different when you wake up, but it isn't. Special? He *admired* me? We'd been lovers for more than two years. Back and forth, me to New York, him to San Francisco. Making excuses for meetings with clients, then staying over an extra day. We talked about moving one day, how we'd completely change our lives together. We would move to Portland. Truth is, I built a whole fantasy life around the way we were going to be. Cozy on the sofa, crackling fire, raining outside, the whole bit. I'd take up painting. I could smell the oil paint and, over that, the smell of Moroccan chicken bubbling on the stove. It was all so detailed, I thought it was real."

It was the first time I'd ever admitted that out loud. But in telling Dave, somehow I saw how running from the pain of Lyle, telling myself he couldn't hurt me, had just been keeping the pain around. I sat a minute with my old fantasy, letting it hurt, letting Dave make it safe to feel pain.

Dave looked like he wanted to beat someone up, but he let me continue.

"I was sure I was over him but, sometimes . . . The wine,

I guess. Certain things. And it all comes roaring back like it happened just last night, and I replay the whole thing, to my everlasting shame.

"For a whole year after that email, when my meds were keeping me up at 2:00 a.m., I'd google medical sites. I was trying to get some definitive answer. Because that whole time I was with Lyle, I didn't actually believe I had cancer. It didn't matter that I had cancer, you know? I had loooove. Then he dumps me and suddenly, holy shit, I'm alone with this thing and I don't even know what it is. So all night long I'm up reading technical abstracts about my type and grade of tumor. I'm looking for the worst-case scenario and then the best. I'd paste the best parts and the worst parts onto a page, as if keeping it all there on my computer would make me comprehend it. As if having all the facts right there would put me back in charge."

"Yep," said Dave. He'd googled too.

"But then, even crazier, I'd switch from Medline to Facebook, and after a few minutes, I couldn't help it, I'd go to Elena de la Pena's page. That was the name Lyle's girlfriend used in Barcelona, not Ellen but Elena de la Pena. God. I hated her for that melodious name."

"Oh, hell yeah," Dave said.

"Sick with shame! Every time I read her insipid Spanish wine blog. Looking to see if she'd mention Lyle. Of course there she is in her picture with that thick, beautiful hair, and I was still bald so I obsessed on her hair."

I pushed away from my temple hair that, two years before, had come back after chemo thick, curly, and all over the place. But by the time I sat there with Dave and the wine it was back to its old straight and brittle self, hanging thin and patchy to my chin, no matter how much I gelled or moussed or blow-dried it, to the point where I considered putting my old wig on again.

Lyle. The time he saw me in the shower bald, head like a baby bird's, four tiny wisps of hair. Was that it?

"I wasted all that time over him!" I said out loud. "Here I'd put off radiation, and then I spent a whole precious year trying to make sense of the thing. Back and forth, Medline, Facebook, stupid fucking wine blog, UCSF medical center, breastcancer. org, wine blog, Facebook, Medline. I just felt worse and worse."

It was such a relief, admitting it all to Dave. I'd never told anyone how obsessed I'd been. When you've got metastatic cancer, try telling some healthy person about another problem you have. Any other. See what I mean?

Dave actually growled, and I thought it was because he was so pissed off at Lyle. I loved him for that. Then he said, "PTSD, hon, PTSD. A convergence of bad things at the wrong time puts you in hell for a bit, and you can get stuck circling round in that hell, for a very long time."

"At least I didn't tell Lyle about my mets," I said. As if that were enough to restore dignity and wipe my mind clean.

"Hell no, you are not going to tell him about your mets!" Dave made the "hell" sound like a gunshot. "None of his goddamn business. You even start to think about telling him, call me first, okay?" His eyes were gray bullets pointing at me.

He didn't say it out loud, but what I heard from Dave was this: Lyle didn't get to know when I died.

I pulled my shirt down flat over my lopsided tits and bunched it up at my hips. Something to hold on to. I said, "I know. Forgiveness. It's hard to admit it, but Christine had a point."

"Not forgiveness. Acceptance," Dave said.

The word seemed to echo, and I remembered how wise I thought Dave was when he said it back in the group at Nordstrom. When it came to me, though, *me* accepting, it sounded like a chapter title or a seminar, a concept worth admiring but out of reach, beyond understanding.

Dave clasped his big hands behind his head and said, "If you must forgive, forgive yourself. Trouble with that is, while you're forgiving yourself, you're telling yourself the same old story.

Telling yourself all you did that was wrong." There was a little mockery in the way he said that, but then his hands dropped down and reached over to mine, pulling my fingers toward him on the table.

"That gives you the excuse to keep telling the story and dragging him back into your head, see? And then on and on it goes. You don't need to forgive either one of you. Just accept and move on. No right, no wrong in any of it. That's the truth."

God, that was wise. I wondered what mental torture he'd had to go through to find that path to peace. If I could accept Lyle, I could accept cancer. If I could accept cancer, I could quit dancing around with Marisa and work on what was real.

"It took me twenty years to figure that out after Vietnam. That long. Slowly killing my own soul over the story about killing over there. Repeating it over and over. It was Robert who helped me figure out the truth, and it's the one truth I know. All there is, is the clean slate of right this minute."

He pulled in air deep and loud, one palm on his chest like he was instructing me in how to breathe. I put my palm on my chest and breathed in with him.

"Don't try to get rid of those thoughts, or they'll keep coming back," Dave said. That was truth I could understand. "Just go ahead and feel what you feel and think the thought. But here's the important thing. Know that the thought is only a thought. The feeling is only a feeling. Neither thought nor feeling is the truth."

Dave said all that. Same guy who'd growled and looked like he was going to pound his fists through the table five minutes before. I wondered if he and Robert had been Buddhists. If they'd sat on tatami mats at home in San Francisco, letting the thoughts pass gently by. That peaceful image stayed with me, and I sat with Dave quietly for a minute or two, feeling my body relax, feeling the pain as a small, manageable ball in my belly and just sitting with it.

Dave stood and reached a hand into his back pocket, then pulled out a leather wallet, tattered and worn almost to the point of falling in two.

"It was Robert's," he said. He dug into a pocket under the billfold and pulled out an even-more-worn piece of college-lined paper, torn from a spiral notebook. He opened it up and I could see it was a list, on both sides of the paper, in different inks. A list of names.

Dave sat down, put the paper on the coffee table, and smoothed it out with both hands. Pulled in a deep breath and looked down at it. I saw the first name, dark and blocky, etched over and over in blue ink: Robert. Then, with a space between each, more names, blue ink, black ink. Sam and Rodrigo and Mom and Katrin and Ed, and more all the way down the page.

"All of them gone," Dave said. "I got to a point, about ten years back. So many gone, sometimes before I'd fall asleep I'd try to count them. To remember, you know? There were so many, I was terrified I'd forget. So I'd count them on my fingers, then crosshatch them by fives on a piece of paper, to remember. I felt so bad when I'd leave someone off. I'd go to sleep with a list and then wake up and think, *Jesus. Mom. I left Mom off the list!* Or my best friend, Eddie. Sometimes you remember the most recent ones, sometimes the ones that hit the hardest, and sometimes it makes no sense, the order of what you remember."

I felt my own breath stop, cold up my back and across my shoulders. The number of names on that list. Both sides of the page.

"Dave," I said. "I'm so sorry. How can you ever?"

"No," he said. He was leaning back on the couch, easy as could be. "I'm not showing you to feel sad," he said. "This list gives me comfort. One thing, I know that everyone's on there, everyone important. They're all written down there, permanent ink, and I carry them with me, no danger of forgetting. It's comforting in another way too. Seeing all the names like that, knowing we all end up there, it makes it feel okay."

Dave's body rocked slowly forward and then back as he stared at the list; then he lifted his head, and his eyes bored right into mine.

"What I want to say is," he said, "maybe you should do the same thing."

I checked off names in my head: Mom. Dad. Lisa, Patti, and Leslie from work. Cam, my housekeeper, a single mom. Carol, my friend from San Francisco State. Doug, my first boss. Susan, who lived across the street from Bradley and me. Cousin Rory, AIDS. My high school boyfriend, Steve. For sure I was forgetting someone.

"Do it," Dave said. "Do it tonight. And when you get to the last name? Add one more. Add Lyle."

It hit me like a terrifying ghoul, dropping from the ceiling onto my head.

"That's right," Dave said. "Put him on there. It'll help. Trust me. You're the only one who'll see it. Eventually he'll be gone for real, so you may as well make him that way now, far as you're concerned."

I was about to say thank you, and promise him I'd do it, when he told me what he'd obviously wanted to say.

"'Course, I put my brother on there, even though he was alive. For years he was on there, far as I was concerned."

He turned the page over. Pointed to the last name on it, crossed out so many times I couldn't tell it said "Brent."

"Turns out I got my brother all wrong," he said. Now it was Dave confessing, lips pressed in, head down, breathing in deeply because now that he'd said that, he had to explain, and explaining was the hard part when it was something you really, really got wrong. But then he sucked it up, looked straight at me, body marine straight. "Had nothing to do with me being gay," he said. "At least that wasn't the main thing. Thing is, I was the one who left him, he feels. I left, enlisted, then went to college out here on purpose. I got into vet school at Davis, then moved to San

235

Francisco and never came back. Mom died while I was in vet school, and then all there was back there in La Porte was Brent and our son-of-a-bitch father. I went back once while Dad was alive, and that was all I could take. Mean, drunken bastard."

Tribe within a tribe. I'd done my version of leaving too. Emotionally AWOL from my family, thinking I was keeping everything in control. All that time Dave had blamed Brent. All that time I had blamed Bradley, and Marisa, for my own inability to be real.

Dave went on, loud monotone, steel-gray eyes looking back into my eyes, tearing up.

"I told Brent back then he should leave, too, but he's a better man, I suppose. Me thinking it was about coming home for Christmas. All those years he was stuck with him. Years and years of it until Dad finally died."

Dave took a deep breath. Squeezed his forehead. I felt that pain in my gut that comes when there's nothing you can do to make a thing better.

"I didn't even go back then," he said. "As if that punished Dad, not Brent. Just left him to deal with the whole thing. Man, I fucked up."

"I'm sorry, Dave." It was all I could say. In the end, it's all anyone can say.

"I can leave him everything I have. Most everything. Some things will go to Lynette. But the house, the Subaru? All Brent's. Won't make up for those years, but might make the rest of them better."

"And Brent's here now? At your place?"

"That's the thing, he is here. And I don't want him to have to go through it all with me. He says he will, but I don't know. We're just getting to know each other again. I forgot the things I liked about him. How funny he can be."

Dave spread the list out with his hands again, hands wrinkled, paper wrinkled, Brent's name crossed off.

"I feel terrible about putting him on there," he said. "I just didn't know the truth."

Then Dave straightened up and pointed at me. "You?" he said. "You know. Go ahead and put Lyle on the list."

The way he said it, so matter-of-factly, felt almost parental. I got up, went to the kitchen counter, and pulled a sheet of notepaper from the grocery pad. I wrote the name in ink. And that was the moment I finally let Lyle go.

Chapter 21

*R*honda was still in the hospital, and Dave, Lynette, and I met at Dave's clinic in the Tenderloin district. Dave's ex introduced herself with a hug, then pulled back to assess me, blue eyes crinkling up in a smile. "Dave's told me such nice things," she said. I instantly warmed to her, not just from the compliment but from the confident, sincere way she came across. I could tell generosity came easily to her. She turned then to the plan, and we practiced our lines.

Dave was to tell Sally how sick her mom was and how we became the Oakland Mets and all, thanks to Rhonda. I'd tell Sally how much her mom cared about her. I'd tell her nothing would make Rhonda happier than to see her daughter get clean, and I'd say I knew that for sure, both as Rhonda's friend and as a mom with a daughter Sally's age. Lynette agreed I could be the closer. I would tell Sally I'd seen Cassie—how adorable she was.

Lynette would tell Sally how she knew the best place to detox safely and without going crazy with the pain of it, and then a better rehab, best in the country and so forth, after that. The idea being that we all understood, we knew she'd relapsed again and again, that was the deal with addiction, but this time could be different and she could have a whole new life. She could be Cassie's mom again.

We never even thought of what to say to her boyfriend, Josh. Didn't even factor him in. We walked all the way down Eddy Street to Sally's block, slow because Dave told us his meds were giving him terrible foot blisters. Every step on his right foot stretched open a sore and punished it with two hundred pounds of Dave. It hurt just to look at him. We'd only gone a half a block when Lynette made him lean on her to relieve the pressure. I was behind them, Dave listing right, his arm around Lynette's strong shoulder, Lynette in charge, on a firm, steady march. Their heads were a matching gray, Dave's hair wiry and thin, Lynette's pulled back in a worn blue scrunchie, thick as a horse's tail hanging midway down her back. Seeing them leaning together, I wished I'd known Dave that way for forty years.

When we got to Sally's block, a skinny-legged drag queen in dreadlocks was dancing around, high as a kite and singing, "You just got to moo-oove!" right in the middle of the street. She danced to the sidewalk and got right in my face to yell, "Yow!" and the smell of BO and Jack Daniel's nearly laid me flat. Her teeth were thick and wide as a donkey's, and she had enormous eyes, drooping then popping wide open, mascara globbed on thick. I could tell they were looking at a vision having nothing to do with me or with any of us. We just kept moving.

We weren't sure which building was Sally's because the numbers were scraped off the metal doors. A whiskery fat guy sat smoking on the steps of one of the SROs nearby. Pale, hairy thigh skin showed through a two-inch hole on the side seam of his faded sweats. When we asked him if he knew where Sally lived, he looked at us through eyes that said there was a time he'd consider killing us just for asking, if there weren't three of us and one of him, and what a wonder it was to be too old now to bother. He jerked a thumb at the brown metal door.

That door wasn't a problem, no lock at all. The problem was the filthy linoleum staircase, the kind that curves around as it climbs, steps getting skinnier and skinnier as they circle around, so skinny you could kill yourself carrying groceries up. I cringed at the thought of Dave with his blisters getting up those stairs. They were too narrow for him to lean on Lynette going up, and there was no railing to hang on to—of course there wasn't. You could see the screw holes where there once had been one.

We all stood there at the bottom looking up, as if looking would help us figure something out. Then Dave hoisted himself up on the first stair. "Uhhn!"

"Wait. I'll go first," I said, figuring that Lynette was a lot stronger than I was and that if Dave slipped back on those stairs, she had a chance of holding him up.

About six stairs up, before the curve, I turned to watch Dave scope out the whole flight ahead of him, then look down at just the one step ahead. Right foot, wince, and big inhale, "uhhn" as his foot touched down, then two stairs one right after another with his face squeezed together in pain. I squelched my impulse to tell Dave to sit at the bottom and wait for us. Instead, I turned and stepped up, waiting every two steps to keep pace with Dave, staying on the first landing until he pulled himself up. Sweat on his forehead. I waited until he jerked his head up at me to go ahead, he'd be fine. None of us said a word going up. We were in unknown territory.

Those stairs wound up to a long hallway painted a green too ugly for any tree. At the end of that hallway there was a guy sleeping or nodding off, I wasn't sure because of the worn-out Giants baseball cap covering his eyes. He was propped against the wall with his legs spread straight out on the floor, under a window made out of stuff they must use in prisons, some kind of milky plexiglas threaded with steel. It let a little light in but then laughed in your face when you tried to see out.

The door of 2B, like all the other ones, was metal with a dead bolt and a doorknob, so it looked as if the way to get in was with a bludgeon, not a key. Plywood two-by-fours were nailed around the doorframe, and stickers and graffiti covered both the wood and metal of the door. The white plastic cover of an ancient doorbell hung by a wire below the tiny smashed-in mechanism.

Dave was a sweating, wincing mess, the canvas shirt with plaid cuffs hanging over his Mets shirt, wet at the neck with perspiration. He straightened himself up, put both feet flat on the floor, and took a couple deep breaths in, out. Then Dave—you just gotta love Dave—put on the biggest smile.

Lynette moved in front of him and gave a social worker rap on the door. Three slow raps, with full knuckles. The knock said business, but not cops, not someone looking for drugs. No answer.

Dave pressed Lynette to the side with a tap of his palm and stepped in front of the door. He tried the same kind of knock, only twice as loud because he was Dave, and in just a couple seconds from behind the door came a man's high voice, a dangerous voice you could tell right off because it was both high-pitched and a young guy needing to prove his manhood. It gave me a chill.

"Fuck you want?"

"Dave here, and two other friends of Rhonda. Sally's mom?"

I jumped in to counteract Dave's deep bellow. "No worries! We just want to talk to Sally, say hi from her mom. Can we speak to Sally, please? Her mom's in the hospital. We want to get Sally some help."

Did I ever blow it, right off the bat mentioning help. I just had to jump in and control the situation. The last thing an addict wants to hear is anything about rehab. You can say all you want that an addict has to *want* to go to rehab, but both Lynette and Dave convinced me that no addict ever wanted to go. Rehab meant not getting high. We'd be lucky if Sally didn't move out that night.

Josh opened the door a few inches. A gold-painted chain lock stretched across the view of his face, sweat on his narrow nose and pointy chin, hair flattened over skinny forehead in oily black strings. Black stubble around his lips. His pupils were pin dots of black in half circles of amber, hooded with lazy lids. Doors to the soul shut for the day. I peeked around Lynette, and over Josh's shoulder I saw part of someone's body, legs in pink sweatpants flat on the floor. The smell of a thousand cigarettes moved into the hallway, past us, and up the next flight of linoleum stairs.

"Sally's not here," Josh said. His voice was like a kid making a prank call, trying to sound low and adult, but the tone so didn't fit what he was saying. There was something terrifying in it. "You fuck off out of here! Now!" He slammed the door so fast I was sure he was going to come back with a gun.

I jerked back, but Dave pounded the door again.

"Jesus, Dave!" I said. "Let's get out of here!"

We heard a woman's voice then, from behind the door.

"Yeah! Fuck off!" she said. It had to be Sally's voice, but for all we knew, Josh was telling the truth and Sally wasn't even there. For all we knew, that wasn't even Josh.

Nothing was going to happen and we knew it, but it took a minute for us to give in, to admit we'd failed. I wanted to scream at Josh, to pound my way inside and blast away at him with his own gun. Or just sit down there on the floor and cry, then wait all night until Sally came out. She had to come out. Dave looked so dejected, slumped over, forehead in his hand. Lynette just looked pissed, staring down that ugly door.

"Let's go," I said.

Dave put his weight on one heel, twisted his body, and planted his other foot so he faced the stairs. Lynette went ahead of him, and this time I followed behind. I thought going down would be easier for Dave, but it seemed to require more weight on his blistered foot. Every few steps when that right foot pressed down it was "Oh, Jesus. Oh, man, uhhn!"

Outside, he leaned on a cement trash can piled high with Chinese take-out boxes and pint bottles from the liquor store next to where the old guy still sat, smoking another cigarette. Dave told Lynette and me to walk ahead while he caught his breath. Leaning on Lynette was probably starting to bug him because when Lynette insisted we wait, Dave growled the way

I first heard him growl back at the Nordstrom table. It was a sound Lynette clearly knew, because she immediately backed off. We walked just a few steps, then turned back to look at him. He was talking to a scruffy guy in burgundy velour pants, white undershirt and a fedora, a hat that had been made the last time fedoras were hip and worn all the years in between till they were hip again. It was faded to nearly gray, with a band of the original black where the ribbon once had been. You could tell something was going on between Dave and the guy, more than just a normal "what's up," the way Dave kept nodding as the guy talked, then patted the guy's shoulder before he turned away and walked toward us. Left toes, right heel, fists by his thighs.

"What'd he say?" I asked.

"He was the one who told me where Sally and Josh were staying in the first place. He said Thursday morning is the time. If it goes like usual, the dealer will come around, and if we can catch them when they're fixed up with enough heroin to mellow out the meth jangles, that's the time," Dave said.

He continued, "They may all be so zoned out, though, that the tough part will be waking Sally up. But we can deal with that as long as Josh is zoned out too."

I didn't know how the scruffy-hat guy knew all this, but I believed it.

"Okay," I said, "we're going back then." No way that little squeaky-voiced twerp was messing with the mission.

I took a shower soon as I got home, washing off the smoke smell, the fear sweat, scrubbing the desperation away. Then I curled myself under the covers and, one ear on my pillow and the other with the phone held against it, I called Marisa. She wasn't in, of course, but while usually I'd leave a message saying, "It's Mom, just checking in," this time I added, ". . . and I just wanted to say how grateful I am that you're my daughter, Marisa. I love you."

he next day, Rhonda was out of the hospital but not up to having visitors at home. Dave and I both talked to her on the phone but didn't tell her what had happened or that we were going to try again. I felt a little guilty about that, but why set her up? Things might not go any better the next time.

I met Dave and Lynette again on Thursday morning inside Dave's clinic on Turk Street. A half dozen destitute men and women waited outside the clinic's locked door. A hunched-over old man in brown plaid pants and a stained sweatshirt rattled the locked door, and a woman—I couldn't tell if she was thirty or sixty—squinted through the window at us through twisty iron bars. She had two missing teeth, and her hair was matted on one side. Bad as I felt for her, we had no time for interruptions. I mouthed, "Not today," and she turned to leave.

Dave ignored the commotion outside. He'd given in to crutches, a giant pair he propped against the one stainless steel table, which was covered in dents.

Good thing Dave had seen someone about the blisters. In addition to the crutches, he had a bandage wrapped around the big, oozing sore smack in the center of his right sole, and he wore one of those clunky black Velcro-on medical sandals to absorb the pressure.

People think it's the big terrible sicknesses that get to you when you have cancer, the nausea and sweats and fatigue laying you flat and all. Those all come, sure; eventually they come.

Sometimes they go and then come back again. Pain comes. But in between the horrible things you expect, it's the blisters, the constipation, the taste in your mouth like you've been chewing cans. The tingling numbness in hands and feet. They're minor annoyances in the grand scheme, but they're the things that drive cancer patients up a wall. Goddamned blisters. They're the dripping faucet from the rusted cold-water pipe, the maddening *drip-drip-drip* until the whole pipe bursts and floods your house while you're asleep.

The clinic smelled like Pine-Sol, and patches of wet cloudy green puddled on the painted concrete floor where it sloped near the drain. I told Dave we shouldn't be discouraged, that most of the time addicts won't go along on the first try.

"We try again is all," I said, mimicking Lynette's social worker's soothing, no-nonsense voice. Dave hung his head down between his shoulders, and his arms stretched out straight to his knees.

"But no expectations, remember," Lynette said. "We're not about kidnapping here."

Lynette stared at me hard from under unplucked gray brows. I was determined, and she knew it. She towered over me in her woven Indian tunic. Everything she wore—the worn black clogs with socks, the baggy knit pants, the tunic—said she'd belonged in that neighborhood for years, since way back when people thought it was a place about love.

I took a deep breath, firing myself up. Dave sat on the exam table, and Lynette paced the concrete floor. It was my idea for us to wear the Mets T-shirts. Something tangible and connected to Rhonda, for Sally to see. Also, probably she wouldn't be so threatened if we showed up looking like dorks.

"Let's do it, then," I said, and without even getting a nod from Lynette, Dave put a crutch on either side of his body and then swung himself down to the floor. Two long vaults and Dave unlocked the door. I told myself the people hanging out in front were poor people with problems, and what was wrong with that? Just people messed up with hangovers or buzzes or worried about their Chihuahua's rheumy eyes.

The man with the plaid pants stood right outside so we could barely get through the door. Dave said, "Yo, Richard, can't help you today, man. You know the hours. Tomorrow at ten."

Richard scratched at his beard and blinked at Dave but didn't say anything back. He scuffed toward the curb where two of his buddies sat, between a pickup and Dave's Subaru. The woman who'd been looking through the bars lifted her Chihuahua and walked the other direction down Turk Street.

Dave leaned on his left crutch, pulled keys from his right pocket, and tossed them to Lynette. She caught them without a blink, opened the driver's-side door, and clicked open the passenger side. They were like an old married couple heading off to Home Depot, only remembering at the last minute that somehow they had to fit me into the cargo area caged off for dogs. I climbed in, and the pain shooting through my collarbone reminded me that I hadn't taken my pain pills. I dug into my jacket pocket for the emergency pill and swallowed it whole and dry. I sat on the hairy carpet with my legs out straight in front of me and pulled Dave's crutches across my lap. It was a pretty good bet nobody in that neighborhood would be busting us for not buckling up.

We circled the block five or six times till Lynette found a spot close enough to the Hyde Street building with no number on the metal front door. She parked in front of Punjab Deli, two doors down from Sally's. I opened Dave's door and handed him the crutches, and the three of us stepped over dog shit—I hoped it was dog shit—on the way to the building door. Flies swarmed the shit. A green plastic bag was sucked against an open vent in the stucco. The old guy on the porch next door was gone, the scruffy-fedora guy was gone, and the drag queen dancing in the street was gone. If anyone was around to see us, they didn't want us to see them.

I opened the door to the building, and there were the damned stairs again. Four flights of treacherous, skinny stairs, this time with Dave on crutches. I started up and waited at the first landing. Dave planted his crutches on the first stair, hoisted himself up, his right knee and bandaged foot up in the air, left foot lightly on the stair. Biting his lower lip, he made it up the second stair. Lynette stayed close behind so she could grab hold of him if he slipped, but up he went, crutch, step, crutch. None of us said a word. Even the crutches sounded like tiptoes.

I wiped sweat from my neck, pressed a palm to my chest to calm my racing heart. We made it to the top and huddled there in a circle to collect ourselves. We had a plan, no need to go over it once again. Lynette smoothed the front of her tunic with her palms, and Dave squeezed on a crutch with his elbow so he could brush his hair back with one hand, as if the addicts might care. We moved all together toward Sally's door. I took off my jacket so the Mets shirt would show. Then Dave pounded on the door so hard it definitely did sound like a cop, but I was the one who yelled, "Sally! We're friends of your mom!"

We heard nothing. According to the scruffy-fedora guy, Sally was supposedly inside getting high right then, probably with Josh and who knew who else. We waited, and waited, and then Lynette tried the social worker knock.

"Sally?" she said. Still nothing.

Dave whispered, "What if they're all passed out? Do we just wait?"

I nodded. We could wait all day.

After another minute, Dave opened his mouth to say something, but before anything came out we heard a whispered "What the fuck?" from the room inside. That was all. It didn't sound like anyone was moving around.

"Sally?" I said softly, and then I put my head down low so I wouldn't jinx the thing. Next to my foot, a hole was worn in the fake tile linoleum, down to the cement floor. Like someone had been standing outside that door knocking for years and years.

Someone was in there, and awake, so I said, neutral as could be, "Sally? Would you mind coming out to talk to us a minute? We're just friends of your mom's."

Just as I was thinking how we'd do this intervention thing standing in the hallway, where Sally could keep shutting the door on us if she ever did come out, or Josh could come out with a gun, or some meth addict could shoot at us right through the door, Lynette yelled at the doorjamb.

"Sally, want to go over to Pearl's Deluxe with us for a burger?"

She knew what she was doing, Lynette. She pulled herself up even taller and breathed her big bosoms out like a shield.

"Best burgers ever, Sally."

Nothing. A whole minute passed, two minutes. Nothing moved, not a sound from Sally or Josh or anyone else. I figured they were all passed out.

Dave was so antsy that, even on crutches, he started to pace. He crutched himself down the hallway, all the way to the window you couldn't see through, and then he turned and crutched himself back. I was nervous, too, but determined to stand my ground. I wiped the sweat above my lip and held my breath, thinking of Rhonda and the despair she covered up with all that Jesus and sweetness and love.

"We just want to tell you how your mom is doing," I said to the door. "Sally?"

I said it gently but afterward bit my lower lip hard.

I stared at the plywood doorframe, just the small piece right in front of me. Purple graffiti, peeling stickers with the names of punk bands: Neurosis, Radioactive Chicken Heads. It seemed we were screwed, and I couldn't believe it. So I prayed, *Just this one thing. God, if you're there, please let us pull it off.* I rubbed my forehead and tried not to cry. Couldn't there be just this one thing? Dave's head was down, shoulders bent over crutches and eyes shut against our failure. Lynette laser-eyed the door, sucking air through her teeth.

A long minute passed like that until I opened my mouth to suggest that maybe we should come back later. Go home, regroup, tend to our own affairs. And just as the words were forming in my head, the way they formed so slowly those days, the metal door opened just a crack.

One inch, two, three between the plywood and the door. A space wide enough for us to see Sally and her to see us. The chain lock crossed her face, but I saw the grooves from her nose down to chalky lips. There were Rhonda's same blue eyes, unfocused, set deep into a face that looked like it was made out of gray paste. Under it somewhere were the high cheekbones and dainty little upturned nose, the cheerleader's lips now pale and thin, wrinkles fanning out on both sides. Sally's skin looked as bad as chemo day plus two. Inflamed pimples on her cheek and chin and eye bags hanging worse than Dave's did when he was lower than low.

I put on the plaster smile, that ghoulish face you can't help putting on when you're more shocked than happy to see someone. She smiled back at me, a slack-jawed stupid smile, two teeth missing on one side, the others cigarette brown. My breath stuck in my throat, and then I remembered why we were there.

Sally unchained the door and opened it the whole way. She stood half in and half out, blinking against the dim light of the hall, looking at none of us in particular. The sleeves of her gray sweatshirt were too long for her arms and filthy at the wrists. She lifted a ropy-veined hand to cover her mouth when she spoke.

"Do you have sixty bucks?"

Her voice was what did it. That little-girl voice, just like Rhonda's, choked me up. I quickly wiped my eye with a knuckle, hoping she wouldn't notice.

"I need to pay a guy, before I see my mom," Sally said. She couldn't care less if I was crying or picking my nose.

"Let's go get something to eat, Sally," I said. "Cup of coffee, okay?"

The fake smile was making my face hurt, but I couldn't help

it. It was just glued on. Dave was plaster-smiling, too, making his eyes big and bobbing his head up and down like you do when an unsteady toddler heads your way. *Come on, come on, that's it, come to me.* Sally stupid-smiled back at us. Lynette was the only one with sense on her face.

"It's just that, just, I can't go anywhere until I pay the guy," Sally said. She kept one hand covering her mouth when she talked, and she waved the other around. Her hair, that beautiful flaxen hair from the pictures, hung dull and flat on her skull, an uneven frizz near her shoulders like she'd cut it herself with a rusty knife.

All I could think of was that we needed to get out of there before Josh grabbed Sally from the doorway or who knows what addict pulled God knew what on us all. I wanted to reach behind Sally and close the door so she'd be out and they'd be in, but I knew that could blow the whole thing. So I stood my ground, sucking in a deep breath, shoulders back, chin out. We wouldn't be buying any addict bullshit. Dave lifted himself up straight. Eyes wide open, hands tight on his crutches, ready to go as soon as Sally opened that door.

"You want coffee, Sally? Breakfast?" I just flat-out ignored what she'd said. I knew enough about addiction to not even try to reason with an addict who was high. I couldn't even reason with Bradley after two Jamesons, and who knew what Sally was on.

"How do you even know my mom? Where is my mom, anyway?"

"Your mother is ill, Sally," I said, moving a couple inches toward her. That close to her, Sally didn't look any more than five feet tall. I felt desperate to connect, desperate to make this right for Rhonda, as if somehow that would also make it right with Bradley, with Marisa, canceling out all the wrong I'd done in my life.

"She has terminal cancer," I said. "She's not well enough to see you unless you're clean." I stopped to let that sink in.

Sally's eyes went from completely dead to scary electrified. Giant black pupils jerked from one side to the other like someone was manipulating them with little wires from behind. She looked at us one at a time, probably wondering which of us had the sixty bucks.

Lynette stretched her arm out to Zen-faced Dave and stupid-smiling me. "These folks are her friends from her cancer group," she said. "They want to do something nice for your mom."

Then sweet Dave jumped in. "The best thing we could do for her is help get you clean, Sally. We know someplace where you'll be comfortable, where you'll be treated well. Better than before."

It didn't seem to register a bit. Sally blinked, stared someplace between Dave and me, and her eyes went dead again. The hallway felt even colder then.

I tried to get us back on track.

"Your mom made our T-shirts!" I said. I pinched mine at the bottom on both sides and stretched it out in front of me so she could see the writing perfectly clear, if she snapped out of her trance long enough to see anything at all. "The Oakland Mets," I said. "Your mom's joke. It's 'mets' for metastatic cancer, Sally."

I didn't have any idea if any of it sank in, but she blinked a couple more times. I put my arm out toward her, wanting her to take my hand. Nothing in those eyes. I grew taller, lifting myself up, and put my hands on my hips, but the voice coming out of me was talking to a three-year-old.

"Why don't you come out and close the door, Sally, so we don't disturb anyone, okay? Thank you."

Just a flicker, the wire pulling Sally's pupils toward me, but that was it. A standoff. But then some force disconnected from Sally's eyes moved her body slightly toward us. She took a step out the door, eyes on Lynette, then Dave, then me. Sally pulled her shoulders in, hugging herself like it was twenty below in that hallway. I sucked in air through a rigid smile.

"That's it," Dave said. His voice was low and calm. Lynette

shot a look at him through slit lids and, sure enough, Dave's voice had been one voice too many. Sally turned her back on us and put a hand on the dented knob.

This was the moment, and none of us made a motion or a sound. No burgers and no rehab if Sally walked back through that door. In my peripheral vision I could see Dave becoming his Marine self, bulked up in his leather jacket, pressing hard on his crutch to stay tall. I knew he was scared shitless, but the mission was underway, god damn it.

"Sally. You want to see your mom before she dies? This is your only chance," Dave said. "You want to see Cassie?"

Then I jumped in. "She's so-ooo cute, Cassie."

The back of Sally's scalp showed in patches under thin, greasy hair. She lifted an old-lady hand and leaned it against the door-frame. All three of us stared at that dented knob as if we could will her from behind, and then she did it. Sally pulled the door closed. She turned to face us.

"Do you have that sixty bucks?"

Lost in her disease. She looked so exposed there, leaning back against the metal door. Her eyes squeezed against even the dim light in the hall.

"You want to see your mom?" I asked again. Sally's head dropped low.

"Let us take you to detox first, Sally," I said, "so you can get ready to see your mom. After you're clean and sober for a little bit, you'll give her a great big hug. You'll get to see Cassie. Nothing would make them happier, Sally. They love you with all their hearts."

I thought, *Jesus, is it stupid to talk about detox right here at the door?* But when I made the switch from burgers to detox just like that, and when we pulled Cassie into it, something clicked. Sally seemed to deflate, to give up and in. She looked more like Rhonda's mother than her child, the way her mouth collapsed over the space where whole teeth should have been. She lifted the filthy gray sweatshirt sleeve to wipe snot and tears.

I moved slowly toward her and rested a hand over her skinny shoulder.

"We know it's hard," I said, almost at a whisper. "We know you can't help it. But right now, you can come with us and get help."

It must have been the "help" that registered, and not in a good way, because Sally flinched back and looked at each of us through her very own undead eyes, as if seeing us and scoping us out for the first time.

It was Dave's turn. He cleared his throat, then said what he'd practiced saying back at the clinic: "We're friends of your mom because we all turned up with cancer at about the same time."

Sally squeezed her eyes closed like she wanted them to go back to that empty space. She shook her head, scratched her scalp through greasy hair.

I brought in the big guns, the closer, the thing we'd practiced the most. Volume up a notch, voice down deep in a place I didn't know I had: "Your choice, Sally. You can help your mom out, or you can keep on suffering and let her suffer until she's gone. Those are the only two choices."

And right then it happened. That high man-boy voice, screaming from behind the door.

"Sally! Fuck are you?"

Sally's eyes opened wide, and the flat darkness disappeared in the clarity of terror. She pressed a bony fist to her mouth, wrapped her other arm tight around herself, and squeezed her elbows as if to make herself small. She turned her head back toward the door. Dave's fists tightened around the grips of his crutches and he lifted his chest up, ready to spring. Lynette stood tall, her face impassive, as if she hadn't heard a thing.

Big tears pooled in Sally's eyes and dripped down the crevices of her cheeks. Just like that, she was full-on crying. Dave moved toward her, moved the left crutch to under his right arm so he could hold both crutches with one big hand. He put his free arm around Sally. She folded herself into him, head under one shoulder and hand up on the other. I waited to hear her sob, but she just breathed into Dave, up, down, slow, deep breaths. Hell, maybe she was falling asleep. At any moment Josh could come swinging through that door. What if he had a gun? But Dave rested there, rocking Sally back and forth, one big palm pressing down her tangled hair. I thought, *We don't have time . . .*

"Let's go," I said. I curled an arm around Sally, and Dave handed Sally off. He put crutches under both his arms and crutched himself back to the skinny stairs. This time, Dave took the lead, and no one was going to slow him down. Hop, lean, hop, lean, hop, lean. Faster than ever, but still too slow down those skinny curving stairs. Halfway down, I heard a loud door squeak and then that voice.

"Sally! Get the fuck back here! I need you back here!" That terrifying voice.

The faster we went, the noisier we were—and we still had one floor to go. Stiff with fear, I handed Sally off to Lynette, whose arms were bigger and steps more solid than mine. At the bottom of the second flight, I looked up, and there were Josh's skinny legs, the bottom of his boxer shorts.

Josh came pounding down the stairs just as we hit the bottom landing. Adrenaline-fueled, I pushed open the heavy metal door to let Sally and Lynette through. Dave, jaw clenched, followed with his crutches, and then I slammed the door behind us all. I didn't know what I was thinking, but I gave a quick look around the sidewalk for something I could pick up and jam against the door, as if there would be a boulder or a log sitting conveniently there instead of just the cigarette butts and dog shit. Lynette pushed Sally by the elbow toward the car. Once Dave was on flat ground, he hauled ass with those crutches, big shoulders heaving up, jeans sagging as he vaulted right past me. I ran to catch up and felt my collarbone throbbing with each long step, worse than before.

Lynette opened the passenger door of Dave's Subaru with one hand, held Sally with the other. Sally looked back at the building but Lynette hunched down in front of her, nudged her into the car, and slammed the door shut. Then Lynette got in the driver's side and I heard the car start. I'd just caught up to Dave, standing by the car door on Sally's side so she wouldn't bolt. Then we heard Josh behind us, screaming.

"Fucking bitches! Sally! Get over here!"

The Subaru still hadn't moved, so Sally for sure could hear Josh yelling at her. There was no time for Dave and me to get in the car, with the crutches and me squeezing into the cage in back. Lynette could get Sally to the detox place on her own.

Skinny-legged, barefoot Josh ran past me, then past Dave.

"Now! Go!" Dave shouted. I heard the clicking of the door lock. Saw Sally's puffy eyes in the window. Lynette turned the steering wheel hard to get out of the parking spot. Josh pounded on the car window with one hand, tried to open the door with the other.

"Get out, you bitch!" he screamed in the high man-boy voice, greasy black hair shaking as he pounded on the car. Lynette cleared the car in front of her and gunned the Subaru, Sally crying, shouting something to Josh through the locked door. We were between them, targets. The back of the Subaru moved down Eddy Street, rolled to the corner, and turned left at the light, heading toward the Bay Bridge. Ten miles to detox and Day One.

Sally was safe, but that maniac addict was just a few yards away from us, a tight wire of rage, stringy hair flying, bad teeth in a growl. Dave on crutches, me with no strength at all, terrified, out of breath, and collarbone throbbing from just that little run. No way for us to get around the corner and back to Dave's clinic faster than Josh.

For a second I froze, thinking what a surprise it was that we'd wind up dying this way instead. And suddenly, at that moment, I didn't mind. We'd done this one thing. Sally was on her way, and I was too elated to be scared.

Josh kicked at Dave's left crutch, knocking it out from under him, and what happened next I guess you'd call a miracle. First, Josh grabbed at me, and when I felt his grimy hands squeeze my arm, a huge, echoing roar erupted from me, I have no idea from what mysterious place.

"*Get* off me!" I yelled. The whole block shook with that yell, I swear to God. I cut hard with my elbow to shake him off, and my bone shot through with pain so bad I screamed. Dave stood up strong on both feet and grabbed the right crutch with both his hands, like a baseball bat. He swung hard at Josh's arm, just above where he had hold of me; Josh screeched and let go. Then he crouched over and moaned—a ruined, angry addict on the sidewalk in pain.

Dave tucked the crutch back under his arm and we got the hell out of there, him vaulting, me trotting along, pain in my collarbone, pain in Dave's face with each step. At the end of the block, we turned to look back. Josh stood, shouting, and then he stumbled toward us. We hadn't even made it around the corner yet.

"Go!" Dave said it loud enough for me but not for Josh to hear, and his crutches went way out ahead of him. Who knew if Josh would forget we were there when he couldn't see us anymore, or whether he fell down again in pain, or whether he'd gone back to the apartment to get a gun. So we kept running, fast as we could for people our ages with mets, one on crutches and both in pain.

Dave propelled himself on the crutches so fast I could hardly keep up. Around the corner, down the block, running and vaulting like Paralympians, all the way across the first crosswalk, cars squealing to a stop. Past the liquor store and dry cleaner and halal meat market. Past ugly apartment buildings and SROs and a Victorian squeezed in between, vault-trot-vault, Dave's pants sagging down, me breathing with my mouth wide open, heart banging, collarbone screaming at me. Still, with all that craziness and fear and pain between us, those six blocks back to Dave's flew by. We were bathed in brilliance, the two of us, after what we'd pulled off.

Never mind how our bodies felt, or the soggy air, or the flat gray sky. I was so pumped that when we got to Dave's clinic, I passed it right by. Dave yelled at me, "Liz! We're here!" and I turned, stopped, and leaned over, holding my knees.

Then out of Dave's mouth came something between a sob and a laugh. The creases by his eyes turned upward, and I could see that his whole big body relaxed over the crutches. He showed his molars in the biggest smile. In seconds we were both laughing, so loud and so hard, doubled over with gulping-air laughter.

"Should we call Rhonda right now?" I asked when we'd gotten it all out.

"No," he said. Deep exhale. "No. We should wait."

Wrung out, at peace, we went through Dave's door.

Inside the clinic, Dave passed the exam table and dug into his jeans pocket for some keys. I hadn't even noticed the door at the back of the room before. It was painted the same battleship gray as the walls and looked like one of those doors to nowhere, painted so many times it appeared welded to the wall, as if you'd need a crowbar to open it and when you did you'd find behind it nothing but concrete. Dave twisted a key into the knob and opened the door to a perfectly lovely room, a funky sanctuary just big enough for an overstuffed sofa and chair plus a sink and long counter over six drawers, the counter and walls painted deep persimmon and the drawers and cement floor a calming sage. There was a mini-fridge, a coffeemaker, and, on the persimmon-colored counter, a little basket filled with herbal teas.

Dave leaned one crutch against the sink and squeezed the other under his left shoulder, and then he hiked his pants back up to his waist with his free hand. "Have a seat," he said. He poured water into a kettle.

I didn't sit. I wanted to help him but didn't want him to think

I was helping him, and, besides, I was feeling so hyped and powerful after what we'd done I could hardly be still, so I just stood there behind him, bouncing on my toes.

"High-test coffee? Herbal tea? Earl Grey?" His back was to me, canvas shirt hanging over his jeans, jeans no longer sagging below his butt, hair grown into steely waves.

We both decided on the Earl Grey, and I asked, "Where are the cups?" because I couldn't stop myself from butting in and helping. I started opening drawers. "I see them," I said before he could answer. Two mugs, the kind I hadn't seen since the 1970s, in a blue and gray and brown starburst print from Japan that was all the rage at Cost Plus, when Cost Plus was all the rage. The mugs felt like home.

I put the tea bags in the cups, poured the water, and then, bossy me, told Dave to sit down in his own room.

"Liz, Liz, Liz," he said. But he sat down in the chair and I brought him his tea. We took a few silent sips, me on the sofa, Dave on the chair, settling in with our feat. I found pain meds stashed in my pocket and swallowed them with the first sip of tea. The pain crashed me down to earth, bringing with it a lead ball of doubt.

"Dave," I said. "What makes us think that this time will be different? I mean, I'll always be glad we tried, but she's already been through rehab more than once, and she wound up right back in that godforsaken shooting gallery with Josh."

All that euphoria was slipping into hopelessness, and Dave must've seen it on my face.

"You can't go there," he said. He gave me that on-the-edge-of-yelling look, steel-wire brows close together, but then, just like that, with a long quiet breath, his face got soft again.

"There is always hope," he said. "Lynette knows her rehabs. She pulled some strings. You can bet Sally will be covered for ninety days, not the useless twenty-eight the insurance companies approve." He took a sip of Earl Grey. "If it comes down to it, I'll pay."

I started to say something about how generous that was, but then I didn't because it sank in why Dave thought he could pay. It stopped my breath for a second, remembering why Dave wasn't saving for the long term. He placed his mug on the floor, calm as could be, and I did the same. I settled back on a flowered cushion. Pain meds kicking in, dulling hopelessness and euphoria alike, putting me into the place of simply okay. Which was the place we both needed to be. The place Dave already was; I could see it then. Could feel it, the soft, slow relaxation of my shoulders, my back, the ease of my next breath. Acceptance.

I breathed in acceptance. Three deep, long breaths, for Bradley, for Marisa, for myself. A kind of relief settled in with the feeling that what Dave had been saying was true. Reality was something you didn't have to like, or change, only accept. I could try improving things with Marisa, but I might not be able to. I took another breath to let that settle in.

"Sally will get clean or she won't," I said. "We'll have to accept it either way. Same as we have to accept whatever happens to us."

"True," Dave said. "You've got to have hope, but sometimes things just don't work out."

Simple as that. Great big beautiful Dave, lifting his mug of tea, the mug so tiny in his fists, his eyes crinkling around the edges. His cheekbones were beginning to show. Sometimes things just didn't work out. I swallowed hard.

Chapter 23

I waited till 8:00 p.m. to call Marisa, imagining she'd be done with work and dinner and, even if she'd brought work home, might be up for a break. She picked up immediately.

"Mom. Are you okay?"

"Good grief. Yes, I'm okay. I just wanted to tell you about my adventure."

It occurred to me right then that I'd never told Marisa about any of my adventures, and I wondered briefly whether it was because I'd never really had any or because, in all our programmed, back-to-back activity, I hadn't really shared much of my life with her.

She seemed genuinely amazed as I told her about what had happened, interjecting, "Are you kidding me?" and, "I don't believe it!" at the tale of Josh, Dave's swinging his crutch, our running away, and Sally going off in the Subaru with a prayer of getting clean.

I gabbed on more than I ever had, finally stopping myself with a great sigh and laughter that trailed off into silence.

"Jeez, Mom. I don't even know what to say," Marisa said. There was a pause then. Disapproval? After all, I'd told her about Dave and Rhonda, but only the bare essentials, and spilling all this out about addicts and whatnot might have given her the wrong idea.

But it wasn't my story she was thinking about.

"I have news too," she said.

"Oh my gosh, a boyfriend?"

I heard her deep sigh. "Why is it when women say they have news, we always assume it's about a guy?"

I was only slightly disappointed. I did hope Marisa would find someone and that I could meet him, know she'd be happy in a relationship. But this was probably about work. A promotion, I expected.

"No, it's about work," she said. Why had I even considered anything else? "I'm quitting the firm, Mom."

My heart stopped a moment. All her life, I'd been wrapped up in Marisa's school, in success after success. I'd always praised her persistence, the way she shot for high goals and didn't stop until she reached them. Now she was an associate at one of the biggest firms in LA, on the partner track.

"You're quitting?" I tried not to sound judgmental, but it probably came across that way.

"I've thought about it a lot," she said. "Don't think I'm just doing it for you." That hadn't even occurred to me. "But that is a part of it. Knowing you're sick made me think about being down here and what I'm doing with my life, and the truth is that I don't like it. At all, Mom. I don't like LA, and I hate working at a big law firm. The sooner I quit, the sooner I'll figure out something else to do. And whatever it is, it's going to be in Northern California, not here. I want to come home."

My God. I didn't know my own daughter. My initial instinct, fear for her jumping off into the unknown like that, almost instantly gave way to joy.

"Marisa! I'm so . . . excited for you! You'll figure it out. You don't need to stay in a job you don't like." How I wish I'd told myself the same, years before. Then the magnitude of it hit me. "Oh my gosh, you're moving back up here?" Tears rolled down my cheeks, and I hoped she couldn't tell that I could barely keep myself from sobbing.

"Yes, and one more thing. I thought that before I get tied down in another job, maybe we could take a trip?"

A trip? But she had to pack up her apartment, and find a place, and move, job hunt . . . I opened my mouth to point this out and shut it immediately, then said, "God, I'd love to," more tears flowing. I covered the phone and blew my nose. Marisa was making possible her version of my experience, sitting on Mom's bed in her precious last months. Now I could see that wasn't codependence; it was simply love. Here I'd been afraid cancer would come between me and Marisa, keep us from getting close, and it was cancer that had opened the opportunity.

"So I've got time to plan," she said. I thought, *Here it comes, the itinerary she's already mapped out and paid for.* But next she said, "I know you like to plan too. Where would you like to go?"

I felt as if my body would float above the kitchen counter, and I could barely speak for smiling so wide.

"How about Alaska?"

Chapter 24

I couldn't wait to tell Rhonda my news. She was home and sounded dreamy and spaced out, her voice thinner, airier than usual, but she exclaimed joyfully when I told her about Marisa. Her own news was good, too, she said. Some people had come over from the choir, and they'd even sung a little together, with Eldon on the piano and Cassie clapping her hands. They sang Rhonda's favorite, "His Eye Is on the Sparrow," full-on gospel version.

"God in the room," Rhonda said. I told her I wished I'd been there.

Lynette told us it was best to wait at least two weeks before letting Rhonda know what we'd done, in case Sally bailed and wound up back with Josh, because that would surely make Rhonda feel worse than if we'd done nothing at all. So Dave and I set the next Oakland Mets meeting for two and a half weeks after picking Sally up, shooting once again for early jazz night at Caffe Trieste.

Dave talked to Rhonda a couple days later and reported back to me. "The nosebleeds keep coming back," he said, "but you know Rhonda; she was all chirpy and worried about us."

Meanwhile, I was back to my routine of walks, talks with Kate and Gabriela and my sister, a couple dinners on the patio. I was finally able to tell Gabriela the truth about Alaska and hear her laugh, "No!" I listened for hours to Kate talking about her latest inappropriate romance, a guy at the office who was separated but not divorced, almost but not quite attainable, like Lyle, like Bradley, like the preceding lovers in Kate's life. When I pointed that out, she got prickly and defensive, so I apologized and decided I'd just listen. "Love you, my friend," I said. "Ditto," she responded again.

I had Whitney Houston in my head, singing "His Eye Is on the Sparrow," for three whole days after talking to Rhonda, and I didn't even know half the words. That morning, I was humming it as I dumped frozen blueberries into the yogurt in the blender and buttered my multigrain toast. I'd planned to call Dave right after breakfast to see how he was doing, but he beat me to it.

"Rhonda's slipping," Dave said.

I sat down right where I was, on my kitchen floor.

He cleared his throat. "Eldon called to say she's back in the hospital." He sniffed. "The nosebleeds wouldn't stop at all this time. And the tumor's sticking out now, beginning to ooze, he said. Eldon was crying, Liz."

I picked at the linoleum with my right hand, left squeezing the phone to my ear.

"So . . . *fast?*" I said. "How could the tumor grow so fast?" I pictured the bad part of Rhonda's face, bulging, and had the desperate thought that doctors must be cutting it out, because surely they could get rid of something sticking right out of her face. And then she'd be better . . . but then Dave repeated himself.

"She's *slipping*, Liz. In and out of consciousness. Family's there and . . . we need to go, now."

Dave said he'd call me as soon as he was across the Bay Bridge, and I said I'd wait for him on the corner of Park Boulevard and East Twenty-Second.

"I got word to Lynette," Dave said. "She'll get Sally if she can."

I rose from the floor, went into the bathroom, filled the sink with hot water, and started splashing my face—scooping the hot water up, splashing, scooping, splashing, over and over again. I scrubbed dry with a towel and ran a brush through my wet hair.

Then I panicked. Had twenty minutes passed? No, just six. It was 9:42 a.m.

I took off my sweatshirt, put on the stretched-out bra, and put the Oakland Mets shirt on over that. *Where the hell is my jacket?* I grabbed my purse and jacket from the sofa, went out the kitchen door, double-locked the door, and then ran down the brick walkway, under the sycamore and across the soggy grass to the sidewalk. Dave was not waiting on the corner. Hondas passed, a motorcycle, a BMW, a Camry. UPS passed. An elderly Chinese woman, hunched over with too many plastic grocery bags, walked past.

Whitney Houston in my head. *His eye is on the sparrow, so something something on me.* I tried to yoga breathe and with the deep inhale felt a stabbing pain on my collarbone. Still, I inhaled breath deep into my chest and down through my torso and both my legs, my feet, through the sidewalk and into the earth. Exhaled breath up from the earth into my legs and torso, on up and out my scalp. Breath back in and down through the sidewalk. I shivered. A Hyundai passed. No Subaru. *Something because I'm free, something something over me.*

Dave pulled up ten minutes or half an hour later. Dave with his Mets shirt on, canvas shirt unbuttoned over that.

I got into the Subaru and he started driving before I buckled in. Neither one of us said a word, but I reached around him and gave his neck a squeeze. He turned to me, lips trembling, then swallowed hard and turned back to the road. I rested my hand on his right shoulder.

Dave drove like a kamikaze, through every single yellow light, and of course every light we came to was yellow turning red. He hunched over the wheel, his whole body pushing the car forward, eyes straight ahead. When we got to the light at Broadway and Pleasant Valley, it had already turned red, but Dave kept right on going. My hands were damp with sweat and my breath went only as deep as my throat. Beside us, the driver of a BMW slammed on the brakes. "Dave! You'll kill us before we get there!" I yelled, but Dave was yelling at the same time. "Out of the way, asshole!" Those were the only words we spoke on that drive.

We got out of the car in the hospital parking lot, slammed the doors, and ran as fast as we could.

Rhonda was in 420A, and the elevator stopped at floors two and three, where a man and pregnant woman got off and an old guy with a walker and six family members got on. One of them pressed the OPEN DOOR button when they figured out the elevator was going up.

"Just stay in!" one of them yelled. I felt my teeth grinding hard, back to front. *Eye is on the sparrow and something something on me.* The elevator buzzed but still didn't move. Dave's shoulder was at the level of my forehead, our bodies pressed together.

On four, the elevator door opened and we were hit with that familiar smell of hospital food and bleach. We'd been down that long shiny hallway, both of us, so many times before. Past the woman in the teddy bear scrubs, past the boy-faced intern carrying a clipboard, past the rolling metal meal cart, plates covered with gray plastic domes.

That morning, all those things were exactly the same as always, but there was something different too; I didn't know what. A huge Spanish-speaking family gathered around 412A, and we had to get by, Dave gripping my arm and pushing me forward, plowing through and saying, "'Scuse us, 'scuse us, please."

Someone called too loudly on the intercom for a doctor to pick up a phone.

We passed 414A, machines beeping, too many people talking, buzzing and lights and rolling carts all at once, and, wait, it was too much, something was wrong. We passed 416A and B and saw a big-shouldered orderly pulling a gurney from the room two doors down. The rest of the gurney appeared, a small long mound with a sheet over it. A woman in green scrubs and purple

Nikes pushed the gurney out of the room as the orderly pulled it around, into the hall.

I wanted them to get out of the way. I turned to Dave, expecting him to be thinking the same thing: *Hurry up and move that thing so we can get in the room to our friend.* Then I felt Dave's crushing grip on my arm, and I looked again at the gurney.

I forgot how to breathe.

Behind the gurney came the people. Eldon, hands over his face, his whole upper body shaking. Eldon who always looked so sharp, wearing a stretched-out Raiders shirt over dirty jeans. A man and a woman who were holding Eldon up, one at each of his arms. Then two other people, a teenager in sweats, a middle-aged woman in a thick coat, hugging her waist. And then Lynette, her arm around a slim blonde woman with a small nose and strong chin, lips squeezed tight and tears streaming down her face.

My cheek pressed into the sleeve of Dave's canvas shirt, but I hadn't even looked up at him because I couldn't stop staring, wondering who those people were and what had happened and how had it happened so fast? Then I realized that the young woman with Lynette was Sally. Sally cleaned up, soft blonde hair to her shoulders, wearing a white blouse, black slacks, and brand-new Puma flats. She turned in slow motion to look toward the gurney as it was pushed down the hall.

Neither Dave nor I moved. We stayed back, hardly breathing, Dave's arm around my shoulder, my arm around his waist, both of us just staring down the hall as the gurney was pushed around a corner and disappeared.

Lynette's face looked older, lined and serious, her thick hair hanging loose over the shoulders of a gray fisherman's sweater, every bit of her gray. When she glanced up from Sally and saw us, Lynette gave a quick lift of her chin and, at the level of her hip, a thumbs-up.

Wondering what she meant, I turned to Dave. For a second I thought she was letting us know it was a mistake, that it wasn't

Rhonda on the gurney. We'd been mistaken. All these people in the hallway were just taking a break. Then I felt a tiny shiver. We weren't mistaken.

I leaned on Dave's shoulder, smelling his sweat and shaving cream and medicine underneath. Somewhere in that deep, enveloping sadness was the briefest feeling that it was all right. I heard myself whisper, "Do you think Rhonda saw her?"

"Maybe," Dave said.

I don't know why the hallway went silent, but the beeping and buzzing and clattering of carts, the talking and announcing on the intercom, it all seemed to have stopped. Lynette guided Sally in the direction of the gurney, and they walked past Eldon and the others and down the hall. The people surrounding Eldon started moving him down the hallway, too, heading the same direction as the gurney, same direction as Sally and Lynette. Dave took one step and I stepped with him. Slow steps forward, then faster toward Eldon and the others.

Dave spoke up then, loud Dave, the only sound in the hallway. "Eldon," Dave said.

Everyone turned.

Eldon looked in our direction, but I could tell he didn't get who we were. His puffy eyes blinked slowly. He opened his mouth and pulled in a sharp, deep breath and then nodded at us. He raised his head and straightened his shoulders, delivering to us the news, repeating the news to himself, saying the news out loud.

"She passed."

His eye is on the sparrow, and I know he watches me.

Chapter 25

I spent the next two days crying, walking, lying on my heating pad, and crying some more until I was hollowed out, in that altered state that comes when death is so close by. It's the sensation that there is no this side or that side or place of passing through. When someone you love dies, it seems like you'll always be in that state. You get it. You believe you'll live better always because of how deeply you've felt, the profoundness of what you've seen. Life has more meaning; colors are sharper and trees more alive. You will live in this altered state forever.

I so wanted to honor Rhonda and stay within the altered state.

I was the one who was crying and Dave sounded hollowed out when he called to say he'd spoken by phone with Eldon, who told him the one thing we both wanted to hear. Dave's voice was soft, barely above a whisper.

"She wasn't in any pain, Liz," he said. "They managed to keep her out of pain."

"And Sally?"

"Lynette got her there in time. Rhonda was barely conscious, but Sally was able to say goodbye."

They say that people on their way out, even when they can't speak or open their eyes, can hear. It's the kind of thing I believe in, but I didn't think Dave would. I could hear him breathe on the phone. We were silent for a bit, and then Dave spoke with conviction.

"I know it," he said. "I know Rhonda heard."

We went to Alive! Ministry of the Word Church together in the Subaru. I'd given up driving altogether because of my meds. Instead of Dave's crutches, there was a wheelchair in back for him, not only because the blisters were bad on both feet by then but also because his hip just gave out all of a sudden two days after Rhonda died. To tell the truth, neither one of us should've been driving at all, but even if we were both stoned out of our minds on meds, there was no way we were going to take a taxi to Rhonda's funeral. It just didn't seem right.

Dave was getting scary skinny too. The grooves in his face were folds.

"She was lucky," Dave said. He kept his eyes on the road.

"She was," I said.

Dave reached over and gave my knee a firm squeeze. He took his eyes off the road just long enough to give me a look that told me that everything I was feeling, he was feeling too: *This is how it will go. I would've gone before lovely Rhonda. I hope she knew how we loved her. Of course she knew how we loved her. Thank God there was no pain. Will there be pain?*

He pressed his lips hard together, eyes red from crying but the steel in them still so strong and fierce. Everything about Dave seemed to be shrinking, but his eyes were bright as ever, piercing from the hollows above his cheekbones.

"Do you feel bad we didn't get to say goodbye?" I asked. "Because that morning when Rhonda died, just seeing her body being wheeled by like that, it felt so horrible. It seemed so wrong. I couldn't get to sleep that night, but when I finally did and then woke up in the middle of the night, I knew for sure. Rhonda didn't want us to have to say goodbye."

Dave let out a noisy sigh. "God. That was so Rhonda," he said.

"And then it hit me," I said. "What have we been doing all this time, anyway? We've been saying goodbye."

Dave nodded, eyes on the road. I didn't expect to see loud, pissed-off Dave anymore. Just this okay-with-it-all Dave. Zen Dave. But there was something I wasn't okay with, and I needed to tell him before we got to the church.

His body hunched over the steering wheel, though we were under the speed limit, slowing for a light.

"Rhonda was a much better person than I am," I said. "I mean, Dave? I do want you to be there."

Dave slowed the car, half a block from the church. We were on busy Fruitvale Avenue, and Dave put on his blinker and cut into the lane on his right, then pulled over to the curb behind a bus stop. He set the parking brake. Then he turned to me, opened his eyes wide, and just stared. It almost scared me, how intense those eyes were. Maybe he wasn't done with being pissed off after all. But then he reached over and lifted my hand and put both of his hands around it. And he spoke in the gentlest voice I'd ever heard.

"No matter who goes first," he said. "We're there."

I leaned over, lifted my chin, and kissed him on his bony cheek.

From the outside, the church looked like a big-box store with a steeple glued on top. The parking lot was huge and packed with everything from scruffy Toyota pickups to brand-new Escalades. We pulled into one of the last spaces, and I got out, opened the hatchback, and took out the wheelchair.

Dave was okay getting into the chair by himself, standing up on both feet just for the second it took to get from car to chair. When he settled in, I grabbed the handles behind him and started to push the chair. Dave turned his head back to me and said, "No, ma'am." His long arms were like sticks, but he pulled them back and then turned the wheels himself.

So in we went, side by side, my steps measured by the rotation of Dave's wheels, until we made it up the handicapped ramp to the crowded foyer of the church. A skinny African American teenager with acne and mustache fuzz stood behind a table. He was wearing a black suit and dress shirt, both a size too big. He handed each of us a program with Rhonda's photograph on the cover. There was a long line behind us, but Dave and I stopped right there, blocking the entrance, staring at Rhonda's face.

"Oh, look at how beautiful she was," Dave said. Rhonda beaming in her choir robe, beaming with her own teeth in her own perfect face.

"Her hair," I said.

I felt a heavy hand on my shoulder and turned to see the big woman we'd met weeks earlier in Rhonda's hospital room. She was wearing a black silk suit, a heavy gold cross dangling over a cream-colored blouse.

Too many feelings at once. Remembering the discomfort at the hospital and realizing we were blocking the line, and that there we were in this woman's church and I couldn't remember her name. I put on the same fake hospital grin and grabbed the handle of Dave's wheelchair to move us along. But the woman pushed out her magenta lips, looked down at me with her huge, penciled-over eyes, and saw straight into my soul, I swear to God. She opened her arms wide, and before I could move she folded me up with her arms and held me, strong and soft, right there in the line. I smelled her Chanel No. 5 and felt the stiff silk of her suit before I finally relaxed in her heavy embrace.

"Oh, baby, I am so sorry," she said. And the way she said it, I could've stayed folded into her that way for the rest of my life. She patted my back a few times, and then she opened her arms, turned, and leaned over to hug Dave, too, down in his chair.

"I am so sorry, baby," she said to Dave.

At home in her church, she was the most welcoming person in the world. I guess she must have hated hospitals too.

"You know Rhonda's in a better place. Yes, she is," the woman said. Faye. That was her name. Oh, to be in the presence of someone who truly believes. What a comfort it is to be wrapped in that certainty when you need it the most. I had no idea how badly I needed it, but there it was, and I was so grateful for the relief that was Faye.

"Now you two come on inside," she said.

We found seats near the back, where there was room for Dave to put his chair next to me on the aisle seat of the worn wooden pew. I put my purse and sweater on the two spaces next to me, saving them for Sally and Lynette. I didn't know for sure if they'd make it to the service, whether Lynette would have a hard time with Sally or the rehab counselors or decide on her own that it was best for Sally not to come. If anything was a recipe for relapse, watching your mother die would have to be it. We couldn't know if Sally would make it at all. Knowing that Cassie was left with Eldon could help her stay clean, or it could give her an out to go back and use again. We couldn't know. But she had looked so good physically in the hospital that morning. There had to be hope.

In the front pew I could see Eldon and, next to him, the top of little Cassie's blonde head. There must have been two hundred people in the church already, Black and white and brown, Asian, Caucasian, African American. A man in a yarmulke and a woman whose headscarf made me think of Rhonda that day at the A's game. All of Rhonda's neighbors and probably everyone who ever worked in the courthouse, plus Eldon's friends and their choir's friends. Practically all of Oakland was there to say goodbye.

One by one the choir filed in, filling the whole of the altar, behind a border of huge floral arrangements: white lilies, gold and white chrysanthemums, yellow gerbera daisies. Dozens of people in deep green robes with stiff ivory collars formed three rows behind the flowers. Every face black or brown. In the front row, two women moved apart, creating a space between them. Rhonda's space. How white she would have looked there, and how at home.

Just as I was about to completely lose it, a drumbeat started. Then horns blared, and in came a saxophone and piano chords. It was a finger-snapping, jump-out-of-your-seat happy sound. Faye, now wearing her choir robe, stepped forward on the altar, opened her arms wide, and sang.

"Every time I look around," Faye sang.

"*Somebody's gone!*" sang the choir.

She sang a verse, and the whole choir responded, and then everyone clapped and the whole room shook with the glorious, enormous sound. Afternoon sun hit the stained glass panels, a multicolored cross behind the choir.

I closed my eyes and saw Rhonda up on the altar singing with those ladies. Singing praise, singing love.

"Well, it's every time I look around!" Faye belted it out, deep.

"*Somebody's gone!*"

"Sooomebody's gone on home!"

Oh, I could barely stand it; the tears just poured from my eyes. I reached over to link my elbow with Dave's, and I felt his body shake from weeping too. But then everyone in the church stood, so I stood with them, and Dave pushed down on the arms of his wheelchair and he stood too. We held each other up and wiped our faces, and then we joined in and clapped, the whole universe clapping with us.

"Somebody's gone on home!" Dave's voice sang so loud, loud as the choir, and that was just fine.

"Going home!" Faye sang. "Going home! I'm going to put on the long white robe!"

Even I sang along with the choir. The piano chords pounded out praise, and a horn played along with the drum. I saw Rhonda in her robe, filling the space left for her on the altar, arms out, singing with the choir.

"*Going home!*"

"Got to go home!" Dave sang it. I sang it. Hundreds of us sang it loud.

"Lay down the heavy burden!"

"*Put on the robe of glory. Shout and tell the story!*"

"Well, the wicked will cease from troubling. And the weary shall be at rest. Shall I meet you there?"

"*Got to go home one day!*"

After

*M*arisa organized everything, of course, mostly according to Liz's wishes. This was the last and smallest Oakland Mets send-off, so it was held in the core of that city, in Preservation Park. The venue, decidedly secular, was a block-sized square of lawn and shrubbery, surrounded by colorful, beautifully preserved Victorian homes, now housing nonprofits and professional offices.

Dressed in a sleeveless black sheath, Marisa carried a mic on a stand to the shaded concrete stage. She had prepared remarks, and she knew Lynette wanted to say a few words. There might be brief remembrances by someone from Liz's work life, though not Lyle, specifically not Lyle.

Dave's brother, Brent, was there, nearly as tall as Dave and a striking contrast to the mostly casual East Bay crowd in a gray business suit. His face resembled Dave's—the unruly eyebrows, the creases from cheekbone to jowl—but his eyes had the vacant look that grief brings. Brent had barely known Liz, but his brother had been gone only six months, the same amount of time they'd had together as adults, truly brothers once again. Liz's passing made his grief fresh, as searing as the day they scattered Dave. Brent wondered where in the Pacific those ashes floated now.

A cellist played Bach at the corner of the stage; this, Marisa had added to Liz's plan. She did go along, though reluctantly, with Liz's food requests, even though they'd argued over the fact that none of the people who'd appreciate the menu's meaning would be present that day. As the cellist played, Cassie ran around on the lawn. Eldon, Sally, Brent, Liz's neighbors, her friend Kate, and assorted strangers from the PR firm settled themselves in white folding chairs. A brown-skinned man in a white shirt, white cap, and black apron prepped the buffet. There'd be a steamer tray of Polish dogs with sauerkraut, plates heaped with churros, and nachos with unreal orange cheese-like sauce, served in red-checked cardboard boats. A keg of beer and pitchers of lemonade sat on a separate table, hung with a bright yellow-and-green-striped cloth. It was all the forbidden food that had tasted so good to Liz, Dave, and Rhonda on their first outing to a ball game, the day Rhonda got the idea to call their group the Oakland Mets.

Marisa gritted her teeth as she watched the caterer dump corn chips into cardboard boats, but the sight triggered a memory of her mother so sharp she began to laugh and sob at the same time. That day they'd argued about the food. All the arguments before. The pride in Liz's eyes. Tears spotted the pages where Marisa had printed her remarks in 16-point type, and she gave herself silent orders: *Pull it together!* At the same time, she felt an arm wrap around her shoulder and turned to look into the dark, kind eyes of Eldon.

"It's okay, Marisa," he said, squeezing her arm. "It's okay." His sympathy would have led Liz to fall apart, and Marisa was no longer impervious to compassionate gestures. She inhaled deeply, gave Eldon a wan smile, and pulled herself up, mumbling thanks. Edging away, she reached into a small black Chanel clutch for a tissue, wiped her eyes, and turned to stride toward center stage.

She tapped the mic, cleared her throat, and said in a clear, strong voice, "Thank you for coming." Soft chatter fell to silence from the few dozens of people in the chairs. She looked at the crowd and saw Bradley, her father, beaming up at her as if she were onstage to receive an award.

"My mother . . ." She caught her breath, then inhaled and

started again. "My mother, Liz, was strong. Growing up, I didn't always see that. It wasn't until recently that I realized how hard she worked to keep it together, how she tried to keep me happy even at times when she was not.

"It wasn't until she got sick that I realized how brave she was."

How was Marisa to know that Liz hated being called brave? No matter, she'd like that her daughter was up there, saying nice things.

Marisa went on about how her mother went overboard sometimes, drawing chuckles with the story about Liz compulsively shopping at J.Crew for a sullen teenager who only wanted to wear torn black jeans. She talked about their trip to Alaska, how Liz had booked two suites on a small ship for a cruise up the Inside Passage, just eighteen months before she died. She hadn't been strong enough to hike, but they'd seen whales and bears. They'd talked and talked, and they'd laughed more than they had in all her time growing up.

"The ship had a schedule of activities for us from morning till night," Marisa said. "And all of you who knew my mom for most of her life would imagine her showing up for every presentation, every zodiac trip, every early morning yoga stretch and afternoon naturalist talk. You'd imagine both of us spending the whole trip like that."

She paused a moment, cleared her throat, and squeezed in her lips. "But you know what?" She cleared her throat again. "This trip was different. For both of us. We waited until the very last minute to decide what we'd do. And half the time the decision was simple. We'd do nothing. Not that looking out the big picture window at glaciers passing by was nothing. It's just that . . . in some ways, her illness was a gift, and Mom recognized that. I was so lucky to share that gift with her.

"And, finally, I need to tell you that in the end of her life, my mom was a member of an exclusive support group—the Oakland Mets. Most of you don't know about that name or the dark joke behind it," Marisa said. "But thanks to Mom's request that we honor their group with the ballpark food here today, it may linger with you longer than you'd like!"

She heard Eldon's high laugh and mutterings from the rest of the crowd. Heads turned to the caterer, who was placing hot dog buns onto a platter.

When Lynette took the stage, in black midi, tights, and thick-soled Mary Janes, she talked about how Liz had brought a special end-of-life friendship to her beloved Dave.

". . . and, at some personal risk, the two of them took it upon themselves to make certain that their friend Rhonda would die at peace."

She hadn't mentioned drugs or the creepy, hopped-up boyfriend, didn't even mention Rhonda's daughter. Lynette managed to give Liz and Dave credit while keeping Sally and her struggles anonymous. She was to be the last speaker, but as Lynette descended from the stage, another woman stood up and walked slowly toward it. She had Rhonda's flawless, creamy skin. Her blonde hair shone, and her cheeks were rosy from a year of healthy habits, but her drug-ruined teeth still needed repair.

"I hardly knew Liz," Sally said, shifting her weight from one foot to the other. "But I know she and her friend Dave did two big things." She paused, gulped, and covered her mouth. Then she gripped her hands at her waist, took a breath, and looked, one by one, into the faces of Marisa, Lynette, and Eldon.

"All I can say is, I'm here because of her and Dave. She brought me back to my family." Her eyes and mouth both squeezed tight. She inhaled deeply and finished through tears. "And that gave my mother some peace. She got to rest. They helped each other to rest."

Acknowledgments

So many people have been supportive of this novel, making it possible for me to make a literary debut after age seventy.

I thank Michael Kennedy, for his expertise in graphics and baseball, and Marlene Vogelsgang, fan and expert on all things Oakland A's. I acknowledge David Jacome and peermusic, for the rights to lyrics from the gospel song "Somebody's Gone on Home."

I thank The Riverside World Affairs Council, without whose encouragement, multiple readings, and patient friendship I may have given up: Mary Ellen Shay, Cindy Zettel, and Karen Swett—RWAC Forever. Sacramento's own Rotting Flesh and friends: Jay Schenirer, Bina Lefkovitz, and Todd and Jennifer Kaufman. Also, Tim and Debbie Zeff, Lynn Belzer, Michael and Barbara Ullman, and Hope and Jeff Rabinowitz, all of whom shared in the ups and downs of this project, along with dear friends Deb Kennedy, Kathleen Golden, Kathie Smith, Suzanne Tacheny Kubach, and Hilary Abramson for their supportive ears and honest critiques. For years, Boston bestie and brilliant writer Martine Tabilio, has never failed to get it.

Deborah Payne and Jane Bergquist, dear friends and cheerleaders forever, kept me going through the pandemic, along with Cheryll Cochrane, writing partner and mischief buddy. My dear friend Larry Smith of Oakland has for years kept my spirits up, helped me regain confidence, and filled my heart with his music. I also thank Hugh Delehanty and Barbara Graham for their encouragement, advice and friendship. My beloved Thursday AWA writing group, a constant source of joy and support: Jan Hartwig, Kay Curtis, Gail Braverman, Inge Taylor, Candace Suerstedt-Eckel, Kathy Jay, Nancy Anton, Becky LaVally, and Elisabeth Kersten.

I am grateful to Tiffany Yates Martin, for her wise counsel and editing expertise, and to Russell Rowland, who steered me through the earliest stages of this project. Shannon Green with She Writes Press has been remarkably responsive and supportive throughout the process of moving from final draft to published book, and I am so thankful she has been my project manager. Publisher Brooke Warner is a marvel, and the She Writes model of collaborative sisterhood has been a joy to experience.

Several writers organizations have given me inspiration, space, and instruction along the way. I thank San Diego Writers, Ink for creating an encouraging and inviting community for writers; the Community of Writers for providing rich and inspiring workshops and a spectacular summer gathering of writers; and Everwood Farmstead for gifting me a beautiful space to write in solitude.

I thank my sisters, Janet Bodle, MD, and Laura Bancroft, RN, who've been a source of friendship and support in both my writing and my health, and Dr. Delphine Ong, oncologist and friend.

This book would not be possible without the loving support of my husband, Irwin Karp, who put up with endless hours of silence, closed doors, and distractedness, nonetheless lauding my progress all the way. I thank my son, Matthew Moore, for his love and the joy of his creative spirit.

About the Author

Photo credit: Barry Carlton

Ann Bancroft was an Army brat who settled in Sacramento as an adult after attending ten schools in seven cities and four states. As a reporter, she worked in the State Capitol bureaus of the *San Francisco Chronicle* and the Associated Press. An alumni of the Community of Writers, the Tomales Bay Writers Workshops, and Everwood Farmstead artist's residency, she has ghostwritten two nonfiction books and was the cowriter, with Father Dan Madigan, of *Many Hands, Many Miracles*. She's written personal essays for the former *Open Salon* and *Cure Magazine*, and her writing has appeared twice in *A Year in Ink*, the annual anthology of San Diego Writers, Ink. *Almost Family* is her debut novel. Ann and her husband split their time between Sacramento and Coronado, California.

SELECTED TITLES FROM SHE WRITES PRESS

She Writes Press is an independent publishing company
founded to serve women writers everywhere.
Visit us at www.shewritespress.com.

Appearances by Sondra Helene. $16.95, 978-1-63152-499-8. Samantha, the wife of a successful Boston businessman, loves both her husband and her sister—but the two of them have fought a cold war for years. When her sister is diagnosed with lung cancer, Samantha's family and marriage are tipped into crisis.

What's Not Said by Valerie Taylor. $16.95, 978-1-63152-745-6. When a middle-aged woman's husband is diagnosed with a life-threatening illness, their secret lives collide head-on, revealing a tangled web of sex, lies, and DNA and forcing her to decide whose life to save—her husband's or her own.

The Convention of Wives by Debra Green. $17.95, 978-1-64742-241-7. A chance meeting fosters a friendship with dire consequences between two women whose lives are unknowingly intertwined. A sweeping saga that follows generations from an Odessa shtetl to comfortable Scarsdale and a Glasgow uprising to servitude in the Caribbean, *The Convention of Wives* is a of a friendship born of shared circumstance and dissolved by betrayal.

Bring the Rain by JoAnn Franklin. $16.95, 978-1-63152-507-0. When sixty-three-year-old psychology professor Dart Sommers discovers that the one thing she has always been able to count on—her brain—is failing her, she struggles to accept the diagnosis, and to let love enter her life.

All the Right Mistakes by Laura Jamison. $16.95, 978-1-63152-709-8. When the most successful of five women who have been friends since college publishes an advice book detailing the key life "mistakes" of the others—opting out, ramping off, giving half effort, and forgetting your fertility—they spend their fortieth year considering their lives against the backdrop of their outspoken friend's cruel words.

Better Than This: A Novel by Cathy Zane. $16.95, 978-1-63152-403-5. When Sarah's seemingly perfect life begins to crumble, she is forced to confront the reality of her abusive marriage and dark past, and it seems all is lost—until she allows the support of friends and a long forgotten, unopened letter to help her find her way back.